Charles Rogers

The Book of Wallace

Charles Rogers

The Book of Wallace

ISBN/EAN: 9783337018658

Printed in Europe, USA, Canada, Australia, Japan

Cover: Foto ©Raphael Reischuk / pixelio.de

More available books at **www.hansebooks.com**

THE
BOOK OF WALLACE

BY THE

Rev. CHARLES ROGERS, D.D., LL.D.

FELLOW OF THE SOCIETY OF ANTIQUARIES OF SCOTLAND; OF THE
ROYAL SOCIETY OF NORTHERN ANTIQUARIES, COPENHAGEN; OF THE
ROYAL SOCIETY OF BOHEMIA, AND OF THE ROYAL HERALDIC SOCIETY
OF ITALY; ASSOCIATE OF THE IMPERIAL ARCHÆOLOGICAL SOCIETY
OF RUSSIA; AND CORRESPONDING MEMBER OF THE HISTORICAL
AND GENEALOGICAL SOCIETY OF NEW ENGLAND; OF THE HISTORICAL
SOCIETY OF BERLIN, AND OF THE ROYAL SOCIETY OF TASMANIA

IN TWO VOLUMES

VOLUME II.

EDINBURGH
Printed for the Grampian Club
MDCCCLXXXIX

"*A fair renown, as years wear on,
Shall Scotland give her noblest son ;
The course of ages shall not dim
The love that she shall bear to him.*"
—JOANNA BAILLIE.

"*A heroic Wallace, quartered on the scaffold, cannot hinder that his
Scotland become one day a part of England: but he does hinder that it become,
on tyrannous unfair terms, a part of it; commands still, as with a god's voice,
from his old Valhalla and Temple of the Brave, that there be a just real union
as of brother and brother, not a false and merely semblant one of slave and
master. If the union with England be in fact one of Scotland's chief blessings,
we thank Wallace withal that it was not the chief curse.*"
—THOMAS CARLYLE.

INTRODUCTION.

POSSESSING a higher culture than that of the elder races which
emanated from Scandinavia, the Normans were content to appropriate territory without expelling the inhabitants ; and so when
William of Normandy conquered England, he granted estates
to his followers, to be held upon the condition that thereupon
they would rear fortalices by the hands of the natives.   In
the reign of Stephen (1135-51) there existed in England eleven
hundred castles, the owners of which exercised upon their
estates a despotic rule,—a proportion of their number being
merciless tyrants, who seized the cattle of the yeomen, plundered
the clergy and the monasteries, and spoiled towns and villages.
But while a portion of the Norman barons grievously oppressed
their subordinates, they themselves groaned under a regal
thraldom ; until, after bearing the yoke for a century and a
half, they wrested from King John the Great Charter.   Yet
in this acquisition the struggle for liberty obtained a start only,
for John's successor on the throne, Henry III., while professing
a milder rule, maintained so lofty a prerogative as to be in
nearly perpetual conflict with his nobles.   More expert in
the art of governing than his father or grandfather, Edward I.
adopted a conciliatory policy.   Affecting to respect the popular
liberties, he summoned a Parliament, and therein introduced

the commonalty, or their representatives. And under the
sanction of this new assembly he proceeded to restrict the
jurisdiction of the older tribunals ; provided that taxes should
not be levied without the common consent; and by the Statute
of Mortmain and other provisions, gave protection against
sacerdotal encroachment. By thus exercising a mild policy
at home, Edward was enabled to effectually prepare for that
vigorous action abroad, whereby he sought to extend his sway
over every portion of the island. He assembled his first Parliament in September 1274, and about two years thereafter—
that is, in November 1276—he declared war against Llewellyn,
Prince of Wales, who, as an independent ruler, had refused
to render him homage. In his conflict with Llewellyn he so
triumphed, that within seven years he was enabled, on the entire
prostration of his antagonist, to appropriate his Principality.
And to impress his power and authority on those who might
venture to resist his arms, he wantonly disembowelled his
adversary and scattered about his remains.

The conquest effected in Wales Edward proceeded to extend
elsewhere. As a first step towards attaining supremacy in
Scotland, he pressed its youthful sovereign, Alexander III.,
to accept him as his liege-lord. The considerations that the
claim of feudal superiority had been resisted on the part
of preceding sovereigns, and that Alexander was his brother-
in-law, did not avail in diverting him from his purpose.
Alexander resisted both blandishments and menaces, but

his premature decease, followed by that of his infant grand-daughter and heir, gave Edward a singular advantage. And when at length the weak king, John Baliol, awoke to the necessity of resistance, Edward improved the opportunity by forcibly asserting his supremacy.

At this stage arose William Wallace, through whose skill and prowess Edward's work of subjugation was effectively arrested. The record of Wallace's achievements we derive from two sources, widely apart. On the side of England we have the contemporary writers, Hemingford and Trivet, also the state papers of the time. Of the latter we have first in order the "Great Roll of Scotland," in which is set forth a narrative of proceedings, from the convention of Norham in May 1291, to the date of Baliol's homage in January 1293. Composed in Latin by Master John of Caen, apostolic notary, the Great Roll narrates the proceedings attested by Master Andrew de Tang, clerk of the diocese of York; and while between the instruments, written in French, on which the narrative is founded, there is an occasional discrepancy, the existence of the originals enables us to attain an approximate accuracy. In illustration of these materials, Sir Francis Palgrave published in 1837 his important volume of "Documents and Records;" and the work of research was afterwards supplemented by the arduous labours of the Rev. Joseph Stevenson. In quest of materials in relation to the War of Independence, Mr Stevenson extended his researches not only into the several record departments in London, but also to public repositories at Paris, Brussels, Lille, and Ghent, and his precious gleanings were in 1870 issued in two octavo volumes.[1] And to these important treasuries of authentic historical information, Mr Joseph Bain has added a most important sequel in his four printed volumes of the "Calendar," published in the Scottish Record Series.

In addition to these more fertile sources, we have on the English side derived some important materials from the *Scala Cronica* of Sir Thomas Gray of Heton, who began to prepare his Chronicle about the year 1355, and whose father, also Sir Thomas Gray, served under Edward I. and II. in their campaigns in Scotland.

On the Scottish side the materials are scanty and imperfect. Such as do exist have under the care of Mr Joseph Stevenson been brought together in a volume entitled, "Sir William Wallace, his Life and Times," which was printed for the Maitland Club in 1841.

The first Scottish historian, John of Fordun, who composed his *Scotichronicon* in the reign of Robert II. [1371-90] presents some ample details in relation to the Patriot; and he is considerably supplemented by Andrew of Wyntoun, who completed his "Cronykil" in 1426. Not, however, until about two centuries after his birth were the hero's achievements

---

[1] Mr Joseph Stevenson's work is entitled "Documents illustrative of the History of Scotland, from the death of King Alexander III. to the accession of Robert Bruce."

detailed in a systematic form. We refer to the well-known poem of Henry the Minstrel, a work composed between the years 1475 and 1488.

Concerning Henry personally, we are, in 1521, informed by Mair, that he was blind from his birth, and that when the writer was a child, he rendered into rhyme legends respecting Wallace, which he derived from the common people. These rhymes, Mair informs us, he recited in the halls of the opulent as a means of support.[1] From the Treasurer's Accounts, we further learn that Henry was some time a pensioner of James IV. In the accounts are contained these entries :—

" 26 April 1490. At the king's command to Blind Hary,	.	xviij[s].
29 Decr. 1490. to Blind Hary,. . . .	.	xviij[s].
5th April 1491. to Blind Hary,.	.	xviij[s].
14 Sept. 1491. to Blind Hary, at the king's command,	. .	v[s].
25 Sept. 1491. to Blind Hary,[2]		ix[s]."

In his poem, Henry describes himself as a "bural man," that is, a humble and unlearned person. He writes—

> " All worthi men at redys this rurall dyt
> Blaym nocht the buk, yet I be wnperfyt."[3]

[1] Mair's account of Henry is contained in these words :—"Integrum librum Gulielmi Wallacei Henricus a nativitate luminibus captus, meæ infantiæ tempore cudit, et quæ vulgo dicebantur, carmine vulgari, in quo peritus erat, conscripsit ; (ego autem talibus scriptis solum in parte fidem impertior) qui historiarum recitatione coram principibus, victum et vestitum quo dignus erat uactus est." (Historia Majoris Britanniæ, ed. 1710, p. 169.) That Henry was blind from his birth has been doubted ; he may early have lost his eyesight, but his descriptions of external nature, together with the extent of his education, would warrant the belief that he was not born sightless.

[2] The precise date of Henry's death is unknown, but the event certainly occurred prior to 1508, when William Dunbar in his *Lament for the Makaris*, includes "Blind Hary" among the departed bards.

[3] Henry's Wallace, B. xi., ll. 1431, 1432, 1461.

But while disclaiming literary pretensions, the Minstrel asserts that he has based his narrative on historical authority.   Thus in reference to the Patriot's kindred, he quotes the chronicle of Conn or Conus,[1] while for the other materials of his poem he expresses himself as indebted to a narrative composed by John Blair, the hero's military chaplain, aided by an associate, Thomas Gray, described as parson of Liberton.[2]   Blair's narrative of the Patriot's life was, according to Henry, composed in Latin, but as it is not quoted by Fordun or Wyntoun, it may be held to have, in the Minstrel's time, been represented in a version written in the vernacular.   And in support of this theory, it may be urged that Wyntoun sets forth that narratives concerning Wallace and Bruce were "contenyd in other bukis" as his reason for not more fully expatiating on their exploits.

That in composing his poem Henry availed himself of written narratives is entirely credible, and in evidence it may be remarked that the localities associated with the Patriot are described accurately.   But whatever were the actual sources of his authority, the Minstrel has, in utilizing them, lapsed frequently into error.   His details consist of a series of episodes brought together without order, or any approach to chronological arrangement, and many of his statements are inconsistent with each other.   The hero, he relates, died at forty-five,[3] while if we accept his details elsewhere, he must

----

[1] Henry's Wallace, B. i., l. 37.   [2] *Ibid.*, B. v., ll. 538-546; B. xi., 1413-1425.
[3] *Ibid.*, B. xi., l. 1427.

have been put to death at twenty-seven, both accounts being inaccurate. The Patriot's father and brother, he describes as obtaining shelter in the fastnesses of Lennox at a time when, according to another of his statements, they were already slain. And while he definitely relates that Wallace's elder brother fell at the battle of Loudoun Hill, we learn on the reliable testimony of Wyntoun that he long survived that engagement. Henry exhibits an utter ignorance of historical personages and events. He describes Aymer de Valence (the Earl of Pembroke) as a recreant Scottish knight, and sets forth that Sir Richard Lundin was the Patriot's companion on the field of Stirling, while he was there conspicuous in the army of Surrey. Among Wallace's antagonists he names a Duke of Lancaster, though, prior to the reign of Edward III., Dukes were unknown in England. Sir John the Graham he asserts received knighthood from King Alexander the Fierce, although that sovereign departed from the scene upwards of a century before Sir John was born. He describes Sinclair as bishop of Dunkeld in the time of Wallace, whereas that churchman did not hold his episcopate till late in the reign of King Robert the Bruce. And without a shadow of foundation, he represents that a "Sir Hugh," Edward's sister's son, was, on entering the Scottish camp as a messenger, beheaded by the Patriot's order. Equally fictitious is his narrative that, at the battle of Biggar, Wallace mortally wounded the Earl of Kent, and that on the same field were slain Edward's second son, also his brother, and his two nephews. In setting forth the Patriot's capture of the pirate, De Longueville, Henry has fabricated an enormous fiction, though one less obviously inaccurate than when he alleges that Edward's Queen had conceived a romantic passion for the Scottish hero at a time when the English sovereign was a widower. But while thoroughly unreliable as an historical guide, Henry's testimony may be fairly accepted in relation to such of the hero's achievements as are confirmed by an intelligent tradition.[1]

In presenting an historical memoir of the Patriot, the writer has, in a brief chapter, extended the narrative beyond the period of his personal career, since the event of his death was attended with a revival of the struggle for independence, in which Scottish valour ultimately triumphed. And in continuing the history to the death of Edward, the writer has been enabled to bring into strong relief the motives and principles of the two great leaders in the international conflict. By a narrative chiefly founded on documents framed under his personal authority, Edward I. is revealed as one who affected piety, only to practise dissimulation, and as a man of inordinate ambition and the most consummate cruelty, who in the immediate prospect of death continued to indulge a ferocious rancour, and to cherish the most terrible revenge.

[1] As a poet, Henry merits commendation, being remarkable for his smooth versification and graceful flow of numbers. Indulging a pleasing alliteration, he strikingly excels in the use of the heroic couplet. His "Wallace" extends to eleven books, and comprehends eleven thousand lines. From its obsolete phraseology the poem has ceased to be generally intelligible, but in Hamilton's modernised version it is widely popular.

In decided contrast to his powerful adversary, the Scottish Patriot shines in the possession of the noblest qualities. Faithful and without reproach, he knew of no sacrifice too costly to be laid on the altar of his country. Indignantly rejecting every offer put forth to induce him to abandon the national cause, he enkindled among his countrymen the decaying embers of their ancient spirit. When the Scottish kingdom was without a king, and the nobles had deserted its standard; when the national revenues were in the hands of a usurper, he revived the popular energies, and only failed to triumph owing to a persistent jealousy, attended by an act of the basest treachery. Under the knife of the executioner he bemoaned his country's miseries rather than his own.

As to the Patriot's physical aspect, it is certain that he presented a commanding presence, and was possessed of a robust and well-built frame. But the different portraits of him are, like Henry's description of his person, wholly imaginary.

According to the English chronicler, Thomas of Walsingham, Wallace received knighthood from a Scottish earl on his becoming leader of the movement against Edward.[1] This statement is obviously conjectural, but in his charter to Alexander Skirmischur of the 29th March 1298, the Patriot styles himself "Willelmus Walays, miles," which would serve to justify his title as Sir William Wallace.

In order adequately to illustrate the leading events associated

---

[1] Hist. Angl., p. 90.

with the Patriot and his work, the writer has added to the historical narrative a series of Appendices, presenting biographical sketches of those conspicuously engaged, whether in maintaining the cause of independence, or in abetting the aggression. In his former volume he has conveyed his acknowledgments to several gentlemen, who have actively assisted him. And he would now express the obligations of the Grampian Club to the Marquis of Bute, for a donation of twenty pounds towards the cost of printing; also his personal thanks to Mr Joseph Bain of London, who has kindly applied his intimate knowledge of the subject in revising the proof sheets of the present volume.

6 BARNTON TERRACE,
EDINBURGH, *November* 1889.

CONTENTS.

CHAPTER | PAGE

I. The Question of England's Superiority and Scotland's Vassalage, 1

II. John Baliol and his Dethronement. The English Subjugation, . 57

III. From the Rise of Wallace to the Battle of Stirling, 87

IV. Wallace Guardian of the Kingdom, . . . 136

V. From the Commencement of the Second War of Subjugation in July 1298 to the Truce in October 1300, . . 160

VI. From the Truce of October 1300 to the Reduction of Stirling Castle in 1304, ... 188

VII. The Patriot's Betrayal and Death, . . . 225

VIII. From the Death of Wallace to the Death of Edward, 239

Appendices :—

I. John Blair, ... 257
II. Sir William Douglas, ... 259
III. Bishop William Fraser of St Andrews, . . 261
IV. Sir Simon Fraser, ... 264
V. Bishop William Lamberton of St Andrews, 269
VI. Bishop Robert Wishart of Glasgow, . . 276
VII. Sir Thomas Charteris, . . . 282
VIII. Alexander Scrimgeour, . . 284
IX. Sir Richard Lundin, . . 287
X. Patrick, Earl of March, . . 289
XI. Bishop Anthony Bek, . . . 292
XII. John, Earl of Warren and Surrey, . 296
XIII. Sir Henry Percy, . . 299
XIV. Sir Robert Clifford, . . 301
XV. Hugh de Cressingham, . . . 304
XVI. Aymer de Valence, Earl of Pembroke, . . 307
XVII. Sir Brian Fitz-Alan, . . . 313
XVIII. Sir Walter de Huntercumbe, . . 315
XIX. Sir John Segrave, . . . 317
XX. Sir Richard Siward, . . 320

Index, 325

ILLUSTRATIONS.

PAGE

1. LETTER FROM SIR ANDREW DE MORAY AND SIR WILLIAM WALLACE TO THE HANSEATIC LEAGUE, . . . 140

2. CHARTER BY SIR WILLIAM WALLACE TO ALEXANDER SKIRMISCHUR, CONSTABLE OF DUNDEE, . . . 146

3. RECOMMENDATION OF SIR WILLIAM WALLACE TO THE POPE BY KING PHILIP OF FRANCE, ... 177

THE BOOK OF WALLACE.

CHAPTER I.

THE QUESTION OF ENGLAND'S SUPERIORITY, AND
SCOTLAND'S VASSALAGE.

Ah! Fredome is a noble thing !
Fredome makis man to haiff liking ; [1]
Fredome all solace to man gifis :
He lives at ease that frely lives.

—*The Brus*, by JOHN BARBOUR.

HE question as to the alleged feudal superiority of
southern rulers over those of the north was practically
solved, first, by Sir William Wallace at the battle of
Stirling Bridge, and next and more amply when King
Robert the Bruce repulsed at Bannockburn the army of
invaders. But apart from its military solution, the question
demands careful inquiry in relation to the early history of the
country, and the investigation has not lost force or interest,
though the peoples of south and north have for nearly three
centuries been united under one sceptre, and in perfect amity.
The question to be considered is this,—whether there is any
evidence, real or constructive, on which it may be held that
the royal power of England extended northward beyond its
actual territory, or, whether the English sovereigns possessed

---

[1] Pleasure or comfort.

A

over the whole length of the island, an authority which might be described as imperialistic.

Dr Freeman, a historian who cannot be charged with partiality for northern claims, asserts, that at the beginning of the tenth century, the Scots were "perfectly independent."[1] But that independence, he holds, was on a public occasion voluntarily surrendered. He reads in the Saxon Chronicle, that in the year 924, Eadward, or Edward, the Elder of Saxony, "went into Peaclond to Bedecan-well [Bakewell-in-the-Peak] and commanded a Burh to be built nigh thereunto and manned. And then chose him to father and lord the King of Scots, and the whole nation of the Scots, and Ragnald and Eadulf's son, and all those who dwell in Northumbria, as well English as Danes, and Northmen and others; and also the King of the Strath-Clyde Wealh, and all the Strath-Clyde Wealh."[2] Satisfied as to the genuineness of his authority, Dr Freeman proceeds to commend the wisdom of the proffered homage. These northern princes adopted, he holds, a judicious policy in meeting half-way one who was meditating the entire subjection of the island, while by acknowledging a protective head, they obtained a strong safeguard against any heathen invasion. The act at Bedecan-well, he adds, was neither "strange" nor "degrading;" "it did not make Scotland a territorial fief; still less did it bring with it any of the feudal incidents, which were invented long after."[3] But we anticipate comment, by presenting the query, Was the homage at Bedecan-well actually made? Doubtless in two MSS. of the Saxon Chronicle, the Benet and Cotton Hurian, the words quoted by Dr Freeman are to be found; but, on the other hand, there is demonstrative evidence that not before the year

---

[1] Dr Freeman in the Fortnightly Review, vol. i., New Series, p. 701.

[2] Chron. Sax., 924.

[3] Fortnightly Review, vol. i., New Series, 703.

927 did the Northumbrian Danes submit to Anglo-Saxon rule, while that submission was yielded not to Edward, who was dead, but to Athelstan his son and successor. Further, we learn on the valid authority of the Irish Annals that Reginald Hy Ivan, who is described as having in 924 commended himself to Edward, had already commended his soul to God, having expired three years previously! And while acts of homage or "commendation" by one sovereign to another, are known only as being rendered upon their frontiers, there is no reason to believe that Constantine II. deviated from the practice by making a pilgrimage into Derbyshire, there to surrender his regal and personal liberty.[1]

Resting on the supposed occurrence at Bedecan-well, Dr Freeman argues that Scotland proper, being that portion of territory to the north of the Forth and Clyde, had in 924, through the voluntary act of the sovereign, surrendered its independence. But Scotland in 924 did not comprehend that superficies which it included subsequently; there were added on the south-east Northern Bernicia or Lothian bordered by the Forth, and on the south-west the kingdom of Strathclyde bordered by the Clyde. But for these territories, Dr Freeman affirms, Scottish sovereigns owned dependence on the English Crown. Lothian, he rightly affirms, was an old Pictish or Celtic possession overrun by the Angles.[2] Subsequently, as is shown by Simeon of Durham, it was ceded to the Scots by Eadulf Cudel in the time of Canute. But it is alleged that Malcolm IV. restored to Henry II. of England the county of Lothian, with other possessions he held in England; and thereupon it has been assumed, that on the territory being

---

[1] Robertson's Scotland under her Early Kings, ii., 395-397. [2] Freeman's Norman Conquest, I., 573, 579.

regranted to him, he must have acknowledged the boon by an act of homage. There is not, however, a shadow of ground for the assertion that Malcolm IV. restored Lothian, or any portion of it, to the English Crown. "If," remarks Dr Hill Burton, "King Malcolm gave up Lothian, history is silent as to how he got it back again, and ruled it, insomuch that some eighty years afterwards, we shall find it as counted within the ancient marches of Scotland." Dr Burton adds, "the old name of Leeds, Leydes, and in Latin, Loidis, is apt to be confounded with the old name of Lothian. We have seen already how Malcolm Canmore was spoken of, as having gone out of Scotland and tarried in Lothian, and that this has been converted into Leeds."[1] Dr Burton, it should be explained, offers these remarks in reference to a quotation from Diceto, which bears that in 1157, Malcolm restored to Henry at Chester, Carlisle, Bamburgh, Newcastle-upon-Tyne, and *comitatus Lodonensis.*[2] But the passage so quoted is clearly an interpolation. The work in question, "Imagines Historiarum," was composed by Ralph de Diceto, Dean of St Paul's, during the reigns of Richard and John, and it begins in 1147, when Robert de Monte finished his chronicle, and concludes in 1198. And to the work has been added by the author, or some other writer, a summary of its paragraphs, under the title "Capitula Imaginarum," but these, though extremely minute in regard to the ordinary contents, present no references in relation to Scottish affairs prior to 1174, nor any allusion to the cession of Lothian in 1157. Not only so, but the portions omitted

---

[1] Burton's History of Scotland, ed. 1873, vol. i., 414.

[2] The words ascribed to Diceto are, "Melchomus Rex Scotorum reddidit ei (Henrico scilicet) civitatem Carleul, Castrum super Tinam et comitatum Lodonensen." There is a doubt as to the reading of the word *comitatum*; if it reads *communitatem*, then it is clear that the County of Lothian cannot be signified. See Lord Hailes' Annals, edit. 1797, vol. iii., app. ii., pp. 125-144.

in the "Capitula" frequently correspond, word for word, with passages in Roger of Wendover's Chronicle, while two errors occur, one relating to the date of Henry's penance at the shrine of Becket, and the other as to the place at which was arranged the treaty, by which William the Lion regained his freedom.[1] And by Roger of Wendover are we first directed to the cession on which he claims Diceto as his authority, for while John of Wallingford (who died in 1258) is content to inform us that the old quarrel,[2] in regard to the possession of Lothian, was settled in the tenth century, when the territory was, as he alleges, conferred by Edgar on Kenneth II., to be held by homage of the English Crown, it was reserved for the monk of St Alban's to devise the relation that Kenneth and his successors became bound to attend the English Court at every solemn festival, while *mansiones* for support of the Scottish train were paid by the English treasury, till the date of the alleged cession of Lothian in 1157. All this is monkish legend. At Chester in 1157, Malcolm surrendered to his cousin-german, Henry II. of England, his claim upon Northumberland, and on Cumbria south of the Solway, and in return for these fiefs he received the Honor of Huntingdon, a gift for which he became liable to the English Crown in military service. And as has been remarked by Mr Robertson, "it is incumbent upon all who maintain the accuracy of Wendover's addition, to point out the period at which Lothian, resigned by Malcolm with the northern counties at Chester, was restored to that king or his successors."[3]

With respect to that portion of Scotland which comprehended the kingdom of Strathclyde, it is admitted by Dr Freeman, that

[1] Robertson's Scotland under her Early Kings, i., 427, 428.

[2] Every chronicler prior to the thirteenth century, both Norman and Saxon, was ignorant of this old quarrel about Scotland (Robertson's Scotland under her Early Kings, ii., 391).

[3] Robertson's Scotland under her Early Kings, ii., 428.

it was originally an appanage of the eldest son of the Scottish kings, but he asserts that it was subsequently incorporated with the kingdom, as a grant from the English sovereign—the gift implying service or homage. But the grant by Edmund to Malcolm I. included only that portion of Strathclyde which formed the county of Cumberland; and this transaction, which was not renewed on Malcolm's death, cannot justify the conclusion that the portion of Strathclyde previously incorporated held of the English Crown.[1]

When William of Normandy obtained by conquest the English throne, he vigorously asserted in all departments his sovereign and seigniorial rights. But he made no pretension to any feudal superiority over the northern kingdom. On the contrary, when aggrieved by the favour extended by Malcolm Canmore towards the Saxon prince, he went to war against him as an independent sovereign; and recognising the Scottish king as such, formed with him the treaty of Abernethy. Upon Malcolm, he, in guerdon of restored friendship, bestowed a grant of manors, and an annual subsidy of twelve marks of gold, while for these the Scottish king consented to render feudal homage, in token that the gift was free, and not an affair of tribute. As the gift was imperfectly renewed, Malcolm, nineteen years afterwards, in reference to the claim, and when William Rufus sullenly demanded an homage more extensive than that due for the manors and rent of twelve marks, rejected the demand menacingly. Nor do we discover that English sovereigns exacted homage from the Scottish kings earlier than in 1126, in which year David I., as an English baron, swore allegiance to Henry I. for the Honor of Huntingdon.[2]

---

[1] Dr Freeman in Fortnightly Review, vol. i., New Series, 703-706.

[2] Robertson's Scotland under her Early Kings, ii., 401, 404, 410.

When on the death of Malcolm IV. in 1165, his younger brother William ascended the throne, he felt himself sufficiently strong to demand from his English neighbour the restoration of Northumberland. And when that demand was refused, he precipitately crossed the Border with an armed force. During the expedition, while he was besieging the castle of Alnwick, he was captured by a troop of Yorkshire knights, and borne as a prisoner to Normandy. At Falaise, on the 8th December 1174, he, in order to his liberation, executed an instrument, whereby he bound himself and his successors to be liegemen to the king of England " for Scotland and his other lands," and in token of subserviency performed fealty to the two Henrys, father and son. Consequent on this obligation, his Scottish subjects became liegemen of the English sovereign, and as vassals were at the English court in frequent attendance upon their liege-lord. But the treaty of Falaise subsisted for fifteen years only, and in 1189, when Richard Cœur-de-Lion succeeded to the throne, one of his early acts was to relieve the king of Scotland and his people from an extorted vassalage. Accepting ten thousand marks as a penalty for the unwarrantable invasion and its consequences, Richard voluntarily discharged the infeudation, and restored the relations between the two kingdoms to their former footing. Thereupon five Scottish strongholds, garrisoned by English troops, were restored, while in the proceedings of revocation no allusion was made as to any further claim upon the Scottish sceptre.[1] Nor was feudal homage to the English sovereign again performed by William, or by his son, or by his grandson.

Apart from the subordination of the Scottish sceptre for the period of fifteen years, dating from the treaty of Falaise, the perfect independence of the northern kingdom may not

---

[1] Burton's History, edit. 1873, ii., 2 ; Fœdera (Record edit.), i., 30, 50.

reasonably be questioned.   If in rendering homage for the Honor of Huntingdon, or other English fiefs, Scottish sovereigns made use of vague or general terms, such a course is not to be attributed to any desire on their part to elude the acknowledgment of a dependence they lacked courage to deny.   The true interpretation is rather to be found in a desire to leave open the question as to the extent of their claims upon the English crown.   The earldom of Northumberland was deeply coveted.[1]

Towards the close of his reign, when King John was becoming involved in trouble with his barons, William of Scotland renewed his hope of regaining both the Anglo-Cumbrian and Northumbrian provinces.   As a first effort thereto he defeated an attempt of the English sovereign to erect a fortress near the Scottish Border.   William died in 1214, and was succeeded by his son, Alexander II., who adopted the same line of policy.   He joined King John's disaffected barons in the hope of securing the northern provinces; and he did secure a formal possession, but failed to maintain it.   Thus, while his troops ravaged Cumberland, King John obtained reprisals by storming Berwick, devastating the Lothians, and burning Haddington and Dunbar.   In association with Louis, son of the French king, Alexander II. renewed his support of the disaffected barons, but the notable disaster which attended the French arms rendered futile a new attempt on the Border provinces.   At length, in 1237, negotiations in regard to these provinces were amicably adjusted; Alexander accepting from Henry III. lands in Cumberland and Northumberland, of the estimated yearly value of two hundred pounds.   For the lands of Penrith, Scotby, and Sowerby in Cumberland, which were assigned him, he consented

---

[1] Robertson's Scotland under her Early Kings, ii., 408, 409.

to yield the usual feudal acknowledgment—the service being compounded by his sending a falcon yearly to Carlisle Castle. The lands of Tynedale and others, granted him in Northumberland, were held on a simple acknowledgment of the English sovereignty, the Scottish King being allowed to administer justice by his own justiciary.[1] On this subject Dr Burton writes, "Handing over the estates on the Border to the King of Scots kept alive the policy of the English court, to have him coming there to do homage for something or other. This was," adds Dr Burton, "perhaps the more desirable that the Honor of Huntingdon had now gone to a collateral—the descendants of Prince David, William the Lion's brother."[2]

Between Henry III. and Alexander II. another conflict arose. At a tournament held in the vicinity of Haddington in 1242, Walter Bisset, a northern Scottish baron, was unhorsed by Patric, Earl of Athole. A feud existed between the families, and as Athole was found murdered in his house, which was set on fire by his assassins, suspicion of the crime fell upon the northern chief. Protesting his innocence, Bisset offered to prove that he was fifty miles distant from Haddington when the murder was committed; he got sentence of excommunication published against the murderers, and made offer to engage in single combat with any one who would charge him with the slaughter. But he declined judgment by an assize. For a time Alexander gave him protection, but at length had to succumb to popular sentiment by condemning the Bissets to forfeiture, and commanding them to make promise that they would repair to Palestine, and there pray for the soul of the murdered earl.

Repairing to the English court, Walter Bisset there sought

[1] Burton's History, ed. 1873, II., 9 ; Hailes' Annals, ii., 169.
[2] Burton's History, ed. 1873, ii., 8, 9.

the support of the vacillating Henry. He assured him that Scotland was but a fief of the English crown, and that the Scottish King, by pronouncing a sentence of confiscation and exile without consulting his superior, was guilty of rebellion. Communicating these sentiments to Alexander II., Henry received from him an indignant denial as to his kingdom, or any portion of it, being a dependency of England. Strife was imminent. Henry sent against Scotland twenty-two Irish chiefs, and himself led to Newcastle a numerous army. Fortifying their Border strongholds, the Scots in large numbers marched into England. But as the two armies came in sight of each other at Ponteland in Northumberland, pacific councils prevailed. At Newcastle was concluded a treaty of peace, while in its adjustment the matter of alleged homage was not so much as named.[1]

Alexander II. died on the 8th July 1249, and was succeeded by his son, third sovereign of the name, a child of eight years.

Five days after his accession, Alexander III. was crowned at Scone, by the Bishop of St Andrews. The Justiciar Alan the Durward, who was in the English interest, adroitly counselled delay, but it was held expedient to complete the ceremony at once. Those who recommended diligence evinced a patriotic foresight, for Henry III. proceeded to request the Pope, Innocent IV., to ignore Alexander's coronation, until he, as Lord Superior of Scotland, granted a formal sanction. The Pope's reply is extant. Dated in 1251, two years after the young Scottish King had received his crown, Innocent informed the English sovereign, that for the gratification of his wish there

---

[1] Fœdera, i., 374, 428 ; Hailes' Annals, ii., 274, 275 ; Burton's History, ii., 16-19 ; Tytler's History of Scotland, ed. 1869, i., 2, 3.

was no precedent.[1] At the same time, a proposal formally made that the sovereign of Scotland should wed the daughter of the English King, was recognised and confirmed.

Disheartened by the Papal missive, refusing to subordinate to his authority the independence of a kingdom ruled by his intended son-in-law, Henry sought to accomplish his purpose after a different mode. On the plea that he was about to make an expedition to Palestine, he induced the advisers of the young king to consent to his nuptials being celebrated while he was only in his tenth year. Accordingly the marriage of Alexander III. with the Princess Margaret was solemnized at York on the 26th December 1251. Amidst the subsequent festivities, Henry required his youthful son-in-law to render homage for his lands at Penrith and Tynedale. This act being performed, there followed the further demand, that Alexander should render homage for his kingdom. As the strategy was anticipated, Alexander's answer was ready : "I came here," said he, "to wed the Princess Margaret, not to treat of affairs of state ; and the step you desire me to take, I cannot even talk of without the advice and guidance of my great council."[2]

On his return to Scotland, Alexander found himself involved between the intrigues of two opposing factions, of which one upheld the independence of the throne, and the other was attached to the English interest. Not long after the proceedings at York, Alan the Durward, Great Justiciary of Scotland, having applied to the Pope for legitimating his wife, a natural daughter of the late king, the Comyns, who led the national party, seized the opportunity of charging him with a design upon the crown. He was consequently removed from office ; but his degradation

[1] Fœdera (Record ed.), i., 277.

[2] Matthew Paris, 329, 330 ; Fœdera, i., 466 ; Fordun a Hearne, pp. 761, 762 ; Wyntoun, B. vii., chap. x. ; Hailes, ii., 179.

was of brief continuance, for in the year 1255, he, at the head of a party of Englishmen, seized the castle of Edinburgh, and under the pretence of increasing the king's personal liberty, took possession of his person.   Foiled in securing the subserviency of those who now directed Scottish affairs, Henry proceeded northward with a powerful force.   To prevent alarm, he, at Newcastle, issued a declaration that he would take no action against the liberties of Scotland, or the independence of its sovereign.[1]   This act did not deceive the Comyns, who attempted resistance, but Henry secured an interview with the young king at Roxburgh, and from thence conducted him to the Abbey of Kelso, where, under the guise of his performing a religious rite, he induced him to acquiesce in certain measures somewhat derogatory to the national honour.   Among other concessions, Alexander was led to appoint a regency favourable to the English interests, and to consent to be guided by their policy till he should attain his majority.   He also consented that Henry should be styled "the King of Scotland's principal councillor." During the following year Henry invited Alexander to England, and then called upon him a second time to render homage for the Honor of Huntingdon.

The Scottish national party regained strength; and on the advice of the king's mother, Mary de Coucy, who, with her second husband, John of Acre, came to Scotland in 1257, they determined to renew the struggle.   Gameline, bishop-elect of St Andrews, had, by the king's English councillors, been set aside, but the Pope, whose favour he had attained, laid his opponents under excommunication.   As the terrible sentence was published by the bishop of Dunblane at Cambuskenneth Abbey, the faithful were adjured to deliver their sovereign from the hands of those

---

[1] Fœdera, i., pp. 560, 561.

who were accursed. To this appeal there was so effective a
response, that the Comyns were enabled to enter the king's
house at Kinross, and seize the sovereign in his bed; they also
possessed themselves of the Great Seal, and by its use proceeded to exercise an authority which speedily overwhelmed
their opponents.

Informed by Alan the Durward as to the triumph of the
national party, Henry had recourse to a policy of dissimulation.
At his counsel, the Durward faction assembled at Roxburgh,
and there made pledge that at a conference to be held at Forfar,
they would publicly yield submission to the new arrangement.
Meanwhile certain English barons were on their way to Melrose,
there professedly to confer with the king, but in reality to
seize his person and convey him to England. Alexander was
on his guard. He invited Henry's commissioners to meet
him in the forest of Jedburgh, in presence of his army. A
compromise ensued, a new regency being appointed, in which,
while the main power rested with the king's mother and the
Comyns, four persons in the English interest were included.[1]

In 1258 Walter Comyn, Earl of Menteith, died somewhat
suddenly, and a suspicion arose that he had perished by poison
administered by the hands of his wife, a base woman, who not
long after his death wedded one Russel, a low-born Englishman.[2]
Chief of the national party, the Earl of Menteith had exercised
a formidable antagonism to the designs of King Henry, and
the event of his death, it was feared by his adherents, would be
attended by further attempts against the national independence.
Accordingly, when, a year afterwards, Henry invited Alexander

---

[1] Fœdera, i., 652, 670; Chron. Melrose, 181; Matthew Paris, 330; Tytler's History, ed. 1869,
i., 7, 183; Fordun a Goodal, ii., 85.

[2] Hailes' Annals, i., 188, 189.

and his Queen to visit him in London, the national party insisted that their sovereign should remain at home, till he received a solemn assurance that he would not, in the course of his visit, be required to treat of national affairs. And as the Queen's early *accouchement* was expected, the regents insisted on a definite pledge, that should she give birth to a child during her visit, it should not be detained in England. Henry made the promises required of him; he also pledged himself to make payment of his daughter's dowry of 5000 marks, which had been withheld hitherto. In February 1260-1, the Scottish Queen gave birth to a daughter; and Henry, her father, content that one of his race was heir of the northern kingdom, ceased for a time to interfere with its concerns.[1]

After an interval of seven years, Henry renewed his interference. He requested that, in obedience to an injunction by Pope Clement IV., the clergy in Scotland should surrender a tenth of their benefices for use in a new crusade. Alexander refused to sanction Henry's demand, but evinced his respect for the Pope by countenancing a crusade originated in his own kingdom; he also with his clergy adopted measures to secure the independence of the Scottish Church, by assembling a council at Perth, under the presidency of a native bishop.[2]

After reigning sixty years, Henry III. died on the 16th November 1273, when he was succeeded by his son Edward, brother of the Scottish Queen. Edward's coronation was appointed to take place at Westminster on the 12th August 1274, but Alexander, whose attendance was invited, made his acceptance conditional on his receiving a written guarantee that his being present would not be construed injuriously,

---

[1] Fœdera, i., 713, 714.; Math. Westminster, 376, 377.

[2] Fordun a Goodal, ii., 109; Hailes, i., 196, 197.

as affecting the independence of his throne.[1] But while the guarantee was yielded, Alexander was persuaded to receive, during his residence in England, a daily allowance of one hundred shillings, for the support of his suite.[2]

Sometime in the year 1277, Edward stated in writing to the Bishop of Wells, that "his beloved brother, the King of Scotland, had agreed to perform an unconditional homage, and that he was to receive it at the feast of Michaelmas.[3] If this statement was well founded, it was to be inferred that Alexander, hitherto keenly sensitive as to the independence of his kingdom, had been cajoled or bribed into its surrender. But did the Scottish councillors, under whose advice he governed, indorse the act? Happily, we are not left in the mazes of conjecture. Considerable correspondence between the sovereigns preceded a visit which Alexander made to the English court, at the period named in Edward's letter. And in that correspondence we remark how, from first to last, Alexander was especially careful not to be inveigled into any act of submission. On the same lines in which he had proceeded four years previously, he, in a message to Edward, despatched in or about May 1278, expresses his willingness "to come to him and to do his pleasure in reason. But," he adds, that "it would greatly satisfy the people of his realm if he had the usual safe-conduct of the English magnates, or a letter from Edward personally, that his coming to England should not hereafter injure him or his heirs." In reference to this request there exist the draft and extended letters-patent by Edward, dated 5th June, bearing that the safe-conduct to be granted to Alexander, should not tend to his prejudice, or that of his heirs.[4]

[1] Ayloffe's Calendar of Ancient Charters, 328, 342 ; Leland's Collectanea, ii., 471.

[2] Fœdera, i., 520 ; Rot. Pat., 4 Edward, m. 36.

[3] Fœdera, ii , 109.

[4] Calendar of Documents relating to Scotland (Royal Letters, 1284, 1288), ii., pp. 26, 27.

On the 29th September 1278, Alexander was present at Westminster, and there by the Earl of Carrick renewed his homage for his lands in England. And in declaring himself a liegeman of the English sovereign, Alexander added by his deputy, "And I shall faithfully perform the services, used and wont, for the lands and tenements which I hold of the said king." In this form the transaction was recorded in the English archives, while Edward thereto added the provision, "saving the claim of homage for the kingdom of Scotland, whenever he or his heirs should think proper to make it."[1] To effect his purpose, Edward adopted other modes. In the Public Record Office there exists a Patent Roll, dated 17th October 1278, in which he affirms that Alexander came before him at Tewkesbury on the preceding day, being Sunday, and offered to do him homage, but as he had not his council with him, he postponed the occasion, and desired that the proffered homage might be rendered in London.[2] As an evidence of real or intended submission this document would have doubtless availed, if by any subsequent procedure the Scottish King had evinced any sign of wavering in his purpose. As this did not occur, a Close Roll was subsequently put forward to show that in his act of homage on the 29th September, Alexander included his kingdom as well as his English possessions. But in examining the instrument we find that the general or extended homage is inscribed on an erasure![3] By Alexander III. and his clergy, Edward's unscrupulous behaviour was abundantly foreseen. Hence the notary of the Abbey of Dunfermline was instructed to set forth in his register a correct narrative of the Westminster proceedings. Accordingly, in the Abbey Register we have the following entry :—"In the

---

[1] Fœdera, ii., 126.
[2] Patent Roll, 6 Edward I., m. 3.

[3] Close Roll, 6 Edw. I., m. 5 dorso ; Allan's Vindication, p. 87.

year 1278, on the day of the apostles St Simon and St Jude,[1] at Westminster, Alexander, King of Scots, did homage to Edward, King of England, in these words, 'I become your man for the lands which I hold of you in the kingdom of England, for which I owe you homage, saving my kingdom.' Then said the Bishop of Norwich, 'And saving to the King of England, if he right have, to your homage for your kingdom;' to whom the King immediately answered, saying aloud, 'To homage for my kingdom of Scotland no one has any right, but God alone, nor do I hold it of any other but of God.' "[2]

While vigorously upholding the independence of his throne, Alexander III. maintained terms of friendship both with Henry and Edward. Like the majority of the line of native princes from whom he descended, he combined the virtues of an enlightened ruler with the chivalrous bearing of an independent sovereign. He advanced agriculture and promoted commerce, and, enacting equitable laws, prudently administered them. In his minority his kingdom was torn by rival factions, but by his urbane and gentle manners he arrested contention and secured concord. Under his sway the country attained to greater opulence than it had possessed heretofore. And there was the promise, that of his goodly stock might be perpetuated a line of princes.

Disappointment and sorrow greatly supervened. On the 26th February 1274-5, Alexander was deprived of his amiable wife, who succumbed to a pulmonary ailment at the age of thirty-five. To her husband she had brought two sons and a daughter. David, the younger son, died in infancy. The elder son, Alexander, wedded, in his nineteenth year, Margaret, daughter

---

[1] The feast of St Simon and St Jude is the 28th October, but it is obvious that the Dunfermline notary refers to the ceremonial which took place at Westminster on the 29th September. In point of fact there was no other.

[2] Register of Dunfermline, 217.

of Guy, Count of Flanders, and by his unpretentious manners awakened a lively hope. He survived his marriage only seventeen months, dying at Cupar-Fife on the 28th January 1283-4, without issue. The King's daughter, Margaret, married, in 1281, Eric, King of Norway; she was in her twenty-first year, while her royal husband was seven years her junior. She preceded her brother to the grave, leaving a daughter, who received her name. This infant, historically known as *the Maiden* of Norway, was, at a Parliament held at Scone on the 5th February 1283-4, acknowledged as heir to the throne, "failing any children whom Alexander might have, and failing the issue of the Prince of Scotland deceased." With prudent foresight, Alexander contemplated a second marriage, and at length fixed his affections on Joleta, daughter of Robert, fourth Count of Dreux, a descendant of Robert the Great, whose father was Louis le Gros, King of France. In the autumn of 1285, the King's nuptials were celebrated at Jedburgh, but the bright garments worn at the marriage feast were soon to be exchanged for vestments of mourning. At the close of a hunt in the forest of Kirkcaldy, the King, on his way to Inverkeithing by the Forth's northern shore, was thrown violently from his horse, and killed by the shock. This sad event, which took place on the 19th March 1285-6, threw the nation into mourning.[1] The earliest strains of our native minstrelsy, of which there is record, are preserved by Wyntoun in memorial of the event. Thus :—

> " Quhen Alysandyr oure Kyng wes dede,
> That Scotland led in luwe[2] and lé,[3]
> Away wes sons off ale and brede,
> Off wyne and wax, off gamyn and glé.

[1] Calendar of Documents relating to Scotland, II., Introd. x., xiii. ; Hailes, i., 200, 201 ; Tytler's History, ed. 1869, i., 22.

[2] Love.

[3] Tranquillity.

> "Oure gold wes changyd in to lede :
> Cryst, borne in to Vyrgynyté,
> Succoure Scotland and remede
> That stad[1] [is in] perplexyté."[2]

Ten days after his demise, Alexander's remains were consigned to the sepulchre of the kings in the church of Dunfermline Abbey. His undoubted heir was his infant grand-daughter, Margaret of Norway, but a powerful body of the nobility had at once determined to exclude her from the throne, and to prefer as her grandfather's successor a remote descendant of the royal house in the person of Robert de Bruce, Lord of Annandale. Dreading an insurrection on Bruce's behalf, the Bishops of St Andrews and Glasgow, and several of the other magnates, held a conference, at which they agreed to report to Edward, as grand-uncle of the young Queen, the imperilled condition of her affairs. In a letter to Edward dated 29th March 1286, they set forth " on behalf of the Clergy, Earls, and Barons, and others of the realm," that they had authorised the Prior of the Dominicans at Perth, also Brother Arnold of that Order, to proceed to the English Court charged with an important message.[3] The message was to be conveyed orally, since the messengers were liable to be captured and searched by members of the adverse faction. But some English writers have groundlessly set forth that the message was a secret one, and as such conveyed to Edward a surrender of the monarchy.

On the 11th April the Estates assembled at Scone, when the infant Margaret was recognised as Sovereign, and six guardians were appointed to administer on her behalf. Three of these guardians—the Earl of Fife, the Earl of Buchan, and Bishop

[1] Placed or standing.
[2] Wyntoun, B. vii., ll. 3619-27.
[3] Original Letter in Public Record Office.

Fraser of St Andrews—were to exercise authority to the north of the rivers Forth and Clyde, and on the south thereof, the three others, namely John Comyn, lord of Badenoch, Bishop Wishart of Glasgow, and the Steward. But while the loyal clergy and barons were concerned in securing a suitable executive on behalf of the infant sovereign, a body of the nobles held their allegiance in reserve. Apart from the malcontents who supported the pretensions of Robert de Bruce, there were not a few who signified their adhesion to the cause of John Baliol, who also asserted a title to the throne.

On the 20th September 1286, a Convention was held at Turnberry Castle. Those present were Patric, Earl of Dunbar, his sons Patric, John, and Alexander; Walter Steward, Earl of Menteith, his sons Alexander and John; Robert Bruce, Lord of Annandale, his sons Robert Bruce, Earl of Carrick, and Richard Bruce; James the Steward and his brother John; Angus, son of Donald of the Isles, and his son Alexander. Their apparent object was the granting of an " Affidatis," by which on oath they bound themselves to assist Richard de Burgh, Earl of Ulster, and Sir Thomas de Clare against the adversaries of the latter, always excepting their respective sovereigns. The throne of Scotland being vacant, and the succession uncertain till it was seen whether the widowed queen of Alexander III. (only six months dead) might have male issue, the person who should succeed was referred to in general terms.[1] The deed is misunderstood by Mr Tytler,[2] who styles it "an important convention that had escaped the notice of Lord Hailes," and argues from it that "there was then a strong party

[1] Three copies of the instrument are contained in the British Museum—Addit. MSS. 15,644, fol. 356; Lansd. 229, fol. 111, and 259, fol. 67. It is not known that the original of the instrument is extant.

[2] Hist. of Scotland, vol. i., pp. 64, 65.

against the Maid of Norway amongst the most powerful of the Scottish barons." His error is demonstrated by John Riddell,[1] who shows that the instrument is simply a Bond of Manrent, by which the several parties bound themselves to aid the English earl and knight. Yet it is far from improbable that the contingencies of the succession were discussed by the subscribing barons, several of whom were interested in it, and all more or less related. Sir Thomas de Clare and his elder brother Gilbert, Earl of Gloucester, were nephews of Isabella, wife of the Lord of Annandale, and support in his claim may have been promised to Bruce in return for his bond. The rules of succession were not then so fixed as to secure the Maiden's absolute right to her grandfather's crown.

In reference to the matter of the succession, Edward was meanwhile preparing for personal action. In the first instance he determined to unite the Scottish kingdom to his own by the marriage of two children—his son, the Prince Edward, and Margaret the Scottish Queen, each about six years old. With this view, he, on the 21st September 1286, obtained from Eric, King of Norway, a receipt for 2000 marks, being the amount of a loan he had given him three months previously.[2] Though nominally a loan, the sum granted was in reality a gift ; and as such it was clearly understood.[3] Eric was expected to satisfy the obligation in another form.

The royal children were cousins once removed, and as a first step to their union a papal dispensation became needful. Accordingly Edward sent to Rome a special messenger, by whom he represented to the Pope Honorius IV., that he could

---

[1] Additional Remarks on Lennox, etc., 1835, pp. 126-128.

[2] Memoranda Roll, 16, 17, Edward I., m. 7 ; also Stevenson's " Documents," i., 24.

[3] Pipe Roll, 21 Edward I.

find no suitable alliances for his children save within the forbidden degrees. Therefore he entreated his Holiness that in relation to the members of his house he would dispense with the impediments of affinity or consanguinity within the fourth degree, or of such marriages legitimate the issue. At Rome, Edward's messengers waited the Pope's reply, and Honorius, on the 27th May 1286, placed in their hands a bull, intended to fully satisfy his royal suppliant.[1]

After an absence in France of three years, Edward, early in 1289, returned to England. On his arrival he received, by the hands of the Bishop of Brechin, a letter from the Scottish guardians, informing him as to the unsettled condition of the country. Edward promised to use his best efforts for the restoration of tranquillity, but the appeal made for his support was obviously pre-arranged. He despatched to Eric of Norway a special envoy. This person—one Richard, a Norwegian—left England on the 8th April, with instructions to orally communicate with Eric as to matters of high import.[2] As a result, Eric, on the 17th of September, sent two special envoys to the English court. Edward gave them letters of protection, and notified their presence at his court to the Scottish guardians, with the intimation that they bore a message to them from the father of their Queen. To the guardians Edward also expressed a desire that they would send commissioners to meet the Norwegian envoys, but in matters of delicacy, such as the interview might involve, he feigned an unwillingness that any of the parties should be restrained by the presence of his court. If the parties met in England, he said, it must be in a locality

---

[1] The original is in the Public Record Office. A leaden bull affixed by strings of crimson and yellow silk still remains.

[2] Patent Roll, 17 Edward I., m. 19.

selected by themselves, and where they would, in counsel and action, be severally free. In a similar strain, Edward communicated with several of the Scottish barons, more especially with the Lord of Annandale. He added that while the convention would be perfectly unfettered, he would yield his highest sanction to its deliberations by sending to it as his representatives his faithful councillors, the Bishops of Durham and Worcester, also the Earls of Pembroke and Warenne.

On the 6th November 1289, the convention so arranged was held at Salisbury. It consisted of Edward's commissioners and those of Eric of Norway; also of the guardians of Scotland, and other magnates of the kingdom. A treaty was formed, in which it was agreed that the young Queen should be sent from Norway to Scotland or England prior to the 1st of November 1290, and that in the interval she should be held free of all matrimonial engagements. If she arrived in England, and the people of Scotland desired that she should be brought thither, then she would be so conveyed, provided that the peaceful condition of the country rendered the course justifiable; also on the further provision, that " the good men of Scotland " should give security to the King of England, that they would not unite her in marriage without his sanction, and that of her father, King Eric. Finally the Scottish commissioners gave solemn pledge that the Queen's presence should not be required in Scotland, until the kingdom enjoyed perfect quiet.[1]

Among the commissioners from Scotland who took part in the treaty at Salisbury was Robert de Bruce. Unaware of Edward's secret negotiations with Eric, and at Rome, the Lord of Annandale was moved by a new ambition. His grandson, Robert, the future restorer of the Scottish monarchy, was then

---

[1] Patent Roll, 17 Edward I., m. 2, 3.

in his fifteenth year. Would not the union of his grandson with the young Queen conclusively establish the kingdom in his family? Edward encouraged the hope while resolutely adhering to his original purpose.

On the 16th November 1289, being the tenth day after the arrangements at Salisbury, Pope Nicholas IV. granted a special dispensation for the marriage of the Prince of Wales with the Scottish Queen—this proceeding on Edward's representation that the offences constantly arising between the kingdoms by reason of their contiguity, rendered such a union most urgent, while any delay, he hinted, might necessitate his intended crusade to be postponed indefinitely.[1] Thus, while by his representatives Edward approved the resolution at Salisbury that the Scottish Queen should not be contracted in marriage for a year after her arrival in this country, his messengers were in progress of obtaining the highest sanction, whereby the infant sovereign of the Scots should, apart from the consent of her people, be at once contracted to his son. In the light of subsequent events, it is abundantly evident, that immediately on the arrival of Eric's envoys in September, he had simultaneously despatched messengers to the Roman Court, and initiated proposals for the Salisbury convention.

Possessed of the papal bull sanctioning the young Queen's marriage, Edward ventured a further move on the political chess-board. To the Estates of Scotland he addressed a communication, in which he counselled them to promote the general concord, and to render obedience to the guardians. And that he might become personally informed of any evils which should be remedied, he promised early to send into the country some

[1] Three copies of the Bull of Pope Nicholas IV., sanctioning the contract of marriage between the Prince Edward and Margaret of Scotland, are preserved in the Public Record Office.

trusted members of his council, who would bring him a report.[1] But these were otherwise instructed, and so on their arrival Edward's commissioners proceeded to set forth that a matrimonial alliance between the two royal families would check any local discord, and induce international harmony. Edward deemed his proposal ripe for publication, when, on the 14th day of March 1289-90, the Estates assembled at Brigham. The Estates had been summoned for the sole purpose of ratifying the treaty of Salisbury; but those members who attended were not unwilling to sanction a further proposal, to which already the guardians had assented. And the guardians had communicated with Edward in these words, "We rejoice to hear the general report, that your Highness has procured a dispensation from the Pope for the marriage of your son, Prince Edward, with our sovereign lady. We beseech your Highness to inform us whether the report be true: if it is, we, on our part, heartily consent to the alliance, not doubting that you will agree to such reasonable conditions as we shall propose to your Council." By the Estates Eric was urged to forthwith send his daughter into England,— these words of menace being added—"Nevertheless if you should fail in granting our request, we must in this exigency follow the best counsel which God may give us, for the state of this kingdom and its inhabitants."[2]

In Scotland Edward had greatly triumphed, since the Estates had not only condoned his lack of candour, but had openly approved it. Further, they had in his favour renounced the custody of their own Queen, electing that she should be sent to England.

Edward instituted preparations for the royal voyage, and

[1] Fœdera, ii., 445. [2] Liber A. (Chapter House), fol. 149ᵃ, 150; Fœdera, I., 700, 701.

in the hope of inducing Eric to accompany his daughter, he arranged that the means of transport should be made abundantly attractive. By his authority a large ship was secured at Yarmouth, and its victualling entrusted to Matthew de Columbariis, the chief butler of his household. Among the articles of victualling were included thirty-one hogsheads and one pipe of wine, ten barrels of beer, fifteen carcases of oxen, seventy-two hams, four hundred dried fish, two hundred stock fish, one barrel of sturgeon, five dozen of lampreys, fifty pounds of whale, together with twenty-two gallons of mustard, and other condiments. There were also many loaves of sugar, and stores of walnuts, figs, and raisins, and twenty-eight pounds of gingerbread. For the Queen's personal use were provided the richest attire, with costly jewelry. The victualling costs amounted to £265, 5s. 9d.[1]

Manned by a crew of forty hands, the vessel sailed from Hartlepool on the 9th of May, and in fourteen days thereafter reached its destination. On board were Edward's commissioners, Henry de Cranebourne, abbot of Welbeck; Henry de Ry, clerk to the Bishop of Durham; and other persons of quality. Having presented their credentials, they placed in Eric's hand a letter, in which Edward asserted the right of at once conveying the Scottish Queen to England.[2] Stunned by the peremptory character of the demand, Eric sought ten days for deliberation, and thereafter refused to surrender his child, or to accompany her to England.

Eric had not forgotten Edward's grant of two thousand marks, and that it had been made recoverable. But, nevertheless, this consideration failed to induce him to entrust his young and fragile child to the custody and control of one, whose chief

---

[1] Wardrobe Book, 18 Edward I.   [2] Patent, 17 Edward I., m. 4, cedula; Fœdera, i., 731.

anxiety was to secure her possessions. In the new emergency, Edward had recourse to the advice of Bishop Bek,[1] and that astute churchman suggested that Eric's private counsellors should be appointed members of the young Queen's household, and pensioned accordingly.[2]

Allowing a suitable interval to elapse, Edward renewed his request. To Eric he strongly represented that the Pope had consecrated the proposed union, that it was desired by the Scots, and further that it was essential to the common welfare. As Eric was at variance with the Pope, the first argument failed. But, as his counsellors now approved of Edward's request, he withdrew his resistance.[3]

Edward next approached the guardians. On the 15th May he became bound to them under a penalty of 3000 marks, that, prior to the 1st of November, the Queen should be landed in Britain, or that Eric and his nobles should take a joint oath to send her thither.[4] Thereupon followed the marriage treaty. This was arranged with the Scottish Estates at a convention held at Brigham on the 18th of July, when Edward was represented by five commissioners, including Bishop Bek. To articles drawn by the guardians, which tended to secure the independence of Scotland under every possible contingency, were added, at the instance of the English commissioners, certain subsidiary provisions, on which Edward might at any time revive his pretension as to feudal superiority. Thus, while in the first and fifth articles it was agreed that the laws, liberties, and customs of Scotland should remain intact, and the kingdom continue to be separate from and without subjection to England,

---

[1] See Appendix.

[2] Patent, Edward I., m. d. ; Fœdera, i., 787.

[3] Fœdera, ii., 473.

[4] *Ibid.,* ii., 479 ; Patent, 18 Edward I., m. 30.

these words were added, " saving always the right of the King of England, and of all others, which, before the date of this treaty, belonged to him, or any of them in the marches, or elsewhere, or which ought to belong to him, or any of them, in all time coming." [1]

Overlooking the force of these subsidiary provisions, to which they rashly assented, the members of the Estates became apprehensive owing to the strong protests of the commissioners, that their own stipulations might be ultimately rejected. They therefore insisted that if their terms were not confirmed by Edward's oath prior to the 8th of September, the entire negotiation should be held as void. But Edward, while disappointed that the Estates had not more fully yielded to his wishes, ratified the treaty. [2]

The marriage treaty provided, that in the administration of Scottish affairs, natives of the country only should be employed. But Edward, when, on the 28th of August, he confirmed the treaty, informed the Estates that he had appointed the Bishop of Durham as lieutenant in Scotland, on behalf of the Queen, and his son, her intended husband. [3] As a next step in subjection, Edward, under the pretence of being disquieted by certain rumours, demanded that all the Scottish castles and strongholds should at once be delivered into his hands. [4]

The Estates received Bishop Bek as their Queen's lieutenant, also the English bishop of Caithness as their chancellor; but the keepers of the national strongholds, led by three patriotic knights —Sir William Sinclair, Sir Patrick Graham, and Sir John Soulis—

[1] Fœdera, ii., 282, *et seq.*

[2] *Ibid.*, ii., 487; Patent, 18 Edward I., m. 9; Public Record Office, Liber A., fol. 154, b.

[3] Fœdera, i., 787; Patent, 18 Edward I., m. 9. To Bishop Bek, Edward, on the 20th February 1290, granted the keeping of the lands in Penrith, Cumberland, and of Tynedale in Northumberland, formerly held by Alexander III. (Patent Roll, 18 Edward I., m. 33).

[4] Fœdera, ii., 488.

declined to surrender them to a foreign power.[1] Edward partially relented, and it was at length arranged that the fortresses should, on the Queen's arrival, be delivered to her and her husband, while if she did not arrive by the first day of November, that the keepers of the strongholds should become bound to retain them for her and the Prince.[2]

Eric elected to send his daughter to Scotland by way of Orkney, on the plea that a longer voyage might be injurious to her health. By corresponding arrangements Edward met the resolution. On the 28th August, he appointed as his procurators for the marriage, John, Earl of Surrey, the Bishop of Durham, and Henry of Newark, Dean of York; and three days thereafter these persons were sent to Scotland to confer with the Estates, and also to arrange with Eric's commissioners.[3] For the Queen Edward provided some costly gifts, these consisting of a pitcher of silver gilt, bearing the royal shield; a cup cochleated with gold; a gilt cup; a cup tallied with gold; a cup of gold, with a shield parted in the midst, displaying the arms of France and Navarre; a double jug, decorated with enamels displaying the arms of France; a jug with lid of gold; a pair of foot lavers, and a pair of basins.[4]

Apart from his special commissioners Edward despatched to Scotland Thomas de Braytoft and Henry de Ry, whom he commanded to proceed to Orkney, there to join the deputies of the guardians in waiting upon the Queen. The itinerary of these two envoys has been preserved. Leaving Newcastle on the 15th September, they proceeded by the east coast to St Andrews, and from thence by Montrose to Aberdeen.[5] Reaching

---

[1] Fordun a Hearne, p. 785.

[2] Fœdera, ii., 489.

[3] *Ibid.*, i., 737; Patent, 18 Edward I., m. 0; Liber A. (Chapter House), fol. 149, 150.

[4] Public Record Office, Liber A., fol. 178, b.

[5] The envoys aspirated the northern capital, and so have put it down as *Haberdone*.

"Schelbotel," that is, Meikle Ferry in Sutherlandshire, on the 1st October, they were there joined by the Scottish deputies.[1] They did not proceed further, nor is the cause stated, for while they continue to record their expenses till they reach England, they enter into no particulars as to their mission.

The Scottish Queen was dead. How and when she parted with her young life is a mystery even now. The sad occurrence was unnotified to the guardians, nor has any record of the event been discovered among the English state papers. Even in the young Queen's native country so great an uncertainty prevailed, that about ten years subsequent to the period when she was placed on shipboard for the Orkneys, a woman from Leipsic ventured to enter Norway, and describe herself as Eric's daughter, and the Scottish Queen. As an impostor, this woman was by Haco, Eric's successor, burned at the stake, but on the spot at Bergen, where she suffered, was afterwards reared a chapel, which was consecrated to her memory. That Margaret from Leipsic was a pretender has been clearly shown. And it seems all but certain that the infant Queen died in Orkney some time in September 1290. Her remains, carried back to Norway, were, it is understood, deposited beside those of her mother in the choir of Christ's Church, Bergen.[2]

Informed of the Queen's death, Edward had, on the 9th of October, the papal bull, sanctioning her proposed marriage to the Prince of Wales, read in the refectory at Westminster, in presence of the Prior and Convent, and a record made of the proceeding.[3]

In Scotland the report of Queen Margaret's death was

---

[1] Public Record Office, Miscellaneous Documents.

[2] Proceedings of Society of Scottish Antiquaries, x., 408.

[3] Memoranda Roll, 18-19 Edward I., m. 2.

attended with an immediate renewal of the conflict as to the succession. On the 7th October, Bishop Fraser of St Andrews, at the counsel of Edward's lieutenant, Bishop Bek, despatched to Edward a letter of the following purport. A rumour had reached him that the Queen was dead, which he hoped was untrue; but it had already led to a course of anarchy. For on the first Sunday of October, when the Estates were assembled at Perth, to be informed as to Edward's contentment as to the strongholds being delivered up to the young Queen and her husband, Robert Bruce of Annandale, who had refused to sanction the arrangement, entered the city with an armed force. The bishop then proceeded, "If Sir John Baliol come to your presence, we advise you to take care so to treat with him that, in any event, your honour and advantage be preserved. If it turn out that our Lady has departed this life, deign to approach towards the march, for the consolation of the Scottish people, and to avoid bloodshed, so that the faithful men of the kingdom may keep their oath inviolate, and set over them for king him who of right ought to have the succession, if so be that he will follow your counsel."[1]

At Bishop Bek's advice Baliol at once journeyed to the English Court. From Edward he, on the 14th of October, received letters of protection from his creditors on the plea that he was about to proceed to the Continent in the King's service.[2] And to Bishop Bek, in acknowledgment of service, Baliol, on the 16th of November, granted the manor of Wark in Tynedale, also the manor of Penrith and others in the county of Cumberland, these having belonged to Alexander III., and which Baliol now claimed as the king's heir. In the instrument of grant he made

[1] Fœdera, ii., 741.
[2] Memoranda Roll, 18-19 Edward I., m. 2 dorso.

provision that should Edward refuse to render the requisite sanction, the bishop should, as an equivalent, receive a portion of land in Scotland of the value of 500 marks.[1]

In renewing his candidature for the throne, the Lord of Annandale again approached Edward with a degrading sub-serviency. On his behalf he drew together his son, the Earl of Carrick, also the Earls of March, Mar, Menteith, Athole, Lennox, and the young Earl of Fife, and causing these to describe them-selves as "the seven earls of Scotland, having the privilege of placing the King of Scotland on the throne," accepted election at their hands, subject to the approval of Edward as Lord Paramount of the kingdom. At his behest "the seven earls" entreated the English King to prevent the further oppression of the Earl of Mar, one of their number; also to restrain Bishop Fraser of St Andrews, John Comyn, and John Baliol, from intermeddling with national affairs. In the earls' memorial Edward was invoked to render his support, inasmuch as not only the memorialists, but the abbots, priors, barons, and free-holders of the kingdom, threw themselves on his protection.[2] On discovering this document in the Treasury, Sir Francis Palgrave was led to assume that the evidence of Scotland's subjection to the English Crown was exhaustively complete;[3] but a little research would have shown that the petitioning earls possessed no elective or legislative function, and that the Scottish earls of the time numbered not seven, but twelve. Nor were the earls personally satisfied as to Edward possessing the authority ascribed to him, since their memorial is accompanied by a parchment in which it is set forth that Edward must certainly

---

[1] From the Campbell Charters in the British Museum, No. 9. A seal in red wax is appended with the Baliol arms, and the legend " + S Johan de Baillovel."

[2] Chapter House, Scots Documents, Box 89, No. 22.

[3] Palgrave's Documents, Introd. viii., i., 14-21.

possess a supremacy over the Scottish sceptre, since Richard I. could not legally release the King of Scots from his subordination to the English Crown.[1]

Added to the wreck of his hopes by the death of the Scottish Queen, Edward was now suffering under severe domestic anxiety. Eleanor, his Queen, to whom he had been married for nearly thirty-five years, had long been in feeble health, and she was now prostrated as an invalid at Hardby manor, near Lincoln. On her death, which took place on the 28th of November, Edward enacted a ghastly ceremonial. Causing the Queen's limbs to be separated from her body, he deposited one in the cathedral of Lincoln, and the other in the church of the Black-friars, London. The mutilated trunk was next borne to West-minster by a procession of courtiers, but was halted at every town so that the clergy might place it in front of the high altar of their principal church. By erecting to Queen Eleanor three costly tombs and twelve monumental crosses, Edward further betokened his grief while he also paraded his magnificence.[2]

According to the usage of the times, it was held proper that one severely stricken as Edward was, should for a time retire from public activities. He rested three months, but when his official mourning was ended, he informed his Council that it was his intention to forthwith subject Scotland to his authority in the same manner in which he had subordinated Wales.[3] As a first step he desired that evidence might be produced to show that Scotland was a fief of the English Crown. Accordingly, in March 1290-1, he enjoined the chapters of his cathedrals and the members of the chief religious houses to institute a search in

---

[1] Chapter House, Scots Documents, Box 1, No. 16.

[2] The Greatest of all the Plantagenets. Lond. 1860, 8vo, pp. 151-155.

[3] Annales Waverleenses, p. 242 ; Script. Brit. a Gale, vol. ii.

their several repositories. And his writs were despatched by special messengers, who were authorised to receive and carry off every ancient document.[1] Of the twenty-two monasteries addressed, the greater number responded, and in their answers set forth that they had found in their registers no single entry bearing upon the feudal subordination of the northern kingdom. It is evident, remarks Sir Francis Palgrave, that if Edward had expected some unscrupulous monk to forge on his behalf, no one was sufficiently criminal or subservient to gratify his purpose.[2]

Foiled in an attempt to induce any portion of his clergy to justify his projected inroad on the liberties of the sister kingdom, Edward proceeded to interpret the letter of Bishop Fraser as a request for his interference made on behalf of the guardians. Accordingly, he, on the 16th April 1291, issued letters of summons to the barons of the northern counties, commanding them to meet him at Norham on the 3d of June, attended by their retainers. Among those summoned were these five barons, who also held land in Scotland, namely,—Gilbert de Umfraville, John de Baliol, Ingram de Gynes, Alexander de Baliol, and Robert de Bruce. The sheriffs of York, Lancaster, Westmoreland, Cumberland, and Northumberland were also strictly charged to secure on the occasion the attendance of all who owed the Crown military service.[3]

Of the proposed formidable gathering, William Fraser of St Andrews, bishop and guardian, could not reasonably complain, for in his letter of October he had suggested the proceeding, though perhaps unwittingly.

---

[1] Great Seal Writs, 18 Edward I.; Privy Seal Writs, 19 Edward I.,—all in the Public Record Office.

[2] Sir Francis Palgrave's Documents and Records, 1837, 8vo, Introd., xcv., xcvi.

[3] Close Roll, 19 Edward I., m. 7 dorso ; Fœdera, i., 752.

Having advised his northern forces to be in readiness for action, Edward, on the 10th May, requested the Scottish Estates to meet him in Norham Castle on the 31st of that month. And to allay the scruples of those who might object to the convention being held on foreign soil, he, in letters of safe-conduct, certified that their present act of attendance should not be quoted to the disadvantage of Scotland's independence.[1]

On the morning of the 31st May, Edward presented himself on a small islet, opposite Norham Castle, in circumstances of imposing splendour. He was attended by his knights, each of whom wore a dark hood, with a coat and breeches of mail, and displayed on his saddle silver spurs, and on his horse the richest trappings. Each knight was attended by his esquire, who wore a blue cap, and a short green gown spotted with white and red flowers, and exhibited from his girdle various ornaments. Edward wore a crown of gold, and a robe of scarlet silk studded with precious jewels, while on his shoulders rested a tabard, of which the front and back were embroidered with the arms of France and Ireland.[2]

When the Scottish Estates, represented by the Bishops of St Andrews and Glasgow and several of the barons, had taken their seats, Edward commanded Roger le Brabazon, Justiciary of England, to open the business. The Justiciary then proceeded to descant on the divine character of justice, and on the blessedness of peace. Next he set forth how that his august sovereign had, on account of the troubles into which Scotland had fallen consequent on the death of Alexander III. and his offspring, been moved anxiously. And in his deep affection for the

---

[1] Patent, 19 Edward I., m. 14 ; Stevenson, i., 227 ; Fœdera, ii., 525.

[2] Jerningham's Norham Castle, Edinb. 1860, 8vo, pp. 129-131

Scottish people, he was now seeking to allay the strife of a disputed succession. As there were several competitors for the throne, he desired to ascertain what were the claims of each, and for that purpose, and in the interests of peace, he had undertaken a long journey in order to be present at the conference. But the duty he felt was incumbent upon him from his relation to Scotland as its Lord Superior. "Whereupon," concluded the Justiciary, "our Lord the King doth require your hearty recognition of his right as your Superior and Overlord."[1]

The assurances of moderation made by Edward through his ambassadors at Perth had, on the part of the Scottish clergy and barons, induced the hope that he would cease from further asserting pretences, which were so utterly obnoxious to them. Under that belief had all the barons now present at Norham undertaken their journey. When, therefore, Edward, by his chief justice, called upon them to abjure their national independence, they felt as men utterly befooled. One baron only was sufficiently composed to express his sentiments, and what he uttered was to the effect, that no answer could be made to Edward's demand so long as the Scottish throne remained vacant. To this remark Edward replied fiercely, "By holy Edward, whose crown I wear, I shall have my rights acknowledged, or perish in the attempt." Consulting together, the Estates pleaded for delay. "I will wait," said Edward, "till to-morrow."

To this impetuous procedure, Edward was advised by Bishop

---

[1] Hemingford, i., 33. The Justiciary's oration, composed in Latin by William Hotham, Provincial of the Predicant Friars, was spoken in Norman French. More discreet than the writer, Brabazon judiciously omitted these words, " The reprobate Saul, from his shoulders and upwards higher than any of the people, oppressed the Israelites ; whereas our Sovereign Lord, by his pious benignity, raises up and supports those over whom the Prince of Peace hath elevated him." Probably the omission was due to the Bishop of Durham, who may have conceived that an allusion to Edward's stature was more likely to excite laughter than promote reverence.

Bek, who, being resident in Scotland as lieutenant, pretended an acquaintance with the national modes, and hence gave the assurance that on strong pressure every Scotsman would yield. But Edward, on having recourse to other counsellors, came to the conclusion that the subjugation of an ancient kingdom could not be attained by bluster and menaces.

Edward found himself in a new difficulty. To him John Baliol had evinced heretofore an entire subserviency, expressing his willingness to receive from his hands the Scottish crown as from a superior and overlord. When, however, the Estates indicated a measure of resistance, Baliol began to demur and hesitate. But the consideration which he had yielded to the representatives of a nation, Edward determined should not be extended to a single individual who was a candidate for his favour.

Baliol was deeply in debt. And as his chief creditor, Edward despatched writs from Norham for the seizure of his lands, and the distraint of his personal estate. These writs were addressed to the sheriffs of Lincoln, Norfolk, Suffolk, Northampton, Bedford, Buckingham, Hertford, Essex, and Middlesex. In especial, the sheriff of Northumberland was charged to seize Baliol's goods and farm produce to the satisfaction of two particular claims,—one, a debt of £633, 3s. 4d., due to the king by his progenitors; the other, an obligation for £601, 19s. 3d., and four tuns of wine, which Baliol owed to Edward personally.[1]

By these severities Edward achieved a twofold purpose. On the one hand he compelled the foremost candidate for the throne to yield unreservedly to his wishes, while on the other he sought to induce a belief on the part of Baliol's rival, the Lord of Annandale, that Baliol was held by him in aversion.

[1] Lord Treasurer's Memoranda Roll, 18-19 Edward I., m. 43, in the Public Record Office.

To the Estates Edward issued a new manifesto. He had, he remarked, sought a public acknowledgment of his authority, in the sole consideration that he might grant feudal possession of the kingdom to one who might be found entitled to the office. And now, in evidence of his moderation, he was ready to receive as competitors, all of the blood royal who, in presenting their claims, were willing to abide by his decision. Nor since the act was obnoxious to them would he further summon Scottish magnates to re-assemble on English soil. He therefore adjourned the Estates, and authorized them to re-assemble within the bounds of Scotland. But, when, on the 2d of June, they again met, their place of assembly was at Holywell Haugh, which is on the north side of the Tweed. And while there under canvas, they met in deliberation, they were within reach of the missiles of Norham Castle, while Edward also paraded before them his stout retainers of the northern counties.[1]

Parliamentary proceedings at Holywell Haugh were commenced by Edward's chancellor, Robert Burnell, bishop of Bath.[2] In sundry documents, said Burnell, it was attested that the English Kings were Lords Paramount of Scotland, while this right, derived from remote ages, they had asserted strongly. Further, that King Edward had lately invited the barons and clergy to produce any evidences or arguments of a contrary sort, but they had offered none; and though the Scottish community had presented a paper, it was not to the point, and

[1] Fœdera, ii., 549.

[2] Robert Burnell attended Edward in Palestine as his chaplain and private secretary, and thereafter continued his chief counsellor. Owner of the Castle of Acton Burnell, near Shrewsbury, he was, in 1274, preferred by Edward as bishop of Bath and Wells. During the same year he was appointed Keeper of the Great Seal, and in the year following obtained the additional office of Lord High Treasurer. He also discharged duty as Archdeacon of York. One of the ablest, he was also the least scrupulous, of Edward's counsellors.

unworthy of attention.[1] Therefore, proceeded the chancellor, the King of England will at once assume his hereditary office, and as overlord of Scotland proceed to determine the question of succession.[2] In the vicinity of an armed force, and of the catapults of Norham, the Estates preserved silence.

In the tent at Holywell, eight persons were, as competitors for the throne, severally introduced to Edward's presence. The first of these was the Lord of Annandale. Since the convention at Salisbury, Bruce had relied more on his personal followers than on the favour of the English King; but when he remarked that Edward was prosecuting for debt his formidable rival, Baliol, he was encouraged to hope that at the English Court his claim would now not be unacceptable. As competitors next followed Florence, Count of Holland; John Hastings; Patric Dunbar, Earl of March; William de Ross, William de Vesci, Walter Huntercumbe, Robert de Pynkeny, and Nicholas de Soulis.

When each competitor had stated his claim, another part of the programme fell to be enacted. A second time called to the front, Robert Bruce was thus interrogated: "Do you freely own and acknowledge Edward, King of England, as Lord Superior of Scotland, and as such are you willing in this cause to abide by his decision?" Bruce answered that he accepted the obligation

---

[1] The Community of Scotland might not be wholly ignored, since Edward had, in the arrangements connected with the intended marriage of the Scottish Queen with his son, acknowledged their legislative existence, and entreated their consent. Yet their protest against Edward assuming the office of overlord has not been preserved! Not long afterwards, we find Edward's notary making complaint, that he had been prevented by the Archbishop of Canterbury from completing notes in reference to Scotland, which he had beside him, and which he only could arrange properly; his meaning evidently being, that, considering the service he could render to the King in relation to Scottish affairs, there would be a fitting policy in upholding his interests (Palgrave's Documents, Introd., lvi., lvii.; Burton's History, ii., 121, *note*).

[2] Fœdera, ii., 544; Dugdale's Chron., series 24.

" sincerely, expressly, and without reserve." [1]   The declaration
made by a competitor whose title to the throne was not remote,
was readily accepted by all the others.

At Holywell, on the 2d of June, John Baliol did not present
himself.   But when the eight claimants had severally acknowledged Edward's superiority, Sir Thomas Randolph set forth
that Baliol was in error as to the day of meeting, and on
this account begged that Edward would adjourn the assembly.
To Randolph's proposal Edward assented, and when next day
the Estates re-assembled, Baliol presented himself.   By Bishop
Burnell he was now asked, as a claimant, to repeat the oath
of submission, which he did after a brief pause and with evident
reluctance. [2]

Baliol's brother-in-law, John Comyn of Badenoch, who had
hitherto resolved rather to sacrifice his claim than acknowledge
Edward's pretensions, next announced himself as a competitor,
and accepted the proffered oath.

By the English chancellor was intimated an act of clemency.
"My illustrious master," he said, " in asserting superiority
over the Scottish kingdom, has no intention of advancing
his claim to heritable proprietorship; this right he would
reserve."   But it was now made evident, that had the infant
Margaret lived to become his son's consort, Edward would have
asserted that her kingdom had, as a fief not descendible to
females, returned to him as overlord.   On this plea he would
have assumed the government, granting the succession to the
Prince of Wales, not as husband of the Scottish Queen, but
as receiving it by his act and will as feudal superior. [3]

When his chancellor had ceased, Edward addressed the

---

[1] Fœdera, ii., 525.   [2] *Ibid.*, p. 549.

[3] Fœdera, ii., 551.

assembly. For the Scottish people, he said, he cherished the deepest affection, as must be evident by the fatigues he had undergone, so as amicably to settle their affairs. And while he would shortly pronounce judgment as to the rightful heir to the throne, he meanwhile would uphold the laws, correct abuses, and promote concord. He added that while his proceedings would be conducted so as to advance the Divine glory, his claim to the property of Scotland would remain entire.

Edward's notary next presented a parchment to which each of the ten candidates was requested to append his seal. It was inscribed thus :—" Forasmuch as the King of England has evidently shown us, that the sovereign seigniory of Scotland and the right of determining our respective claims belong to him, we freely, and without compulsion, agree to receive judgment from him as our Lord Paramount, and we bind ourselves to submit to his award."[1]

Edward closed the proceedings by a further profession of clemency. Though by the competitors accepted as judge absolute, he would be guided by assessors, these to be for the most part selected by the claimants personally. Therefore he made request of Baliol, and his brother-in-law John Comyn, on the one part, and of Bruce upon the other, each to make choice, with approval of the other competitors, of " forty discreet persons " as commissioners of assize. To these he would add twenty-four persons of his own nation, skilled in legal questions, who should deliberate with them in common as to the preliminaries of judgment.[2]

Pleased by his conciliatory modes, the Estates ceased to regard Edward with distrust. And so, when at an adjourned meeting

---

[1] Hemingford, i., 34 ; Fœdera, ii., 529 ; Chapter House (Scots Documents), No. 18.

[2] Scots Documents in Chapter House, Box 16, No. 11 ; Fœdera, i., 764-766.

held on the 4th of June, he urged that in order to his judgment
being followed by execution, he should obtain sasine of the lands
and fortresses, his demand was readily conceded.   By the
previous refusal of the Estates to surrender the strongholds
Edward had been deeply offended, and now that he had secured
his purpose by a vote, he determined that the resolution should
be legally consummated.   So by letters patent prepared on the
instant, the Scottish castles were delivered into his hands.[1]   And
the act of the Estates passed on the 4th was on the two
following days sanctioned by the competitors, who thereupon
renewed their fealty.[2]   On the morning of the 6th, Edward
announced that he would give judgment as to the succession at
Berwick-upon-Tweed on the 2d of August.[3]

From Norham Castle, on the 11th June, the Scottish guardians
issued a manifesto approving the act of the Estates, and thereupon, in the jargon of feudal law, granted Edward "real and
corporal possession of the kingdom."   The guardians, originally
six, had by the decease of the Earls of Fife and Buchan been
reduced to four, these being Bishops Fraser and Wishart,
John Comyn of Badenoch, and James the Steward.   Edward
now added Brian Fitz Alan, an English officer, to whom he
soon afterwards committed the governorship of four principal
fortresses.

Invested by the guardians in feudal possession of the kingdom, Edward on the 12th June presented to them, in presence
of the competitors, as their chancellor in Scotland, a half
educated churchman, Alan of St Edmond, whom lately he had
intruded into the bishopric of Caithness.   And as Alan was,
apart from his subserviency, unequal to the duties of his new

---

[1] Scots Documents in Chapter House, Box 16,
No. 16.

[2] *Ibid.*, No. 18 ; Box 88, No. 20.
[3] *Ibid.*, No. 19.

office, Edward associated with him Walter of Agmundesham, an English notary.[1]

Edward now demanded a surrender of the Scottish castles by addressing his summonses to their governors. But in the assertion of his right he proceeded warily. In the preamble of his summons he described himself as "Edward, King of England, Lord of Ireland, and Duke of Guienne," but in relation to Scotland, as "Sovereign Seygnur." One governor only held out—Gilbert de Umfraville, who, in right of his mother, was Earl of Angus and keeper of the castles of Dundee and Forfar. On receiving letters of indemnity from the Estates, Umfraville afterwards surrendered.[2] To this remarkable baron we shall refer subsequently.

Those members of the Estates who had not yet submitted to his authority, Edward summoned to attend him at Holywell on the 13th of June. Twenty-seven persons assembled and severally rendered homage. But as Lord Hailes remarks, "the only ecclesiastic who performed the disgraceful ceremony was Mark, bishop of Sodor."[3] A herald having proclaimed King Edward as Lord Paramount of Scotland, the Estates adjourned to meet at Berwick on the 2d of August.[4] Edward now commanded that the proceedings relative to Scotland's subordination should forthwith be engrossed in the registers of all his monasteries.[5]

The complete subjection of Scotland had become Edward's chief concern and settled purpose. From Berwick, on the 3d July, he issued a manifesto, setting forth that while he was willing that judgment as to the succession should be pronounced in Scotland,

---

[1] Scots Documents in Chapter House, Box 16, No. 20 ; Fœdera, i., 768.

[2] Fœdera, i., 756.

[3] Hailes' Annals, i., 227.

[4] Fœdera, i., 76 ; Chapter House (Scots Documents), Box 16, No. 9.

[5] W. Hemingford, T. i., p. 36 ; Chapter House (Scots Documents), No. 19; also Box 100, No. 163.

he would not be debarred from giving judgment in England if he thought fit. He at the same time ruled that the writs of the Chief Justice of England should pass current in both kingdoms, since, in respect of the superiority over Scotland which the King of England possessed, the two countries were practically one.[1] Attended by John de Seton, a recreant Scotsman, Edward now made a journey into Scotland under pretence of honouring by a visit his correspondent Bishop Fraser of St Andrews,[2] but in reality for the purpose of securing the allegiance of certain barons and other notables who had not attended at Holywell. Before leaving Berwick, he there extorted homage from Henry, prior of Coldingham, Sir Alexander de Bonkyl, Agnes de Bernham, prioress of the nuns, also from the mayor and eighty burgesses. On the 5th July, when in his northern progress, visiting Sir Walter de Lindesay of Thurston, he received homage from Sir William Douglas, already known as *the Hardy*, on account of his prowess. And on the 8th July, in St Margaret's Chapel in Edinburgh Castle, he was acknowledged as Scotland's overlord by Adam, abbot of Holy Rood, and by Sir Richard Fraser.[3]

Proceeding to Stirling, Edward, on the 12th July, received to his allegiance in the castle, William, bishop of Dunblane, Malise, Earl of Strathearn, Geoffry of Moubray, and William of Ruthven. And on the same day, he, in name of the prelates, guardians, and other magnates, ordained all who were bound to allegiance to a native sovereign, to transfer it to himself. He further stipulated that all who attended on his summons, but refused to render homage, should be detained till performance ;

[1] Fœdera, ii., 573.

[2] Exchequer, Q. R. Memoranda, 18 and 19 Edward I., m. 14 dorso.

[3] Chapter House (Scots Documents), Box 16, No. 2.

that such as did not come, but sent excuse, should be subjected to trial by the Estates; and that those who neither came, nor sent excuse, should be thrown into prison.

From Stirling Castle Edward promulgated a further rule. He enjoined that in a central town of each district, all the clergy and landowners and principal burgesses should render homage either to himself personally, or through the instrumentality of his commissioners. And all were strictly charged to obey this command, before the Estates should, on the 2d August, assemble at Berwick.

On the 17th July, Edward brought to his homage at Dunfermline, at the great altar of the abbey, or in the chapter house of the monastery, the leading barons of western Fifeshire. Among these were Ralph the abbot, Sir Andrew Fraser, Sir William de la Haye, Sir Andrew of Moray, and Constantine de Logher, sheriff of Fife. At Kinghorn on the 19th, he, in the parish church, received fealty from Sir John of Moray, Sir Michael Scot, Sir Aco de Kinross, Sir Robert Horethe, Sir William Leighton, and other barons. At St Andrews on the 22d, he, within the chapter house, received homage from John, prior of the monastery, Sir Adam de Ratray, Sir William de Maule, Sir Alexander de Abernethy, Sir Hugh de la Haye, Sir John de Haye, Sir Henry de Anstruther, Sir Alexander de Airdrie, and Sir Robert Bethune. On the 23d, at the great altar of the abbey of Lindores, he received allegiance from Sir John the abbot, Sir William de Fenton, Sir Symon Fraser, and others.[1]

At Perth, in the cemetery of Blackfriars monastery, Edward received fealty from John of Perth and other seventy burgesses, and thereafter in the church of the monastery

---

[1] Chapter House (Scots Documents), Box 16, No. 2.

obtained homage from the abbot of Cupar; also from Maria, Queen of Man, Countess of Strathearn.[1] Within the King's chamber at Perth, he next admitted to his allegiance Friar Thomas, abbot of Scone, and Sir John, son of Alexander of Argyll.[2]

From Perth Edward moved southward. Reaching Linlithgow on the 28th July, he there received homage from one who commanded wide influence from her reputed sanctity, the Lady Christina, prioress at Manuel. On the 29th, he, in St Margaret's chapel in Edinburgh Castle, admitted to his fealty John, abbot of Newbottle; Ralph, Master of Soltre; Walter, Master of Balnecryfe; and Alicia, prioress of Haddington. And on the same day, in the royal chamber, he accepted as homagers Alexander, prior of the Hospital of St John of Jerusalem, and Brian, Preceptor of the soldiery of the Temple.[3]

Meanwhile Edward's commissioners were at the populous centres receiving to his homage those who were possessed of substance, or were otherwise entitled to consideration. The barons of Perthshire were in their county town accepted to homage by Bishop Fraser, John Comyn of Badenoch, and Brian Fitz Alan. Within the new castle of Ayr oaths of fealty to Edward were administered by Bishop Wishart of Glasgow, James the Steward, and Nicholas de Segrave. In the commission for Galloway, William de St Clair was conjoined with William de Boyville,[4] and these were specially instructed to secure the fealty of the Bishop of Whithorn. The Earl of Sutherland, the sheriff and other magistrates of Inverness-shire,

---

[1] Chapter House (Scots Documents), Box 16, No. 2.

[2] *Ibid.*

[3] *Ibid.*

[4] An Englishman appointed by Edward Keeper of the castles of Dumfries, Wigtown, and Kirkcudbright—Chapter House (Scots Documents), Box 100, No. 187.

were enjoined to personally render homage, and thereafter as commissioners to secure the submission of their neighbours,

Personally, and by his lieutenants and commissioners, Edward had greatly triumphed. At Holywell Haugh had succumbed the guardians, the competitors, and the members of the Estates. And between the 24th of June and the beginning of August, upwards of two hundred chief persons in Scotland had taken the oaths. Among the latter were nearly all the bishops, abbots, and friars, and the heads of military orders; also Maria, Queen of Man, the Earls of Strathearn and Ross, and thirty-six knights and barons.

On the 3d of August, the Estates assembled at Berwick, in the chapel of the castle. Edward, who was present, at once instructed his commissioners, numbering one hundred and four persons, to proceed to the church of the Dominican monastery, there to receive the competitors. Twelve persons now appeared as such, and by Edward's notary they are thus described :—

Florence, Count of Holland, great-grandson of Ada, daughter of Henry, Prince of Scotland, and sister of William the Lion.

Robert de Pinkeny, great-grandson of Marjory, daughter of Prince Henry, and sister of William the Lion.

Patric Dunbar, Earl of March, great-grandson of Ada, daughter of William the Lion.

William de Vesci, grandson of Marjory, daughter of William the Lion.

William de Ros, great-grandson of Isabella, daughter of William the Lion.

Nicholas de Soulis, grandson of Marjory, daughter of Alexander II., and wife of Alan Durward.

Patric Galythly, whose father, he alleged, was the lawful son of William the Lion.

Roger de Mandeville, who maintained a descent from Aufrica, whom he affirmed to be a daughter of William the Lion.

John de Hastings, son of Ada, third daughter of David, Earl of Huntingdon, brother of William the Lion.

John Comyn, Lord of Badenoch, who claimed descent from Donald Bane, who for a time occupied the throne ; and as descended from Marjory, younger daughter of Margaret, eldest daughter of David, Earl of Huntingdon.

Robert de Bruce, son of Isabel, second daughter of David, Earl of Huntingdon.

John de Baliol, grandson of Margaret, eldest daughter of David, Earl of Huntingdon.

Nine days were occupied in stating claims and adjusting them. Robert Bruce presented four series of pleadings, all composed in Norman French. On the 12th August, Edward, attended by his nobility, and by the members of the Scottish Estates, gave the claimants an audience. Having received their petitions from his deputies, he ruled that the entire process should be deposited in a bag, under the seals of the Bishop of St Andrews and the Earls of Buchan and Mar, until further light should be cast upon it. And professedly in order thereto, also that a missing document, which the Count of Holland alleged gave support to his claim, might be discovered, he gave authority that the repositories of the national records should be strictly searched. And as searchers he commissioned three Englishmen, namely, Sir John de Lithegreynes, Master William of Lincoln, and Thomas of Fisseburn, who were to associate themselves with the abbots of Dunfermline and Holyrood, also with William of Dumfries, Keeper of the Scottish Rolls. And all records and parchments were to be gathered up,—first those in the Royal Treasury, afterwards those contained in the monasteries and other public receptacles.[1]

This deliverance being intimated, a decision on the claims was adjourned to the 2d of June 1292,[2] prior to which date the

[1] Chapter House (Scots Documents), Box 1, Nos. 10, 11, 13, 21 ; Box 4, No. 21.

[2] Ignoring the revelations of the Record Office, Mr Clifford declares the adjournment was caused on account of tidings received by Edward as to his mother's illness—also to the necessity laid upon him of suppressing a violent feud which had broken out between the Earls of Hereford and Gloucester (The Greatest of the Plantagenets, pp. 189, 190).

commissioners of search were charged to produce their report. Privately they were enjoined to promptly convey every available parchment or other record into the castle of Berwick.

For the execution of their purpose in securing and carrying into England the national records of Scotland, Edward's commissioners possessed abundant facilities, for those kept in the Royal Treasury at Edinburgh Castle were already under the control of Ralph Basset of Drayton, the English governor. The commissioners proceeded actively, so that on the 23d of August, or eleven days after they had received their instructions, they bore the civil records to Berwick, and on the 3d of September completed an inventory of their contents.[1] That, in the records, Edward sought to discover some pretence for the assertion of his high-handed policy, his commissioners well knew. Hence in reference to King Richard's act revoking the vassalage extorted from William the Lion, they were careful in the inventory to report as to the defective nature of the seal. They describe the instrument thus :—"Litera Richardi Regis promissoria Regi Scotiæ quod restituet ei omnia jura sua ; *sed vix apparet sigillum.*"[2]

Notwithstanding the influence of Bishop Fraser, put forth on Edward's behalf, the commissioners were in relation to the ecclesiastical records unsuccessful, for, amidst the general defection, a large portion of the clergy still adhered to the national cause. Among the church records preserved was the Register of Dunfermline, which contains an entry of the attempt made by Edward in 1275 to induce Alexander III. to include Scotland in the possessions for which he rendered homage.

One of the chief purposes assigned by Edward for adjourning

---

[1] Chapter House (Scots Documents), Box 3, Nos. 53, 54, 58. The inventory is to be found in the "Fœdera" and the "Rotuli Scotiæ ;" also in Robertson's "Introduction to the Index of Charters ;" also *Instrumenta*, etc., in the first volume of the Statutes.

[2] Burton's History, ii., 108.

his decision was, that he might allow his hundred and four deputies leisure for deliberation. His real motive was widely different. For he well knew that so long as the matter of succession was open and unsettled, his personal authority was safe, while a display of eagerness to fully inform himself as to the subject of arbitration was likely to induce towards him confidence and favour.

When, on the 2d of June 1292, Edward again met the Estates at Berwick, the competition had materially narrowed. Of the twelve claimants, the Earl of March, William de Vesci, William de Ros, Patrick Galythly, and Roger de Mandeville, were found to descend from illegitimate children of William the Lion, and Nicholas de Soulis from an illegitimate daughter of Alexander II.; while of Margery, daughter of Prince Henry, through whom Robert Pinkeny assumed descent, there was found no trace. The Count of Holland's claims were overlapped by those possessed by the descendants of his ancestress's brother, David. On the two grounds on which John Comyn based his claim, the first was found to be untenable, and in the latter he was preceded by Baliol. Only on the plea that the kingdom was partible among the representatives of the three daughters of the Earl of Huntingdon, could John of Hastings' claim be held tenable, and as this doctrine was not to be sustained, the competition became restricted between the remaining candidates, Bruce and Baliol.

Meanwhile a new competitor arose; for Eric, King of Norway, father of the late Queen, was made to present a claim as his daughter's heir. It was probably put forth under Edward's connivance, as a plea for further delay, but inasmuch as Eric was authorized to receive a portion of his wife's dowry still unpaid, it was at once withdrawn.[1]

[1] Patent, 20 Edward I., m. 7.

As a first step towards giving judgment, Edward called the Scottish commissioners to the front, and publicly asked them how they would advise as to the claims of Bruce and Baliol? Then their pre-arranged answer was promulgated, which was that in a case so difficult, and without precedent, they could impart no counsel, more especially that in regard to Scottish laws and usages they differed among themselves, therefore they claimed the assistance of the English deputies.

With the English deputies the Scottish commissioners now held conference. "If you had agreed," said the deputies, "then we would have advised the king to confirm your judgment; but since you disagree we would not be justified in offering counsel. Besides, our numbers are few, and the king would do well, in so grave a question, to delay expressing a deliverance till he has obtained counsel from his Parliament." To counsel which he had secretly inspired, Edward had no difficulty in assenting. He adjourned the proceedings till the 15th day of October; at the same time expressing his anxiety that all present would in the interval consider how judgment should be given.

In October, when Edward again met the Estates at Berwick, he proceeded to renew his former policy. To his English deputies he propounded these two questions. *First*, "By what laws and practices ought judgment to be given; or if there are none such, or if the laws of England and Scotland differ, what was to be done?" *Secondly*, "Was the kingdom of Scotland to be regarded as a common fief, and the succession to the crown regulated by the same principles which were applicable to earldoms and baronies?" To these questions the pre-arranged answers of the deputies were in these terms,—that the king should decide according to the laws and usages of the kingdoms over which he reigned, and that if there existed no law adapted

to the case, he should frame a new law suited to the emergency.
Further, that the succession to the Scottish crown should be
decided in the same manner as the succession to earldoms,
baronies, and other indivisible inheritances.[1] Determining these
questions as his deputies had advised, Edward next invited
Bruce and Baliol to present their pleadings.   Bruce, it will be
remembered, was son of Isabel, second daughter of the Earl
of Huntingdon ; Baliol, grandson of Margaret, the earl's eldest
daughter.

On behalf of the Bruce it was urged that Alexander II.,
despairing of heirs of his own body, had accepted the Lord of
Annandale as his heir, and that Alexander III. had informed his
familiars that failing his own issue, Bruce should become his
successor.   On Bruce's behalf it was further pleaded, that
succession to a kingdom should be decided, not by the principles
which regulated the succession of vassals and subjects, but by
the law of nature, which suggested that the nearest heir of blood
is to be preferred.   And the mode of regal succession in
past times, it was held, justified this doctrine, inasmuch that on
the death of Kenneth M'Alpine, his brother Donald was allowed
the sceptre in preference to his son Constantine ; and that when
Constantine died, his brother Edh was preferred to his son
Donald. Further, on the death of Malcolm III., his brother
was preferred to his son as his successor.   It was further
alleged that in Spain, Savoy, and several other countries, the
son of the second excluded the grandson of the eldest daughter.
And it was contended lastly, that a woman is incapable of
governing, and as at the death of Alexander III., Devorgoil, the
mother of Baliol, was then living, and could not reign, the

---

[1] Fœdera, ii., 528.

kingdom had devolved upon Bruce as heir-male of the royal house.

In his pleadings Baliol made no answer in respect of the alleged preference of the two preceding kings. The claimants, he submitted, were in the court of their Lord Paramount, who would give judgment as in the case of any other tenements depending on his crown. And by the law and practice of England, the eldest female heir was preferred in the succession to all inheritance indivisible as well as divisible. In reply to Bruce's plea as to the ancient modes of succession, he maintained that if the brother was preferred to the son of the king, the example militated against the pleader, inasmuch as the son was nearer in degree than the brother, yet the brother was preferred. On the death of Malcolm it was acknowledged that his brother had occupied the throne, but on a complaint by Malcolm's son to the King of England, the usurpation was overcome. And when on the death of Malcolm's son, the former usurper again seized possession of the crown, the English King again dispossessed him, and placed on the throne Edgar, Malcolm's second son. The laws of succession in foreign countries, Baliol held, were inapplicable. That a woman ought not to reign was an argument inconsistent with Bruce's own claim, for if Isabel, his mother, could not legally govern, she could not transmit to her son the right on which he founded. But Bruce, it was contended, had acknowledged the validity of female rule by taking the oath of allegiance to the late Queen.[1]

To those assembled, Edward now addressed the question,— "By the laws and usages of both kingdoms does the issue

---

[1] Fœdera, T. II., 584.

of the eldest sister, though more remote in one degree, exclude the issue of the second sister, though in one degree nearer?"[1] There was elicited the response, that the issue of the elder sister was to be preferred. Again Edward prorogued the assembly.

To a meeting of the Estates which he held at Berwick on the 6th of November, Edward summoned all the competitors. He indicated that Bruce's claim was inferior to that of Baliol, but before pronouncing a final judgment, he expressed his desire to receive pleadings from the other claimants. Accordingly, John of Hastings, as the representative of the third daughter of David, Earl of Huntingdon, now set forth that the kingdom of Scotland was divisible, and ought, according to the laws of England as to partible fiefs, to be equally divided among the descendants of the three daughters.[2] To this, Bruce adhered, and therefore demanded a third of the kingdom as descended from the second daughter, reserving to Baliol, as representative of the eldest daughter, the title of King and the royal dignity. Having put to his commissioners the question as to whether the kingdom of Scotland was divisible, and received an answer in the negative, Edward made a further adjournment.

At Berwick Castle on the 17th of November, Edward re-assembled the competitors. Eight of their number, Eric, King of Norway, Florence, Count of Holland, William de Vesci, Patrick, Earl of March, William de Ros, Robert de Pinkeny, Nicholas de Soulis, and Patrick Galythly formally withdrew. By non-appearance John Comyn and Roger de Mandeville were

---

[1] *Fœdera*, ii., p. 586.

[2] On the 14th June 1292, Florence, Count of Holland, and Robert Bruce of Annandale executed an indenture, whereby they became bound to stand by each other, he who succeeded to the throne consenting to assign one-third of the realm to the other—the division to be settled by eight men of law to be named on each side (*Cottonian Charter*, British Museum, vii., 15).

held to have retired. Edward now gave judgment. The kingdom of Scotland, he said, being indivisible, the King of England was bound to judge the rights of his subjects according to the laws and usages of the people over whom he reigned, by which laws the more remote in degree of the first line of descent is preferable to the nearest in degree of the second. Therefore he gave his decree that John Baliol ought to have sasine of the kingdom of Scotland, with reservation of the right of the King of England, and of his heirs, when they shall think proper to assert it. Baliol was now called upon to indicate his willingness to receive his kingdom as a fief of the English crown, by paying to the Lord Chamberlain of England a fee of service. The precise amount of this exaction not being found by precedent, it was fixed at twenty pounds, or double the fee exacted on homage from an English earl.[1]

Exhorting his vassal to exercise discretion in his office, Edward commanded the five guardians to give him sasine of the kingdom, and instructed the governors of the several strongholds to surrender them into his hands.[2]

On the 20th November, Baliol rendered homage to Edward as overlord, and according to practice the notarial instrument which authenticated the proceeding should have borne the seal used in connexion with the fief, of the possession of which the act of homage was a symbol. But the seal of Scotland bore that it was that of a kingdom, and therefore its waxen impression would have negatived the concessions of the homager. In the circumstances, Edward ruled that Baliol should use his private seal, and that the Great Seal of the kingdom should be destroyed.[3] The

---

[1] Fœdera, ii., 591, 592.

[2] *Ibid.*, ii., 590.

[3] On the reverse of the seal was engraven the figure of St Andrew, with this inscription—"Andreas Scotis Dux est et compatriotis" (Anderson's Diplomata Scotiæ, No. 38).

act was performed in Baliol's presence. The Great Seal was broken into four pieces, and the fragments placed in a leather bag to be deposited in the English Treasury. For this procedure two reasons were urged—one, that questions relating to the validity of writs would be obviated, and further, that the broken seal would become a permanent token of the English superiority.[1]

[1] Rishanger's Chronicle, 368.

————o————

CHAPTER II.

> " Right to devoted Caledon
> The storm of war rolls slowly on
> With menace deep and dread ;
>
> .   .   .   .   .   .
>
> And O ! amid that waste of life,
> What various motives fired the strife !
> The aspiring Noble bled for fame,
> The Patriot for his country's claim."
>
> *—Lord of the Isles.*

EDWARD gave judgment in favour of Baliol solely as
a matter of policy. For six years and nine months
subsequent to the death of Alexander III., he had
been endeavouring to bring Scotland under subjection ; and to this end his decision in favour of Baliol
materially tended.   For in subordinating the northern kingdom
his chief obstacle lay in the resistance of the common people,
and these he concluded might succumb to the wishes of a native
prince.   And Baliol's personal obedience was in a measure
secured, since he was led to clearly understand that his reten-
tion of his kingly office depended on his procuring for his accepted
overlord the entire submission of his people.

When at Norham on the 20th November 1292, Baliol rendered
homage for his kingdom, Edward granted a feudal writ authorising him to receive the crown.   The privilege of placing
the crown on the head of the Scottish sovereign devolved

hereditarily on the Earl of Fife, but on the pretence that Duncan, holder of the title, was a minor, Edward instructed Sir John de St John, an English knight, to perform the act. At the hands of St John, as Edward's commissioner, Baliol was content to receive the regal symbol. The ceremony was enacted at Scone on the 30th of November.

By the bulk of the people, Baliol was held as a poltroon, for they were not uninformed that he had accepted as counsellors persons in Edward's pay, or immediately under his control.[1] Among these were his own brother-in-law, John Comyn of Badenoch, who as recompense received from Edward upwards of fifteen hundred pounds; Bishop Wishart of Glasgow, who received a land rental of £100 ; also James the Steward, the Earl of March, and Sir William de Soulis—all whom were compensated with English gold. To Sir John de Soulis, William de St Clair, and Patrick de Graham, also counsellors of the Scottish king, were granted yearly allowances of 100 marks.[2] And though the strongholds were nominally placed under Baliol's authority, they remained with his consent in the keeping of English governors.[3]

Edward summoned Baliol to present himself on the 26th December at Newcastle to renew his act of homage.[4] Under this command there lurked a secret purpose. Reminded that by the treaty of Brigham, Scotland was to be governed by its own laws, Edward determined to get rid of this embarrassing

---

[1] Rishanger, 371.

[2] Rotuli Scotiæ, i., 24 *et passim.*

[3] Fœdera, ii., 500 ; Rotuli Scotiæ, i., 11. From writs issued by the Guardians to the Chamberlain, directing him to make payment of salaries due to the keepers of the royal castles, we find these strongholds thus enumerated:—In the southern division, Edinburgh, Berwick, Roxburgh, and Jedburgh; in the western, Kirkcudbright, Wigtown, Dumfries, Dunbarton, Ayr, and Stirling; and in the northern, Inverness, Dingwall, Cromarty, Kincardine, Aberdeen, Cluny, Aboyne, Forfar, Dundee, Banff, Nairn, Elgin, and Forres. Other powerful castles, such as Caerlaverock, Turnberry, and Dirleton, were in the hands of the nobles.

[4] Fœdera, ii., 593 ; Rotuli Scotiæ, i., 11.

obligation, and an opportunity of re-opening the question had occurred conveniently. Margery Moigne, a widow at Berwick, had granted to a goldsmith, a burgess of the place, the loan of one hundred and eighty pounds, the property of her sons. The goldsmith died, and his executor Roger Bartholomew took possession of his estate, without satisfying the widow's claim. In his defence Bartholomew pleaded that the goldsmith's estate had a claim for the maintenance of the widow's sons, and that the widow had possessed herself of the balance due by snatching it from a strong-box. A decree in favour of the widow having been pronounced by the Court of Custodes at Edinburgh, Bartholomew, under the advice of certain Englishmen, appealed for redress to Edward as Lord Paramount. Entertaining the appeal, Edward resolved to sit in judgment upon it at Newcastle, and so desired to secure Baliol's presence as a party in the action. In support of the decision by the Edinburgh tribunal, Baliol referred to the treaty of Brigham, which provided that judgments pronounced in the Scottish Courts were not to be reviewed by those of England. In reply, Edward insisted that the treaty of Brigham was framed when the Scottish throne was vacant, but as now there was a king who owned vassalage, the condition was changed. He further insisted that he was hearing an appeal from judges whom he had personally chosen. He now made a fashion of consulting with some of the Scottish barons, and thereafter exhorted his Council to decide as they approved.[1]

To the subject of the Brigham convention Edward further returned, by maintaining that it should no longer be thrown in his teeth, especially when he was performing an act of justice. So far, he added, from rejecting appeals from the Scottish tribunals, he would hear all of them ; he would also assert the right

---

[1] Ryley's Pleadings in Parliament, 147.

of summoning Scottish prelates and nobles to attend him in England, as he thought fit. And as an earnest of the authority which he proposed to exercise, he summoned Baliol to attend him in his chamber on the 31st of December. When Baliol attended on the appointed day, he was informed by Edward's Justiciary that his royal master would not hold himself bound by any promises, which implied that he was to decline appeals from the country of which he was overlord, and that all deeds or legal instruments which implied a negative must be discarded or recalled. His dominion over Scotland, Edward then personally intimated, he would exercise when and where he pleased; nor would he hesitate to summon his vassal to attend him in England as occasion served.[1]

Baliol succumbed. By a legal instrument, dated 2d January 1292-3, he renounced the treaty of Brigham for himself and his successors; he also relieved Edward from all other obligations which might be pleaded against his exercising an unlimited authority over the Scottish sceptre. To this humiliating document, which was extended both in Latin and in Norman French, Baliol pledged himself that the Scottish magnates should append their seals in addition to his own. And he fulfilled his engagement, inasmuch that soon afterwards the instrument was sanctioned by the Bishops of St Andrews and Glasgow, John, Earl of Buchan, Patric, Earl of March, Gilbert, Earl of Angus, John, Earl of Athole; also by John Comyn the younger, Alexander de Balliol, Geoffry de Moubray, Patric de Graham, William de St Clair, and Thomas, son of Randolph.[2]

To Baliol as his vassal, Edward extended certain acts of courtesy. Having in the year 1290 taken under his protection

---

[1] Fœdera, ii., 507; Tyrrel's England, iii., 74.

[2] Chapter House (Scots Documents), Box 100, No. 90 and No 29.

the Isle of Man, he now relinquished it to Baliol, who thereupon acknowledged him as overlord.[1]   Next, for Baliol's special use, he delivered to his chamberlain, Alexander de Balliol, certain public records, also the rolls of causes decided by the guardians.[2]

With occasional acts of courtesy, Edward continued to pursue his aggressive policy.   In a letter, dated at Cupar-Fife, 20th April 1293, Baliol ventured to entreat him to forego his attending a justice ayre to be held in Yorkshire in the following month, to which he had been summoned.   And as a ground of excuse he ventured to remind his overlord of a promise made by him in the previous December, that he would in future dispense with all ordinary attendances.[3]   As an act of favour, Edward yielded assent to Baliol's entreaty, but he forthwith devised measures to intensify the burden of his vassalage.   At Westminster on the 3d of May, in presence of his Privy Council, he authorised his escheator to surrender to Baliol the lands of Tynedale, held by King Alexander III. on the condition that he did homage for the same " before or in the quinzaine of St Michael."[4]   And on the 12th of May, while ostensibly relieving Baliol of an irrecoverable obligation for £3000 charged for the relief of his late mother's lands in Scotland, he in the same instrument provided that other heavy obligations should be paid him by yearly instalments.[5]

The earldom of Fife has been referred to.   Duncan, Earl of Fife, died in 1288, and was succeeded by a son, also named Duncan, who, being a minor, was placed under the protection of Bishop Fraser of St Andrews.   The lands of the earldom having been usurped by one Macduff, the young Earl's granduncle, this person was ejected by the bishop ; but, on the order of Edward,

---

[1] *Fœdera*, ii., 402, 602.

[2] *Ibid.*, ii., 602.

[3] Tower Miscellaneous Rolls, No. ⁴⁵⁄₁₇.

[4] Close Roll, 21 Edward I., m. 9.

[5] Patent Roll, 21 Edward I., m. 19 ; Fine, 21 Edward I., m. 16, 17.

to whom he appealed, he was restored by the guardians. When, on the 10th February 1292-3, Baliol held his first Parliament at Scone, Macduff was required to answer for holding forcible possession of the lands of Reres and Croy, which, since the death of the last Earl of Fife, were in the hands of the king. An irrelevant defence which he put forth being repelled, he, as a trespasser, was committed to prison.[1] Liberated after a short detention, he petitioned Baliol for a re-hearing of his claim, and such being refused he appealed to Edward. Pleased with the opportunity of further asserting his authority as overlord, Edward summoned Baliol to appear before the English Parliament on the 24th of March.

Conceiving that the summons was issued as simply a matter of legal form, Baliol did not enter an appearance. But when the case was called in Parliament, Edward ordered an adjournment, that the Scottish king might present an attendance. Edward afterwards renewed his summons, charging Baliol to appear before his Parliament on the 14th of October.[2] From the Scottish Courts other appeals to Edward rapidly followed, and as in connexion with each Baliol was summoned to Westminster, it became necessary, as Lord Hailes remarks, "that the Scottish king should reside in England rather than in his own kingdom."[3]

By the members of his second Parliament, held at Stirling on the 3d of August 1293, Baliol was counselled to assert his personal liberty, also his regal authority. Accordingly, when in October he was, in presence of the English Parliament, called on to answer in the Macduff appeal, he ventured to maintain his independence. "I am King of Scotland," he said, "and to the complaint of Macduff or of any other, I cannot answer without

---

[1] Fœdera, ii., 604 ; Acta Parl. Scot., i., 89 et 509.

[2] Ryley's Placita, 151.

[3] Fœdera, ii., 605-607 ; Hailes' Annals, i., 250.

consulting my people." "What means this refusal?" exclaimed Edward. "Are you not my liegeman? You have done homage to me, and on my summons you are here." Baliol answered, "In matters which concern my kingdom, I neither dare nor can answer in this place, without the advice of my people."[1] As it was evident that Baliol spoke as directed by the Estates, Edward, with a show of justice, signified his willingness that he should again consult his clergy and barons. But Edward's lords of Parliament were inexorable. They reversed the judgment of which Macduff had complained, and, amercing Baliol in damages, ruled that until he humbled himself the Scottish fortresses should be wrested from his authority, and appropriated by his overlord. Entreating that judgment might be stayed, Baliol rendered homage for the lands of Tynedale and the manors of Sowerby and Penrith, and also gave a further homage for the Honor of Huntingdon.[2] And before leaving for Scotland, he became bound by an oath that he would appear before the English Parliament on the day after the Feast of the Trinity.[3]

For a time Edward was diverted from concentrating his attention on Scottish affairs. A ship from Normandy and an English vessel having sent their boats ashore in the neighbourhood of Bayonne in quest of water, a scuffle arose in which a Norman sailor was mortally injured. Informed of the fatal encounter, Philip spoke of revenge, and the Norman seamen, believing that they were allowed to seek reprisals, forthwith boarded an English ship and hanged one of the sailors at the yard-arm. By this unexpected outrage the naval

---

[1] Ryley's Placita, 158.
[2] Close Roll, 21 Edward I., m. 2; Fine, 22 Edward I., m. 22.
[3] Ryley's Placita, 152, 160; Prynne's Edward I., p. 554.

authorities at the Cinque Ports were deeply incensed, and proceeded to attack every French vessel which appeared in the Channel. Within a short space sixty English ships were found to have destroyed the cargoes of two hundred French trading vessels, also to have killed or cast overboard many of their seamen. In answer to a demand for compensation, Edward sent to the French king the Bishop of London as a special envoy, with the offer that he would render justice in his own courts, or would submit the cause to arbitration. Rejecting both proposals, Philip called upon Edward, as his vassal for the province of Gascony, to answer personally for his misconduct. Desirous of averting a rupture which might interfere with his intended operations in Scotland, Edward despatched to the French Court his brother Edmund, who, as husband of Philip's mother, was likely to secure favourable terms. Philip now agreed to an accommodation, on Gascony being temporarily surrendered to him. The concession was yielded, but as Philip thereupon proceeded to annex the province to his dominions, Edward prepared for war.

Notwithstanding his rupture with France, Edward did not abate his rigour towards Baliol. On the 2d of April 1294, he charged him to appear before his Parliament at Westminster on the morrow of Ascension Day. And on the occasion he was called upon to plead as defender in a new appeal, in which one John Mason was complainer against the executors of Alexander III. From the proceedings of the Scottish Estates in reference to the claim, it appears that a balance of £100 due to Mason had been offered him, but the sum was claimed by his creditors, and latterly he had (at the instance of Edward's emissaries) refused a settlement on any terms.[1] In promoting the appeal

---

[1] Chancery Miscellaneous Portfolios, No. 11 ; Royal Letters, Nos. 1311, 1312, 1313.

Edward secured a further point in his claim of superiority, since the respondents were executors of the deceased king, and as such were held as consenting to the English jurisdiction.

Baliol arrived at London in May, and on the 20th June executed a chirograph whereby he surrendered the liferent of his manors of Penrith, Scotteby, Salkeld, Sowerby, and others.[1] These he conveyed nominally to Bishop Bek, but in reality as a subsidy to Edward so as to aid him in carrying forward his military operations against the French king.

In proportion to the subserviency of the liegeman was the oppression of the overlord.[2] On the 27th June 1294, Edward despatched to Baliol and eighteen of his nobility a military summons, charging them to appear with their forces at London on the first day of September to take part in his expedition against France.[3] And along with the acts of summons, Baliol and his nobles were apprised that the reeves and community of Berwick had made complaints as to their administration.[4]

Baliol's servility had meanwhile aroused among his people a general discontent. At a Parliament held at Scone, a majority of the assembled barons desired him to inform his overlord that they were unequal to the task of bringing a number of fighting men into the field; they also declared that out of an impoverished exchequer they were unable any longer to provide salaries or pensions to those natives of the south who held among them offices of state. These messages Baliol refused to convey, and in token of obedience expressed his consent that so long as hostilities prevailed between England and France, the Bishop of Carlisle should, on Edward's behalf, retain in keeping the castles of Jedburgh, Roxburgh, and Berwick.[5]

[1] Patent, 22 Edward I., m. 3.
[2] Fœdera, ii., 635, 1000.
[3] Gascon Roll, Tower Miscellaneous Rolls, ⁴⁄₂.
[4] Chancery Miscellaneous Portfolios, No. 11.
[5] Fœdera, ii., 692.

In subordinating Baliol and subverting his authority, Edward advanced steadily. On the 1st of October 1294, he, as " overlord of Scotland," empowered Walter de Kambok, his warden in Fife, to deliver to "his dear friend" the Bishop of Glasgow, the lands of Calder. At Edward's instance the warden subsequently presented against the Scottish Estates, a heavy bill of costs.[1]

So long as Baliol remained a free agent, his barons now foresaw that Edward would, by practising upon his fears, rapidly subvert his rule. Therefore, for his own safety and that of the realm, they determined on his seclusion, while they appointed as governors in his stead, a committee of four bishops, four earls, and four barons.[2] Though not demurring to his restraint, Baliol was withal apprehensive that he might nevertheless be associated with acts which would compromise him with his overlord. He therefore secretly despatched to the English court his secretary, Henry of Aberdeen, with an oral message expressive of his fidelity. And as it was his interest to play off the Scottish king against those who had assumed the government in his name, Edward cordially reciprocated his message. Thus, in his reply, dated at Westminster 23d August 1295, he informed his "illustrious liege" that his approving sentiments would be conveyed by the messenger.[3]

Excluded from the power of governing, Baliol began to reflect on the difficulty of his situation. By adhering to Edward, he clearly foresaw that he would remain a king only in name; while by independently exercising the royal function, he might regain his authority. At length he was prevailed on by the Committee of Estates to take decisive action. On the 3d of

---

[1] Privy Seals (Tower), 22 Edward I., Bundle 3; Exchequer, 2 R. Miscellanea (Army), No. 7.

[2] Matthew of Westminster, 425; also Rishanger and Hemingford, anno 1295.

[3] Close Rolls, 23 Edward I., m. 7 dorso.

July he accredited ambassadors to the French king, bearing proposals for a treaty between the kingdoms.[1] In this treaty (which was concluded at Paris on the 23d of October) Baliol expressed himself as so grievously offended at the undutiful behaviour of Edward to the King of France, his liege lord, that he conceived himself bound to render assistance to the latter in the event of the former invading the territory of France. And reciprocating this pledge, the French king made an engagement that should Edward invade Scotland he would yield active aid, either by causing a diversion, or sending succours. It was also further arranged that the bonds of amity should be further strengthened by a matrimonial compact—Philip consenting that his niece, the eldest daughter of Charles, Count of Anjou, should wed Baliol's son and heir, while Baliol pledged himself, in the interest of his son and daughter-in-law, not to enter into a second marriage without the consent of his ally.[2] To the treaty were appended the seals of the burghs of Edinburgh, Aberdeen, Perth, Stirling, Berwick, and Roxburgh, in evidence that the Scottish community approved the arrangement.

Deeply offended by Baliol's defection, Edward, on the 11th of October 1295, instructed the sheriffs of the several English counties in which his estates lay, to instantly seize his lands and goods, also the possessions of those Scottish barons who adhered to or co-operated with him.[3] The sale of the estates was some time deferred, but on the 19th February 1295-6, Edward ruled that it should be proceeded with.[4]

Resuming the consideration of the Macduff appeal, Edward summoned Baliol to appear at Newcastle on the 1st March as a defender in the cause.[5] And as he failed to present himself,

---

[1] Chancery Miscellaneous Portfolio, $\frac{1}{17}$; Fœdera, i., 822, 823, 830.

[2] Fœdera, ii., 695; Hemingford, i., 66; Acta Parl. Scot., i., 95.

[3] Fine Roll, 23 Edward I., m. 3.

[4] Memoranda Roll, 24 Edward I., m. 12.

[5] Prynne's Edward I., 537.

Edward put himself at the head of an armed force and marched northwards. At Newcastle he was, in response to a military summons, joined by a contingent of light-armed auxiliaries from Wales.[1] Thereafter Bishop Bek added his forces, consisting of 1500 infantry. Before entering Scotland the invading army numbered 30,000 foot and 5000 horse.[2]

In embodying his troops, Edward gave forth that his sole purpose was to bring into submission his vassal, King John, but when it became suspected that the expedition was intended to effect the subjugation of Scotland, the greater part of the army were inclined to return home. Edward now proceeded to arouse a general ardour by the proclamation that he and his forces were engaged in a species of crusade, since in their march floated over them the consecrated banners of St John of Beverley and of St Cuthbert of Durham.[3] And in token of the sanctity which he attached to these consecrated banners, he publicly announced that he would confer on Gilbert de Grymmisby, a churchman, one of the bearers, the first benefice which fell vacant in Scotland.[4]

Crossing the Tweed at Coldstream on the 28th March, Edward led his army to the north-eastward. On the second day resting at Hutton, near Norham Castle, he, on the third day, reached the neighbourhood of Berwick.

Before his seclusion by the Estates, Baliol had offered to place the castles of Berwick, Jedburgh, and Roxburgh in

[1] Thierry's Norman Conquest, Lond. 1847, ii., 299, 300.

[2] Hemingford, i., 87-93. In regard to the number of Edward's army, also in reference to the places visited by him during the course of his expedition, and the dates at which these visits were made, we have followed the entries in a journal of the fourteenth century, found by Mr Joseph Stevenson in the National Library at Paris (Fonds Lat., 6049, fol. 30 b.), and which, accompanied by translation from the original French, he has included in his "Documents Illustrative of the History of Scotland," vol. ii., 25-32.

[3] Rymer, ii., 732; Prynne's Edward I., 667; Hemingford, i., 89.

[4] Fœdera, ii., 732.

Edward's keeping as a pledge of his fidelity, and as his promise had not been fulfilled, Edward resolved in the first instance to secure these castles by force. Encamping close by the town of Berwick, he summoned the magistrates to an immediate surrender. On receiving a refusal, he caused the officers of his store ships to attack and destroy all the merchant vessels lying in the harbour. This effort failed, since, in the defence of their shipping, the burgesses succeeded in setting on fire three of the English vessels, and compelled the others to withdraw. In violent rage, Edward now assailed the city, first by his archers, and afterwards by his cavalry. And as he gave orders that no quarter should be given, aged men and women and children were slaughtered in large numbers. Those who sought refuge in churches were dragged forth and butchered. Every dwelling was a scene of carnage, and the streets became as a pool of blood.[1]

At Berwick a body of Flemish merchants occupied a fortified structure called the Red Hall, which by their charter they were bound to defend. True to their engagement, thirty of their number held out after the city had fallen; but at nightfall Edward set fire to the fabric, and destroyed the inmates. The castle was some time vigorously defended by Sir William Douglas, but as he agreed to surrender it, and render homage, he was allowed to quit the stronghold with military honours.[2]

Berwick was seized and wrecked on the 30th of March 1296. By some writers Edward's severities have been ascribed to his

---

[1] Hemingford, i., 90; Fordun a Goodal, ii., 159; Langtoft's Chronicle, ii., 272; Knighton apud Twysden, p. 2480. According to the Chronicle of Lanercost, the conflict continued for a day and a half, and was attended with the slaughter of 15,000 persons (Lanercost Chronicle, 173). The historians, Wyntoun, Fordun, and Boece, reckon the number slain at 7000 or 7500.

[2] Hemingford, i., 91.

seeking revenge on the minstrels of the place who had satirized him in these caustic rhymes,—

> " What wende the Kyng Edward
> For his langge shanks,
> For to wynne Berewyke
> Al our unthankes?
> Go pike it him,
> And when he it have wounc
> Go dike it him." [1]

For his inhumanities Edward had other motives : he sought to revenge the French alliance, and to alarm into an abject submission Baliol and his adherents. Besides, in wrecking Berwick he destroyed the chief mart of Scottish commerce, and largely conduced towards the impoverishment of a people he sought to subjugate.[2] As a further step in conquest, he caused the place to be fortified as an English town.

Through the wanton destruction of Berwick, Baliol was aroused to a vigorous resistance. Notwithstanding his assertion to the French king, that Edward had forfeited every title to his allegiance, he had yet allowed his act of fealty to remain undisturbed, and he continued in the condition of one who under the sanctity of an oath was bound to uphold the cause of the slaughterer of his people. His several acts of homage he now determined formally to renounce. On the 5th of April he attached his seal to an instrument of renunciation, in which he declared that Edward had forfeited the privilege of continuing his overlord by the flagrant abuse of his prerogative. Edward, he particularly set forth, had summoned him to his courts on

[1] From an old French Chronicle, quoted by Burton, ii., 168 ; Wallace Papers, 142.

[2] According to the Chronicle of Lanercost, Berwick was in extent of commerce a second Alexandria, and it was certainly a principal outlet for skins and wool, by the export of which many Scottish merchants derived their wealth.

trifling excuses, seized his estates, and appropriated his castles ; he had also imprisoned his subjects, and subjected them to plunder, and when his perfidy and violence were complained of, he, instead of granting redress, had entered Scotland with an army, and caused anarchy and bloodshed.[1]

With respect to the special nature of his renunciation, Dr Burton contends that Baliol had arrived at a conclusion inconsistent with feudal logic, since, if the homage and fealty were the fulfilment of Edward's rights, they could not be legally withdrawn.[2] Under the stringency of feudal law this view is admissible, yet Baliol's procedure in renouncing his homage was afterwards justified when Charles I. was beheaded at Whitehall, and James II. was forced into exile. It is also to be remembered that the nation of which Baliol was the representative, had not consented to any abnegation of its privileges.

Not without a measure of hope that Edward would be inclined to an amicable adjustment, Baliol sent to the English court his instrument of renunciation by the hands of his former secretary, Henry, now abbot of Arbroath. Henry had in 1292 accepted Edward's fealty, and the king on a former occasion had talked with him familiarly, while the abbey he represented enjoyed special trading privileges in England.[3] But Edward on this occasion received the abbot coldly, and in answer to his message said tersely, "The foolish traitor, if he will not come to us, we must go to him."[4]

For some time prior to Edward's expedition to Berwick,

---

[1] Fœdera, ii., 707 ; Fordun a Hearne, 969.

[2] Burton's History, ii., 170.

[3] Register of Aberbrothoc, 330. The author of Edward's "Itinerary" represents Abbot Henry as having held up to ridicule the English nation, by charging them with effeminacy. This is difficult to account for, since, on the 7th July 1296, he renewed to Edward personally, at Arbroath, his oath of homage.

[4] Fordun a Hearne, 969.

military preparations were actively prosecuted in Scotland. The Earls of Menteith, Strathearn, Lennox, Ross, Athole, and Mar had collected and armed their retainers, while William and Ralph Moncrieff, William de St Clair, Richard Siward, and John Comyn the younger took under their command bodies of well-equipped burgesses. In the course of a few months the Scottish army, numbering 40,000 foot and 500 cavalry, assembled under the leadership of John, Earl of Buchan, otherwise known as John Comyn the elder.[1]

Under Buchan the Scots marched to Berwick, and as the place was strongly garrisoned by Edward, they proceeded thence to Carlisle, which they entered about the end of March. Finding the place unprotected, they set it on fire, but on a strong muster of the inhabitants, they were compelled to retreat.[2] Investing the castle of Wark, they were admitted by the governor, Robert de Ros, a Scotsman, who, renouncing Edward's fealty, attached himself to his countrymen. Assisted by this person, the Earl of Buchan repulsed a large body of English troops assembled at Prestfen, many of whom were slain.[3] Penetrating into Redesdale and Tynedale, he dilapidated the monasteries of Lanercost and Hexham.[4] Attempting to storm the castle of Harbottle, he was forced to retreat. But his movements had excited a measure of alarm, for, on the 11th of April, we find Edward offering at Newcastle a free pardon to criminals and

[1] Matthew of Westminster, 427 ; Hemingford, i., 87.

[2] Hemingford, i., 87 ; Scalacronica, 122 ; Rishanger, 156. Buchan's inroad into the northern counties has, by other English writers, been mixed up with Wallace's expedition into England, subsequent to the battle of Stirling. Among the Historical MSS. of the See of Carlisle, there are frequent references to expenses incurred during a siege ; and it is probable that these were incident to Buchan's attack—the Bishop being then Warden of the Castle (Ninth Report of Royal Commission on Historical MSS., Part i., 181 *a*).

[3] Burton's History of Scotland, ed. 1873, vol. ii., p. 197, note.

[4] Fœdera, ii., 887 ; Trivet, 291 ; Langtoft, ii., 291 ; Hemingford, i., 93.

vagrants, on condition of their assisting in the expulsion of the Scots.[1]

Withdrawing from England, Buchan encamped his army in the vicinity of Dunbar, in the belief that should Edward, on completing the fortifications of Berwick, venture northward, he would effectively arrest his progress. Dunbar Castle was the possession of Patric, Earl of March, who served with Edward at Berwick; but the Countess, who was left in occupation, gave her adhesion to the national cause. Admitting into the castle Buchan and his officers and principal adherents, she dismissed those of her attendants whose fidelity was doubtful. Informed of the countess's defection, Edward lost no time in sending from Berwick to Dunbar the Earl of Surrey at the head of ten thousand foot and one thousand cavalry. Commencing his attack on the castle on Monday, the 23d of April, Surrey prosecuted the siege so vigorously, that on the second day the garrison offered to surrender unless relieved within three days. At this stage, Buchan drew up his troops in a strong position on the heights near Spot, and the imposing spectacle which he presented induced some members of the garrison to make sport of their besiegers.[2] But large and well appointed as his army was, Surrey discovered that he was incompetent as a leader, and so had recourse to a stratagem. Having strongly advanced as if he intended an attack, he next made a feint of allowing his men to fall into confusion, or of making a retreat. As he had anticipated, Buchan conducted his troops into the valley to repulse the enemy whom he believed to be in flight. Surrey now put his men in order, and advanced resolutely. There was a strong resistance, but in a few hours the Scots were driven back, while

[1] From the Pardon Roll, 24 Edward I., m. 6. [2] Fordun a Goodal, vol. ii., 165; Hemingford, i., 95.

many of their number were slain.[1] Among those who fell was Sir Patrick de Graham, whose feats of valour had attracted admiration even from the enemy. Marching towards Dunbar with fresh levies, Edward rested at Coldingham on the evening of the 27th, and was there informed of his lieutenant's triumph.

On the day after the battle, the garrison of Dunbar made an unconditional surrender, the prisoners including the Earls of Ross, Athole, and Menteith; the barons William St Clair, Richard Siward, John de Mowbray, and John Comyn the younger; also seventy knights. By Edward's order the more notable captives were laden with fetters and sent as prisoners to different fortresses in England and Wales.[2]

Entering the castle of Dunbar, Edward remained there till Wednesday, the 2d of May, when he moved to Haddington. On Sunday, the 6th May, he entered Lauder, and on the following day lodged with the Friar Minors at Roxburgh. On Tuesday, the 8th May, he approached Roxburgh Castle, when the Steward, who acted as governor, invited him to enter. In the "Submission Roll" it is intimated that at Roxburgh, on the 13th May 1296, "Sir James the Steward of Scotland, knight, of his own free will, renounced the league with the King of France, and swore fealty *tactis sacrosanctis*, and kissing the Holy Evangels." At Roxburgh on the 15th, John, brother of the Steward, swore fealty, and there, on the 4th June, Sir Thomas de Somerville, a considerable baron, also rendered homage.[3] From Roxburgh Castle, the Steward addressed missives to his companions urging a voluntary submission to Edward's authority. In conformity with his strong appeal Sir Ingram Umfraville, who was now

[1] MS. French Journal in the National Library of Paris; Stevenson's Documents, ii., 26.

[2] Hemingford, i., 96; Langtoft, ii., 277; Matthew of Westminster, 427; Fordun, xi., 24, 25; Scala Cronica, 123; Rotuli Scotiæ, i., sub. Ed. I., 25, 644.

[3] Prynne's Edward I., 649; Ragman Roll, m. 1, 2.

governor of Dunbarton Castle, intimated his surrender of the place, and in token of personal submission sent to Edward as hostages his daughters Eva and Isabel.[1]

Having remained at Roxburgh Castle nearly two weeks, Edward, on the 22d May, moved to the castle of Jedburgh, of which the governor gave him possession. Thereafter he received the keys of the fort of Castleton, in Liddesdale. At Castleton he remained from Thursday, the 24th May, till the following Sunday, when he returned to Jedburgh.[2] At Roxburgh Castle, on Friday, the 1st June, he held a special conference with the Steward, and on the following day visited the fort of Lauder, resting on the banks of the Leader, on the spot now occupied by the castle of Thirlestane.

After obtaining shelter for a day and a night with the monks of Newbattle, Edward, on Wednesday, the 6th of June, entered Edinburgh, and there took up his abode in the abbey of Holyrood. At Holyrood Abbey he took possession of an ecclesiastical symbol, wherewith he hoped anew to excite the ardour of his troops. This was *The Black Rood*, a supposed fragment of the true cross, brought to Scotland in a shrine of gold by Queen Margaret, and in honour of which, her son David I., under the belief that it had preserved his life when in hunting he was attacked by a stag, had reared the abbey of Holyrood. Aware of the reverence in which it was held as the national palladium, Edward caused it to be conspicuously borne in his march, so that, from the natives as well as his own followers, he might claim the sanction of religion. On the Black Rood of Scotland he caused all who afterwards accepted his fealty to make oath.[3]

[1] Rotuli Scotiæ, 22 Edward I., m. 8 dorso.
[2] MS. Journal at Paris, formerly quoted.
[3] Liber Cartarum Sanctæ Crucis, Preface; Miscellany of the Bannatyne Club, ii., 13.

Within Edinburgh Castle were deposited the crown plate and jewels, and chiefly on this account the Scottish governor, when summoned to surrender the place, gallantly refused. Proceeding to the reduction of the castle, Edward erected against the walls three powerful engines, which, casting formidable missiles, led the defender to surrender on the fifth day. Edward now seized the treasure, and, depositing it in three large chests, caused it to be removed to London.[1] The regalia were evidently broken up. A crown of gold afterwards found among Baliol's effects was, by Edward's order, hung up at the tomb of Thomas à Becket, in the Cathedral of Canterbury.[2]

At Edinburgh, on the 10th June, Edward caused Sir William Douglas to renew his homage,[3] and he remained in the city several days till he was joined by the main body of his army. Having assigned Edinburgh Castle and the neighbouring strongholds to the care of Walter de Huntercumbe, an English knight,[4] he now marched northward. On Wednesday, the 13th June, he reached Linlithgow, and as the castle held out, he at once proceeded to its reduction. By casting missiles into the structure, he, in a single night, effected his purpose. Next day he reached Stirling, where he found the castle unoccupied—the garrison having fled at his approach. At Stirling he received homage from the Earl of Strathearn, Sir John de Calantyr (Callander), William de Colnehath, John de Lamberton, Sir William de Rotheven, Sir William de Garden (Jardine), Sir Walter de Corrie, and Sir Michael de Wemes (Wemyss).[5]

[1] Joseph Hunter's Paper on King Edward's Spoliations in Scotland, Art. in Arch. Journal, xii., 245.

[2] Burton's History, ii., 171.

[3] Ragman Roll, m. 2.

[4] Fœdera, ii., 731. At Berwick, on the 28th August 1296, Walter de Huntercumbe was, by Walter de Ibernia, pursued for 100s., the value of sixteen oxen and ten cows belonging to him, which Huntercumbe had snatched from a moor near Aberdeen. Huntercumbe denied the charge, and his trial was ordered (Placita Roll of the English Army in Scotland, m. 9).

[5] Ragman Roll, m. 2, 3.

Joined at Stirling by the Earl of Ulster at the head of a powerful reinforcement, Edward tarried in the place five days, resuming his march on Wednesday, the 20th of June. Crossing the Forth, described by the writer of the " Itinerary " as " the Scottish sea," he thereafter rested at Auchterarder Castle, a royal hunting seat, and from thence marched to Perth.

Edward now perpetrated an act, whereby he caused the external destruction of the monarchy. Already he had broken up the Great Seal, plundered the national records, appropriated the Black Rood, and borne off the jewels of the crown. But the coronation stone of the kings yet remained, where for centuries it had stood, within the venerable abbey of Scone, within a few miles of the city of Perth, and there Edward effected a further deed of spoliation.

The Scottish coronation stone, a rectangular block of conglomerate rock, borne from the Argyleshire coast to its original site in Dunstaffnage Castle, was popularly believed to have been that on which the patriarch Jacob rested his head at Bethel when he had the vision of angels ; further that it was brought to Scotland by a daughter of one of the Pharaohs, and that it was afterwards used as a pillow by Saint Columba. And so long as the stone rested on Scottish soil, the legend also set forth, a native line of princes would occupy the throne. From Scone, Edward caused the coronation stone[1] to be transported to

---

[1] Hemingford, i., 37, 100; Harding's Metrical Chronicle MS., Bed. Sold. B. 10 ; Fordun a Goodal, book xi., chap. xxv., vol. ii., p. 166. Edward placed the Scottish coronation stone in the Abbey of Westminster, as an offering to Edward the Confessor, a dedication inappropriate to an act of plunder. In his monograph on the coronation stone, published in 1869, Dr William Skene presents a minute description of its aspects. In length 26 inches, by $16\frac{3}{4}$ inches in breadth, and $10\frac{1}{2}$ in depth ; it is a dull reddish or purplish sandstone, in which a few pebbles are imbedded. It was, remarks Dr Skene, evidently prepared in imitation of the Lia Fail of Tara in Ireland, and may have been constructed so early as the reign of Nectan, the Pictish king, in the eighth century. Associated with the stone is a metrical couplet embodying a monkish prophecy—

Ni fallat fatum Scoti, quocunque locatum
Invenient lapidem, regnare tenentur ibidem.

Westminster Abbey, and there to be placed under the chair on which the English sovereigns received their symbols of authority.   And that in its absence from Scone, no trace might remain of its original purpose, he also appropriated the Abbey Register, together with the corresponding writs.[1]

Having plundered the abbey of Scone, Edward next proceeded to the neighbouring monastery of Cupar, where he robbed the monks of their furniture and jewels.[2]

With his acts of spoliation Edward frequently blended the observances of religion.   In his journeys he bore with him several casks of wine for use in the sacrifice of the Mass; also iron vessels specially fabricated for baking the consecrated wafers.   Having despoiled the abbeys of Scone and Cupar, he gave order that the Feast of the Nativity of the Baptist, held on the 24th of June, should be observed with more than wonted solemnity; and on the same day caused a banquet to be provided to his knights lately associated with him in his acts of plunder and sacrilege.

At Perth he received fealty from various barons, among whom were Sir Robert Cambron (Cameron), lord of Balnigrenach; Sir Robert Cambron, lord of Balnely; Sir Alexander de Abernethy, Sir John de Hay, Sir John de Moncriefe, and Hugh de Urre.[3] He also received messengers from Baliol tendering his submission, and desiring to be informed when and how he could renew his fealty.   To this message he replied haughtily, "Let him present himself within fifteen days at Brechin Castle, and then the Bishop of Durham will inform him as to our intentions."

Leaving Perth on the 25th of June, Edward resumed his

[1] Chartulary of Scone, p. 26 ; Innes's Critical Essay, Notes and Illustrations, letter G.

[2] Wardrobe Account, Edward I., Addit. MSS., British Museum, 7965.

[3] Ragman Roll, m. 3.

march. Visiting Kinclevin Castle, on the banks of the Tay, he there planted a garrison. At the castle of Cluny, a stronghold in Stormount, he remained five days, and there received homage from Sir Gilbert de Glenkerny, Sir Archibald de Livingstone, Sir John de Stirling, and Eustace de Bickerton, rector of the church at Auchtermuchty, also from other magnates.[1] He planted garrisons at Cluny, and in the castle of Inverquiech, and thereafter marched to Forfar.

Within the castle of Forfar Edward received fealty from Sir William Fraunceys, Sir Andrew Beton, Hugh de Moray, and others.[2] After three days he proceeded to Aberbrothoc, where the members of the convent rendered him fealty. He next visited the castle of Farnwell, and there received other submissions.[3]

Having halted at the town of Montrose, Edward from thence, on the 7th July, despatched Bishop Bek as his commissioner to further humiliate the already degraded Baliol. Bek caused the suppliant king to meet him in the lonely churchyard of Stracathro, and there, at the hour of vespers, to denude himself of his royal robes, and make an abject surrender of his fief. The commissioner next insisted that his former friend should, on his knees, render penance for venturing to contract his son with the niece of the French king, and also solicit pardon for the act.

The process of feudal degradation initiated at Stracathro was consummated in the castle of Brechin, where, on the 10th of July, the dethroned sovereign was made to emphatically set forth that "through wicked counsel" he had become guilty of renouncing his fealty, also of invading the territory of his overlord. Next, expressing an approval of Edward's career of plunder, he resigned into his hands the royal dignity, also his lands and goods. And

[1] Ragman Roll, m. 5. [2] *Ibid.*, m. 6.
[3] *Ibid.*, m. 8.

finally he signified his gratitude that the offence of resisting his overlord had not been visited with personal restraint. These several acknowledgments were embodied in a legal instrument, which Baliol attested, declaring that he had executed the same of his own free will. And having affirmed the document by an impression of his seal, he agreed that Edward's attorney should in his own presence break it up as the last symbol of his authority. Baliol then delivered up to Bek, to be detained as the English king saw fit, his only son Edward, as a pledge of his submission.[1]

That Baliol escaped sentence of death is not to be ascribed to Edward's clemency. Irrespective of the consideration that he had a son to claim his inheritance, his death by violence Edward foresaw would excite the common people to insurrection, and also revive the ambition of the Lord of Annandale. Secretly the dethroned king was conveyed to England. On the 22d November 1296, he appears as resident at Hertford, with the privilege of keeping a huntsman and ten hounds.[2] On the 28th January 1296-7, he seems to have received a further authority to hunt in the royal forests south of the Trent and within twenty leagues of London.[3] But these privileges were not long to be continued. By Edward's order the exiled king was, on the 6th August 1297, transferred from his abode at Hertford to the Tower, and there committed to the charge of the constable.[4] In the Tower his allowance was restricted to nineteen shillings a day, along with a moderate retinue.[5]

---

[1] Ragman Roll, m. 8 ; Fœdera, ii., 718 ; Fordun, xi., 26 ; also the French Itinerary. The instrument of Baliol's homage is preserved in the National Archives at Paris, section J., carton 631, No. 6. See Stevenson's Documents, ii., 59-61.

[2] Close Roll, 25 Edward I., m. 25.

[3] Patent Roll, 25 Edward I., m. 19.

[4] Pipe Roll, 27 Edward I.

[5] Expenses of John de Baliol in the Tower of London. Original in the Public Record Office.

In his efforts for the renewal of the French alliance Edward had resolutely persevered, and he was now in terms for a definite treaty, to be cemented by his espousing Philip's sister. And as an early step towards the proposed alliance, he, to suit certain requirements made by Philip's envoy, gave consent that his prisoner, the dethroned Baliol, should be transferred to the keeping of Raynald, bishop of Vincenza, appointed by the Pope as his delegate for promoting amity between the two countries. Baliol was accordingly borne to Wissant and from thence to Cambrai, where the bishop of Vincenza received him as a lodger.[1] Subsequently, residing under papal sanction in one of the manors of the abbot of Cluni, he there executed an instrument empowering the King of France to arrange with Edward as to his affairs in England.[2] Consequently he was, in November 1302, allowed to reside on his lands in Picardy, where he remained till his death, which took place in 1315, after he had learned that the grandson of his rival, the lord of Annandale, had won by the sword a crown which he had forfeited by his pusillanimity.

While Bishop Bek was occupied at Stracathro and Brechin in effecting Baliol's feudal degradation and permanent dethronement, Edward tarried at Montrose. There, on the 10th July, he received to his fealty the Earl of Buchan, who led the Scottish army at Dunbar,[3] Sir Alexander Balliol, Sir Herbert de Maxwell, Sir John the Marischal, Sir John de Moray, Sir Nicholas de Haye, Sir John Sinclair, Sir Hugh Rydel, Sir John le Botelier, Sir Nicholas de Rotherford; also many of the dignified clergy.[4]

Garrisoning the castle of Montrose with English troops, Edward marched from thence on the 11th July to the strong

<hr>

[1] Addit. MS., Brit. Museum, 15, 365, fol. 73, 80.
[2] Imperial Archives at Paris, Carton 633, No. 5.

[3] Ragman Roll, m. 8.
[4] *Ibid.*, m. 10, 11.

castle of Kincardine, which he also garrisoned. Next in his northward route occupying the castle of Glenbervie, he, on the 13th, reached Durris. On the following day he marched from Durris Castle to Aberdeen, where, remarks the author of the "Itinerary," he found "a good castle and a good town upon the sea."

At Aberdeen, Edward remained six days, receiving submission from many of the clergy and barons. Among the clergy who rendered homage were Henry the Bishop, Sir Walter of the Blakwater, the Dean, Sir Henry de Crambathie, Dean of Dunkeld, and William Comyn, brother of the Earl of Buchan, Provost of the monastery at St Andrews. Among the lay homagers were Sir Norman le Lechelyn, Alexander de Lamberton, John de Glenesk, John Stirling de Moray, Thomas the Durward, Gilbert de la Haye, John de Cambo, John de Kyros, John, son of Herbert de Makeswelle [Maxwell], William de Montalt [Mowat], Sir John Fleming, and Sir William de Moray.[1]

Leaving Aberdeen on the 20th July, Edward marched to Lumphanan Castle, where Sir John de Maleville [Melville] tendered his submission.[2] On the 21st he garrisoned the castle of Fyvie, and on Sunday the 22d occupied the castle of Banff.[3]

Edward now moved westward, garrisoning in his progress the fort at Cullen. On the 24th he encamped on a common bordering the Spey, and next day, crossing the river, he rested at Rapenach (Lossiemouth) in Morayshire. From thence he marched to the castle of Elgin, where he received homage from the Earl of Menteith, whom he consequently released from forfeiture.[4]

At Elgin Edward began his journey homeward, resting on Sunday, the 29th July, at Rothes, a strong castle on the Spey. Thence he despatched three knights—Sir John de Cantelow, Sir

---

[1] Ragman Roll, m. 14.
[2] *Ibid.*, m. 14.
[3] *Ibid.*, m. 15.
[4] *Ibid.*, m. 16.

Hugh le Spencer, and Sir John de Hastings—to inspect the district of Badenoch. He now detached a considerable body of his troops under Bishop Bek, while he personally led the main body through the range of the Grampians by the Pass of Inverchanach. On the 31st July reaching the castle of Kildrummie, in Strathdon, he there rested. His next stage was the hospital of Kincardine O'Neil, and on the 3d August he arrived at Brechin Castle.

On the 4th of August Edward marched to Aberbrothoc, where he lodged in the Abbey. On the 6th he occupied the castle of Dundee, rested at Baledgarno or "Red Castle" on the 7th, and on the following day reached Perth. He now crossed the Tay and entered Fife, sojourning on the 9th and 10th August at the abbey of Lindores. Leaving Lindores early on Saturday the 11th, he on the same day reached St Andrews, which in the "Itinerary" is described as "a castle and good town." Leaving St Andrews, he on the following day halted at Markinch, which consisted only of "the minster and three houses." On the 13th he entered the abbey of Dunfermline, where, the author of the "Itinerary" remarks, "nearly all the kings of Scotland lie." Edward now passed to Stirling, and from thence to Linlithgow, Edinburgh, Haddington, Pinkerton near Dunbar, and Coldingham. On the 22d he reached Berwick. The author of the "Itinerary" remarks, as a sequel to his narrative, that Edward "conquered the realm of Scotland, and searched it . . . within twenty-one weeks, without any more."[1] At Berwick, on the 28th August, he held a Parliament. Among those summoned were the representatives of burgesses, who were styled "sovereigns of the people." About two thousand Scotsmen now rendered homage, these assembling from every district of the

[1] French Itinerary: Stevenson's Documents, ii., 25, 31.

country. Among the homagers were Mary, Queen of Man, the Earls of Mar, Strathearn, Menteith, Lennox, Sutherland, Angus, and March, also Robert Bruce, the younger, Earl of Carrick. The submitting ecclesiastics included the bishops of Glasgow, Aberdeen, and Whithorn; also the abbots of Holyrood, Dunfermline, Dryburgh, Jedburgh, Kelso, Melrose, Arbroath, Lindores, Sweetheart, Paisley, Tongland, Dundrennan, Cambuskenneth, Balmerino, Kinloss, Cupar, Scone, Newbattle, Deer, Holywood, Iona, Kilwinning, and Holmcultram; the priors of St Andrews, Canonby, Restennet, Whithorn, and Ardchattan; and the prioresses of Haddington, Manuel, Berwick, and Lincluden. There also rendered homage the Master of the Chivalry of the Temple in Scotland, and the Warden of the Hospital of St John; and in fealty-making were represented by their provosts or aldermen the burghs of Edinburgh, Perth, Stirling, Montrose, Dumfries, Roxburgh, Jedburgh, Haddington, Peebles, Linlithgow, and Inverkeithing.[1]

Towards those who rendered fealty, Edward acted with his usual tact. Homagers who pledged themselves to attend a Parliament to be held at St Edmunds on the 1st November, he allowed to retain their lands and goods, while to the widows of barons, who had died prior to the alliance with France, he restored the family estates, unless they had contracted second marriages with non-homagers. Edward also made a small provision for the wives of several barons detained in English prisons. In restoring the lands belonging to the Church, he stipulated that those English ecclesiastics who had been removed from benefices should be admitted; also that the bishops should possess the privilege of bequeathing or otherwise alienating their

---

[1] Ragman Roll, m. 21-35.

endowments. And in relation to provincial or local magistrates, he ruled that those only who acknowledged his authority should continue in office.

Edward assigned to Englishmen the highest offices of state by appointing as guardian the Earl of Surrey, Hugh de Cressingham as treasurer, and William Ormesby as justiciary. And at Berwick he constituted an exchequer for receiving the rents which he claimed as sovereign. English governors he appointed to the principal forts, these including Walter Tonke to the castle of Roxburgh, Osbert de Spaldington to the castle of Berwick, Thomas de Burnham to Jedburgh Castle and the Forest of Selkirk, Walter de Huntercumbe to the castles of Edinburgh, Linlithgow, and Haddington, and Sir Henry de Percy to the castle of Galloway and the sheriffdom of Ayr.[1]

At Berwick occurred an incident which might have been attended with confusion. In resenting the imputation of covertly abetting the national cause Sir Gilbert de Umfraville, son of the Earl of Angus, publicly assailed Sir Hugh de Lowther, Edward's sheriff of Edinburgh. Arraigned before Edward, De Umfraville acknowledged his offence, while De Lowther expressed himself content.[2]

After remaining at Berwick twenty-four days, Edward departed for London on Sunday, the 16th of September.[3] On his arrival in the metropolis, ensigns celebrating the conquest of Scotland were floated from the Tower, also from the Abbey of Westminster. But in accepting the honours of a conqueror Edward was not unaware that a kingdom could only be permanently subdued when was wrested from the inhabitants the last shred

----

[1] Prynne, iii., 652; Fœdera, ii., 714, 716, 717, 723, 727, 729, 731; Rotuli Scotiæ, i., 29-35.

[2] Close Roll, 24 Edward I., m. 4.

[3] French Itinerary: Stevenson's Documents, ii., 31, 32.

of their liberties. He had, therefore, begun to ingraft upon the Scottish national system new and Anglican modes. As a first expedient he caused all legal writs to be drawn in an English form.[1] And in a mandate issued at Montrose on the 10th July 1296, he enjoined his chancellor and others to introduce the English judicial system. Further, he established at Berwick new Courts of Chancery and Exchequer.[2] And the existence of these Courts he caused to be felt, by exercising through their instrumentality a course of rigorous oppression.[3] On the 9th October 1298, the custom-house officer at Berwick made report to him that he had sequestrated the goods of certain burgesses, and that he thereanent waited further instructions. The offence of the distrained persons consisted in that, while the royal mills were, through heavy floods, rendered incapable of use, they had prepared meal in mills of their own, and on this account declined to pay the customary tax.[4]

[1] Forms of Writs to be used in Scotland; Public Record Office ; Rotuli Scotiæ, i., 26.

[2] Treasurer's Memoranda Roll, 24, 25 Edward I., m. 28.

[3] *Ibid.*, m. 40 ; 26 Edward I., m. 72, 100.

[4] Original Letter in Public Record Office.

—o—

CHAPTER III

RISE OF WALLACE, TO THE BATTLE OF STIRLING.

" Wallace, unstained illustrious name,
   My country's honour and her shame."
                    —MS. poem by JAMES HOGG.

" Oh Scotland ! proud may be thy boast
     Since Time his course through circling years hath run,
   There hath not shone, in fame's bright host,
     A nobler hero than thy patriot son."
                    —JOANNA BAILLIE.

"MOST of the noble and ancient families of Scotland," observes Sir Walter Scott, "are reduced to the necessity of tracing their ancestors' names in the fifty-six sheets of parchment which constitute the degrading roll of submission to Edward I." In a sense true, Sir Walter's deduction is nevertheless considerably overstrained ; the parchments of submission actually number thirty-five, and these contain not more than two thousand names, inclusive of those English ecclesiastics who held the principal benefices, also of Norman barons who possessed land in England ; together with a body of knights, esquires, and municipal officials, under the direct influence of the Norman nobles. And as the population of Scotland at the close of the thirteenth century did not exceed 400,000, there might remain, after deducting children and other non-combatants, and the homagers, about 160,000 persons unsubdued. To these—that is, to the bulk of the people—the competitors for the crown made no reference in their pleadings, since each claimant was willing that the kingdom should be regarded as an estate, which, with those dwelling on its surface, might be disposed of at the will of a superior. This ignoring of the rights of citizenship formed one of the grounds for protest on behalf of the Commons, which, on being presented to him at Norham, Edward caused to be destroyed as "irrelevant."

To the popular section belonged William Wallace, through whose patriotic ardour and unflinching courage were effectively revived the national energies. Though ranking only as a common citizen, Wallace was of gentle birth. Sprung from that eastern race which peopled Strathclyde, usually known as the southern Picts,[1] his progenitors were for about a century considerably conspicuous. In guerdon of service they received lands from David I., and in the reign of Alexander III. were possessors of large estates.

Younger son of Adam Wallace of Riccarton, the Patriot's father, Malcolm Wallace, held the lands of Auchinbothie in Ayrshire, and the barony of Elderslie in the county of Renfrew. His wife, Margaret Craufurd, was daughter of Sir Hugh Craufurd of Loudoun and Corsbie, scion of an Anglo-Danish family, who, driven into Scotland at the Conquest, became owners in Edgar's reign of a considerable territory. Wyntoun refers to the hero's lineage in these lines :—

> " He wes cummyn off gentillmen,
> In sympill state set he wes then :
> His fadyre wes a manly knycht ;
> Hys modyre wes a lady brycht." [2]

---

[1] By more than one writer Sir William Wallace has been described as of "Norman blood," his ancestry being assigned to one of the barons who accompanied the Conqueror. This is in direct variance with historical evidence. By Henry the hero is described as

"Of hale lynage, and true line of Scotland."—B. i., 23.

[2] Wyntoun's Cronykill, B. viii., 2017-2020. For a detailed account of the Patriot's ancestors see vol. i., pp. 1-20.

William Wallace was born in the manor house of Elderslie, but the year of his birth is uncertain. According to Henry, he had, at his death in 1305, attained his forty-fifth year; but the Minstrel's statement of his age is inconsistent with the details of his history. From a general examination of the events which occurred in his early life, his birth may be assigned to the year 1270.

As a younger son, the future Patriot had before him two alternatives—one, that of expending his activities in the hunting field; the other, that of preparing himself for the Church or other clerkly employment. For at his period scholastic knowledge was sought for by those only who intended thereby to earn the means of subsistence. Of the famous Archibald Douglas, Earl of Angus, who flourished two centuries later, it is recorded that he publicly expressed his satisfaction that of his four sons, none save Gavin (the bishop of Dunkeld) could write their names, or otherwise use the pen.

With a view to his education, the younger son of Malcolm Wallace was by his father placed under the care of a relative (probably his mother's brother), the priest of Dunipace. For many years the native clergy, with a few exceptions, strenuously upheld the national liberties. When Turgot, the pious confessor of Queen Margaret, was, in the year 1109, elected bishop of St Andrews, he accepted consecration from the Archbishop of York, and the proceeding was, by the southern clergy, construed into an acknowledgment of subordination to an English hierarch. And the assumed supremacy afterwards came to be so resolutely maintained, that when Henry II. had extorted from his prisoner, William the Lion, a surrender of the civil liberties of his kingdom, he next insisted that the Scottish clergy should acknowledge the superiority of the English bishops. The latter demand was keenly resisted, and when the king, on re-obtaining his independence, proceeded to erect the abbey of Aberbrothoc, he, on the advice of his clergy, dedicated it to Thomas à Becket, the notable opponent of the English sovereign. From repeated attempts to render them subservient to the English prelates, the Scottish clergy at length obtained a decisive triumph when Pope Celestine III. issued a decree that the Scottish Church was "by special grace the daughter of Rome."[1]

Apart from successfully maintaining an unflinching struggle with their English brethren as to the independence of their order, Scottish ecclesiastics advanced the cause of liberty by initiating the emancipation of the serfs.[2]

But circumstances rendered the cleric home at Dunipace a special nursery of patriotism. Misled by a confused tradition, Henry the Minstrel represents the young hero as faring prosperously at Dunipace, since his "eyme" [uncle] was "a man of gret richess,"[3] an assertion evidently founded on a legend that, while early prosecuting his education, the Patriot was under the protection of a person of rank. Important particulars in regard to the chapel at Dunipace, and a family of rank and political importance, by whom it was endowed, have recently been opened up.

A kinsman and chief associate of William of Normandy, Sir Robert de Umfraville, styled "Robert with the Beard," received, on the conquest of England, the lands of Redesdale in Northumberland ; and his grandson, Gilbert de Umfraville, had granted to him by David I. of Scotland the lands of Dunipace.[4] Gilbert's

---

[1] This act of grace was not improbably procured through the good offices of Gilbert de Umfraville, who strongly upheld the interests of the Scottish Church.

[2] Social Life in Scotland, vol. i., 187-191.

[3] Henry the Minstrel, B. i., l. 299.

[4] Dugdale's Baronage, Lond. 1675, vol. i., 504-508 ; Register of the Monastery of Cambuskenneth, 44, 108, 112.

grandson, Richard de Umfraville, gave a vigorous adherence to those who maintained the struggle with King John, and to whom in 1215 that sovereign granted the Great Charter at Runnymede.[1] His son, Richard, made Scotland his head-quarters, and in the words of Matthew Paris became "the chief flower of the north."

Gilbert de Umfraville, eldest son of the second Richard, became second husband of Matildis, Countess of Angus, receiving with her extensive lands in Angus, also the custody of the royal castles of Dundee and Forfar. At his counsel the youthful Alexander III. averted the insidious attempt of Henry III. to induce him to render fealty for his kingdom. And as a baron of England, he personally resisted Henry, when he menaced a departure from the provisions of the Great Charter.

By his wife, the Countess of Angus, Gilbert de Umfraville had a son, also named Gilbert, who became eighth Earl of Angus. Taking his father's place as a royal counsellor, he was one of the nobles who, in 1281, agreed on oath to ratify the marriage contract of the king's daughter, Margaret, with Eric, King of Norway,[2] while in 1284 he joined the other nobles of Scotland in a formal recognition of the Princess Margaret of Norway as heir of the throne.[3] Prior to the young Queen's death, he succeeded to his hereditary office of governor of the castles of Dundee and Forfar; and this function he was exercising, when, on the 12th June 1291, the several custodiers of Scottish strongholds were required to surrender their offices to Edward, prior to his giving judgment in the matter of the succession. But the earl would renounce

---

[1] Dugdale's Baronage, i., 504-509.   [2] Fœdera, ii., 1052.

[3] *Ibid.*

his office only when his act was indemnified by the guardians, a proceeding which, Lord Hailes remarks, "proved him the only Scotsman who acted with integrity and spirit, on this trial of national integrity and spirit."[1] On account of the earl's influence in both kingdoms, Edward persistently sought his favour. On the 28th of June 1292, he instructed the guardians to allow the earl *misas et expensas* for keeping the castles which he had reluctantly surrendered.[2]

In terms of a royal summons, the Earl of Angus attended at Portsmouth, on the 1st September 1294, with horses and arms to aid in the intended expedition to France, and his fidelity was rewarded, on his being, on the 22d January 1294-5, presented with a tenth part of the taxation of Redesdale. And when his Scottish title was afterwards rejected by the English Parliament, Edward gave it his sanction. But, while willing to acknowledge Edward's authority in all reasonable concerns, the earl continued to support the Scots in their rights and aspirations. He died in 1307.[3]

Another descendant of the patriotic baron who successfully resisted the despotism of King John, was Sir Ingram de Umfraville.[4] In his sixteenth year, Prince Alexander, son of Alexander III., addressed, on the 29th March 1275, a letter to his uncle King Edward, begging that he would grant the petition which Sir Ingram de Umfraville is about to make for possession of lands which had belonged to his late father, Sir Robert de Umfraville. On Sir Ingram's behalf a similar application was made to Edward by King Alexander III.[5] In 1295, Sir Ingram became principal negotiator in the alliance between

---

[1] Fœdera, ii., 531; Hailes' Annals, ed. 1797, i., 227.

[2] Rotuli Scotiæ, i., p. 9ª.

[3] Dugdale's Baronage, i., 505; Sutherland Additional Case, v., 11; Wyntoun, ii., 55.

[4] Fœdera, ii., 695.

[5] Royal Letters, No. 1299.

Scotland and France, and in a writ, dated 20th of February 1298-9, he is described as an enemy of and rebel against the King of England, and as such is deprived of lands in England and Scotland, to which he had succeeded as heir of Ingelram de Baliol—these lands being conveyed to Sir Henry de Percy.[1] In a report made to Edward in August 1299 by Sir Robert Hastang, his sheriff at Roxburgh, Sir Ingram is named as Scottish sheriff of that county, and as one of a party of prominent Scotsmen, who had at Peebles fallen into contention, on account of Sir William Wallace proceeding abroad without the sanction of his compeers.[2] A son of Sir Ingram de Umfraville, bearing the same name, joined in the famous letter presented to the Pope in 1320, asserting the national independence.

These details are not inappropriate. On the 13th May 1195, Pope Celestine III. confirmed the foundation of a chapel at Dunipace, which the founder, Gilbert de Umfraville, had granted to the abbey of Cambuskenneth.[3] But in conveying to the abbey the means of endowment, the founder did not contemplate that a chapel constructed for the use of his domestics should be subordinated to conventual supervision. Accordingly, against certain ecclesiastical interference, Gilbert, great-grandson of the founder, son and heir of the Countess of Angus, made complaint to the diocesan, Bishop Gameline of St Andrews. Having made inquiry through Robert, dean of Linlithgow, as his commissioner, Bishop Gameline proceeded, on the 6th May 1267, to issue letters of judgment. He decerned that the place of worship at Dunipace was a mother church, since it had not

---

[1] Patent Roll, 27 Edward I., m. 36.
[2] Scots Documents, Public Record Office · National MSS. of Scotland, ii., No. viii.
[3] Register of the Monastery of Cambuskenneth, pp. 42,46.

rendered procuration to the bishop, whether entire or partial.[1] And on this deliverance, the chapel at Dunipace came to enjoy the same immunity from ordinary ecclesiastical control, as that which had latterly been accorded to the chapel royal at Stirling.[2]

To two charters of Gilbert de Umfraville, " Roger," described as " his chaplain," appears as a witness. In the earlier charter, Gilbert de Umfraville, as titular Earl of Angus, grants to Duncan, the king's dempster in Angus, a charter of the lands of Pitmulin ; in the latter he, on the 18th October 1271, grants at Ballendaloch in Stirlingshire, to Alexander of Alredas, the lands of Inverquharity, in the county of Forfar.[3] That Roger the chaplain usually resided at Dunipace may be inferred, since his chapel stood in that neighbourhood. In connexion with their lands at Dunipace the barons of Umfraville occupied Torwood Castle, an erection of the twelfth century, of which the foundations are yet traceable. And at Torwood, traditions respecting the Patriot long survived. Near the remains of the castle stood a gigantic oak, in the hollow of which he was held to have concealed himself when pursued by the English. The stem of this oak, forty-two feet in girth, was cut down in 1779, when portions were distributed among the curious. A snuff-mull formed of it was presented by the Earl of Buchan to General Washington, by whom it was bequeathed to the donor. Another portion was by Sir James Dunbar of Mochrum presented to Robert Wallace of Holmstone, who therewith framed a supposed portrait of the hero, procured in France and presented to one of his predecessors.

When as a youth William Wallace entered upon his education

[1] Reg. of Monastery of Cambuskenneth, p. 112.
[2] Hist. Chapel Royal of Scotland, Intro. xxxiii.
[3] The Douglas Book, by Sir William Fraser, vol. iii., pp. 4, 353, 354.

under the priest of Dunipace, Torwood Castle was probably the residence of Sir Ingram de Umfraville the elder, since, as a younger son of the house, he might reasonably be called upon to occupy the family mansion, while the elder representative had established his headquarters on those lands in Forfarshire which his wife, the Countess of Angus, had added to his family estate. And if we may estimate Sir Ingram's private character from the recorded incidents of his patriotism, we are prepared to expect that he would elect as his domestic chaplain one who shared his political sentiments. "Roger the clerk" was one of the Scottish prisoners in the Castle of Nottingham on the 1st of May 1298, and was retained in ward while one of his two companions was, at Michaelmas 1299, set at liberty.[1] Almost certainly he was captured at the battle of Dunbar in April 1296, and his designation and the enterprise with which he was associated may serve to identify him as the chaplain or priest of Dunipace. But apart from this connexion it is historically certain that the priest of Dunipace imbued the youthful Wallace with sentiments of patriotic ardour. A Latin couplet which the priest gave forth in his prelections, was often quoted by the Patriot, and has been transmitted to our times. The lines are these:—

> " Dico tibi verum, libertas optima rerum,
> Nunquam servili sub nexu vivito, fili." [2]

Wallace next appears as attending a school at Dundee. For this, indeed, our sole authority is Henry, but the Minstrel's assertion is confirmed by an emphatic tradition.[3] The young hero's removal from Dunipace to Dundee may easily be

---

[1] Chancery Miscellaneous Portfolios, No. 11.

[2] Majoris Historia, ed. 1740, p. 160. Rendered into English the couplet reads:—"Believe me, my son, freedom is the best of all possessions; never then subject yourself to the oppressor's yoke."

[3] Henry's Wallace, B. i., l. 155.

accounted for. To the nephew of his family chaplain, Gilbert de Umfraville, Earl of Angus, would, in his castle of Dundee, be disposed to yield a generous hospitality. And there was a schoolmaster in the place to whom the earl might desire to entrust the youth's education.

Some time prior to 1178, David, Earl of Huntingdon, brother of King William the Lion, founded a church at Dundee, in gratitude for his escape from shipwreck. That church he dedicated to the Virgin, attaching its temporalities to the monastery at Lindores, also his foundation. In connexion with the principal churches, schools were associated so early as the age of St Columba, and in the thirteenth century, burghal and other seminaries were superintended by the vicars.

About the middle of the thirteenth century, William Mydford, Master of Arts, was, by the monks of Lindores, appointed their vicar at Dundee, but, on entering upon his duties, he came to realise that the respectable endowment attached to his office was almost wholly appropriated by his patrons. And in the belief that the small portion of tithes which he received would prove unequal to his maintenance, he complained to his diocesan, the bishop of St Andrews, and as that prelate decided adversely to his claim, he presented an appeal to the Papal Court. By a rescript, dated 10th April 1256, Pope Alexander IV. confirmed the bishop's judgment,[1] with the result that the appellant became obnoxious to his clerical superiors at Lindores, also to his bishop, thereby arresting his ecclesiastical advancement. And if Wallace proceeded to Dundee when the eighth Earl of Angus was governor of the castle, that is about the year 1290, he is likely to have entered

---

[1] Chartulary of the Abbey of Lindores, pp. 10, 13, 14, 16, 18 ; Laing's Lindores Abbey, Edinb. 1876, pp. 57, 58.

the burgh school during Mydford's incumbency. If so, he would, by an instructor who so fearlessly contended for his rights, be further indoctrinated into a wholesome resistance of every species of oppression.

In June 1291, Gilbert de Umfraville, Earl of Angus, relinquished the governorship of the castle of Dundee, when it fell under Edward's control until the 18th November 1292, when, with the other strongholds, it was transferred to Baliol. During the seventeen months that the castle was in Edward's power, it was placed by him under the care of Brian Fitz Alan, a Yorkshire baron. And as that baron was also entrusted with the governorship of the castles of Roxburgh, Jedburgh, and Forfar, he discharged his function at Dundee by means of a substitute.

We are informed by the Minstrel that when Wallace was prosecuting his studies at Dundee, he was, in the place of sport, rudely accosted by a youth named Selby, son of the English constable of the place. By this person he was challenged for wearing green vestments as unbefitting his social rank ; also for being armed with "a knife," or dagger, which his assailant called upon him to deliver up. Incensed by the attack, Wallace fell upon his antagonist, and with his dagger smote him mortally.[1] The bold act, proceeds Henry, aroused the members of the garrison, and led the valiant Scotsman to flee for his life.[2] According to tradition, Wallace fled to the westward, and out-distancing his pursuers, reached the hamlet of Longforgan, six miles distant. There, in a state of exhaustion, he, at the door of a crofter's hut sat down to rest on the grainknocker, which stood near. The crofter, whose name was Smith, was absent in the field, but his wife, whose maiden name was

Henry's Wallace, B. i., ll. 192, 203-228.   [2] *Ibid.*, B. i., ll. 229-250.

Aimer, on being informed of the youth's extremity, offered help. Disguise being a first necessity, the kindly matron enveloped the fugitive in a loose spinning garb, which the fluff from the wheel speedily covered over. The pursuers entered, but in the stalwart spinner failed to recognise the object of their search. On their departure, the fugitive was, by the crofter and his wife, hospitably entertained, and in the evening conducted to Kilspindie.

In evidence of the event, the grain-knocker or bear-stone associated with the hero's name was, by the crofter's family, preserved at Longforgan for nearly six centuries, and by the last representative was in 1862 presented to the neighbouring proprietor, Colonel Paterson of Castle Huntly.[1]

According to the Minstrel, Wallace was at Kilspindie sheltered by his mother and uncle. After an interval, his mother accompanied him to Dunfermline to the tomb of Queen Margaret, both being clothed as pilgrims. As such they crossed the Tay by the boat passage at Lindores abbey. After a short visit to Dunfermline, they removed to Dunipace.[2]

Henry's narrative as to the Patriot's conflict with young Selby and his subsequent flight has clearly an historical basis. Many of those Englishmen whom Edward sent into Scotland to discharge public functions were connected with the northern counties. Fitz Alan, governor of a group of castles of which Dundee was one, was a Yorkshire man, and there were several northern families named Selby, from the members of which he might for his duties at Dundee have selected a deputy. Sir Walter de Selby of Northumberland was held by Edward in special favour. Another family of the name possessed lands in

[1] Warden's History of Forfarshire, v., 261-263.

[2] Henry's Wallace, B. i., ll. 150-154, 193-228, 276-298.

Cumberland. And Richard of Seleby, master of "la Blie" of Newcastle, is named on the 12th November 1305 as being actually in the employment of Edward's government.[1]

At Kilspindie, where our hero, in escaping from young Selby's avengers, found refuge, stood the house of Evelick, a seat of the Lindsays. To the baron of Evelick, Mydford's scholar may have been made known when in June 1291 the Earl of Angus ceased to occupy the castle at Dundee, since we learn from the Minstrel that the knight of Kilspindie was in the habit of visiting Dundee, and had there a town house or "lodging."[2]

But the Selby adventure, while resting on a basis of truth, is associated with circumstances which are evidently fictitious. If, as Henry represents, the hero attended the school of the place, his clothing must have been of dark serge, and he would also be unarmed. On the other hand, that in revenge for some taunt as to the abject condition of his country he struck down young Selby, is not improbable; and it is to be remarked that he first appears in history as in rebellion against English rule. Further, in reference to the episode, it is not without significance that Edward, when on his visit to Dundee in 1296, evinced a desire to revenge some insult to his authority by wrecking the church of St Mary.[3]

The Selby incident must have occurred between the months of June 1291 and November 1292, when the castle of Dundee was in the hands of an English governor. And the question at once arises as to how our hero was employed, or sheltered, between the date of the Selby encounter and of his consequent outlawry, and the time of his appearance as a military or popular leader. If we accept the Minstrel's authority, his military efforts were,

[1] Exchequer Q.R. Memoranda, 33 Edward I., m. 72, dorso.

[2] Henry's Wallace, B. i., l. 233.

[3] Walcot's Scoti-Monasticon, p. 30.

from the time of the Selby incident, continuous and persistent. For Henry conducts the hero from Dunipace into Ayrshire, and there presents him as chief of a band of patriots, which made rough havoc among parties of English troops who had, under Sir Henry Percy, their headquarters in the castle of Ayr.[1] But Percy was appointed governor of Ayr not before the 8th September 1296,[2] that is, about four years subsequent to the possible occurrence of the Selby incident!

And in the further prosecution of the inquiry, it may be asked, if the son of the English Constable of Dundee was slain by our hero, at the only period when such an event could have taken place—that is between June 1291 and November 1292— how did Baliol, who, at the latter date, came to the throne, permit the slaughter of a follower of his overlord to pass unavenged? We offer the explanation, that in the encounter, Selby was wounded and disgraced, but not injured mortally. Further, that subsequent to the event, his assailant may have experienced protection at the hands of some one politically powerful. Now, from the scene of strife, Henry conducts the hero to Dunipace, and a tradition exists that Wallace, on being pursued thither, concealed himself within the hollow trunk of an oak near the castle of Torwood. Torwood Castle was a seat of the Umfravilles, and as such, a home of the Patriot's relative, the priest of Dunipace; while the owners of the castle, owing to their influence in both kingdoms, Edward desired to conciliate rather than provoke. Under the circumstances, Wallace, outlaw as he was, might have been comparatively safe. On the other hand, it is unreasonable to suppose that one so much imbued with patriotic ardour, would for a series of years have been content to remain in

---

[1] Henry's Wallace, B. ii., l. 23.   [2] Rotuli Scotiæ, 24 Edward I., m. 7.

a state of inactivity. Nor, with his manly nature, was he likely to contemplate without protest the unworthy subserviency of Baliol. And if so, may it not be assumed, in the light of his subsequent negotiations with Philip of France, that he was an active adviser of that policy which secluded Baliol from the conduct of affairs, and thereupon initiated the league with France?

In subordinating the country, subsequent to the victory at Dunbar, Edward experienced a measure of restraint in the southern and western districts. In Galloway, Robert Bruce of Annandale, and his son, the Earl of Carrick, exercised a chief influence; and Edward foresaw that in the wide territory under their control, he would more easily secure a submission to his authority, by stimulating their ambition. On the 6th October 1295, he appointed the elder Bruce to the keepership of Carlisle Castle,[1] while on the 12th of February 1295-6, he remitted a debt due by him to the Crown.[2] And subsequent to the battle of Dunbar, he empowered the two barons, father and son, to receive to his allegiance the inhabitants of Annandale and Carrick.[3] Edward's policy was attended with evident success, inasmuch as among those who, at Berwick on the 28th August 1296, rendered homage, we find the names of "Robert de Brus le Veil," and "Robert de Brus le jeovene."[4]

But submission to his rule on the part of the house of Bruce, Edward well knew rested solely on self-interest, and was consequently uncertain. Therefore, among other arrangements for the subordination of the kingdom, which, on the 8th September 1296, he published at Berwick, was that of placing south and western Carrick under an English governor. Accordingly, he forthwith appointed Sir Henry de Percy as warden of Galloway,

---

[1] Patent Roll, 23 Edward I., m. 5.
[2] Memoranda Roll, 24 Edward I., m. 12.
[3] Prynne, iii., 652.
[4] Ragman Roll.

and governor of the south-western castles of Ayr, Wigtown,
Cruggelton, and Botel [Buittle].[1] The chief function of the
new warden was to subordinate to English rule owners of
land and other prominent persons. Among the landowners
of Ayrshire, who now, or formerly, acknowledged Edward's
authority, were the following who thus described themselves :—

> " Adam le Waleys, del counte de Are.
> " Aleyn Waleys, tenant le Roi du counte de Are.
> " Nicol le Waleys, del counte de Ayr." [2]

But a kinsman of these persons, Malcolm Wallace of Elderslie,
still held out. And according to the Minstrel, he was on account
of his recusancy exposed to a rigid persecution. Driven from
home, his wife obtained shelter from the baron of Kilspindie,
while he was necessitated to conceal himself in the uplands
of the Lennox. The territory of Lennox was on the east
skirted by the forest of Torwood and the lands of Dunipace. But
Henry's narrative in relation to Malcolm Wallace is singularly
disjointed. At first we are informed that he was slain by the
English, and that consequently the hero was led, immediately
after his flight from Dundee, to assume arms to avenge his
death. Subsequently, forgetful of what he had written, the
Minstrel relates that Malcolm Wallace fell at the battle of
Loudoun Hill, fought some time afterwards.[3]

Next in the order of his narrative, Henry sets forth that
the hero's uncle at Dunipace endeavoured to dissuade him
from a further resistance of English rule, and jointly with his
mother entered into negotiations to secure his freedom. At
Elderslie they had an interview with Sir Reginald Craufurd,
whom, in his capacity of sheriff of Ayr, they induced to plead

[1] Exchequer L.T.R., "Nomina Villarum," No. 455.
[2] Ragman Rolls, 137, 148.
[3] Henry's Wallace, B. i., l. 319.

with Sir Henry Percy, that his sentence of outlawry might be revoked.[1]

Henry's narrative has probably a basis of truth. In describing the hero's uncle at Dunipace as "a man of gret richess," and "a mychty persone,"[2] it is evident he rested on a tradition which had confused the individuality of the priest and his patron. Now, on the 8th September 1296, a warrant was issued by Edward in favour of Sir Ingram de Umfraville, whereby the sheriffs of Ayr and other counties were authorised to restore his lands, inasmuch as he had surrendered Dunbarton Castle, which he held under Baliol, and had also done homage.[3] And having thus yielded to the English king, Sir Ingram might consequently proceed to intercede on behalf of the adventurous youth who for a course of years had been his companion, counsellor, and friend.

Sir Reginald Craufurd, sheriff of Ayr, had with several of his kinsmen rendered fealty to Edward, their names thus appearing in the homage roll :—"Reinaud de Crauford, del counte de Are;" "Johan de Crauford, tenant le Roi du counte de Are;" "Roger de Crauford, del counte de Are;" "William de Crauford."[4]

According to Henry's narrative, Sir Reginald Craufurd, anxious for his nephew's safety, gave him shelter at his house of Corsbie, situated within five miles of the town and castle of Ayr. But while accepting his uncle's protection, the young hero resolutely refused to acquire favour with the English government by acknowledging Edward as his sovereign—a resolution which led Sir Reginald to inform him that he dared not longer yield to him harbour or entertainment. So saying,

[1] Henry's Wallace, B. i., ll. 326-334.
[2] *Ibid.*, B. i., ll. 299-300.
[3] Exchequer L.T.R., Nomina Villarum; No. 455.
[4] Ragman Rolls, 129, 137, 142, 146, 161.

Sir Reginald conducted him to Riccarton, and there placed him under the care of Sir Richard Wallace, his father's brother. Sir Richard was old and blind.[1]

Riccarton Castle stood on a gentle eminence, at a place now known as Yardside, on the margin of the river Irvine. There, according to Henry, the Patriot arrived in the month of February, and sojourned till the following April. One morning, when, with a single attendant, he was net-fishing in the Irvine, a body of English troopers on the march from Ayr to Glasgow, suddenly came up. Five of their number lingering behind demanded of the angler a share of his fisher's creel, as an offering to Saint Martin.[2] Not indisposed to a proposal associated with a religious rite, Wallace was proceeding to hand over a portion of his draught, when the troopers insisted on receiving the whole. Informing them that he was fishing on behalf of an aged knight, who (the season being Lent) was that day observing the offices of religion, the angler mildly expostulated as to the unreasonableness of the demand. On this one of the troopers approached menacingly with his sword, when Wallace wrested it from his grasp, and with it hewed down his assailant. Two of the other troopers now rushed upon the angler to avenge their comrade's death, but the defence was maintained so effectively that one was slain and the other prostrated. The two other troopers rode off precipitately, and on applying to their leader for a reinforcement to avenge their associates, were informed that five men-at-arms should have been able to cope with an unarmed fisherman, and that no support would be allowed.[3]

---

[1] Henry's Wallace, B. i., ll. 327, 364.

[2] Martin was a military saint held in reverence by English soldiers. He was represented as dividing his cloak with a beggar at the gate of Amiens, and in allusion to this legend the English troopers seem to have urged their claim on the Scottish angler.

[3] Henry's Wallace, i., 367-434. A thorn-tree on the bank of the Irvine formerly marked the scene of the hero's exploit.

The encounter into which he had reluctantly been drawn Wallace apprehended might, in the event of his longer remaining in the locality, endanger the safety of his aged relative at Riccarton ; also, in the event of pursuit, place himself untowardly. He therefore, as Henry relates, left Riccarton, and on the horse of one of the slain troopers rode hastily to Auchincruive. The castle of Auchincruive, occupying the site of the present mansion, rested on the precipitous bank of the river Ayr. The owner, Aleyn Wallace, was one of Edward's homagers, and, like the sheriff of Ayr, dreaded to actively harbour a kinsman who was under outlawry. But that shelter which he felt bound to refuse in the castle, he was willing to yield him in the thicket. And included in his broad demesne was an ancient forest, styled the Laighlyne, or low-lying woods. There, according to tradition, Wallace, in April or May 1297, first drew together the nucleus of that national army of which he became the leader.

Within the forest of Laighlyne, at a bend of the Ayr stream, and close to its bank, is a spot styled *the Wallace Seat.* Protected overhead by a projecting cliff, it is approachable from one point only, while by a powerful resistance from within an intruder would certainly be precipitated into the surge. Here the hero rested at night, and in circumstances of danger. And it may not historically be overlooked, that to these scenes, associated with the national Patriot, the great Caledonian bard resorted early in life, in order to be imbued more ardently with the love of country. In his letter to Mrs Dunlop of November 1786, Burns writes thus :—" I chose a fine summer Sunday, the only day my line of life allowed, and walked half a dozen of miles [from Mount Oliphant] to pay my respects to the Leglen wood, with as much devout enthusiasm as ever pilgrim did to Loretto ; and as I explored every den and dell where I could suppose my heroic countryman to have lodged, I recollect (for even then I was a rhymer) that my heart glowed with a wish to be able to make a song on him in some measure equal to his merit."

According to the Minstrel, Wallace, while under shelter at Laighlyne, ventured forth at intervals, and then performed prodigies of valour. Attended by his groom, he visited Ayr, where at the market cross he found a sturdy Englishman making offer on a wager to allow any Scotsman to strike him on the back with a thick rod which he bore in his hand. Discovering that the rod on being raised bent up and fell lightly, Wallace deposited his forfeit and offered to make trial. He then grasped the rod above the place where it was intended to give way, and dealt a blow so forceful as to prostrate the boaster lifeless at his feet. To avenge their companion a body of English soldiers surrounded the smiter and vigorously attacked him. Having struck one across his basinet, which he shivered into fragments, and smote four others, the hero mounted his horse, and effected his escape.[1]

At Ayr an English buckler-player, boasting of his skill, challenged to single combat all who approached him. He had some time maintained his superiority, when Wallace, who was in Ayr in disguise, bade him defiance. A combat followed, when the Patriot, parrying his antagonist's powerful thrusts, penetrated his helmet and brought him to the ground. Wallace was accompanied by fifteen followers, and his party being surrounded by a large body of English soldiers, a general conflict ensued. After striking down twenty-nine of their opponents, the hero and his followers effected a retreat.[2]

A story setting forth that Wallace was imprisoned at Ayr, cast out as dead, and afterwards restored by his nurse, is circumstantially related by Henry, who, with his details, mixes

---

[1] Henry's Wallace, B. ii., 1-80.   [2] *Ibid.*, B. iii., 353-404.

up a tradition relative to Thomas the Rhymer and the monks of Fail.[1] The episode possesses a curious interest, inasmuch as it was the special privilege of monks of the Mathurin order, to which those of Fail belonged, to rescue persons in captivity.[2] But the Minstrel's narrative is evidently apocryphal.

Having satisfactorily evidenced his prowess, the Patriot at length obtained countenance from several of his kinsmen. Among these were the three sons of Sir Richard Wallace of Riccarton, Adam, Richard, and Simon; also Edward Litill and James Cleland.[3] Litill is by the Minstrel described as the hero's sister's son, but there is no evidence that he had a sister; and, considering his own age in 1297, it is doubtful whether the son of a sister could have at that time been able to carry arms.

On the 14th December 1366, Martin Lytill was witness to a charter whereby David II. granted to Sir William Douglas the lands of Aberdour in Fife;[4] while in the sixteenth century a family of the name possessed the lands of Liberton in the county of Midlothian.

The family of Cleland took their designation from a portion of land in the county of Lanark. According to the Minstrel, James Cleland was the Patriot's cousin, and by a modern genealogical writer he is described as son of Alexander Kneland or Cleland, of that Ilk, by his wife Margaret, daughter of Adam Wallace of Riccarton.[5] By the Minstrel, Cleland is described as supporting the Patriot at the battles of Loudoun Hill and Stirling Bridge, as being present with him at the battle of Falkirk, and as accompanying him to France. With his eldest son he aided Bruce at Bannockburn, and being there wounded received in compensation a portion of lands at Calder in the county of Linlithgow.

[1] Henry's Wallace, B. ii., 141-359.
[2] See Wallace of Failford, vol. i., p. 117.
[3] Henry's Wallace, B. iii., ll. 43-58.
[4] Robertson s Index of Charters, 81, No. 156.
[5] Anderson's Scottish Nation, i., 648; ii., 617.

Besides his supposed relatives, Wallace obtained the adherence of Robert Boyd, whom the Minstrel describes as "gud and worthi and wight."[1] In the year 1205 Sir Robert Boyd was witness to a contract between Bryce de Eglington and the town of Irvine; and his son, Sir Robert, made a prominent figure at the battle of Largs in 1263. A son of the hero of Largs, also Sir Robert, was, it is believed, Wallace's companion in arms. In August 1296 he appears as one of Edward's homagers; and he seems to have joined Wallace in the course of the following summer.[2] With Sir Robert Boyd as his lieutenant, Wallace took command of a small band of patriots. And at this stage the hero is by the Minstrel described thus :—

> " Gude lycht harness, fra that tyme, wayt he cuir,
> For sodeyn stryff, fra it he wald nocht scuir
> A habergione vndyr his gonne he war
> A steylle capleyne in his bouet but mar ;
> His glowis of plait in claith war couerit weill,
> In his doublet a closs coler of steyle ;
> His face he kepit, for it was cuir bar,
> With his twa handis, the quhilk full worthi war,
> In to his weid, and he come in a thrang :
> Was na man than on fute mycht with him gang.
> So growane in pith, off pouer stark and stur,
> His terryble dyntis war awful till endur.
> Thai trast mar in Wallace him allane
> Than in a hundreth mycht be off Ingland tayne."[3]

For a time Wallace repulsed parties of English troops issuing from the castle of Ayr, but when he had organised a considerable force, he sought to disturb the garrison more effectively by cutting off their provisions. Aware that their chief supplies were obtained from Carlisle, and ascertaining when a victualling party was in motion, he assembled his followers at Mauchline Muir.

[1] Henry's Wallace, B. ii., l. 430.

[2] Crawfurd's Renfrewshire, 55; Dalrymple's Collections, 80; Crawfurd's Peerage, 242; Prynne's Collections, iii., 656.

[3] Henry's Wallace, B. iii., ll. 85-98.

Having ascertained at an inn that the victuallers' mounted pioneers had passed forward, he concealed twenty of his men in a plantation which skirted the thoroughfare. As at early morn the waggoners with their escort passed into a narrow defile, he caused his party to obstruct the passage. Foremost in the encounter, he unhorsed the leader, and having rescued Boyd, his lieutenant, who was thrown down and wounded, he was forthwith aided by Adam Wallace, younger of Riccarton, who slew one Beaumont, an English knight. Ultimately the brave strategist routed the victuallers and seized their supplies.[1] At the east of Loudoun Hill, a precipitous bank on the margin of an ancient road is pointed out as the spot whereon the Patriot and his followers lay in ambush.[2] According to the Minstrel, the conductor of the waggoners bore the name of Fenwick, and had incurred Wallace's resentment as leader of that attack upon the Scots in which his father was slain. A family named Fenwick flourished in Northumberland, but only in the pages of the Minstrel does the name appear in connexion with the War of Independence. That an English commander of the name was concerned in the slaughter of the Patriot's father is extremely improbable, for, while Henry relates that Malcolm Wallace was killed in a former battle at Loudoun Hill,[3] he offers no details of the conflict, and its existence is more than doubtful.[4]

The seizure of the English waggons at Loudoun Hill tended to stimulate the energies of those who were inclined, under favourable circumstances, to support the national cause, while a large booty, including victuals, horses, military stores, and a portion of money, proved of the utmost avail to those who had hitherto served without pay and subsisted upon scanty rations.[5]

[1] Henry's Wallace, B. iii., ll. 100-203.
[2] New Statistical Account, Ayrshire, v., 836.
[3] Henry's Wallace, B. i., l. 319.
[4] *Ibid.*, B. iii., ll. 111-116.
[5] *Ibid.*, B. iii., ll. 220-221.

Penetrating into Lanarkshire, Wallace sheltered his troops in the forest of Clydesdale. And obviously at this time (though Henry presents a different connexion) occurred that conflict at Lanark which has commonly been described as the hero's first great stroke on behalf of his country. The affair at Lanark is set forth by Wyntoun; but Henry, who has adopted his narrative, adds some most improbable details. According to Wyntoun, the Patriot, appearing in a street of Lanark clad in green and bearing a great sword, was by an English soldier charged with arrogance. And when the hero retorted on his churlish assailant, he discovered that his antagonist belonged to a party of English troops gathered in the market-place. Wallace now brought together a body of his followers, and a conflict ensued. After this had some time continued, he, overpowered by numbers, withdrew, and in the house of his "lemman" or mistress effected shelter or escape. During the scuffle, the English sheriff was absent from the place, but on his return he caused the hero's protectress to be inhumanly slaughtered. Informed of the tragic event, Wallace re-entered the town, and with thirty of his followers broke into the sheriff's residence, and there effected his death.[1]

According to Henry, Wallace and his associate, Sir John the Graham, were, on leaving Lanark church, in which they had been worshipping, upbraided by Hesilrig, the English sheriff, also by Sir Robert Thorn, an English knight.[2] A conflict following, Wallace and Graham, at the head of twenty-four Scotsmen,

[1] Wyntoun's Cronykil, Edinb. 1872, B. viii., chap. xiii., ll. 2029-2138.

[2] The upbraiding words used are given by the Minstrel, but vary in different editions. Dr Jamieson has the following :—

"Gud deyn, dawch Lard, bach lowch banyoch a de,"

implying a mixture of Scottish and Gaelic, probably the speech of a portion of the Lowlands when Henry wrote. The first four words may be rendered from the Scottish, "Good evening, lazy laird"—the other words synonymous with the Gaelic l' a ail luibh, beaunach a De, – that is, "If you please, God bless you."

repelled two hundred English soldiers, and slew fifty of their number. Thereafter the two Scottish leaders were, with their followers, enabled to retreat through the kindly offices of a gentlewoman, who admitted them into her demesne. Next hastening to Cartland Crags, they there fully eluded their pursuers. Meanwhile, learning that his benefactress was put to death, Wallace, to avenge the atrocity, slew Hesilrig and his son, while Graham, also returning to Lanark, set on fire the dwelling of Sir Robert Thorn, who perished in its ruins. Thereafter, according to Henry, the Lanark burgesses commenced a general slaughter of the English troops, and terminated in the place the Edwardian rule.[1]

In connexion with the incident that a Scottish gentlewoman at Lanark conduced to the Patriot's escape, the Minstrel has fabricated a web of fiction. He corrects Wyntoun as to his deliverer being his "lemman," or mistress, asserting that she was his lawful wife. And the circumstances of the union he poetically sets forth. The gentlewoman, he alleges, was the only child of Hew Bradfute of Lamington, and had in early youth lost both her parents. By incidentally seeing her in church, Wallace had become her admirer, while his affection was afterwards intensified by his becoming acquainted with her personally. He now, on the advice of his friend Kerlé, pressed his suit, when the gentlewoman informed him that she had been urged by Hesilrig to wed his son, and that though she was resolved not to comply, she dreaded openly to avow herself the wife of another. But she espoused Wallace in secret, and the union resulted in the birth of a daughter, who became the wife of a landowner named Shaw.[2]

---

[1] Henry's Wallace, B. vi., 107-262.   [2] *Ibid.*, B. v., 584-721 ; vi., 65-73.

This matrimonial incident is clearly fictitious, but the occurrence of a struggle between the Scottish Patriot and the soldiers of the garrison at Lanark, in which the English sheriff was killed, is fully attested. Fordun refers to the event, and there is other evidence.[1] In an inquiry instituted at Michaelmas 1304 as to money in the keeping of Hugh de Cressingham, Edward's treasurer in Scotland, which after his death in September 1297 had gone amissing, it is set forth that about the 15th of August preceding, the lost treasure was deposited in Werkworth Castle in dread of the Scots, who had commenced an insurrection, and slain the English sheriff of Lanark.[2] And sixty years later, Sir Thomas de Gray, a Northumbrian knight, relates in his "Scala Cronica" that in May 1297, when his father was in garrison at Lanark, Wallace fell at night upon the English quarters, killed the sheriff, and set the place on fire. He adds, that in the conflict his father was wounded, and left on the street as dead, and that he would have perished, had he not been rescued by William de Lundy, his companion.[3] And as a chronicler Gray's testimony is supported in the fact that, in acknowledgment of special services against the Scots, Edward II. in 1319 granted his father and his heirs a considerable portion of land.[4]

Hesilrig, the English sheriff or military governor at Lanark, was member of a landed family in Northumberland. By an inquisition held at Newcastle on the 14th March 1318-19, it was found that the late William de Heselrig was seised in the fourth part of the Manor of Akild, in Northumberland, in which he was succeeded by his son John, a minor.[5]

---

[1] Fordun a Hearne, p. 978.

[2] Exchequer Q. R. Memoranda, 33 Edward I., m. 37.

[3] Scala Cronica, 124.

[4] Burton's History, ed. 1873, ii., 184, *note.*

[5] *Inq.* ad quod damnum, 12 Edw. II., No. 82.

About the same time John of Hesilrygg petitioned Edward II. for compensation, inasmuch as that he, at the "descomfiture" of Stirling, had lost horses and armour of the value of two hundred marks, and being captured by the Scots, had suffered imprisonment for two years, and had paid two hundred marks as ransom, and had further sustained the loss of the profits of his 40 mark land in Northumberland for the space of five years.[1]

On the 20th November 1360, Edward III. granted to William of Heselrig the lands in Weteslade South, in Northumberland, for his good services in the Scottish wars, and also in compensation of losses which he had sustained therein.[2]

Prior or subsequent to his attack on the English headquarters at Lanark, Wallace concealed his followers amidst the rocky depths of the Cleghorn woods. According to tradition, he some time sojourned at Lanark in a dwelling at the head of the Castlegate.

Subsequent to the affair at Lanark, Wallace marched to Biggar, twelve miles distant, and there received a reinforcement under Sir John de Graham, son of the baron of Dundaff, in the district of the Lennox. At the head of a considerable force, moderately equipped, he now proceeded northward. On his attacking the castle of Dunbarton, the English garrison made a surrender. Roseneath Castle, which he next assailed, also submitted to his valour. He rested at Faslane, where, by the Earl of Lennox, he and his followers were hospitably entertained. Returning to the midlands, he next marched eastward to Stirling, and in his progress attacked the small fort or

---

[1] Parliamentary Petitions, No. 4316.　　　[2] Patent Roll, 34 Edw., p. 3, m. 8.

peel of Gargunnock. By Henry the structure is described thus :—

> "On Gargownno was byggyt a small peill
> That warnyst was with men and wittaill weill,
> Within a dyk, bathe closs, chawmer, and hall ;
> Capteyne tharoff to nayme he hecht Thrilwall."[1]

For the admission of workmen who were repairing the structure, the drawbridge being frequently lowered at night, Wallace waited his opportunity. Made aware, by the kindling of a fire in the vicinity, that the drawbridge was lowered, he suddenly attacked the place before day-break. There was a gallant resistance, but the garrison was ultimately overwhelmed. By his own sword he struck down Thornton,[2] the governor, but forthwith provided for the safety of his widow and three children. He now demolished the fort. The conical eminence on which it stood is still pointed out.

After hunting for some days in the forest of Kincardine, Wallace crossed the Forth at Kildean, and marched into Strathearn. During his sojourn at Berwick, in August 1296, Edward had charged the principal burgesses and more opulent traders, to join the clergy and barons in testifying their allegiance. Many rendered a ready compliance, while those who refused or hesitated were menaced with heavy penalties, or with the punishment of outlawry. And in order to effect his purpose, Edward appointed William de Ormesby, an Englishman, as a special Justiciary, to impose penalties upon recusants. Ormesby held his principal courts in the monastery at Scone, a structure hallowed not more by religious association than by regal and patriotic memories.

Informed of the tyranny at Scone, Wallace hastened north-

---

[1] Henry, B. iv., ll. 213-216, 269.

[2] Hemingford, i., p. 118 ; Trivet, 200. According to Henry, the governor's name was Thrilwall.

ward, and, being joined at Perth by Sir William Douglas with a considerable body of followers, he marched to Scone, and succeeded in breaking up the English court, and putting to flight the Justiciary.[1]

Having assisted Wallace in the displacement at Scone, Sir William Douglas forthwith departed into Dumfriesshire, where not long afterwards he reduced the English garrisons at Durrisdeer and Sanquhar.

From Perth, Wallace marched towards the castle of Kinclaven. Ascertaining that the English garrison planted there were expecting a reinforcement, he waited its approach, and then with a party of troops issuing from a thicket by the wayside, suddenly attacked a body of ninety troopers, two-thirds of whom he smote or unsaddled. Thereafter he reduced the castle, and destroyed the structure by fire.

Among the slain troopers was their leader Sir James Butler, an English knight. To avenge his death, his son, Sir John Butler, proceeded with two hundred men-at-arms to make a vehement pursuit of Wallace and his followers. A first attack the Patriot vigorously repelled, seriously wounding the opposing leader. But there was a succession of encounters, and in these Wallace suffered heavily, till his force was reduced to about forty. With these he sought shelter in Elcho Park, on the Tay's northern bank, but his place of hiding being discovered by Sir John Butler, he, in effecting his escape, had to sacrifice nearly the entire body of his adherents. Taking a concealed route by the north bank of the Earn, he sought the unoccupied fortalice of Gask, amidst the woods of Gascon Ha'.

---

[1] Trivet, 299; Hemingford, vol. ii., 128. According to Hemingford, the attack on the Justiciary by "the two Williams," took place on the 1st of August (feast of St Peter *ad vincula*), when the Earl of Surrey and Cressingham had proceeded southward to attend a Parliament in London. Hemingford's date is clearly erroneous.

At this point the Minstrel introduces into his narrative a thrilling adventure. In ascending an eminence at Gask, one of the hero's followers, an Irishman named Fawdoun pleaded his inability to proceed further, when, suspecting him of treachery, Wallace smote him mortally. When his remaining followers —now reduced to thirteen—had reached the castle, he invited them to repose under its shelter, while he personally undertook to act as sentinel. Falling into a reverie, he reflected on Fawdoun's death, and awakening suddenly there burst upon his ears a sound as of shouting and dog-baying, and the blowing of horns. Arousing two of his followers, he despatched them in quest of intelligence, and as they did not return he sent out the others in pairs to make search, till he remained unattended and alone. And now he was further distracted by the head of Fawdoun being cast into the fire near which he rested, the figure which bore it rapidly making off. The Minstrel now explains that a sleuth-hound belonging to Sir John Butler had stopped at Fawdoun's body, when a party of English soldiers, who came up, concluded that Wallace had perished at the hands of his followers. Hence one of their number took up the head, and was bearing it to Gask Castle, when, on discovering Wallace seated by the fire, he hastily threw it down and betook himself to flight.

Tidings of the Scottish insurrection Edward received with some degree of incredulity, since he had fully persuaded himself that the last embers of the national ardour were being extinguished under Ormesby's uncompromising exactions. He was conscious only of one peril—that which arose from the ambition of Robert Bruce, the young Earl of Carrick. Robert Bruce, known as the Lord of Annandale, was dead, and his son Robert, the elder Earl of Carrick, had some time resided in England content in the possession of his personal estate. But the earl's son Robert, third of the name, remained in Scotland, and his plans and purposes were uncertain. Besides he had vast resources, inasmuch as his father, content with being known as the elder Earl of Carrick, claimed no share of the lands or any other concern in the earldom. The younger Bruce therefore bore rule over a district extending from the Solway to the Clyde, which implied the power of bringing many fighting men into the field. As a first step, then, in dealing with the Scottish insurrection, Edward resolved to make sure of Bruce's fidelity. Summoning him to Carlisle, he commanded him there to renew his homage. And on this occasion he was called upon to render it by kneeling on a portion of armour represented as the consecrated sword of Thomas à Becket. This test fulfilled, Edward gave him a further opportunity of proving his fidelity by commissioning him to hotly pursue Sir William Douglas so as to disperse his followers, and secure his lands and goods. Accepting the mission, Bruce forthwith made an attack on Douglas's territories, and, scattering his followers, threw his wife and children into prison.

On the subjection of Sir William Douglas, Edward inclined to believe that the Scottish revolt was all but suppressed, hence his preparations for an expedition to Flanders, some time in progress, he vigorously continued. But when he afterwards learned that discontent prevailed in the west country, he, on the 24th of May, put himself into active communication with Hugh de Cressingham, his treasurer of Scotland, also with Patric, Earl of March, and others of his principal adherents.[1] And letters to these persons were accompanied with certain messages to be delivered orally.[2] These letters, in the light of future events,

---

[1] Hemingford, i., 119, 120.

[2] Close Roll, 25 Edward I., m. 27. The period of summons is described as "after Sunday next following the octaves of the Nativity of St John Baptist."

evidently suggest the secret capture of suspected persons, and offer a recompense to those who should engage in the service.

Meanwhile, in the belief that disaffection in the west might be crushed by a decisive movement, Edward instructed the bishop of Durham to proceed to the scene of revolt at the head of an hundred and twenty cavalry. Among those who had joined in the western insurrection was Robert Wishart, bishop of Glasgow, a powerful churchman, and by his overthrow Bek hoped to strike a universal terror. Accordingly, on his arrival in Glasgow, he at once invested Wishart's episcopal palace, and in the bishop's absence secured its possession. At this time, Wallace was engaged in besieging the new castle of Ayr, but informed of the disaster at Glasgow he resolved to raise the blockade and to concentrate his energies in resisting Bek's military progress. Having by a night march reached Glasgow, he arranged his men in two columns, one of which he placed under the command of his uncle, the laird of Auchinleck, the other under that of his valiant lieutenant, Sir Robert Boyd. As the English troops still held possession of the bishop's palace by closely environing it, the hero's uncle, who was familiar with the locality, moved towards them by St Mungo's Lane and the Drygate, thereby causing a diversion. Another attack was made by Sir Robert Boyd, who proceeded to the scene of action by the course of the High Street. A violent conflict followed, at a spot long known as "The bell o' the brae;" the Scots under Wallace ultimately achieving a decided victory. Among Wallace's captives was Henry of Horncester, an English monk eminent for his military prowess.[1]

[1] Henry's Wallace, B. vii., ll. 492-600 ; Carrick's Life of Wallace, ed. 1840, pp. 42, 43 ; Glasghu Facies, vol. i., pp. 53-55. The sole authority in relation to the *Battle o' the Brae*, is Henry. In our narrative we have excluded many details which are obviously fictitious. That an engagement disastrous to the English did take place, may be assumed from the circumstantial character of the tradition ; also from Bek's speedy return to England, and its consequences.

Escaping from the disaster which overwhelmed his troops, Bishop Bek hastened to England bearing to Edward the intelligence that the Scottish insurrection had assumed formidable proportions. Consequent on this report, Edward, on the 4th June, granted a special commission to Sir Henry Percy, governor at Ayr, also to Sir Robert Clifford, charging them to suppress all national gatherings, and to arrest those who took part in them.[1] And on the 10th of June he empowered his several tax collectors in Scotland, to raise in their several localities the sum of £2000, for the immediate use of Hugh de Cressingham, his treasurer.[2] Edward next invited the young Earl of Carrick to put forth his utmost efforts towards restraining discontent and advancing order. In his commission as drafted by the clerk, Bruce was instructed to bring into the field as many fighting men as he could conveniently muster, but Edward personally interpolated the injunction that he should at once enter the field at the head of a thousand men, to be specially selected by him from the several districts under his control, including Kyle, Cunningham, Cumnock, and Carrick.[3] To other magnates in Scotland and in the north of England, Edward also issued summonses, alike emphatic and peremptory. He enjoined Gibbon Fitz Kan and Duncan Macdowal, two powerful Gallovidian chiefs, to recruit one thousand, but in the revised draft, two thousand men. From Sir Richard le Brun, in Cumberland, he demanded a thousand troops; from Sir Robert Lengleys and Walter de Stirkeland, in Westmoreland, a thousand, but on revision, nineteen hundred men; from Sir John de Hodelstone, five hundred; from Sir William de Dakre, at Lancaster, seven hundred, or on revision, one thousand more. Commands for

---

[1] Patent Roll, 25 Edward I., Part 1, m. 6.   [2] Liberate Roll, 25 Edward I., m. 3 in scedula.
[3] Original Memoranda in the Public Record Office.

levies Edward also addressed to Sir Marmaduke Twenge, and other Yorkshire barons; also to Sir Walter de Huntercumbe, in Northumberland, and to John le Fitz Marmaduke, in the county of Durham. From the Earl of Angus he demanded three hundred foot, and he interpolated the provision, that if he could not attend personally he should provide a substitute in his son. For fortifying purposes, the public authorities of Northumberland and Yorkshire were charged to provide a body of masons and ditch-workers.[1]

Of his new and powerful force, Edward, on the 14th of June, entrusted the command to the Earl of Surrey, his guardian in Scotland.[2] Replying to a letter of instructions, Surrey expressed his belief that the Scottish rising did not warrant such ample preparations, and could certainly be suppressed apart from his personal service. Bishop Bek, he added, had returned from the north, not on account of a reverse, but owing to the force under his command being inadequate for its purpose. A sufficient force he added would be despatched forthwith.[3]

About eight days after the date of his letter to Edward, Surrey sent into Scotland Sir Robert Clifford, in command of forty thousand foot and three hundred cavalry. From Berwick, Clifford marched his troops through Annandale to the district of Lochmaben, where he encamped. Hitherto he had met with no obstruction in his progress, but he now experienced a vigorous night attack upon his tents, which could be repelled only by his setting on fire a portion of his huts, so as to obtain light wherewith to discover the motions of the aggressors. Striking his tents he hastily departed for Ayr.[4]

---

[1] From the original Memoranda in the Public Record Office.

[2] Patent Roll, 25 Edward I., Part 1, m. 2.

[3] *Ibid.*, Part 2, m. 1.

[4] Knighton, p. 2515.

Edward suddenly changed his policy. Probably from some circumstances in connexion with the conflict at Glasgow, he had been led to suspect that natives of the north, while nominally yielding him allegiance, would not hand to hand resist those of their brethren who were contending for personal or national freedom. Accordingly he recalled his orders to the leading magnates that they should bring together their followers to aid in checking the insurrection, and gave command that they should be severally ready to accompany his army into Flanders.

Rashly instituted, Edward's new movement excited a vehement discontent, inasmuch as those chiefs who had yielded to the English rule began to suspect that they were distrusted, and further that the scheme was put forth covertly, so as to decoy them from their homes. And it is also probable that they cherished an apprehension, that an appropriation of their territories might, in their absence, follow the seizure of their country. Firmly declining to accompany the English army into Flanders, they assembled their troops, and therewith lingered in the vicinity of the patriotic army, now in Ayrshire, under the command of Sir William Douglas and other leaders. At this stage a friendly coalition would have materially availed, but this became impracticable owing to a strong contention as to the chief command, for each body of patriots held resolutely that its leader should submit to no authority but his own. Dissension as to the leadership had become wildly acrimonious, when the confederates in their camp at Irvine came to understand that the English army under Clifford had reached Ayr, four miles distant. Disgusted by the unseemly contention, Sir Richard Lundin, a valiant knight, who had hitherto warmly espoused the national cause, joined the English army at Ayr; while, by messages to Clifford, the Earl of Carrick, James the Steward, and his brother John, Sir Alexander Lindsay, and Sir William Douglas, tendered their submission. At Irvine, on the 7th July, the several leaders issued a declaration, in which they represented to the Earl of Surrey, the English guardian, that they had assumed arms solely in the belief that Edward had determined to draft all able-bodied Scotsmen into his army for service abroad, and that, if the rumour proved to be unfounded, they would at once return to their allegiance.[1]

But Percy and Clifford, Surrey's deputies at Ayr, were in no temporizing mood, and the supplicants were emphatically assured that their destruction would be averted only by an unconditional surrender. Accordingly, on the second day after their original proposition, the confederates appended their seals to an instrument drawn in Norman-French, in which they acknowledged that they were rebels against their lawful sovereign, and had in their insurrection been guilty of murder and other crimes; therefore they rendered an absolute submission, save on certain points only, described as reserved in an instrument given under the hands of Percy and Clifford. In token of his personal submission, the Earl of Carrick offered, as a hostage, his daughter Marjory; while Bishop Wishart of Glasgow, James the Steward, and Sir Alexander Lindsay, bound themselves, under pain of forfeiture and death, to fulfil their pledges.[2]

[1] From an original document in the Public Record Office.

[2] The first of the instruments at Irvine is written on a small membrane polled at the top—four seals in red wax being appended—the first bearing the device of a lion upon a field, ornamented with scrolls, and surrounded with the inscription *Secretum Secretorum.* The second instrument is polled at the top, but the seals have been lost. In transferring the former document into his "Fœdera," Rymer has in the word *Irewin* mistaken a partially-effaced flourish of the capital *I* for an *S*, and the three parallel strokes of the concluding syllable *in* for the letter *m*, thus altering the word to Sirewm. Having made this preliminary blunder, he proceeds to divide the word into *Sire Willaume,* and so forms his printed text. The words *Sire Willaume* were held to denote Sir William Wallace, the last name being supposed to be

Wallace was not present in the camp at Irvine. From his successful conflict with Bishop Bek, near the palace of Glasgow, he proceeded northward, closely following Edward's route of the preceding year. At his first stage from Perth, he lodged in the Abbey of Cupar, the monks, who had succumbed to Edward, making flight at his approach. The castle of Forfar he recovered from the English. He next reduced the castle of Brechin, and thereafter laid siege to the powerful castle of Dunnottar. According to Henry, a portion of the English garrison of Dunnottar sought refuge in the parish church, which they abandoned on the structure being set on fire. That, as Henry asserts, the Scots slew all the soldiers of the garrison, and

> " Quhen this was done, feill fell on kneis doun
> At the byschop askit absolutioun,"

bears its own refutation. Henry, it is not improbable, had misinterpreted a tradition that Wallace, unable to control the violence of his followers, had compelled those who exercised an indiscriminate slaughter to publicly express their penitence. The parson of Dunnottar, Wautier de Kerington, was one of Edward's homagers at Berwick.[1]

On arriving at Aberdeen, Henry relates that the Patriot found that the English troops sought to effect their escape by their ships in the harbour, but that he destroyed the vessels and appropriated the cargoes, amidst a terrible slaughter. He adds that priests, women, and children were, in terms of Wallace's order, fully protected.[2]

incidentally omitted. Lord Hailes, deceived by the misreading, was led to write thus :—"The meaning is, as I presume, that the barons had notified to Wallace, that they had made terms of accommodation for themselves and their party " (Rymer's Fœdera, i., 868, or ii., 774, 775; Hailes' Annals, i., 272 ; Documents and Records, Introd., cxxiv., cxxv.).

[1] Jervise's Angus and Mearns, 444 ; Henry's Wallace, vii., 1044-1064.

[2] Henry's Wallace, vii , 1065-1077.

In the northern counties, Wallace obtained a large addition to his followers. And in Aberdeenshire his movements assumed such an important character, that Edward specially directed the bishop and sheriffs to have recourse to a violent resistance, also to guard the castle of Urquhart, held by William de Warrene, against an apprehended attack.[1]

Wallace marched into Buchan,—John Comyn, Earl of Buchan, who had espoused the English interest, retiring to Slains, and afterwards proceeding to England.

Resisting a body of English troops at Cromarty, the Patriot returned to Aberdeen. He now marched to Dundee, which he reached on the 31st of July.[2] As his successes became known, several of those who had subscribed the submission at Irvine delayed to produce hostages, or otherwise to fulfil their engagements.

Meanwhile, Edward became satisfied that his expedition of the preceding summer had proved ineffective, and that if Scotland was to be annexed to his sceptre, the people must be subdued not by extorted pledges, but actually by force of arms. Accordingly intermitting his activities in relation to his Flemish campaign, he diligently prepared for a Scottish war. On the 12th July he commissioned several barons and other notable persons in the counties of Northumberland and Cumberland to act as officers of his Scottish army, and at the same time appointed Walter de Agmondesham, administrator of military finance.[3] With Hugh de Cressingham, his treasurer in Scotland, he held a special correspondence. In a dispatch written at Berwick on the 23d July, Cressingham informed him that he had received his instructions as to making sure of the submission of the Earl

[1] Rotuli Scotiæ, vol. i., pp. 41, 42.

[2] Henry's Wallace, vii., 1088-1092.

[3] Royal Letters in Public Record Office, No. 3362.

of Carrick, also of the Steward and his brother, and, with that view, of offering gifts in circumstances of urgency. By Cressingham Edward was also informed that on the 17th inst. he had a force of three hundred horse and ten thousand foot assembled at Roxburgh ready to proceed northward, but that their advance had been delayed owing to a report made by Percy and Clifford that the Scottish insurgents to the south of the Forth had already submitted themselves. In his dispatch Cressingham adds that the king's enemies to the north of the Forth should not be allowed to escape, more especially the large company who, under William Wallace, held out resolutely. In conclusion, the Treasurer assured his royal master that he would remain quiescent till the Earl of Surrey's arrival.[1]

At this stage Bishop Wishart of Glasgow appears in an unfavourable light. An adviser of the submission at Irvine, he had already sought through Cressingham to procure restoration to Edward's favour. He now dispatched to Cressingham at Berwick a further communication, which, though undated, was evidently written early in August. In this missive he thanks the Treasurer for orally communicating with him through Sir Reginald Craufurd, in spite of the reports spread to his disadvantage, and proceeds to recommend to his confidence his messenger and clerk, Master Walter de Camoys, who, he adds, would fully interpret his sentiments.[2] Wishart did not profit by his policy of tergiversation, for, utterly distrusted by the Anglican authorities, he was, by Edward's orders, warded in Roxburgh Castle, while, in punishment of his abandoning

---

[1] Tower, Miscellaneous Rolls, No. 474. Cressingham, who writes in Norman French, describes Wallace as being present with his company on the other side of the sea of Scotland, that is to the north of the Forth, and as lingering in the forest of Selechirde, that is Selkirk. As Wallace was then in Morayshire, a forest in that district is clearly intended.

[2] Royal Letters, No. 3362.

the national cause, Wallace afterwards made an attack upon his palace, and took his nephews prisoners.[1]

On the 24th July, Sir Osbert de Spaldington, governor of Berwick, sent to Edward, by a special courier, an important dispatch. Confirming Cressingham's statements made on the preceding day, he proceeds to report that Percy and Clifford had brought with them to Berwick two persons lately in rebellion, viz.—Sir Alexander Lindsay and Sir William Douglas. As the latter had not fulfilled his covenants, the writer had detained him in Berwick Castle, and though he much chafed under restraint, he, the writer, would not advise his liberation. Finally, De Spaldington entreats the king that the vacant church of Douglas, with its revenue, exceeding 200 marks, should be conferred upon Cressingham, whose fidelity he commends.[2]

On the same day on which the governor of Berwick informed Edward as to Sir William Douglas being a prisoner in the castle, and begged that his parish church should be bestowed upon Cressingham, that functionary reported his recent diligence; but in an answer to the king's dispatch of the previous day, instructing him to impose a tax on the issues and rents, he stated that such an operation was impracticable, since the greater number of county collectors had, by the Scots, been deprived of life, or thrown into prison; while the holders of bailiwicks had renounced their offices, and dreaded to return. In certain counties, he added, the Scots had expelled both magistrates and ministers; indeed, there was disorder everywhere, save in the shires of Roxburgh and Berwick. Cressingham concluded his missive by expressing his belief that, with

---

[1] Hemingford, ii., 133. If Wishart did, in reality, sustain the force of Wallace's resentment, this must have happened subsequent to the battle of Stirling. The bishop afterwards proved a consistent adherent of King Robert the Bruce.

[2] Patent Roll, 25 Edward I., Part ii., m. 1.

the Divine help, the campaign about to be commenced under the leadership of the Earl of Surrey, Sir Henry de Percy, and Sir Robert de Clifford, would lead to the restoration of order.[1]

From Berwick, on the 1st of August, Surrey communicated with Edward that he expected to meet there within a week the bishop of Glasgow, the Earl of Carrick, and the Steward. After completing their treaty of obedience, they would, he believed, materially aid the force under his command in effecting the suppression of revolt. To Edward, his lieutenant also reported that the Earl of Strathearn had captured Macduff and his sons, and that on his being brought to Berwick, the former would be punished as a traitor; further, that as Sir William Douglas had failed to produce his hostages, he had been thrown into irons.[2]

While deeply impressed with the importance of fully re-asserting his authority in Scotland, Edward was primarily concerned in efficiently carrying out his continental policy; he therefore proposed to relieve Surrey of his northern command, in order to utilise his experience in the Flanders campaign. His intention as to a change in the Scottish lieutenancy having become known, the governor of Berwick, ever ready to be helpful to his friend, the Treasurer, dispatched to Edward, on the 4th of August, a familiar letter, in which he suggested that unless some "great lord" was already in view as Surrey's successor, Cressingham should be entrusted with the chief command.[3] Meanwhile, Edward in view of

[1] From the original in the Public Record Office. The letter to which it is an answer is contained in Rotuli Scotiæ, i., 42, col. 2.

[2] *Ibid.* On the 12th of October, Douglas was committed to the Tower (Close Roll, 25 Edward I., m. 4).

[3] From the original in the Public Record Office.

The letter recommending Cressingham as lieutenant of Scotland is unsigned, but the writer is obviously Sir Osbert de Spaldington, governor of Berwick. In communicating with Edward, De Spaldington usually commences his letters with the words "Dear Sire."

economising his public expenditure, had already nominated as his Scottish lieutenant Brian Fitz-Alan, governor of the castles of Roxburgh, Jedburgh, Forfar, and Dundee, in the hope that he would discharge the duties of the new office without expecting an increase of emolument. In acknowledging the offer, Fitz-Alan, in a letter dated the 5th of August, respectfully informed his royal master, that his accepting office must, owing to his restricted fortune, be contingent on his receiving the same remuneration as that granted to his predecessor.[1] Here negotiations ceased, since, in view of disquieting rumours from the north, Edward resolved that Surrey should be relieved of employment in the Flemish expedition. Personally Edward embarked for Flanders on the 22d of August,[2] after instructing Surrey to assist the Prince of Wales in the re-subjugation of Scotland.[3] This operation seemed comparatively easy, since Edward bore with him to Flanders the most powerful and opulent Scotsmen, captured at Dunbar, while their eldest sons remained in England as hostages for their fidelity.[4]

Consequent on the surrender at Irvine, the defection of Bishop Wishart, and the imprisonment of Sir William Douglas, the Scottish army had collapsed, apart from the force led by Wallace. Wallace's progress we have already traced to Dundee. There, under the conduct of Alexander Scrimgeour of Dudhope, he was joined by a large body of the burgesses.[5] And he was engaged in storming the castle of Dundee, still in the hands of the English, when he learned that the Earl of Surrey was at the head of a powerful army, advancing towards Stirling. In

---

[1] Royal Letters, No. 2586.

[2] Rotuli Scotiæ, 44, 45 ; Trivet, 301.

[3] Tyrrel, iii., 120.

[4] Rotuli Scotiæ, 47, 48.

[5] Wallace, on becoming governor of Scotland, appointed Scrimgeour to the office of Constable of Dundee, and as an endowment granted to him certain lands and tenements on the north side of the town (Acta Parl. Scot., i., 97 ; iv., 90).

the hope of presenting an effective resistance at the passage of Forth, he deputed to Scrimgeour, as his lieutenant, the future conduct of the siege, and by rapid marches hastened south-westward.[1]

During the thirteenth century, the ordinary mode of crossing the Forth in the route from the south to the north of Scotland, was by means of two fords, one at Manor, half a mile to the east of Stirling; the other at Kildean, about one mile to the west of that town. According to tradition, the Romans threw across the ford of Kildean a narrow bridge of timber, and a structure of this sort became permanent. But by such an inconsiderable appliance, the passage of the river was necessarily tardy, and in the case of war a small body of troops could readily impede the progress of a numerous force.

On reaching the Forth's northern shore, Wallace proceeded to encamp his troops at the Abbey Craig.[2] This craggy eminence presents on the south-west a precipitous front to the height of three hundred feet, and it is on the north and north-east separated by a narrow strath from the Ochil hills. Approaching the crag through a pass of the Ochils, Wallace distributed his men on its north-eastern slope, his movement being unobserved by Surrey's army, which was drawn up on the Forth's southern shore in the vicinity of Kildean.

The movements of the English army are described by Hemingford. When, he relates, Surrey had reached the town of Stirling, he was there met by the Steward, the Earl of Lennox, and certain other Scottish noblemen, who entreated him to forbear hostilities, as they would endeavour to induce their

---

[1] Fordun, xi., 29. Buchanan erroneously asserts that Wallace was besieging the castle of Cupar, when he was informed of Surrey's march to Stirling.

[2] Abbey Craig derives its appellative from its proximity to the Abbey of Cambuskenneth.

countrymen to offer their submission. Surrey granted delay, but on the 10th of September was informed by the Steward and his friends that, as they could not persuade their countrymen to yield, they would on the following day personally join the English force with sixty armed horse.

On the same evening, according to Hemingford, the Earl of Lennox came up to a party of English troopers, when, promoting a quarrel, he seriously wounded one of the number with his sword. Indignant at the unexpected maltreatment, the troop to which the wounded man belonged bore him to Surrey's presence on a litter, and demanded revenge. But Surrey recommended forbearance pending the issue of a general engagement.[1]

Having come to understand that the great Scottish leader had brought together a powerful force on the north-eastern slopes of the Abbey Craig with a view to dispute the passage of the river, Surrey, on the morning of the 11th September, despatched to him two predicant friars with the offer of terms on his surrender. Wallace's reply was bold and uncompromising. "Go back and tell your masters," said he, "that we came not here to treat of peace, but to avenge our wrongs. Let your masters advance, and we will meet them." In the English camp these defying words engendered division—the inexperienced section counselling an immediate attack, while the more prudent advised caution. Among the latter was Sir Richard Lundin, who, according to Hemingford, spoke thus:—"My Lords, if we go up to the bridge we are dead men, for we cannot pass over but two at a time, and our enemies will come down upon us in one great front." He then, proceeds the English chronicler, spoke of a certain ford near at hand, where the English army

[1] Hemingford, vol. ii., pp. 134-137.

might safely wade sixty abreast ; while he personally made offer, that if he received the command of five hundred horsemen and a small body of foot, he would approach the Scots from behind, so that when they were occupied in defending themselves, the rest of the army could cross the Kildean bridge in perfect security. Lundin's counsel as to utilizing the ford at Manor was rejected, Cressingham emphatically giving forth, that the proposal implied a useless expenditure of the royal treasure, since there was no necessity for dealing with the enemy otherwise than by force of numbers. "Let the king's troops," he said, "cross at Kildean, and an easy victory is assured." Adopting his counsel, Surrey, early in the forenoon, deployed his columns by the bridge under the care of one of his experienced lieutenants, Sir Marmaduke Twenge. When about five thousand had crossed, the Scots descended swiftly from their position on the crag, and by a flank movement planted a body of spearmen so as to secure possession of the bridge.[1]

[1] In relation to the passage of the bridge, Hemingford presents two narratives. In one of these he sets forth, that after five thousand troops, chiefly Welsh, had gone over, they were ordered back by Surrey, as the passage had been made without his authority, and even before he had risen from bed. In connexion with the counter movement of the Scots, there prevails a popular error. According to a legend, Wallace, in anticipation of the English movement, caused the main beam of the bridge to be sawn across, and the broken portion to be temporarily sustained by a pin, which, on a signal, was drawn out by one who, suspended in a basket, sat beneath. Henry sets forth the legend in these lines :—

" On Setterday on to the bryg thai raid,
Off gud playne burd was weill and junctly maid ;
Gert wachis wait that nane suld fra thaim pass.
A wricht he tuk, the suttellast at thar was,
And ordand him to saw the burd in twa,
Be the myd streit, that nane mycht our it ga ;
On charnaill bandis nald it full fast and sone,
Syne fyld with clay as na thing had beyne doue.
The tothir end he ordand for to be,
How it suld stand on thre rowaris off tre,
Quhen ane war out, that the laiff doun suld fall ;
Ther self wndyr he ordand thar with all
Bownd on the trest in a creddill to sit,
To louss the pyne quhen Wallace leit him witt.
Bot with a horn, quhen it was tyme to be,
In all the ost suld no man blaw bot he

.   .   .   .   .   .

Fra Jop the horn he hyntyt and couth blaw
Sa asprely, and warned gud Jhon Wricht.
The rowar out he straik with gret slycht ;
The laiff yeid doun, quhen the pynnys out gais.
A hidwyss cry among the peple raiss ;
Bathe horss and men into the wattir fell."

—Henry's *Wallace*, vii., 1147-1162, 1180-1185.

Mr John Wright of Broom, who died at Stirling about thirty years ago, was familiarly known as "Pin Wright," on account of his claiming descent from a person of the name, employed by Wallace in the destruction of Kildean Bridge, during the progress of the battle.

In relation to the progress of the conflict Hemingford continues his narrative in a dramatic form. Remarking the capture of the bridge, and the separation of those who had crossed from the great body of the army, Sir Marmaduke exclaimed, "Is it not time, brothers, that we should ride against them?" Those so addressed rode forward hastily, inflicting some injury on the Scots, who, however, rallied so effectively as to thoroughly repel their assailants, and cause a precipitate retreat. Amidst the confusion Sir Marmaduke was thus addressed by one holding a subordinate command, "The way to the bridge is closed against us, and we are intercepted; it is better, therefore, that we trust ourselves to the water, if haply we may be able to cross, than to make a fruitless attempt to penetrate the wedged ranks of the enemy." To this oration Sir Marmaduke responded, "Truly, my dearest comrades, it shall never be said of me that I would recklessly perish in the flood; and be that purpose far from you. Follow me, and through the midst of them I shall bring you safely to the bridge." Then spurring his horse, Sir Marmaduke broke violently upon the enemy, and by dexterously wielding his sword formed a wide passage for his followers. While thus valiantly leading, Sir Marmaduke's nephew was unhorsed by the Scots. Entreating his uncle's assistance, Sir Marmaduke called on him to mount behind him, but as, from the severity of his wounds, he was unable to do this, he was, by one of Sir Marmaduke's officers, borne onward to the bridge. In the vicinity of the bridge the conflict was vigorously maintained, for Wallace now despatched to the assistance of his spearmen a large portion of his army, under his chief lieutenant, Sir Andrew de Moray, who, fetching a compass on the north and north-west, assailed the enemy with consummate vigour. According to Hemingford, nearly all who had passed to the Forth's northern shore were struck down in the field, or, in attempting to escape, perished in the water. These included five thousand foot and one hundred horsemen.[1] The nephew of Sir Marmaduke Twenge was mortally wounded.

Having wrecked that section of the English army which had crossed at Kildean, Wallace now contrived to effect an easy passage at Manor Ford, when, with his reserve, he attacked the remainder of the English force, which Surrey held in his personal command. By the Steward and the Earl of Lennox, he was assisted powerfully. After a disastrous defeat, Surrey rode solitarily from the field. According to Hemingford, his force consisted of fifty thousand foot and one thousand horse, while, by the same authority, the Scottish army numbered forty thousand infantry and one hundred and eighty cavalry. The computation is clearly exaggerated; it is certain that the Scottish army did not exceed ten thousand men, of whom a very few were mounted. Among the slain was Hugh Cressingham, whose rashness had largely contributed to Surrey's defeat. Hemingford asserts the Scots flayed his body to revenge his acts of extortion.

By Wyntoun, the battle of Stirling Bridge is described in these lines :—

> " This Willame Walays off Dundé
> Assegeand [2] the Castelle wes, quhen he
> Herd, that thare come ane new ost
> Owt off Ingland wyth gret host,
> Wyth thys Schyr Hw of Karssyngame.
> This ilke Walays than Willame,
> A payne [3] off lyff and lyme bathe he
> Bade the burges off Dundé,
> At that assege that thai suld ly,
> And kepe that castell rycht stratly,
> Quhill that thai wan the Inglis men,

---

[1] Hemingford, ii. 133-136.   [2] Besieging.   [3] Penalty.

> That occupyid that castell then.
> And wyth his court than alsa fast
> Till Stryvelyne this Willame Walays past :
> And at the Bryg of Forth Willame
> The Walays met wyth Karssyngame.
> Thare thai mellayd [1] in to fycht,
> Quhare mony dowre [2] to ded wes dycht ; [3]
> Thare thai layid on alsa fast :
> Thare Karssyngame at the last
> Wyth the mast part off his men
> Slayne besyd that bryg wes then.
> And all the lawe [4] owt off that stede
> Than turnyd the bak, and away flede.
> The Scottis folowyd fast on then :
> Quhare evyr thai ouretuk the Inglis men,
> Thai sparyd nane, but slwe all down.
> Walays off this had gret renowne
> For all hale the wyctory
> The Scottis had off this juperdy ;
> And few wes slayne off Scottis men.
> Bot Androwe off Murrawe slayne wes then :
> Fadyre till gud Schyre Androw he
> Wes, and prysyd off gret bownté.
>   This dyde Walays at Strevelyne
> And hely [5] wes commendyt syne.
>   Fra wencust [6] he had Karssyngame,
> Heyare,[7] and heyare ay wes hys fame ;
> And, throwe the kynrik [8] as he past,
> The statis till hym bowyd fast." [9]

Less moved by the discomfiture than was Edward's lieutenant, Sir Marmaduke Twenge, on escaping from the field, entered the castle of Stirling in the hope of stimulating the English garrison to maintain a resistance. But the effort was unavailing, for the garrison had, in witnessing the complete overthrow of the English power on the adjoining field, determined to yield themselves

[1] Joined in battle.
[2] Brave.
[3] Sent to death.
[4] Remainder.
[5] Highly.
[6] Vanquish.
[7] Higher.
[8] Country.
[9] Wyntoun, B. viii., ll. 2147-2186. Sir Andrew of Moray was severely wounded in the battle, but was not slain.

to the victor. Wallace therefore obtained a surrender of the castle on the day succeeding the battle. Secured as a prisoner, Sir Marmaduke Twenge was under an escort sent to the fortress at Dunbarton, where he remained till April 1299, when he was exchanged for Sir John de Moubray, a Scottish knight in the hands of the English.[1]

The formidable character of the Scottish insurrection had induced the Prince of Wales, as regent, to issue a mandate on the 12th of September charging the Earl of Surrey not to leave Scotland till the mutiny was suppressed.[2] But Surrey did not receive the message till the kingdom was wrested from his control.

A few days after the battle of Stirling, the English garrison at Dundee surrendered to Alexander Scrimgeour, who, taking possession of the fortress, was afterwards constituted governor. The castle of Dunbar, held in the English interest by the Earl of March, was soon yielded up. Roxburgh Castle surrendered in October, the townsmen complaining to the king that they had, by the bailiffs of Berwick and Newcastle, been prevented from baking or making merchandise for their support at these places, to which, after the surprise by the Scots, they had escaped only with their lives.[3] Berwick was by Wallace captured soon afterwards, and at his instance occupied by Sir Henry de Haliburton.[4] "The loss of Berwick," writes Dr Hill Burton, "was very vexatious to Edward, for he had given instructions to make it impregnable with stone walls in addition to its earthen mound, and the instructions had been neglected."[5]

[1] At Westminster, on the 7th April 1299, Edward, on the petition of Mary, wife of William Fitz Warin, and other friends of prisoners in Scotland and England, empowered Anthony, bishop of Durham, John de Britannia, and William le Latimer, *senior*, to negotiate the exchange, "body for body," of William Fitz Warin for Henry de Scinteler, *Marmaduke de Twenge for John de Moubray*, also various others (Patent Roll, 27 Edward I., m. 31).

[2] Close Roll, 25 Edward I., m. 5.

[3] Royal Letters, No. 4694.

[4] Scala Cronica, p. 124.

[5] Burton's Hist. of Scotland, ed. 1873, ii., 194.

CHAPTER IV.

> " He strode o'er the wreck of each well-fought field
> With the yellow-haired chiefs of his native land ;
> For his lance was not shivered on helmet or shield,
> And the sword that was fit for Archangel to wield
> Was light in his terrible hand."
>
> —CAMPBELL's *Dirge of Wallace.*

> " Heroic Wallace ! while the tide
> Of Time shall onward roll,
> A land of freemen will admire
> Thy great and gallant soul ! "
>
> —ALEXANDER LOGAN.

POWERFULLY assisted at the battle of Stirling by Sir Andrew de Moray, Wallace subsequently took him as his coadjutor in the management of affairs. Moray's personal history has recently been ascertained. In reference to the desertions at Irvine, Lord Hailes remarks that "the only baron who then remained faithful to Wallace was Sir Andrew Moray of Bothwell;" he adds, that on his death at the battle of Stirling, the Patriot took as his partner in command, his son, "the young Sir Andrew Moray." And until lately historical writers have accepted this narrative. But it has now been shown, that, while the barony of Bothwell was confiscated by Edward, its titular lord, whether father or son, was not Wallace's associate. Sir William de Moray, lord of Bothwell, swore fealty to Edward on the 1st of August 1291, and again on the 28th of August 1296. In the instrument recording the first act of submission, he is named as "the rich," evidently to distinguish him from the three other Sir Williams, of Drumsargard, Sandford, and Tullibardine.[1] Heir of the opulent and powerful Walter de Moray, lord of Bothwell, Sir William became a victim to Edward's cupidity. Deprived of his Scottish estates, he retired to his manor of Lilleford in Lincolnshire, where he experienced further attainder, since, prior to the 3d February 1295-6, he shared the fate of several Scottish magnates whose English possessions Edward had confiscated by enjoining his Treasurer and his Barons of Exchequer to sell their goods, reserving only their oxen and implements of husbandry.[2] And on the 8th of January 1298-9, Edward made record that, in the exercise of his compassion towards Sir William de Moray, who was detained in England, south of the Trent, and was receiving no benefit from his lands, he had caused his Treasurer and Barons to issue to him the means of sustenance. From the sheriff of Lincoln, Moray, consequent on this order, received an allowance of £25.[3] He died prior to the 10th November 1300.[4]

Having traced the career of Sir William de Moray of Bothwell, we would now advert to the movements of two of his contemporaries, each designed Andrew de Moray, and both of whom took part in the national struggle. Sir Andrew de Moray, "knight," and his son, Andrew de Moray, were taken prisoners at the battle of Dunbar, and, on the 16th May 1296, were sent for detention, the former to the Tower, the latter to Chester Castle.[5] On the 6th November 1297, the Sheriffs of

---

[1] Chapter House, Scots Documents, Box 16, No. 2 ; Ragman Roll, p. 196.

[2] Privy Seal, 24 Edward I., bundle 5 ; Close Rolls, 24 Edward I., m. 10.

[3] Exchequer Q. R. Miscellanea, 27 Edward I., m. 26, dorso ; 27-28 Edward I., m. 63.

[4] Inq. post mort., November 28, 1300, 29 Edward I., No. 10.

[5] Close Rolls, 24 Edward I., m. 6, 7.

London were commanded to grant Sir Andrew Moray, as prisoner in the Tower, an aliment of fourpence daily.[1] His son, Andrew de Moray, was, after a short detention, liberated from Chester Castle, and being permitted to return to Scotland, was, on the 28th August 1297, allowed a safe-conduct to enable him to visit his father in the Tower.[2] He did not avail himself of the privilege, being already a lieutenant in Wallace's army. In an inquisition *post mortem*, dated 28th November 1300, twelve jurors in the Court of the Sheriff of Berwick served, as heir to William de Moray, Andrew de Moray, an infant, who is described as grandson of Sir Andrew de Moray, and son of Andrew de Moray, "interfectus apud Strivelyn contra Dominum Regem,"—that is, slain at Stirling fighting against the king.[3] But in referring to Andrew de Moray, who was engaged at the battle of Stirling, Fordun writes, "cecidit vulneratus,"—that is, he fell wounded.[4] And this statement solves a difficulty, inasmuch as Andrew de Moray, who, on the 11th October 1297, is described as Wallace's military colleague, appears to have survived the battle, and by his friend to have been made a sharer in the government.[5] His son, Andrew de Moray, named as an infant in 1300, was not born until Pentecost 1298.

In effecting Surrey's defeat on the field of Stirling, Wallace was enabled to appropriate his military stores ; he also obtained a portion of treasure which was borne by Cressingham and his staff. When tidings of the discomfiture at the Forth reached Dundee, the English garrison in the castle surrendered to the valiant Scrim-

---

[1] Exchequer Q. R. Memoranda, 26 Edward I., m. 109.

[2] Patent, 21 Edward I., Part ii., m. 1.

[3] Inq. p. m., 29 Edward 1., No. 10.

[4] Fordun, edit. 1871, i., 329.

[5] In official documents Wallace generously placed the name of his gallant associate first in order, while both are described as *duces exercitus regni Scotiæ*.

geour ; and Wallace proceeded with his followers to reduce the English garrisons at Edinburgh, Dunbar, Roxburgh, and Berwick.

From the reduction of Berwick, returning northward, Wallace halted at Haddington, and there in St Duthac's monastery invoked the Divine blessing upon his recent victories.[1]

Since the destruction of Berwick and the overthrow of Baliol's government foreign trade had almost wholly collapsed, and the people were suffering from an oppressive indigence. Wallace clearly foresaw that so long as a condition of poverty prevailed, national independence was practically valueless. He therefore hastened to communicate with the members of the Hanseatic League, praying for a renewal of commercial relations. This act demands a special explanation. So early as the reign of Macbeth Scottish commerce was considerably prosperous, while under the government of Malcolm Canmore it obtained a new impulse, since, at the instance of Margaret, his pious queen, foreign merchants were encouraged to bring into the kingdom the more precious wares. A most enterprising sovereign, David I., gave to every mercantile community and body of traders a special protection. Under his encouragement arose in the kingdom two commercial confederacies —one to the north of the Grampians, the other comprehending the burghs of Berwick, Roxburgh, Edinburgh, and Stirling. And the mercantile system which King David organized was by his grandson, William the Lion, developed and extended. Incorporating as royal burghs many populous places and centres of trade, William authorised the inhabitants to elect magistrates and exercise self-government.

From the twelfth century the course of Scottish trade may be

[1] St Duthac's monastery was erected by Alexander II., and then, or subsequently, became known from the splendour of its perpetually burning lamps, as the "Light of Lothian" (Walcot's Scoti-Monasticon, 345).

traced definitely. Prior to the year 1191 the monks of Melrose sent wool to the Netherlands, and had from Philip of Flanders the privilege of conveying their goods through his provinces without cess. And in the reigns of Alexander II. and Alexander III. Flemish traders effected settlements on the Scottish seaboard, and at Berwick established a notable emporium. That emporium being wrecked by Edward in the spring of 1296, was yet unrestored. Such a restoration Wallace sought for. His letter to the Hanseatic League was written from Haddington[1] on the 11th of October, and in the manner of the times was composed in Latin. The document, which is extant, proceeds thus :—

" Andreas de Morauia et Willelmus Wallensis, duces exercitus regni Scotie, et communitas eiusdem regni, prouidis viris et discretis ac amicis dilectis, maioribus et communibus de Lubek et de Hamburg salutem et sincere dilectionis semper incrementum.

" Nobis per fide dignos mercatores dicti regni Scotie est intimatum, quod vos vestri gratia, in omnibus causis et negociis, nos et ipsos mercatores tangentibus, consulentes, auxiliantes et favorabiles estis, licet nostra non precesserint merita, et ideo magis vobis tenemur ad grates cum digna remuneracione, ad que vobis volumus obligari; rogantes vos, quatenus preconizari facere velitis inter mercatores vestros, quod securum accessum ad omnes portus regni Scotie possint habere cum mercandiis suis, quia regnum Scotie, Deo regraciato, ab Anglorum potestate bello est recuperatum. Valete.

" Datum apud Hadingtonam in Scotia, undecimo die Octobris, Anno gracie, millesimo ducentesimo nonagesimo septimo. Rogamus vos insuper vt negocia Johannis Burnet et Johannis Frere, mercatorum nostrorum promouere dignemini prout nos negocia mercatorum vestrorum promouere velitis. Valete. Dat. ut prius." [2]

Freely translated, the letter to the Hanseatic League reads thus :—

---

[1] The place from which Wallace's letter proceeded was long represented as " Badsington," from a misreading of the document.

[2] From the " Urkundliche Geschichte des Ursprunges der deutschen Hanse," of G. F. Sartorius, part ii., pp. 188, 189; Lappenberg's edition, 1830.

Andreas de Moravia et Willelmus Wallensis, duces exercitus Regni Scocie, et communitas eiusdem Regni, providis viris et discretis dominis maioribus et communibus de Lubek et de Hamburgh, salutem et sincere dilectionis semper incrementum. Nobis per fidedignos mercatores dicti Regni Scocie est intimatum quod vos consulitis estis in omnibus causis et negociis nos et ipsos mercatores tangentibus consilentes auxiliantes et favorabiles estis licet nostris profestent merita et sino magis vobis tenemur ad grates ad dignam remuneracionem ad quas vos volumus obligari. Rogantes vos quatinus promiseritis facere velitis ut mercatores vestri quatinus accessum ad omnes portus Regni Scocie pusint habere cum mercandiis suis quia Regnum Scocie Deo gracias ab Anglorum potestate bello est recuperatum. Valete. Datum apud Haddingtonn in Scocia undecimo die Octobris. Anno gracie millesimo ducentesimo nonagesimo septimo. Rogantes vos insuper ut negocia Johannis Burnet et Johannis Frere concivium nostrorum promovere dignemini prout nostra negocia racionabiliter exigunt. Prout pronam voluntatem valetis. Datum ut supra.

Andrew de Moray and William Wallace, leaders of the army of the kingdom of Scotland, and the community of that kingdom, to their prudent, discreet, and well-beloved friends, the mayors and citizens of Lubeck and Hamburg, greeting; and with a sincere desire for the increase of friendship. By trustworthy merchants of ours we have been informed that you have been favourable and assisting to our merchants in the affairs of commerce, though we have had no reason, on account of anything we had done, to expect such kindness; we are therefore bound all the more to render you thanks and recompense. This we willingly bind ourselves to do, and we therefore request that it be widely made known among your merchants, that they will now have safe access to all the ports of Scotland, as the kingdom, blessed be God, has by arms been recovered out of the power of the English. Farewell. Given at Haddington in Scotland, this eleventh day of October, in the year of grace one thousand two hundred and ninety-seven. We request, moreover, that you will see good to forward the interests of our merchants, John Burnet and John Frere, as you wish us to forward the interests of your merchants here.

Despatching to Hamburg the Scottish merchants Burnet and Frere, so as at once to secure the resumption of commerce, Wallace next gave orders for the proper cultivation of the fields. From the Continent he procured needful supplies of grain and seed-corn.

In a letter to the Earl of Surrey, dated 24th September, the Prince of Wales referred to certain rumours as to the disturbed condition of Scotland, and charged him to remain in the country until tranquillity was restored. The Prince also instructed Sir Robert Clifford and Brian Fitz Alan to forthwith co-operate with Surrey in suppressing the revolt.[1] He also enjoined the sheriff of York and thirteen barons in the north of England to aid in the Scottish expedition.[2]

On the 25th September the Prince intimated to the Scottish magnates who had adopted the Anglican policy, that as the

---

[1] Close Roll, 25 Edward I., m. 5, dorso.   [2] *Ibid.*

Earl of Surrey had resigned the lieutenancy,[1] Brian Fitz-Alan had been appointed his successor, and he strongly desired them to assist the new lieutenant in suppressing the insurrection. Among those so addressed were John Comyn of Badenoch; Patric, Earl of Dunbar; Gilbert, Earl of Angus; Alexander, Earl of Menteith; Malise, Earl of Strathearn; James the Steward; John Comyn, Earl of Buchan; Malcolm, Earl of Lennox; William, Earl of Sutherland; Nicholas de la Hay, Ingram de Umfravillo, Richard Fraser, and Alexander de Lindsay.[2]

Wallace made preparations for a general defence. He caused muster rolls (matriculas) to be drawn in every parish, bearing the names of every male between the ages of sixteen and sixty, capable of bearing arms. In accomplishing this purpose he experienced strong resistance from a section of the barons, who insisted that their vassals were subject only to their own personal authority. But the military Governor of Scotland did not pause to discuss the special requirements of feudal law, but renewed his order that all able-bodied persons should assemble to the national defence, or be strung up on gibbets which he reared in every county.[3]

Assembling his troops on Roslin Muir, near Edinburgh, Wallace determined in the first instance to procure the necessary supplies by forthwith penetrating into England. According to Hemingford, he entered Northumberland on the Feast of St Luke, that is, on the 18th of October. Establishing his headquarters in the forest of Rothbury, he from thence made

---

[1] The only extant document in relation to Surrey's defeat at Stirling is a letter from him, dated the 27th of September, in which he informs Langton, the English chancellor, that he had left Sir William Fitz Warin keeper of Stirling Castle, in place of Sir Richard Waldegrave.—*Original Letter in the Public Record Office.*

[2] Rotuli Scotiæ, i., 49.

[3] Fordun a Goodal, ii., 172.

incursions into the fertile regions by which it was environed. Obtaining large booty, he, in order to its safe transmission, made collections at convenient centres, from which he sent waggons to Scotland at convenient intervals.[1]   Having ravaged Northumberland and Cumberland from Inglewood Forest to Derwentwater and Cockermouth, he next penetrated into Durham, but his further progress, remarks Hemingford, was interrupted by the severity of the weather, owing to the miraculous intervention of St Cuthbert.[2]

With his usual respect for the ministers of religion, Wallace granted to the prior and monks of Hexham, a letter of protection.   That document proceeds thus :—

"Andreas de Moravia et Willelmus Wallensis, Duces exercitus Scotiæ, nomine præclari Principis Domini Johannis, Dei gratiâ, Regis Scotiæ illustris, de consensu communitatis regni ejusdem, omnibus hominibus dicti regni ad quos præsentes literæ pervenerint, salutem.   Sciatis, nos, nomine dicti Regis, Priorem et Conventum de Hexhildesham in Northumbria, terras suas, homines suos, et universas eorum possessiones, ac omnia bona sua, mobilia et immobilia, sub firma pace et protectione ipsius Domini Regis, et nostra, justè suscepisse.   Quare firmiter prohibemus, ne quis eis in personis, terris, seu rebus, malum, molestiam, injuriam, seu gravamen aliquod, inferre præsumat, super plenaria forisfactura ipsius Domini Regis, aut mortem eis, vel alicui eorum, inferat, sub pœna amissionis vitæ et membrorum ; presentibus post annum minimè valituris.   Dat apud Hexhildesham, vii. die Novembris."[3]

Freely translated, the letter of protection may be thus rendered :—

Andrew of Moray and William Wallace, leaders of the army of Scotland, in name of the illustrious Prince John, by the grace of God king of Scotland, with the consent of the commons of the said kingdom, to all men of that kingdom to whom these letters may come, greeting.   Know ye, that we have

---

[1] Hemingford, i., 131.   [2] *Ibid.*, i., 132.   [3] *Ibid.*, i., 135.

taken the Prior and Convent of Hexhildesham in Northumberland, also their lands, men, possessions, and goods, under the protection of the king; wherefore we strictly forbid you to hurt or do injury to them, in their persons, lands, or goods, under penalty of forfeiture of your own goods and estates, or to kill them, or any of them, under pain of death. These presents to remain in force for one year and no longer. Given at Hexhildesham, the 7th day of November.

With respect to the protection extended to the monks of Hexham, Hemingford seeks to detract from the Patriot's benevolence. On first reaching the monastery, the Scots, he represents, snatched the principal treasures; nor did their leader offer any reparation. When after an interval the Scots returned to the monastery, several of their number entered the chapel, and there found three monks employed in repairing the recent devastation. Threatening the monks with their lances, the intruders demanded treasure. "As you have already snatched our treasure," replied one of their number, "you ought to know where it is now." At this stage Wallace came up, and, restraining his followers, asked one of the monks to celebrate mass. As the monk was preparing for the service and Wallace had retired to lay aside his arms, one of his followers snatched the chalice and plundered the missal. Informed of the outrage, Wallace, proceeds Hemingford, granted by way of expiation to the institution, his letter of protection. In denouncing the alleged sacrilege, Hemingford remarks that it was the more unpardonable, inasmuch as the monastery of Hexham was dedicated to the patron saint of Scotland, and had received from King David a perpetual protection. This portion of Hemingford's narrative is evidently fictitious.

While the Scottish hero was vigorously wasting the northern counties, the English government were not inactive in devising methods of resistance. That portion of Surrey's army which had escaped from the field of Stirling disappears from the scene. But the several English counties bristled with military preparation. On the 23d of October William de Ormesby, the English Justiciary in Scotland, was called upon to exercise a new function by raising an army to revenge himself on the adventurous Scotsman who had displaced him at Scone; he was enjoined to raise one thousand men in Northumberland, four thousand in Yorkshire, and one thousand in the counties of Derby and Nottingham. Under different barons, Lincolnshire was ordered to provide three thousand men, Cumberland five thousand, Westmoreland three thousand, Shropshire three thousand, Staffordshire one thousand, Worcester one thousand, and Gloucester two thousand. From North Wales was required a contingent of two thousand, and from Cheshire four thousand.[1]

Ormesby did not assume office as a military leader, but Sir Robert Clifford in command of a body of troops considerably impeded the Scots in their homeward route, and afterwards penetrated into Annandale.[2] According to Hemingford, Wallace reached Carlisle on the 11th of November,[3] and Wyntoun informs us that he remained in England till Yule.[4]

Sir Andrew de Moray, colleague of Wallace in the government, was alive on the 7th November, when the letter of protection was granted to the monks of Hexham, but he seems to have succumbed to his wounds not long afterwards.[5] Finding him-

---

[1] Patent Roll, 25 Edward I., Part ii., m. 3.

[2] Knighton, p. 252.

[3] Hemingford, i., 133, 134.

[4] By Henry, Wallace's expedition into England is made the subject of one of his most extravagant flights. He represents him as pursuing a victorious progress through Yorkshire and the Midland Counties onward to St Albans, where, as he was arranging an attack upon London, he was waited upon by the Queen, who, attended by fifty of her ladies, invoked his clemency. In 1297, when Wallace penetrated into England, Edward was a widower.

[5] Moray had a posthumous son, born in May 1298, who became brother-in-law of King Robert the Bruce, and was also regent of Scotland (Calendar of Documents relating to Scotland, vol. ii., Introd. xxx.).

self alone in office, and without other warrant than his sword,
Wallace now summoned the Estates to meet him in the Forest
Kirk—being, the parish church of Carluke—when by those
present he was confirmed as guardian.   Writes Henry—

> " Syne couth to Braidwode fayr,
> At a conuceill thre dayes soiornyt thar ;
> At Forest Kirk a motyng ordcend he,
> Thar chosit Wallace Scottis wardand to be." [1]

The Earl of Lennox was the only person of noble rank who
attended, but a rumour spread among the common people that
Saint Andrew, the patron of the kingdom, was there in person,
and presented the hero with a consecrated sword. [2]

At a convention of the Estates, held in the Preceptory of
Torphichen on the 29th of March 1298, Wallace placed in
offices of trust those who in the recent struggle had been
prominently useful.   Among those appointed was Alexander
Skirmischur or Scrimgeour, who was confirmed as constable
of Dundee, also as hereditary standard-bearer of Scotland, with
a portion of land in recompense.   His charter proceeds thus :—

" Willelmus Walays, miles, Cuftos regni Scociæ, et Ductor exercitus
ejufdem, nomine præclari principis domini Johannis, Dei gratia regis Scociæ
illuftris, de confenfu Communitatis ejufdem regni, omnibus probis hominibus
dicti regni, ad quos præfens feriptum pervenerit, æternam in Domino falutem.

" Noverit univerfitas veftra, nos, nomine prædicti domini noftri regis Scociæ,
per confenfum et affenfum Magnatum dicti regni, dediffe et conceffiffe, ac
ipfas donationem et conceffionem præfenti carta confirmaffe, Alexandro dicto
Skirmifchur fex marcatas terræ in territorio de Dunde, fcilicet, terram illam
quæ vocatur Campus Superior, prope villam de Dunde ex parte boreali, cum
acris illis in campo occidentali, quæ ad partem regiam fpectare folebant,

<hr>

[1] Braidwood named by the Minstrel is within
a mile of Carluke. The site of the Forest Kirk
was on the south-west corner of Mauldslie garden, at the base of Ha'hill—a spot formerly
known as "the Abbey Steads." The position of
the ancient church is indicated in the Ordnance
Survey, and is marked on the plan, " St Luke's
Church and Cistercian Abbey."

[2] Fordun a Goodal, 170.

Willelmus Walays miles. Custos regni Scoc' et ductor exercitus eiusdem. nob
Omnibus probis hominibus dicti regni ad quos presens scriptum pervenit etiam in d
sensum magnatum dicti regni dedisse et concessisse ac ipsas donatione et c
in territorio de Dunde scilicet terram illam que vocatur campus superior
spectare solebant ipse villam de Dunde ex parte occidentali. Et etiam pratum
pertinentiis libertatibus et aisiamentis sine aliquo retinemento. p homag
cursu suo predicto regno impenso portando vexillum Regium in exercitu
predicto domino nostro Reg' et heredibus suis ut suis successoribus. libere quiet
tis ad dominicam terram et pratum prenotatum. et prefatam constabulariam spe
Reg' et heredibus suis ut suis successoribus scilicet p predictis ter. prato. et
tam constabulai' tantum. p omnibus que de predictis exigi poterit in fu
appositum. Datum apud Torphichin. xxix. die Martii. Anno gracie M

...clar' principis dni Joh'is dei gra Reg' Scot' illustr' de consensu comitis eiden regni

...galm. Voluit vniuersitas vra nos noie pd'ca dni nri Reg' Scot' p consensum et af-

...ssione psenti carta confirmasse Alexandro d'co skirmschur sex marcatas tre

...villam de Dunde ex pte boriali cu acris illis in campo occidentali que ad pte Regia

...egni in pd'co territorio de Dunde. Et etiam Constabulariam castri de Dunde cu suis

...reddo dno Reg' et heredibz suis ut sui successoribz faciendo et p fideli seruicio et suo

...de tempore confectonis psentiu. Tenend et habend pd'co Alex et heredibz suis de

...regie pacifice et honorifice in pptuu cu omnibz ptinen libertatibz et aspame-

...ntibz ut quocuq modo spectare valentibz in futuru faciendo inde annuatim dno

...stabulari cu suis ptinen libertatibz et aspamentis seruiciu qd ptinet ad dic-

...irii. In cui rei testimoniu sigillu comune pd'ci regni Scot' psenti scripto est

...[millesimo] ducentesimo nonogesio octauo.

prope villam de Dunde ex parte occidentali, et etiam pratum regium in prædicto territorio de Dunde, et etiam Conftabulariam Caftri de Dunde, cum fuis pertinenciis, libertatibus et afyamentis fine aliquo retinemento, pro homagio prædicto domino Regi et heredibus fuis, vel fuis fuccefforibus, faciendo, et pro fideli fervicio et fuccurfu fuo prædicto regno impenfo, portando vexillum regium in exercitu Scociæ tempore confectionis præfentium. Tenendas et habendas prædicto Alexandro et heredibus fuis de prædicto domino noftro Rege et heredibus fuis, vel fuis fuccefforibus, libere, quiete, integre, pacifice et honorifice, in perpetuum, cum omnibus pertinenciis, libertatibus et afyamentis ad dictam terram et pratum prænominatum, et præfatam Conftabulariam, fpectantibus, vel quoquo modo fpectare valentibus in futurum, faciendo inde annuatim domino Regi et heredibus fuis, vel fuis fuccefforibus, fcilicet, pro prædictis terra, prato et Conftabularia cum fuis pertinenciis, libertatibus, et afyamentis, fervicium quod pertinet ad dictam Conftabulariam tantum pro omnibus quæ de prædictis exigi poterunt in futurum.

"In cujus rei teftimonium, figillum commune prædicti regni Scociæ præfenti fcripto eft appofitum.

"Datum apud Torpheichyn, vigefimo nono die Marcii, anno Graciæ millefimo ducentefimo nonogefimo octavo."[1]

Abbreviated, and in an English dress, the charter appears thus: —"Sir William Walays, guardian of the kingdom and leader of the armies of Scotland, in the name of Prince John, by the grace of God the illustrious king of Scotland, with the consent of the community of the said kingdom, wishes to all true men of the kingdom, to whom the present writing may come, eternal salvation in the Lord. Be it known to you all, that, in the name of the foresaid king, with consent of the nobles of the said kingdom, we grant, and hereby confirm, to Alexander, surnamed Skirmischur, six marks of land in the district of Dundee, namely, that land which is called the Upper Field, near the town of Dundee, on the north side, with those acres in the west field, which used to belong to the royal grounds, and also the royal

---

[1] Acta Parl. Scot., i., 453; iv., 90.

meadow in the foresaid territory ; also the constabulary of the castle of Dundee, with the rights, liberties, and privileges belonging thereto, without any reservation whatsoever, on performing homage to the king, and his heirs or successors ; and for the faithful service and assistance rendered to his kingdom in bearing the royal standard in the army of Scotland, at the time the present writing has been drawn up ; securing and preserving to the foresaid Alexander and his heirs free, quiet, peaceable, and honourable possession in all time coming, together with all the rights, liberties, and privileges belonging thereto. . . ." The charter bears, in conclusion, that thereto had been affixed " the common seal of the kingdom of Scotland," and that it was " given at Torphichen, on the 29th of March, in the year of grace 1298."

In the course of a military progress, Wallace proceeded to remove the last vestiges of Anglican authority. Journeying from Perth to the abbey of Lindores, and thence to Cupar, he there rescued the castle from an English garrison. He next visited St Andrews, where, as a first step towards the proper resumption of ecclesiastical order, he deposed the bishop.

On the death of Bishop Fraser in 1297, the Culdean chapter of St Andrews had, under Edward's sanction, claimed the privilege of electing his successor, and to the episcopal office had preferred their conventual chief, William Comyn, provost of Kirkheugh, brother of the Earl of Buchan. This ambitious churchman rendered homage to Edward at Montrose in July 1296,[1] and had since keenly adhered to the English policy. When Wallace entered the city, he, anticipating deposition, hastily quitted the place, first proceeding to London and afterwards to Rome.[2]

---

[1] Chapter House (Scots Documents), Portfolio 4, No. 6 ; Fœdera, i., 842.

[2] Henry, b. ix., ll. 1119-1135 ; Lyon's History of St Andrews, vol. i., 140-142.

Having deposed Bishop William Comyn, Wallace enabled the canons-regular of St Andrews to elect as bishop his friend William de Lamberton, then or formerly chancellor of the diocese of Glasgow. This eminent person had, in August 1296, become one of Edward's homagers, but he had already renounced his fealty, and on Wallace's behalf was now at the court of France entreating Philip's support to the cause of his country.

At St Andrews the guardian next proceeded to execute an order of the Estates whereby English churchmen appointed by Edward to parochial and other cures were deprived of their offices. Hemingford reports, on the authority of an English priest, that, from the menaced violence of the guardian, three English churchmen sought personal safety by retreating to a hallowed stone in the neighbourhood, known as the Rock or Needle, but that nevertheless he caused them to be slain.

On the south-east margin of the bay at St Andrews stands a majestic concretion of basalt, known as the Rock and Spindle, but it is not traditionally associated with the solemnities of religion. And the narrative that Wallace at the spot authorised the slaughter of three English churchmen is inconsistent with the act whereby he protected the monks of Hexham, also with the testimony of Fordun that he cherished a deep reverence for those serving at the altar. It is also inconsistent with an incident which Hemingford afterwards relates, that when on his return to Perth two English monks from St Andrews were arraigned before him for disobeying the order of the Estates, he was content to relieve them from discharging a penalty by accepting their promise that they would depart for England.

To the cause of Scottish liberty the political condition of the south had been singularly opportune. On embarking for Flanders

on the 22d August 1297, Edward entrusted the administration
of affairs to a council of regency, and this body, on learning of
Surrey's disaster at Stirling Bridge, convened a Parliament, which
was held at London on the 10th of October.[1] Among those
who attended were the Earl of Norfolk and the Earl of Hereford,
who successfully urged that no levies should be granted till the
Great Charter, and the Charter of the Forests, were ratified by
the king, with an additional clause which should prohibit any aid
or tallage being exacted, apart from the consent of the clergy,
nobles, and freemen. Informed of the determination of his Parliament, Edward evinced a strong displeasure, but after the
expiry of three days he acceded to the demand. He confirmed
the charters at Ghent on the 5th of November.[2] Pending the
approval of a Parliament summoned to meet at York on the
14th of January, the English council of regency evinced various
activities. Money was urgently required. At Norham in June
1291, Edward appointed as chancellor of Scotland, Alan of St
Edmunds, an obscure churchman, whom he also nominated
bishop of Caithness. Cognizant of Alan's inefficiency, he conjoined with him in the chancellorship, Walter de Agmondesham,
one of his chaplains, whose salary was after a brief interval
advanced from ten marks to five pounds weekly.[3] Agmondesham
was afterwards constituted sole chancellor, therewith receiving
the church living of Kinross,[4] and on the death of Cressingham at
the battle of Stirling he was appointed treasurer. As treasurer,
he, in December 1297, was authorised by the council of regency
to receive from Thomas Corebridge, bishop-elect of York, a

<hr>

[1] Hemingford, i., 139.

[2] Tyrrel, iii., 124; Hemingford, i., 138;
Trivet, p. 309; Rymer, new ed., i., Part ii., p.
880.

[3] Chapter House, Scots Documents, Box 16,
No. 20, 14; Box 94, No. 8, 5.

[4] *Ibid.*, Box 94, No. 5; Close Rolls, 24
Edward I., m. 7; Compotus of Robert de
Cotingham, fol. 10.

subsidy granted by the clergy of his diocese for use in making war upon the Scots.[1]

On the 10th of December the council of regency called upon the people of Wales to proceed against the Scots as a nation of "robbers, homicides, and fire-raisers," and for that purpose to send levies to Durham or Newcastle not later than the 13th of January.

Parliament met on the 14th January. Among those who attended were the Earl Marshal and the great Constable, also the Earl of Surrey, the Earls of Gloucester and Arundel, Sir Henry Percy, John de Wake, Sir John de Segrave and Guido, son of the Earl of Warwick.[2] But the Scottish nobility, though charged on their loyalty to be present, were wholly unrepresented, an occurrence which more emphatically than any other incident shows the confidence which at this period Wallace had inspired.

Under the sanction of Parliament, Surrey was restored to his command, and William le Franks, a military purveyor, was authorised to procure, in the counties of Lincoln and York, the necessary supplies, which he was instructed to convey into Scotland, both by sea and land.[3]

On the 19th of January, a body of 11,300 Welsh troops arrived at Newcastle,[4] and there a few days later Surrey assumed the command of a large force which included 2000 heavy cavalry and 2000 light horse.

Marching into Scotland, Surrey at once relieved the castle of Roxburgh, and, repelling a body of Scottish troops at Kelso, returned to Berwick, which he restored to English rule.[5] But

[1] Exchequer Q. R. Memoranda, 33 Edward I., m. 37 ; Close Roll, 26 Edward I., m. 17.

[2] Tyrrel, iii., 129 ; Fœdera, i., Part ii., 890 ; Palgrave's Parliamentary Writs, Chron. Abstract, p. 38 ; Rotuli Scotiæ, 26 and 27 Edward I.

[3] Memoranda Roll, 26 Edward I., m. 105.

[4] Patent Roll, 26 Edward I., m. 31 ; Memoranda Roll, 26 Edward I., m. 106.

[5] Knighton, p. 2525 ; Trivet, p. 311.

his further progress was unexpectedly arrested, for Edward communicated to the council of regency that he had determined to effect the subjugation of the Scots in person, and that for this end he had concluded a truce with the French king, whereby their differences were referred to the arbitration of the Pope.

Edward landed at Sandwich on the 11th of March.[1] He was received with acclamation, and he increased his popularity by remedying the complaints made against his purveyors, who had been victualing his army, by a course of military seizure. Requiring a convention to meet him in York at Pentecost, he addressed letters of summons not only to the lords of Parliament, but also to residents in counties and burghs, whom he empowered to elect representatives. To the convention he also summoned the nobles and barons of Scotland, who were warned that if they absented themselves, they would be dealt with as defaulting vassals.[2] It is creditable to the Scottish magnates that they severally disobeyed. Even those who had recently been released from English prisons refused to actively acknowledge the subjection of their country.

Receding from his ratification of the charters, Edward's popularity considerably waned, hence his earlier writs summoning a military force were imperfectly responded to. Fertile in expedients, he, in providing army supplies, indulged a lavish expenditure. He extended his commission to Ireland, authorising his treasurer at Dublin to send to Carlisle supplies of corn, oats, malt, and wine.[3] His expedition he also proposed should march to conquest under saintly tutelage. In moving his army to Scotland in 1296 he had raised the standard of St John of Beverley, and in consideration that the saint's virtues were believed to have

---

[1] Fœdera, new ed., i., Part ii., 887-889.   [2] Hemingford, i., 158.
[3] Memoranda Roll, 26 Edward I., m. 116.

availed heretofore, and were generally revered in the northern counties, he paid a visit to his shrine at Beverley again to invoke his protection.

But a semblance of devotion sufficient to dazzle an unreflecting soldiery failed to satisfy the barons, who continued to insist that the Great Charter and the Charter of the Forests should be fully ratified prior to their taking any part in the new campaign. Finding conciliation necessary, Edward consented that the Bishop of Durham and the Earls of Surrey and Norfolk should give an assurance, " on the king's soul," that, on returning from Scotland a victor, he would confirm the charters.[1]

In raising a national army Wallace was beset with difficulties. The burgesses readily joined his standard, but the rural population, though equally ardent in maintaining the national liberties, were restrained by their feudal superiors, not a few of whom apprehended the forfeiture of their English possessions. By strong measures and menaces Wallace had snapped a few links of the feudal system, but the great chain remained unbroken.

According to Fordun, he ranked his followers in two divisions —those who came up to a particular standard of height, and those beneath it. Next, he divided his army into regiments, appointing to each thousand men a commander, styled a chiliarch. These principal divisions were next subdivided into sections of one hundred, which again were redivided into parties of twenty, and ten, and five.

For the invasion of Scotland Edward's preparations had materially advanced. To meet him at Chillingham, in Northumberland, he, on one of the latter days of June, summoned 30,000 foot, also large troops of heavy and light horse ; but the force actually secured is extremely uncertain. Marching north-

---

[1] Hemingford, i., 159.

ward, he reached Roxburgh Castle on the 3d of July, remaining there till the 6th, when he obtained fresh levies.[1] Meanwhile the guardian, adopting the method of defence practised by the Caledonians against the Roman invaders, had caused the inhabitants of the Border counties to destroy their huts and homesteads, and to lay waste their fields—a politic movement which probably induced the Earl of March to style Wallace king of Coille —that is, king of the Forest, in allusion to his skill in converting inhabited and fertile districts into a condition of waste.[2]

Edward's route is minutely recorded. On Monday, the 7th July, he encamped at Redpath, near Melrose, and on the 9th in the vicinity of Lauder.[3] At Dalhousie on the 10th, he next day rested at Braid,[4] arriving soon afterwards at Templeliston,[5] now known as Kirkliston, near South Queensferry, where he expected his fleet with the requisite provisions. But the fleet had not arrived, and there was consequently a general discontent from lack of food, while the Welsh troops complained so boisterously, that Edward, dreading a mutiny, caused several casks of wine to be appropriated to their use. This mode of remedy proved worse than unavailing, for, drinking heavily, a body of the malcontents became violent, and, fixing a quarrel on their English comrades, stormed their quarters. Eighteen priests who sought to restore order were mercilessly struck down, and eighty persons perished in the conflict. By incursions from the neighbouring woods the Scots also caused considerable havoc.[6]

At the expiry of six days, three of Edward's provision ships arrived at Queensferry with tidings that the remainder of the

---

[1] MS. Itinerary in the Record Office. Probably the whole of Edward's army did not exceed 40,000.

[2] Henry, B. viii., 1. 39.

[3] MS. Itinerary ; Prynne, iii., 788.

[4] Rotuli Scotiæ, i., 51 ; Historical Documents, ii., 87.

[5] Historical Documents, ii., 88.

[6] Hemingford, i., 160, 161 ; Walsingham, 75.

fleet, which had suffered from tempestuous winds, would not proceed further than the port of Leith. Edward accordingly proposed to move thither, when, as we learn from Hemingford, the Earls of March and Angus informed Bishop Bek that the Scots were posted at Falkirk, a few miles to the westward. On obtaining this intelligence, Edward determined on making an immediate attack, and with that intention proceeded to move his troops towards the west. On the evening of the 21st July he rested his army on a heath at Linlithgow. As at night he lay on the ground he sustained a serious accident, two of his ribs having been broken by a kick from his horse.[1] A rumour that he had been treacherously wounded having arisen, he in the morning showed himself on horseback, so as to dispel the panic. And, after a few hours' march on the morning of the 22d, he brought his troops into the presence of the patriot army.

According to the native historians, the Scottish army at Falkirk did not exceed ten thousand foot and one thousand horse. On the field their position is by Hemingford so minutely described, as to imply that the chronicler derived his information from an eye-witness. On a slightly-inclined plain the infantry were divided into four schiltrons, or compact circles, the men of the first line kneeling with their lances pointing outwards, while those in the interior were compactly posted. Resting on Hemingford's description, Langtoft writes :

> " Ther formast conrey,[2] ther bakkis togidere sette
> Ther speres poynt ouer poynt, so sare and so thikke
> And fast togidere joynt, to se it was ferlike
> Als a castelle thei stode, that were walled with stone
> They wende no man of blode thorgh tham sud haf gone."[3]

[1] Walsingham, 75.   [2] Clump or compact mass.
[3] Langtoft, ii., 304, 305.

Between the schiltrons were arranged the archers, who were in the rear supported by the cavalry.[1]

Having so disposed his troops, Wallace addressed them familiarly, using a mode of expression common at the time. He said, "I have brought you to the ring, hop if you can."[2]

Aware of Wallace's skill as a military leader, Edward at first proposed to postpone the engagement, but as his nobles insisted on action, he ordered an advance. At the head of his first division Bigot, the Earl Marshal, and the Earls of Hereford and Lincoln marched directly towards the Scots, but their progress being impeded by a morass, they by a circuitous movement advanced on the westward. Perceiving this evolution, Bishop Bek, who commanded the second division, led up his cavalry on the east, a movement which, with the third division, Edward rapidly followed up. Though assailed on both flanks, the Scottish schiltrons kept vigorously together, resisting both infantry and horse, while the archers, chiefly drawn from the forest of Selkirk, fought courageously. But on the death of their leader, Sir John Stewart of Bonkill[3] (brother of the Steward), the archers gave way, while soon afterwards the entire body of horse under John Comyn of Badenoch hastily withdrew.[4] For

---

[1] Hemingford, i., 163.

[2] Walsingham, 75; Matthew of Westminster, 451; Langtoft, ii., 305. Lord Hailes has (Annals, i., 283, 284) expended considerable learning in rescuing Wallace's address from misrepresentation. Of the three chroniclers by whom the speech is quoted, Walsingham, who affects to quote the vernacular, substitutes "king" for "ring;" and Langtoft uses the word "renge"—that is, kingdom. But Matthew of Westminster translates the word *annulum*, clearly showing that Wallace was quoting a proverb in allusion to a rustic dance.

[3] Henry represents that at the commencement of the battle Sir John Stewart disputed with Wallace as to the leadership. The explanation is this—Lacking fertility of invention, the Minstrel, when he desires to cause surprise, reproduces old incidents in a new connexion; hence the controversy as to the leadership at Irvine had suggested to him the notion of a similar difference at Falkirk. As Wallace was the recognised guardian of the kingdom, and leader of the national army, a brother of the Steward could have had no plea for questioning his authority.

[4] Fordun a Hearne, p. 981; Hemingford, 161; Wyntoun, lib. 8, chap. 15, l. 47; also Chron. de Lanercost, p. 19.

some time the schiltrons continued to stand firm, but at length they yielded to a combined attack by the English archers and stone-slingers and the heavy armed cavalry. There was a terrible slaughter, but that portion of his troops which survived the conflict, Wallace conducted to safe shelter in the adjacent forest.

Along with Sir John Stewart, perished on the field the guardian's attached friend and early comrade, Sir John de Graham.[1] The remains of the two heroes were committed to the dust in Falkirk churchyard. There the leader of the archers is commemorated by a small block of sandstone bearing the words, "Here lies a Scottish hero, Sir John Stewart, who was killed at the battle of Falkirk, 22d July 1298." A small altar tombstone in memory of Graham bears this inscription—

> "Mente manuque potens, et Vallæ fidus Achates
> Conditur hic Gramus, bello interfectus ab anglis."

Graham's tombstone has been twice renewed, the older erections being also preserved. The last renewal, as an inscription bears, was effected by William Graham of Airth in 1772, and upon its margin appear these lines :—

> "Sir John the Grame, baith wight and wise,
> Ane of the chiefs reskewit Scotland thrise ;
> Ane better Knight not to the world was lent,
> Nor was gvde Grame of trvth and hardiment."

At the highest point of the Wallace Ridge, an elevated portion of ground about two miles to the south-east of the town of Falkirk, a plain obelisk, reared about half a century ago, denotes that Wallace stood there during the battle. Upon a chief scene of

---

[1] Till within the last forty years, a large yew-tree at Grahamston, near Falkirk, marked the spot where Sir John de Graham received his death wound.

the conflict has been reared the modern village of Grahamston ;
it was formerly known as Graham's Moor. In an adjoining
marsh portions of armour have frequently been dug up.

Fighting on the English side at the battle of Falkirk fell
Brian le Jaye, Prior of Torphichen, and formerly Master of the
Scottish Templars. This military cleric received from Edward,
on the 12th December 1291, letters of protection.[1] Advanced
to the office of " Master of the Temple in England," he was, by
Edward, on the 30th September 1295, authorized to appoint two
attorneys to act for him in Scotland.[2] Brian le Jaye fell at
a spot, still denoted, to the east of the hamlet of Bainsford
village.

From the forest of Torwood, Wallace marched to Stirling,
which he laid in ruins; he then hastened to Perth, which he also
rendered unprofitable to the invaders. Soon afterwards he
retired from the guardianship, not owing to the event of his
defeat at Falkirk, but consequent on the circumstances with
which it was attended. Governing on behalf of Baliol, he had
latterly associated with him in the leadership of the royal army,
John Comyn, the husband of Baliol's sister, and when Comyn
withdrew his cavalry from the battlefield and thereby rendered
impracticable any further effort of defence, he regarded the
incident as a virtual confirmation of Baliol's submission. And if
Baliol ceased to rule, it was obvious that no one could legally claim
his sanction in upholding his authority. Writes Wyntoun—

> " Efftyr that batalle few dayis
> This forsayd Willame the Walayis
> Persawyd,[3] how he wes in gret leth[4]
> Had wyth the Cwmynys, in thare wreth,

---

[1] Patent, 20 Edward I., m. 28.   [3] Perceived.
[2] Patent, 24 Edward I., m. 8.   [4] Hatred.

And in dowt off tresown stad
Be swylk [1] taklus as he had
Besyd the wattyre off Forth he
Forsuk Wardane evyr to be,
Or swylk state in Scotland hald ;
Tak thai curys[2] quha evyr wald ;
For leware he had to lyve symply
Na wndyre sic dowt in senyhowry,[4]
Na the lele comownys off Scotland
He wald noucht, had peryst wndyr his hand." [5]

[1] Such.
[2] Charge.
[3] Preferably.

[4] Power.
[5] Wyntoun, B. viii., ll. 2285-2306.

—————o—————

CHAPTER V.

FROM THE COMMENCEMENT OF THE SECOND WAR OF SUBJUGATION
IN JULY 1298, TO THE TRUCE IN OCTOBER 1300.

"The star of the unconquered will
He rises in his breast,
Serene and resolute and still
And calm and self-possessed."

—LONGFELLOW.

SUBSEQUENT to his victory at Falkirk, Edward remained in the vicinity of the place four days waiting for the additional supplies which some time he had expected at Leith. As the supplies were not forthcoming, he, on the 26th July, led his army to Stirling, but there finding no provisions, the town and castle being in ruins, he despatched foraging parties into the surrounding country. Consequent on the accident which he had sustained on the eve of the battle, he felt that rest was essentially needful; hence he effected lodgment in the Dominican monastery.[1] Having repaired the walls of the castle, he appointed to the office of governor, John Sampson, an Englishman, who had, prior to the preceding October, been several years custodier of the fortress at Scarborough. To the new governor, he, on the 8th August, granted for use in the chapel of the castle a chalice of silver, a sacerdotal vestment, two towels, a missal, a portoise, an

---

[1] Trivet, 373, 374.

antiphoner, a troper, and two cruets of pewter ; also provisions, consisting of live and dead stock.[1]

Leaving Stirling on the morning of the 9th of August,[2] Edward in the evening of the same day reached Torphichen.[3] At Torphichen he instructed John de Langton, his chancellor, to confer on William Bakun, an Englishman, the vacant precentorship in the cathedral of Dunkeld.[4] From Torphichen he, on the 11th, removed to Abercorn Castle,[5] and there gave sanction to an obligation, whereby Aymer de Valence agreed to bestow upon Sir Thomas de Berkeley certain remuneration for service under his banner.[6]

On the 19th August, Edward encamped at Braid, near Edinburgh, where he gave audience to ambassadors specially sent to him by Philip of France. Both to Philip and Edward, the war in Flanders had proved most inopportune, for while the resources of the former were almost exhausted, the arms of the latter had in Scotland suffered an all but overwhelming reverse. On the 9th of October 1297, the royal belligerents therefore consented to a truce, which should certainly subsist for two years,[7] and might form the basis of a permanent peace.[8] With a view to a final reconcilement, Philip, in April 1298, put forth certain proposals which included the provisions that Baliol should be liberated from the Tower, also that all the Scottish prisoners detained in England should, on the delivery of hostages, be immediately set free. When these two propositions were first made to him, Edward was preparing for his expedition to Scotland, and in order to await the issues of his new campaign, he pleaded that he would

[1] Exchequer, Q. R. Miscellanea (Army), No. $\frac{2}{3}$, m. 13.

[2] Close Roll, MS. Itin.

[3] Historical Documents, ii., 289.

[4] Privy Seals (Tower), 26 Edward I., File 8.

[5] Close Roll, MS. Itin.

[6] Exchequer, Treasury of Receipt, Miscellanea, No. $\frac{1}{13}$.

[7] Fœdera, new ed., ii., p. 878.

[8] Ibid., pp. 906, 952.

require time for deliberation.[1] And on similar pleas he postponed his answer, till, on achieving the victory at Falkirk, he evinced his willingness to finally express his views. As then at Braid he gave audience to Philip's envoys, he emphatically refused to deliver up Baliol, or to include in the truce the liberation of the Scottish nobles. When, he remarked, the articles were originally drawn, the French king did not consider the Scots as his allies, nor was Baliol even named;[2] while as to any alliance or compact between Baliol and Philip, if such had any actual existence, it had already been renounced.

Moving from Braid on the 21st August, Edward marched first to Glencorse, and from thence to Linton, in Peeblesshire, where he encamped.[3]

Wallace, to whose proceedings we revert, had, we find, after rendering Stirling and Perth useless to the enemy, returned with his followers to the Torwood. From thence he followed on Edward's track, and about the end of July held personal communication with Sir Simon Fraser in the forest of Selkirk.

After the manner of the Lord of Annandale, his grandfather, the young Earl of Carrick had greatly vacillated. With his father, the second Robert Bruce, he, at Berwick, had sworn fealty to Edward in August 1296, but in June 1297 he, under the plea of resisting foreign service, allied himself to Douglas's section of the national army. Thereafter he prominently took part in the capitulation at Irvine, when he became bound to attend at Berwick on the 8th August, there to ratify his submission.[4] This act he had evidently postponed, since, on the 14th of November, the Prince of Wales is found

---

[1] Fœdera, new ed., Part ii.
[2] *Ibid.*, p. 598.
[3] Prynne, iii., 703; Close, Patent, Fine Rolls, and MS. Itin.
[4] Stevenson's Historical Documents, ii., 217-226.

giving authority to the Bishop of Carlisle and Sir Robert Clifford to receive him to the king's peace.[1] He must again have vacillated, for, on the 4th June 1298, Edward instructed the Sheriff of Essex to distrain the goods in his bailiwick, inasmuch as in the sums of £295 and £359, 14s. 1d. he was indebted to the Crown.[2] Re-attaching himself to the English interest, he, on the 8th June, received from Edward a safe conduct to enable him to take part in the proposed expedition against Wallace and his followers.[3] In the Falkirk Roll his name is not entered, but as this includes the names of those only who commanded detachments, the omission does not prove his absence, while Wyntoun and Fordun not only affirm his presence, but refer to his prowess in the field.[4] To his energy, Fordun ascribes the Scottish defeat. He writes, "It is commonly reported that Robert of Bruce—who was afterwards King of Scotland, but then fought on the side of the King of England—was the means of bringing about this victory, for while the Scots stood invincible in their ranks, and could not be broken by either force or stratagem, this Robert the Bruce went with one line, under Anthony of Bek, by a long road round a hill, and attacked the Scots in the rear; and thus those who had stood invincible and impenetrable in front, were craftily overcome in the rear."[5] In a note on Fordun's narrative, Mr Stevenson remarks that it was most probable that Bishop Bek would have Bruce in his retinue, inasmuch as the latter owned considerable estates at Hartlepool, within the bishop's palatinate.[6]

Bower and Henry the Minstrel severally affirm that subsequent to the battle of Falkirk Wallace and Bruce had an interview on

---

[1] Fœdera, ii., 799.
[2] Memoranda Roll, 26 Edward I., m. 117.
[3] Rotuli Scotiæ, i., 151.
[4] Wyntoun, B. viii., ll. 2253, 2254.
[5] Fordun, ed. 1871, I., 300.
[6] Wallace Papers, 112, footnote.

the banks of the Carron.   By Henry the interview is described
in these lines :—

> " Wallace commaundyt his ost[1] tharfor to byd ;
> Hys ten he tuk, for to meit Bruce thai ryd.
> Sowthwest he past, quhar at the tryst was set ;
> The Bruce full son and gud Wallace is met.
> For loss of Graym[2] and als for propyr teyn,[3]
> He grewyt[4] in ire, quhen he the Bruce had seyn.
> Thar salusyng[5] was bot boustous[6] and thrawin.
> ' Rewis[7] thow,' he said, ' thow art contrar thin awin ?
> ' Wallace,' said Bruce, ' rabut[8] me now no mar ;
> Myn awin dedis has bet me wondyr sayr.'
> Quhen Wallace hard with Bruce that it stud sua,
> On kneis he fell, far countenaus can him ma[9]
> In armes son[10] the Bruce hes Wallace tane ;
> Out fra thair men in consalle ar thai gaue.
> I can nocht tell perfytly thair langage ;
> Bot this it thair men had off knawlage :
> Wallace him prayit ; ' Cum fra yon Sotheroun king.'
> The Bruce said, ' Nay that lattis me a thing,
> I am so boundyn with wytnes to be leill,[11]
> For all Ingland I wald nocht fals[12] my scill.
> Bot off a thing I hecht[13] to God and the,
> That contrar Scottis agayn I sall nocht be ;
> In till a feild, with wappynnys[14] that I ber
> In thi purpos I sall the neuir der,[15]
> Gyff God graunts off ws our hand till haif,
> I will bot fle myn awin selff for to saiff ;
> And Eduuard chaip,[16] I pass with him agayn,
> But I throu force be ether tane or slayn
> Brek he on me ; quhen that my terme is out,
> I cum to the, may I chaip fra that dout.'
> Off thair consaill I can tell yow no mar.
> The Bruce tuk leyff[17] and cum till Eduuard's fayr
> Rycht sad in mynd for Scottis men that war lost." [18]

That Bruce desired to take counsel with the Scottish guardian

[1] Host.	[7] Regret.	[13] Promise.
[2] Graham.	[8] Repulse.	[14] Weapons.
[3] Sorrow.	[9] More.	[15] Adventure.
[4] Groaned.	[10] Soon.	[16] Escape.
[5] Saluting.	[11] Faithful.	[17] Leave.
[6] Menacing.	[12] Falsify.	[18] Henry, B. x., ll. 587-619.

subsequent to the battle of Falkirk is sufficiently probable. According to the English historians, Bruce, at the close of the conflict, returned to Edward's headquarters, when an episode occurred which the chroniclers relate variously. In one version Bruce is represented as seated at dinner in the royal camp, when Edward remarking his gore-stained hands, exclaimed derisively, "See how that Scot eats his own blood!" In another version, Bruce is described as reminding Edward of his promise to appoint him king, when he received the haughty rejoinder, "Do you think I have no more to do than to conquer kingdoms for you?" Owing to whatever reason, it is absolutely certain that soon after the battle of Falkirk Bruce espoused the national cause. Under his change of sentiment, he would naturally enough seek an interview with the recognized leader of his countrymen. That, between Bruce and Wallace, there came to subsist a common understanding, would appear from subsequent events.

Retiring from Edward's camp, Bruce established his headquarters at his castle of Turnberry—Wallace by a series of night marches following him into Carrick. We next hear of the two leaders in connexion with an attack on the English quarters at Ayr, Bruce at the head of his followers demolishing the new castle, while Wallace seized and set on fire the English barracks of the place.[1] According to Hemingford, five hundred soldiers were cut off.

The new castle of Ayr was reared by William the Lion, and occupied a site near the place now known as Cromwell's Fort,

[1] The English historians refer solely to Bruce in connexion with the attack on the castle and barracks at Ayr (Hemingford, 63; Rishanger, 188); while Scottish writers assign the operation to Wallace only. In reality both heroes were concerned in the work. From Barnwell Hill, about four miles to the southward, where a monumental tower in his honour now stands, Wallace is traditionally represented as having watched the progress of the conflagration, and by exclaiming "The barns burn weil," to have suggested the name afterwards given to his scene of observation.

but every vestige of the structure has latterly disappeared. The English barracks stood in Barns Street, at the western part of the burgh.

In his narrative as to the destruction of the English barracks at Ayr, Henry alludes to certain persons as having assisted the hero in his enterprise. To a niece of the patriot he refers without supplying her name, and he causes the guardian to address Wallace of Auchinleck as his uncle, and Adam, son of Richard Wallace of Riccarton, as his cousin; but these had in August 1296 become homagers to Edward. He names one Craufurd, obviously one of Wallace's maternal kinsmen, but who also seems to have rendered fealty to the English king. By the name "Jop" Henry refers to the hero's faithful associate, the brave Alexander Scrimgeour of Dundee.[1]

While, in reference to Wallace's associates in the work of destroying the barracks at Ayr, the Minstrel may be approximately correct, he is obviously confused in his details. The date of the conflagration he erroneously assigns to the 18th of June 1297. And on that day, he sets forth that an assize was to be held at Ayr, under Arnwlf, an English judge, to which were summoned the principal barons of the neighbourhood, so that each might render fealty to the English king. The convention, he proceeds, was expected to assemble in four great barns or barracks, constructed by Edward, when he was on a visit to the place. Meanwhile Wallace passed to the parish church of Monkton, and there had a vision—the angel-genius of his country granting him distinguished recognition, and a special commission. Thereafter he proceeded to join his uncle,

---

[1] Henry, B. vii., 154-227. In the "Relationes" of Arnald Blair, it is set forth that in destroying the barracks of Ayr, Wallace was accompanied by Sir John the Graham and Sir John Menteith, while, as we know, the former fell at the battle of Falkirk.

Sir Reginald Craufurd, in attending the assize, but finding that his relative had forgotten his parchment summons, he rode to his residence at Corsbie to procure it for him. The place of assize, adds Henry, was guarded by men in armour, while the entry was so constructed that

> " No man enter micht
> But ane at anys, nor haill off other sicht."

In the interior a beam crossed the entrance bearing running nooses for the seizure and suspension of those who entered. Being first called, Sir Reginald had, on crossing the threshold, a noose slipped over his neck, by which he was hoisted upward, and strangled. In like manner were done to death all who entered, including Sir Bryce Blair, Sir Neil Montgomery, and several members of the resident families of Stewart, Kennedy, Campbell, Berkeley, and Boyd. And Wallace, according to Henry, burned the barns to avenge the butchery. In reality, the Minstrel wildly interweaves several distinct occurrences. Not improbably a special assize was held at Ayr about the 18th of June 1297; and it is obvious that the judge named Arnwlf[1] was Sir William Ormesby, whom Wallace had expelled from Scone, and who might have continued his exactions in a locality where the English rule was still upheld. In connexion with the date which Henry assigns to the Ayr assize, it is to be remarked that on the 11th of June, Edward granted to Sir Reginald Craufurd letters of license, authorizing him to return to Scotland from a visit to the southern kingdom.[2] On the other hand we know certainly that Sir Reginald Craufurd and Sir Bryce Blair did not perish in June 1297, since the

---

[1] "The Burning of the Barns of Ayr," by John, Marquess of Bute, 50-66. Lord Bute shows that the name Arnwlf has evidently been substituted for Ormesby by some inattentive transcriber.

[2] Patent Roll, 25 Edward I., Part i., m. 4.

former was executed at Carlisle on the 17th of February 1307 ; and the latter was alive on the 13th October 1306, and was by Edward's order executed in a barrack at Ayr some months later.[1]

On the 26th of August 1298, Edward reached Ayr, when he found the castle a ruin, and the barracks a wreck. For a time he and his army severely suffered, a portion of the troops owing to lack of provisions becoming turbulent and unmanageable. He lost several of his best horses.[2] On the 31st he gratified his revenge by granting to Sir Alexander de Lindesay a castle which had formerly belonged to the Steward.[3] During his sojourn at Ayr, there arrived at the Isle of Arran from Ireland, Thomas Bysset, an opulent baron, who had intended to give his support to the Scots, but who, under the circumstances, joined the invader. In recognition of service, Edward bestowed upon Bysset the lands of Arran, an act which Hemingford remarks was discourteous to the Earl Marshal and the Earl of Hereford, since he had promised to make no grants of land in Scotland without consulting them.[4]

According to Hemingford, Edward continued in Ayr about fifteen days, but the "Itinerary" informs us that he departed on Monday, the 1st of September, after a residence of five days only. *En route* for Carlisle, he passed through Cumnock and Sanquhar, reaching, on the 3d, Tibbers Castle, near Thornhill. Both at Tibbers and at Dalgarno he lost horses.[5] Arriving at Lochmaben on the 4th,[6] he there rested till the 6th, when he marched to Dumfries. On Sunday the 7th, he embarked on the

---

[1] In the circumstance of Sir Bryce's perishing in a barn at Ayr, there is a further illustration of the Minstrel's tendency to mix up and confuse the facts traditionally presented to him.

[2] Horse Roll.

[3] Chapter House (Scots Documents), Box 99, No. 99.

[4] Hemingford, i., 166.

[5] Horse Roll.

[6] *Ibid.*

Solway at Carlaverock, and reached Carlisle on the following day.[1]

At Carlisle on the 9th September, Edward presented Robert de Wodehouse, an Englishman, to the church of Ellon in Aberdeenshire; also John de Crosseby, a native of England, to the church of St Mary, in the forest of Selkirk.[2] On the 10th he conferred on Adam Pouray, clerk, the church of Kirkton, and on Henry de Craystocke the church of Arbuthnot, both in the diocese of St Andrews. And on the same day, he instructed John de Langton, his chancellor in Scotland, to alter the terms of the presentation of John de Benestede to the Provostry of St Mary, at St Andrews, formerly held by William Comyn, inasmuch as the office should have been called "The Provostry of the King's free chapel at St Andrews," attached to the royal dignity, and exempt from ordinary jurisdiction.[3] On the 11th he presented Thomas de Chelreye to the church of Little Yetham, in the diocese of Glasgow;[4] on the 20th, Thomas de Querle to the church of Ratho;[5] and on the 25th, Master William de Rus to the church of Auchtermuchty, in the diocese of St Andrews.[6]

At Carlisle Edward held a Parliament, when he bestowed on certain of his leading nobles the estates of several Scottish barons, which he had exposed to forfeiture.[7] On the 25th of September he granted to Guy, Earl of Warwick, 1000 marks

---

[1] MS. Itinerary; Lord Bute's "Barns of Ayr," p. 40.

[2] Exchequer Q. R. Miscellanea (Army), No. 23, m. 5.

[3] Privy Seals (Tower), 26 Edward I., File 11.

[4] *Ibid.*, Files 10, 11.

[5] *Ibid.*, File 11.

[6] *Ibid.* Besides the gifts enumerated, Edward presented, in the year 1298, English churchmen to the churches of Carnmoel, Sanquhar, Bothwell, Stobo, Douglas, Monimail, Kirkpatrick-on-the-Clyde, Kinkell, Selkirk, Ellon, Ratho, Kirkmahoe, and Tynningham (Patent Roll, 26 Edward I., m. 25).

[7] Hemingford, i., 166.

of the lands of Geoffry de Moubray, in Scotland (excluding the manor of Eckford near Roxburgh), and of the lands of Sir John de Stirling, also the castle of Amesfield and the land of Drungrey, belonging to Andrew de Chartres.[1]

In his progress, Edward is found at Berwick on the 9th October;[2] at the castle of Jedburgh on the 16th and 18th,[3] and on the 20th at York.[4] On the 21st of October he sent a mandate to John de Halton, Bishop of Carlisle, authorizing him to reimburse Sir Henry Percy in fifty marks, towards payment of his outlays in defending the city against the Scots.[5]

On the 25th October Edward moved from York to Chester, and subsequently into the county of Durham,[6]—from whence he marched to Newcastle, where he issued some important writs. On the 19th of November he appointed Patric, Earl of March, captain of his forces on the eastern march, with special instructions as to making forays upon the Scots.[7] On the 20th, he requested Ingram de Gynes and Walter de Teye and their lieutenants, at Westerker in Eskdale, to render obedience to Simon de Lindesay, whom he had appointed captain in those parts.[8] On the 24th he granted to Gilbert de Umfraville, Earl of Angus, the manor of Faudon, in Northumberland, seized from Sir William Douglas.[9] On the same day he authorized Sir Robert Clifford to secure as homagers the men of Nithsdale; also John de Kingston, his constable of the castle, and sheriff of the county of Edinburgh, to receive the fealty of all persons in his constabulary and county, whose

---

[1] Chapter House (Scots Documents), Box 93, No. 16.

[2] Tower Miscellaneous Rolls, No. 474.

[3] Exchequer Q.R. Miscellanea (Army), No. 23/25, m. 13.

[4] Tower Miscellaneous Rolls, No. 117.

[5] Exchequer Q. R. Memoranda, 26 Edward I., m. 109.

[6] *Ibid.*, m. 8 ; Privy Seals (Tower), 26 Edward I., File 13.

[7] Patent, 26 Edward I., m. 2.

[8] *Ibid.*

[9] Close, 27 Edward I., m. 20.

possessions exceeded the yearly value of twenty shillings, apart from earls, barons, knights, and freeholders.[1]

To the people of Annandale and other borderers, Edward, on the 26th October, issued a proclamation charging them to serve under the standard of Sir Robert Clifford, his lieutenant, in contending with "the rebels."[2] On the same day, he invited Sir Simon Fraser, whom he described as "his friend and liege," to assist John de Kingston, constable and sheriff at Edinburgh, in making a raid upon the Scots with twenty barbed horses.

On the 26th October, Edward granted to John de Kirkby, sheriff of Northumberland, an allowance for certain costs incurred by him in fortifying the castle of Newcastle-on-Tyne, from the 30th September to the 2d November 1297, when the place was besieged by the Scots.[3]

After a campaign of six months, Edward returned to London early in December. With the young Earl of Carrick, he sought to avoid any absolute rupture. Among "the Miscellaneous Documents" preserved in the Tower is a letter in Norman French written at Dumfries on the 6th August, which, though not further dated, may certainly be assigned to the year 1298. In this communication the writer, Hugh de Nauntone, reports to Sir Walter de Bedewynde, for Edward's information, some facts as to the political situation.[4] "The great man" to whom he had been accredited, had, he set forth, yielded him a courteous reception, and at meeting, he would fully explain to his correspondent the subject of their talk. His words, he adds, were abundantly

[1] Patent, 27 Edward I., m. 40.

[2] *Ibid.*, m. 41.

[3] Exchequer Q. R. Memoranda, 27 Edward I., m. 47 dorso.

[4] Sir Walter de Bedewynde, who was an ecclesiastic, had, two days before the date of De Nauntone's letter—that is, on the 4th August— been appointed by Edward to the vacant church living of Kirkpatrick-on-the-Clyde. He remained in Edward's military service, and attended him at Stirling in 1304 (Privy Seals (Tower), 26 Edward 1., File 9 ; Tower Miscellaneous Rolls, No. $\frac{5}{6}$).

reasonable, and pervaded by an evident sincerity. He then intimates that King Edward had gone to the new castle of Ayr, there to receive homage.[1] Now it seems all but certain that "the great man" interviewed by De Nauntone was the second Robert the Bruce, husband of the Countess of Carrick, and that on account of his favour for English rule, the reporter had concluded that his son, the young Earl of Carrick, then at the new castle of Ayr, would, on Edward presenting himself there, cordially renew his fealty. On the personal adherence of the second Robert Bruce, Edward continued to place the fullest reliance, since in certain " memoranda " relative to a contemplated expedition to Scotland, he in the winter of 1298-9 remarks that he expected the Earl of Carrick and others would raise upwards of 8000 foot soldiers from the parts of Carlisle, also from Galloway and Nithsdale and other portions of the northern and midland counties.[2]

When at Rome, obtaining confirmation of his election, Bishop Lamberton had succeeded in inducing Boniface VIII. to uphold the cause of Scottish independence, and his policy seemed to attain a further triumph, as, on Philip's suggestion, Edward consented to submit their differences to the Pope's arbitration. Informed by Boniface that his favour in the adjustment of the disputes would largely depend on the liberation of Baliol, Edward haughtily answered that the Pope might have him, as a perjured man and a seducer of the people.[3] Practically he agreed to place Baliol in the hands of the Papal legate, the Bishop of Vicenza.

In the belief that negotiations with Edward had advanced towards ratification, Philip proposed to accredit to the English

---

[1] Tower Miscellaneous Rolls, No. 1½8.

[2] *Ibid.*, No. 474. The second Robert Bruce died in 1304.

[3] Walsingham, 76, 77; Prynne's Edward I., 797, 798; Trivet, 315.

Court the bishop of St Andrews, the abbots of Melrose and St Andrews, Sir John de Soulis, and others, as the representatives of Scotland. Edward did not ostensibly object, but, on the 8th July 1299, he instructed the men of Yarmouth, and other masters of shipping, to arrest the Scottish envoys—pointing out in his manifestoes that they were likely to embark at Dam in Flanders; he also commissioned a vessel specially to effect their seizure.[1]

The Scottish deputies eluded capture; but, in Lamberton's absence from the French court, Edward contrived to evade certain conditions in the proposed treaty. Liberated from the Tower, Baliol was, in July 1299, conveyed by Sir Robert Burghersh, constable at Dover, to Whitsand near Calais, where he was met by the Papal legate, who received him under the express condition that the Pope should not be expected to recognize his sovereignty.

Receding from his stipulations as to the independence of Scotland, Philip, on the 19th June 1299, entered into a treaty with Edward, in which it was stipulated that, in order to a better understanding between their kingdoms, Edward should espouse Philip's sister, and that Isabella, Philip's daughter, should become the wife of the Prince of Wales.

On his return to London, Edward began to prepare for a new campaign, in the course of which he hoped that Scotland would be finally subdued. In a letter to the sheriff of York, dated the 12th of December, he desires him to provide for the expedition 1200 quarters of wheat, 1500 quarters of oats, 1000 quarters of barley, and 500 carcases of oxen. Such provisions he specified should, carefully sifted and properly packed, be

---

[1] Patent Roll, 27 Edward I., m. 20.

conveyed to Berwick not later than Whitsunday.[1]   Edward similarly instructed the sheriffs of Lincoln, Norfolk, Suffolk, Cambridge, Huntingdon, Essex, Surrey, Sussex, Nottingham, and Derby; also his principal functionaries at Southampton, Holderness, Ely, Yarmouth, the Isle of Wight, and in different parts of Ireland.[2]

On the 19th of December Edward appointed the Earl of Surrey as commander of the expedition.   And entreating the co-operation of the Earls of Norfolk, Suffolk, Gloucester, Hertford, Warwick, Hereford, and Essex, the Earl Marshal, the Constable, and Sir Henry de Percy, he charged them conjointly to provide five hundred barbed horse, towards the cost of which they were authorized to draw in certain proportions the sum of £7691, 16s. 8d. from the subsidy for the War granted by the province of Canterbury.[3]

On the 23d February 1298-9, Edward issued a pardon to a person convicted of murder, inasmuch as he had afforded aid in the Scottish War.[4]   He also made a journey to St Albans to invoke on his new campaign the sanction of its tutelary saint.[5]

But in proceeding to renew his hostilities Edward experienced a variety of difficulties.   Philip of France urged pacific counsels, while his barons strongly complained as to a heavy and arbitrary taxation, and began to insist on his restricting his prerogative, also that the bounds of the royal forests should be reduced.   At a Parliament held at Westminster, the Earls of Hereford and Norfolk renewed a demand for a confirmation of the charters, also for a perambulation of the forests.   Edward granted confirmation, but by adding the words "salvo jure coronæ,"

---

[1] Patent Roll, 27 Edward I., m. 40.

[2] *Ibid.*, m. 39.

[3] Exchequer Q. R. Memoranda, 26 Edward I., m. 106, dorso.

[4] Patent Roll, 27 Edward I., m. 34.

[5] Chronica S. Albani, quoted by Tyrrel, vol. iii., p. 134.

attempted to avoid the consequences of his act. As, however, in the hall of Parliament the contending earls expressed a menacing resentment, he, at another Parliament, which met after Easter, confirmed the charters unreservedly.

In arranging the peace of July 1299, Philip proposed that Edward should grant to the Scots a truce of seven months, and as Edward rejected the demand, those specially concerned in maintaining the national independence again became hopeful that Philip would withdraw his negotiations with the English court, and return to his ancient alliance. About this time Wallace proceeded to the French court. Respecting this movement, we are informed, in a letter addressed to Edward on the 20th August 1299, by Sir Robert Hastang, governor of Roxburgh Castle. Sir Robert reports that the Scots had, under Sir Ingram de Umfraville, Sir William Balliol, and others, made an inroad into Selkirk Forest, of which Sir Simon Fraser was keeper; and further that a convention had been held at Peebles, attended by Bishop Lamberton, the Earl of Carrick, and by the Earls of Buchan, Menteith, and another, whose title is indecipherable, also by Sir John Comyn "le Fiz," and the Steward of Scotland. The object of the convention, proceeds Sir Robert, was to concert measures for reducing Roxburgh Castle, but a spy had ascertained that dissension had arisen consequent on a demand by Sir David de Graham for the lands and goods of Sir William Wallace, who was going abroad without leave, Graham's demand being resisted by Wallace's brother, Sir Malcolm. The contending knights, Hastang continues, had called each other false, and had drawn their swords, and the confusion was augmented by Comyn seizing young Robert the Bruce by the throat, and Lord Buchan collaring the bishop of St Andrews. Concord being at length restored,

Bishop Lamberton, Robert the Bruce, and Sir John Comyn were thereafter appointed guardians of the realm, the bishop receiving charge of the strongholds. On the members separating, Robert the Bruce and Sir David de Brechin proceeded to Annandale and Galloway, the Earl of Buchan and Comyn to the north of the Forth, and the Stewart and the Earl of Menteith into Clydesdale. Sir Robert adds, " The bishop of St Andrews remains at Stubbowe [Stobo], Umfraville is made sheriff of Roxburgh, and Sir Robert de Keith, warden of Selkirk Forest, with one hundred barbed horse and fifteen hundred foot besides the foresters, these being expected to make raids on the English march, for which object each lord left a body of men with Umfraville." Hastang concludes by referring to negotiations for an exchange of prisoners.[1]

According to Hastang, Wallace was at the Peebles convention charged with going abroad without leave, and as the act implied forfeiture, Sir John Comyn the guardian desired that his lands and goods should be granted to Sir David Graham. Sir David was captured by Edward at the battle of Dunbar, and had along with Comyn been a prisoner in the Tower.[2] Subsequently he was removed to St Briavels Castle;[3] and, on the 30th July 1297, was liberated by Edward on the condition of his serving against France in the Low Counties. From the Flanders campaign he returned to Scotland. His attempt through Comyn to obtain Wallace's possessions seems to have conduced to the guardianship being established on a wider basis, Comyn being now associated with the young Earl of Carrick and Bishop Lamberton.

---

[1] Scots Documents in the Public Record Office. The letter is printed in the National MSS. of Scotland, ii., No. viii.

[2] Close Roll, Edward I., m. 7 and 6.

[3] Liberate, 25 Edward I., m. 5.

RECOMMENDATION OF SIR WILLIAM WALLACE

BY KING PHILIP OF FRANCE

Phus dei gra Francie Rex dilcis et fidelibz .. Geneibz suis ad Romam Curiam accedentibz etc edilt mandan9
uob gñate .. Summnю Pontificem rogauitus / ut dileccm nrm Guillm le Walois de Scocia militem nrrmes
dñm regem ṛ hijs q ap eum habuit expedne .. Dat ap Pontissonem ꝗ die post festum scm Sancrosp.

On obtaining a share in the government, Lamberton made known to the French king that Wallace's protection at his court was essential to the continuance of friendship between the kingdoms. We now quote from the Cottonian MS. :—

" When he (Wallace) came to the town of Amiens, it was immediately told to the king of France that an enemy of the king of England had arrived ; upon which he ordered him to be detained and kept in prison. Then the king of France sent a letter to the king of England, saying, that if he thought good, he would send him William le Walcis, the conqueror of Scotland ; and the king of England wrote back, returning him many thanks, and entreating, in the most pressing manner, that he would send the said Wallace." [1]

This statement is anonymous, and is at variance with the evidence presented in a document extant in the national archives. That document, dated at Pierrefonds on the 1st of November, and addressed by Philip to his agents at Rome, proceeds :—

" Philippus Dei gratia Francorum rex dilectis et fidelibus gerentibus meis ad Romanam curiam destinatis, salutem et dilectionem. Mandamus vobis quatenus Summum Pontificem requiratis ut dilectum nostrum Guillelmum le Waleis de Scotia, militem, recommendatum habeat in hiis que apud eum habuerit expedire. Datum apud Petrafontem die Lune post festum Omnium Sanctorum."

Translated into English, Philip's letter reads thus :—

" Philip, by the grace of God King of the French, to my loved and faithful, my agents, appointed to the Roman Court, greeting and love. We command you to request the Supreme Pontiff to hold our loved William le Waleis of Scotland, knight, recommended to his favour in those things which he has to transact with him. Given at Pierrefonds on Monday after the feast of All Saints." [2]

[1] Cottonian MS., Claud D., vi., fol. 163.

[2] We present a facsimile of Philip's letter from a carefully executed lithograph contained in Part I. of "The National MSS. of Scotland." As the document is preserved among the other public writs of the reign of Edward I.,

Immediately before he left Scotland for France, Wallace, who had long been hovering with his followers in the fastnesses of the Torwood, succeeded in forcing the English garrison at Stirling Castle to surrender, by cutting off their supplies. The garrison consisted of ninety persons; these including John Sampson, the constable, three knights, a chaplain and his groom, a clerk and his groom, a master engineer with four companions, and two janitors or gate-keepers. One member only, William of Lanark, bore a Scottish surname.[1]

In connection with the surrender of Stirling Castle, Sampson, the constable, in a statement of "losses" presented by him to Edward at Dover, on the 19th July 1305, sets forth the following particulars. When by the king's order he surrendered the place to Gilbert Malherbe,[2] he sustained losses in horses, armour, robes, etc., to the value of £61, 13s. 10d., among these a bay horse, which cost £13, 7s. 8d., and which was eaten in lack of other food; also a " ferrant " horse, which cost £8, and a mare bought from Gilbert le Braconer for one mark, which also were eaten; a "bausan" horse, which cost 40s., and was ridden by Sir William Danant towards the king for news of the castle and of the country, which was lost at Lundr'; and a "liard" horse, which cost four marks, and was lost on a Saint Bartholomew's day, when William le Waleys came to take away their supplies. He

it is nearly certain that it was not borne by the Scottish Patriot to the Court of Rome, and it is probable that at his capture it was found in his possession, and was in consequence deposited among the English state papers.

[1] Exchequer Q. R. Miscellanea (Army), No. 23.

[2] Gilbert Malherbe was a landowner in Stirlingshire. One of Edward's homagers in August 1296, he was, on the 24th May 1297, commanded to prepare for taking part in the expedition to Flanders (Close Roll, 25 Edward I., m. 27). On returning from the Continent he joined the national cause, but abandoned it prior to the 20th April 1304, when he received from Edward a grant of the goods of Sir William Oliphant, governor of Stirling Castle (Privy Seals [Tower], 32 Edward I., file 5). By Edward's order his lands were also restored to him (Close Rolls, 32 Edward I., m. 13).

also lost, when leaving the castle, two "aketons," which cost him
more than 40s.; two "gambesouns," more than £4, with "cotes
armeres;" one "jupel feytis," more than 20s.; a hauberk and
a haberchion, price 15 "soldz;" a "pisane," and "cape de
hust," which cost him 10s.; a "jambers quisez," which cost more
than 8s.; a "chapel de feer," price 20s.; a "chapel de nerfs,"
price 40d.; gauntlets (gantz de fer), which cost him 5s.; a pair
of "plates," which cost him more than a mark; a pair of
"treppes," price two marks; three swords, a "misericord," and
two anlaces with ivory handles, price 10s.; two sumpter and two
hackney saddles, costing him more than 24 "soldz;" two sacks,
"a draps de quir," with "houces" and appurtenances, price
16 soldz; a gentleman's bed and all appurtenances, price 53s. 4d.;
two robes, "un falding," price 30s.; two "naps," two "touailles,"
price 6s. 8d.; "lyngedraps," cut and uncut, price half a mark;
"livres, forcers, besas, lanoir, batin, barriz, mazre, potz darreine,"
and "mult des hustilementz come appent a gentil home," to the
value of 26s. 8d. and more; two buckles of gold, price 10s.;
eleven gold rings, price 22s.; two "correys de say," mounted
with silver, price 10s.; three silk purses, price 3s.; ten silver
spoons, price 12s.; a [canvas] tente, price 33s. 4d., and 10s.
silver at leaving the castle. When Alexander le Convers
brought money for robes then wanted, he had four valets for
whose robes he paid the 30s., which came to him for his robe,
and 2s. more to these four to keep peace. To divers messengers
to the king in England, 12s. "par treiz cez;" divers spies, 9d.;
during the truce between Herbert de Morham and the castle,
for hay for the cart and other horses, 14s.; for beef, 16s.; mutton,
9s. 5d.; milk, 5s.; butter, 9d.; cheese, 10s.; flour, 33s. 6d.;
fish, 16s.; "canure" and "lynes" for the crossbow strings, 4s. 5d.
Edward's barons found Sampson entitled to his claim, more

especially that he had suffered personal injury in the royal
service in Scotland.[1]

At Canterbury on the 10th September 1299, Edward espoused
the Princess Margaret of France, and on the seventh day
thereafter summoned the Earl of Cornwall and some others
to meet him at York on the 10th of November,[2] equipped for
a new expedition to Scotland. About the end of October he
received a despatch from Sir Robert de Feltone, who commanded the English bowmen at Lochmaben Castle, reporting
that he had seized the castle of Carlaverock, and having slain the
constable, Robert de Coningham, nephew of the husband of
the Steward's sister, had placed his head on the entrance tower
of the castle of Lochmaben. The Scots, Sir Robert added, were,
on account of the French alliance, deeply dejected; he pleaded
that he might be supplied with garments, and that the king
would hasten his journey northward.[3]

For the success of his projected expedition, Edward caused
prayers to be offered in every parish church; he also specially
instructed the Friars Predicant to intreat heaven on behalf of
his enterprise.

Cognizant of the formidable preparations, the Scottish
Guardians assembled at the Torwood a considerable army, but,
learning from the French ambassador that Edward had at length
assented to a seven months' truce, they, by a special messenger,
expressed their acquiescence.[4] But Edward, notwithstanding
his pacific professions, continued his hostile preparations, and
in evidence that he had not receded from his warlike purpose he
prohibited tournaments and jousts in his several counties, until

[1] Exchequer Q. R. Memoranda, 34 and 35
Edward I., m. 5.

[2] Fœdera, i., Part ii., p. 913, new ed.; Palgrave's Parliamentary Writs, p. 42, Chron.
Abstract.

[3] Tower Miscellaneous Rolls, No. $\frac{4}{0}\frac{8}{1}$.

[4] Chapter House (Scots Documents), Box 14, No. 14; Fœdera, i., 915, new ed.

Scotland was thrown into subjection.[1] At York on the 13th of November, he mustered a body of troops, and, notwithstanding the terms of the truce, he prepared at once to proceed north-ward. As an obstacle, his barons pleaded the severity of the weather, but he would permit of no delay, on the plea that unless speedily relieved Stirling Castle would fall into the hands of the enemy.[2] Hastening to Berwick, he there received a reinforcement of fifteen thousand infantry.[3] But the barons again protested. Ignoring the breach of the truce, also the rigorous condition of the weather, they powerfully set forth that Edward had, while ratifying the recent Parliamentary acts, continued to restrain their liberties and assert his prerogative. And as no remedy was forthcoming they proceeded to cause their followers to withdraw from the royal army. With the small force that remained to him, Edward determined to press forward, but, learning that the Scots were strongly posted at the Torwood, he followed his barons in their march southward.[4]

In view of a further expedition against the Scots, Edward came to realize the necessity of making concessions to his barons. Accordingly at a Parliament held at Westminster, he, in respect of the Charters of the Forests, sanctioned the provision that prizes were to be taken solely by the royal purveyors, on the production of sufficient warrants ; while he also became pledged that the proper perambulation of the forests would become the subject of an early statute. Relying on these new pledges, the recusant barons returned to their allegiance, and pledged their aid in the Scottish war.

While his affairs with his English nobility were yet unsettled,

---

[1] Fœdera, i., 916, new ed.

[2] Edward was certainly not unaware that Stirling Castle had already capitulated.

[3] Fœdera, i., 915, 916, new ed.

[4] Langtoft's Chronicle, p. 309.

Edward, on the 17th January 1299-1300, addressed letters to his principal subjects in Ireland, requesting a subsidy to be used against "the Scottish rebels," and informing them that he had appointed the Earl of Ulster, his Justiciar, and five barons of Exchequer in Ireland, to make the necessary arrangements.[1]

In a letter, dated the 1st March, Edward instructed Sir John de St John, his lieutenant in Cumberland and Annandale, to supply the castle of Dumfries with provisions, so as to prepare against a probable insurrection.[2]   On the 30th of April he directed the Sheriffs of Derby, Nottingham, Lancaster, Cumberland, Westmoreland, and Northumberland, to assist his knights in providing well-armed levies to be sent to Carlisle prior to the 28th of June.[3]   On the 24th of June he held a rendezvous at Carlisle, and a few days later divided his forces into four squadrons.   The third squadron he took under his personal command.   To the command of Bishop Bek he assigned a separate or auxiliary force.

Wallace had returned from France, and, in anticipation of Edward's expedition, had marched from the Torwood into the southern counties.   Seizing the castle of Tibbers, also other strongholds in Nithsdale, and routing a party of English soldiers at Dalswinton, he rested at Carlaverock Castle, then in possession of the Scots under Sir Herbert de Maxwell.[4]

Edward recovered several of the Dumfriesshire strongholds. Having occupied the castle of Lochmaben, he from thence proceeded to the castle of Carlaverock, to which he laid siege. This powerful stronghold, situated on the coast of the Solway, rose in the form of a triangle, with a tower at each side of the

---

[1] Patent, 28 Edward I., m. 28.
[2] Close, 28 Edward I., m. 13.
[3] Patent, 28 Edward I., m. 16.

[4] The Book of Carlaverock, by Sir William Fraser, Edinburgh, 1873, 4to, vol. i., pp. 43, 44.

broader angles, also two towers flanking the great entrance gateway, the structure being surrounded by a rampart. As a first step in the siege, Edward cut down the brushwood by which the castle was surrounded; making way for the erection of huts, from which his troops might cast into the fortress stones and arrows. After a time he received from the vessels on the Solway a supply of war engines. These included three of great power, which, delivering formidable strokes, wrecked whatever they struck. A vigorous attack upon the gate by Richard of Kirkbride rendered further resistance unavailing. The governor surrendered, and on entering the stronghold Edward was surprised to find that the defence had been maintained by a party of sixty.

The siege of Carlaverock was in progress on the 14th July, when Sir John Segrave certifies that Henry de Middeltone bore Edward's standard, displaying three leopards in fine gold set in red.[1]

Removing into Galloway, Edward was by parties of armed Scotsmen frequently deprived of his supplies, and otherwise attacked. Mediation between the belligerents was attempted by Thomas, Bishop of Galloway, one of Edward's homagers, but unsuccessfully. At length, when his progress was considerably impeded, Edward was waited on by Sir John Comyn, one of the regents, accompanied by his cousin, the Earl of Buchan, when they offered that resistance would cease on the conditions that Baliol was restored to his freedom and throne, and that the lands of Scottish barons lately bestowed upon English nobles

---

[1] Chancery Miscellaneous Rolls, No. 474. A metrical history in Norman French, entitled "The Siege of Carlaverock," and supposed to be written by Walter of Exeter, a Franciscan friar, has been printed in the Antiquarian Repertory, vol. iv., p. 469; also by Sir Nicolas Harris Nicholas, who presents the Norman original with a translation, and accompanied with a facsimile of the achievements. In 1864 Mr Thomas Wright issued an edition in which the achievements are blazoned in colours.

were restored to the rightful owners. These proposals Edward received with derision, and marching to Irvine, there obtained an ample supply of provisions from his ships, which lay on the coast. At Irvine he remained eight days, a body of Scots under Wallace hovering on his rear. Attacked by the Earl of Surrey at the head of a powerful force, Wallace found refuge for his followers on a heath skirted by marshes on every side. Edward returned to Dumfries, reducing in his progress several strongholds in Galloway. But he now experienced an unexpected restraint, the result of Scottish negotiation.

Owing to the necessity laid upon him of returning to the leadership of the national army, also to other considerations, Wallace did not proceed to Rome in person, but he continued to actively move the Pope on behalf of his country's independence. And as Bishop Lamberton was one of the guardians, under the bishop's authority he got despatched to the court of Rome three envoys,—viz., Baldred Bisset, William Eaglisham, and William Frier, Archdeacon of Lothian.[1] On receiving from their hands a strong appeal despatched by Bishop Lamberton and the other guardians, Boniface VIII., on the 27th of June 1300, addressed to Edward a powerful re-monstrance. This he despatched to Robert Winchelsey, Archbishop of Canterbury, with the request that he would personally deliver it into the hands of the king.[2] In dread of Edward's violent displeasure, Winchelsey at first declined, but as the Pope was inexorable, and as Edward had already entered on his Scottish campaign, he prepared to follow him in his route. After occupying some time in making arrangements for his journey, Winchelsey set out with an imposing retinue. In his journey from London to Carlisle he occupied about

---

[1] Fœdera, ii., 883-971.   [2] Ibid., i., 907.

twenty days. When Edward entered Galloway, he proposed to join him, but finding that parties of armed Scotsmen were sweeping the country, he determined to proceed cautiously. Finding that the English army had returned from Irvine to Dumfriesshire, he despatched to the king two of his retinue, who, after encountering some difficulties in their progress, gave notice of his approach. Not uninformed of his purpose, Edward urged Winchelsey to postpone his advance till his escort was joined by that of the queen, who was also journeying northward. But the legate unheeding the suggestion, hastened to Edward at the castle of Carlaverock, which he reached by the Solway towards the end of August.

To the archbishop, as the Pope's legate, Edward gave a solemn audience in presence of the Prince of Wales, and his nobles and knights. In proceeding with his mission, Winchelsey referred to the duty of a reverent submission to the head of the Church, remarking that Jerusalem would not fail to protect her citizens, and to cherish those by whom she was obeyed. To the king he then handed the Papal bull, which, on being read, proved of the following purport :—" Only to the Holy See did Scotland owe allegiance, inasmuch as it had been miraculously converted to the Christian faith by the relics of Saint Andrew." Boniface then charged Edward with violating the liberties of Scotland, both ecclesiastical and civil, since neither he nor any of his predecessors "held over the kingdom any actual superiority." " Your father, Henry, king of England, of glorious memory," proceeded the Pope, " when in the wars between him and Simon de Montfort, he requested the assistance of Alexander III., king of Scotland, acknowledged by letters-patent that he had received such assistance not as due to him, but as a special favour. And when you yourself invited King Alexander to attend your coronation, you made the request as a matter of favour and not of right. Further, when the king of Scotland did homage to you for his lands in Tynedale and Penrith, he publicly protested that his homage was rendered not for his kingdom, but for these lands only, since as king of Scotland he was independent. Again, when King Alexander died leaving an heiress to his crown, a grand-daughter in her minority, the wardship of this infant was not conferred upon you, which it would have been had you been lord superior, but was given to certain nobles of Scotland chosen for the office." Referring to the preliminary negotiations for the projected marriage between the Prince of Wales and the Maiden of Norway, Pope Boniface reminded Edward that he had in these acknowledged the independence of Scotland. Next, in the matter of his arbitrating in the competition for the crown, he had declared to the Scottish nobility, who repaired to his court, that he received their attendance as a favour, and not as a right. Boniface set forth that if any innovations had lately been made on the rights and liberties of Scotland, with consent of a divided nobility, or of the person to whom Edward had committed the charge of the kingdom, these ought not to subsist, having been extorted by force and intimidation. The Pope then exhorted Edward, in the name of God, to discharge from prison the bishops of Glasgow and Sodor, and other ecclesiastical persons whom he had incarcerated, and to remove all officers whom he had delegated to govern the nation under him. In conclusion, Boniface added that if Edward had any pretensions to the whole or any part of Scotland, his proctors should be sent to him, and he would determine according to justice.[1]

---

[1] Add. MS. 15,365, f. 63, British Museum;   Knighton, p. 2529; Prynne's History, Edward Fœdera, vol. i., part ii., p. 907, new ed. ;   I., p. 883.

On hearing the Pope's letter, Edward expressed himself violently. "I will not," he said, "be silent or at rest, either for Mount Sion or for Jerusalem ; but as long as there is breath in my nostrils, will defend what all the world knows to be my right." [1] After a pause he requested the archbishop to retire, that he might consult the nobles. And at the succeeding conference he was reminded that a rupture with the Pope would be inconvenient, since the province of Gascony still remained in his hands, Boniface not having yet decided as to whom it should belong. When Winchelsey was recalled, Edward therefore addressed him in these conciliatory terms :—"My Lord Archbishop, you have delivered to me on the part of my superior and reverend father, the Pope, a certain admonition touching the state and realm of Scotland. As, however, it is the custom of England, in matters which relate to the state affairs, to take advice from all who are concerned, and since the present business not only affects Scottish affairs but the rights of England—and since many prelates, earls, barons, and great men are now absent, without whose advice I am unwilling, finally, to reply to my Holy Father, it is my purpose, as soon as possible, to hold a council of my nobility, and by their joint advice and determination, to transmit an answer to his Holiness by my own messengers." [2]

In October Edward closed his campaign, granting a truce to the Scots to continue till Pentecost, which he alleged proceeded solely from his desire to gratify his ally and brother-in-law, the king of France.

[1] Walsingham, p. 78.

[2] Patent, 28 Edward I., m. 3 ; Fordun a Hearne, p. 983 ; Wyntoun, vol. ii., p. 104.

CHAPTER VI.

FROM THE TRUCE OF OCTOBER 1300 TO THE REDUCTION OF STIRLING CASTLE IN 1304.

HIS truce with the guardians having been duly ratified, Edward issued letters-patent at Dumfries on the 30th October 1300, by which he disbanded his army. But the disembodiment was incomplete, for on the plea that he was under the necessity of watching the movements of the Scots, he retained of his force, one hundred men-at-arms, also three hundred foot soldiers, whom he instructed under one of his Wardens to inspect the several castles and fortresses so as to ascertain whether the truce was being observed. He also ruled that such English garrisoned strongholds as were beleaguered by the Scots at the date of the truce should continue to steadily hold out. He also commissioned Sir John Segrave to plant with English troops the castles of Roxburgh, Edinburgh, Linlithgow, Stirling, and Kirkintilloch ; Sir Robert de Clifford, the castles of Carlaverock, Dumfries, Dalswinton, and Tibbers; Sir John de St John, the castles of Lochmaben and Buittle; Sir Henry de Beaumont, the castle of Jedburgh; Patric, Earl of March, the castle of Dunbar; Sir John de Vaux, the castle of Dirleton; and Sir Aymer de Valence, the castle of Selkirk. Further, he instructed the English residents at Perth, Dundee, Ayr, and Banff, to remain in these places till the expiry of the truce, and the anglicised Scots outside the castles, which had not yielded to the guardians, to exhibit a good front to the enemy.[1]

To conciliate the Pope and gratify the clergy, he released from imprisonment the Bishop of Glasgow, but only after he had at the abbey of Holme Cultram renewed his allegiance.[2]

Edward now convened a parliament to meet him at Lincoln on the 20th of January 1300-1, expressing in his letters of summons his strong desire that measures should be passed for upholding the dignity of England in opposition to the representations which, on behalf of the Scots, had been made at the court of Rome. And in order that the regal and national honour might be properly sustained, he requested the universities of Oxford and Cambridge to delegate as their representatives their most expert civilians, whom he specially expected to testify as to the supremacy of the English crown over that of Scotland. He also instructed the heads of religious houses to attend the parliament provided with such excerpts from their chronicles as might serve to indicate the alleged domination.[3] To gain favour with the people, Edward also summoned to the parliament at Lincoln representatives from one hundred and thirty-seven cities and boroughs. For the entertainment of the members he largely provided, by commanding the sheriffs of Lincolnshire

---

[1] Tower Miscellaneous Rolls, No. $\frac{45}{7}$.   [2] Fœdera, ii., 867.

[3] *Ibid.*, iii., 146.

to procure for this purpose four hundred quarters of corn, four hundred quarters of barley, and one thousand quarters of oats and hay, one hundred cattle, three hundred sheep, and one hundred pigs. For the use of the members the sheriffs were also to provide four hundred horses.

When Parliament met, Edward in the first instance endeavoured to gain the favour of his barons. He approved the reports of the committee on disforesting, and in the matter of perambulation allowed a precedence to the earls. He then addressed the assembly. At the court of Rome, he said, an attempt had been made to degrade the monarchy by depriving the sovereign of his privileges. Then causing the Pope's letter to be read, he remarked that his law-officers had prepared an overwhelming rejoinder, but he desired that before its transmission it should obtain the sanction and authority of Parliament. After much debate as to the form of procedure, Rishanger, the clerk, was authorised to formulate the parliamentary answer. His missive was vehemently assertive. Commending the Roman Church on the caution she exercised in maintaining national rights, he, in name of the Parliament, declared that the letter from the Holy See contained in relation to Scotland new and untenable propositions. The communication proceeded that a superiority over Scotland by the English sovereign was recognised throughout the world, and had been duly exercised in the removal and appointment of its rulers, while the various acts of homage granted by the kings of Scotland to those of England were not, as had been asserted, for private fiefs, but for crown and kingdom. The Treaty of Brigham, in which the Scots asserted a separate nationality, Rishanger continued, was virtually an act of homage, inasmuch as the Scottish Estates approached their lord superior and solemnly rendered fealty.

Embodying a narrative of the competition for the crown, the writer stigmatised Baliol's assertion of independence as an act of wicked effrontery and unnatural rebellion. By the pen of Rishanger Parliament next charged the Scots with perpetrating outrages on English religious houses, every act of clemency being carefully concealed. In conclusion, the secretary of the Lincoln Parliament presented to the Pope the following remonstrance :—" By a custom which has been inviolably observed, a privilege arising from the pre-eminence of the regal dignity, the kings of England have never pleaded, or been bound to plead, respecting their rights in regard to Scotland, or any other their temporal rights, before any judge, ecclesiastical or secular; wherefore, having diligently considered the letters of his Holiness, it was the common and united resolve, and by the grace of God shall for the future remain such, that with respect to the rights of his kingdom of Scotland, our lord the king shall not answer judicially before the Pope, nor submit to his judgment, nor suffer his right to be brought into question by any inquiry. . . . . Neither do we permit the king to do, or attempt to do, such strange and unheard-of things, even if he were willing so far to forget his royal rights. Wherefore we reverently and humbly entreat your Holiness to permit the king to enjoy his rights in peace, without disturbance or diminution." [1] This manifesto, dated 15th May 1301, and bearing the seals of one hundred and four of the nobility and barons, was dispatched to Rome by a special embassy, accompanied by a letter to the Pope from Edward personally. In that letter Edward asserted as veracious the following fables :—In the time of the prophets Eli and Samuel, there lived an illustrious person named Brutus, who, on

[1] Fœdera, ii., 097, or 875, now ed.; Chapter House (Scots Documents), Box 1, No. 8; Box 100, No. 118. A translation of the text into French is printed in Palgrave, pp. 231-234.

the destruction of Troy, quitted the city along with a band of
noble Trojans, and having put to sea, at length discovered the
island of Albion, then tenanted by giants. Brutus smote the
giants, and in his honour his followers designated the captured
island Bruton, or Britain. They also reared the town of Trino-
vantum, afterwards called London. Upon his three sons Brutus
afterwards settled his possessions, giving England to Locrin the
eldest; Albany, or Scotland, to Albanac, the second; and to
Camber, the third son, Cambria, or Wales. At Troy, Edward
proceeded, it was the invariable practice that the eldest son and
his line should bear rule over the younger brothers and their
descendants; hence Locrin maintained a superiority over his
brothers, his descendants continuing in the island to hold supremacy. Edward next introduces King Arthur, who, as Locrin's
representative, he describes as punishing the Scots for an act of
turbulence by displacing their king and appointing in his stead
Anselm, one of his followers, while to Arthur Anselm rendered
homage for his kingdom. As to the Pope's claim to the
possession of Scotland, founded on the miraculous relics of Saint
Andrew, Edward held that the right was negatived by another
miracle, the particulars of which he thus detailed:—King
Athelstane of England overcame the Scots in a battle fought
under the auspices of St John of Beverley, and on completing
his victory he prayed, through St John's intervention, that he
might receive a visible token whereby future generations might
be assured that the Scots were actually subject to English rule.
His prayer was answered, for while he stood in front of a rock
at Dunbar, and struck it with his sword, he made an impression
which proved to be of the precise length of an ell measure. And
the truth of this miracle was attested by an existing weekly
service in St John's church at Beverley. But the Athelstane

miracle, Edward is careful to remark, he set forth not as an answer to any plea, but simply to relieve the conscience of his Holiness.[1]

With a view to the resumption of the war, Edward on the 1st March issued summonses to the Earl of Lincoln, the Earl of Lancaster, the Earl of Gloucester and Hertford, the Earl of Arundel, and twenty other barons and knights, charging them to meet him at Berwick on the 24th of June. He specially commanded the Earl of Lincoln to attend with a superior force, since he proposed to grant him the privilege of accompanying the Prince of Wales, who, being now in his sixteenth year, was to enjoy the distinction of "taming the pride of the Scots," by entering their country from Carlisle.[2] For his own troops at Berwick, Edward levied supplies in the counties of Essex, Norfolk, and Suffolk, and from the towns of Derby, York, and Yarmouth; he also provided a strong fleet to meet him at various harbours on the coast. For the contingent under the Prince of Wales, he gave orders that supplies should be furnished from Lancaster and Chester, also from the principality of Wales.[3] And on the 3d April he commanded his Justiciary, and Chancellor, and Treasurer in Ireland, to provide from that country for the use of his army 3000 quarters of wheat, 3000 quarters of oats, 2000 quarters of malt, 500 quarters of beans and pease, 200 casks of wine, 10,000 hard fish and 5 lasts of herrings. Of this supply one-half was to be shipped for Skinburness, the other for a port in Arran.[4]

In a letter to his English chancellor, John de Langton, dated the 25th of April, Edward informs him that the parlance on Scottish affairs, which was to have been held at Canterbury between his people and those of the king of France, was, much

---

[1] Fœdera, ii., 883, or new ed., vol. i., part ii., 932; Tyrrel, ii., 147.

[2] Close, 29 Edward I., m. 15 dorso.

[3] Chancery Miscellaneous Portfolios, No. 1⁄2⁄3.

[4] Patent, 29 Edward I., m. 19.

to his advantage, broken off. He then charges the chancellor to summon the Earl Marshal to prepare for joining him in Scotland; also to amend the letters to the Pope, as circumstances might justify.[1] By public letters issued on the 12th of May, he gave orders that 12,000 men should meet him at Berwick on Midsummer day—these to be levied in Shropshire, also in the counties of Stafford, Hereford, Worcester, Gloucester, Nottingham, Derby, York, and Northumberland.[2]

To solemnize his acts, Edward now made pilgrimages to the shrine of St Thomas à Becket and other holy places, and shortly after Midsummer he reached Berwick. There on enumeration his force was found to consist of 7000 foot soldiers and 40 light horsemen or "hobelars;" together with a body of foresters from the counties of Roxburgh and Selkirk. All had practised as archers, with the exception of twenty persons, who used the crossbow. In his train he also included a small body of masons and miners; and in order to the ignominious destruction of inconvenient prisoners, he had attached to each of the companies a "logeman" or executioner. His body-guard consisted of twenty persons.[3]

From Berwick Edward detached a party of troops to occupy the castle of Bonkyl, belonging to Sir John Stewart, brother of the Stewart.[4] His progress northward is noted in the Pay Roll. Subsequent to the 14th of July he marched by the valley of the Tweed to Selkirk, where he encamped on the 25th. He reached Peebles on the 8th August where he also rested. At Peebles on the 10th August, he granted to Sir Aymer de Valence a charter of the barony of Bothwell, which had belonged to the late

---

[1] Privy Seals (Tower), 29 Edward I., file 1.
[2] Patent, 29 Edward I., m. 14.
[3] Exchequer Q. R. Miscellanea (Army), No. ⁷⁄₈.

[4] Chron. Abingdon, quoted in Tyrrel, iii., 148; Trivet, 331, 332; Hemingford, i., 196; Langtoft, ii., 315, 316.

Sir William de Moray.[1] Entering the vale of Clyde, Edward may now have had that encounter with the Scots, which the Minstrel describes as the battle of Biggar.

Early in September Edward learned from Sir Robert de Tilliol, his warden at Lochmaben, that Sir John de Soulis and the Earl of Buchan were posted at Loudoun; also that Sir Simon Fraser, Sir Alexander de Abernethy, and Sir Herbert de Morham were in command of a strong force at Stonehouse on the Avon.[2] On the 10th of September, De Tilliol further reported that Sir John de Soulis and Sir Ingram de Umfraville had, with 240 men-at-arms and upwards of 7000 footmen, burned the town of Lochmaben, and made an attack upon the castle; they had also marched to Annan, and there obtaining supplies were now resting at Dalswinton, *en route* for Nithsdale and Galloway.[3] Alarmed by the unexpected intelligence, Edward commanded Sir Robert Hastang to make an immediate attack, which in a despatch from Roxburgh, on the 13th September, he promised to do.[4] But the English garrison at Berwick mutinied for want of pay, and though money was sent promptly, the leaders of the revolt continued to evince a gloomy discontent.[5]

In fulfilment of his mission, the Prince of Wales marched at the end of June from Carlisle to Dumfries, and from thence into Galloway. His further movements are unreported till the 21st of September, when Edward was, in a despatch from Sir William de Durham, his warden at Peebles, informed that a spy had arrived from Nithsdale, with tidings that the Scots had in course of retreat been on the preceding Sunday at "les Kellys," and would on the next day arrive at Glencairn. To

---

[1] Chapter House (Scots Documents), Box 93, No. 1.

[2] From original in Public Record Office.

[3] Royal Letters, No. 3415.

[4] *Ibid.*, No. 2585.

[5] Chancery Miscellaneous Portfolios, No. $\frac{41}{100}$.

Edward, Sir William further communicated a report, that the Scots having heard that the Prince of Wales was in pilgrimage to St Ninian's image at Whithorn, had removed the image to New Abbey, but that it had returned miraculously. At the close of his despatch, Sir William complains that money was lacking ; he also suggests that the troops should be paid daily.[1]

On the 1st October, the Prince of Wales had granted to him, fifty-nine casks of red wine for his use at the castles of Ayr, Turnberry, and Lochryan.[2] On the following day the Earl of Lincoln, writing on his behalf from the Water of Cree, congratulates the king on the surrender of Bothwell Castle, and begs that if the Castle of Inverkip is taken, it may, in anticipation of the Prince's arrival, be duly garrisoned.[3] Writing from Carlisle on the 5th, the Prince informed his father that he was in good estate, adding that the messenger would orally communicate the wishes of his attendants.[4] In reality the Prince was retreating from a formidable peril, since in an undated letter, which seems to have been despatched on the 5th, Sir Montesin de Noillan, constable of Ayr, also others upholding the English rule in Kyle and Cunningham, communicated to Edward that on Tuesday the 3d a body of 400 armed Scots had attacked Turnberry Castle, and had also attempted to reduce the new castle of Ayr. By the writers, Edward was therefore begged to send succours, since the Scots had collected in such force that they could be repelled only with difficulty. From the Earl of March, who was intrusted with the keeping of the district, the reporters added, no intelligence had been received. Not long afterwards, the earl with a powerful

---

[1] Tower Miscellaneous Rolls, No. $\frac{452}{5}$.

[2] Chancery Miscellaneous Portfolios, No. $\frac{1}{1}$.

[3] Royal Letters, No. 2635.

[4] Chancery Miscellaneous Portfolios, No. $\frac{1}{1}$; Royal Letters, No. 2635 ; Tower Miscellaneous Rolls, No. $\frac{452}{4}$.

force relieved the English garrison at Turnberry, and he, on the 21st February 1301-2, recommended that subsidies should be granted to Sir Montesin de Noillan and others who, in defending the castle, had suffered loss.[1] In his progress, Edward rested his army at Glasgow on the 22d of August, and reached Dunipace on the 29th of the same month.

By a letter from Sir Robert Hastang, dated at Roxburgh on the 30th September, Edward was informed that the writer had sent out scouts to warn the country, and that Sir Alexander de Balliol of Cavers, custodier of Selkirk Forest, had undertaken when the Scots returned from Galloway, to give early information as to their route.[2]

In October Edward planted his troops at Linlithgow and Falkirk.[3] To his Treasurer in Scotland he, writing from Falkirk on the 20th October, requested a supply of materials for constructing crossbows to be used at Linlithgow.[4] Intending to pass the winter at Linlithgow, he there erected a residence.[5]

Meanwhile an English fleet under command of Sir Hugh Bisset cruised from Bute to Kintyre.[6] And on the 17th November Sir John de St John received instructions to provide a hundred men-at-arms to make forays on the Scots in Galloway; while the castles of Lochmaben and Dumfries were each garrisoned with men-at-arms, besides one hundred foot soldiers.[7] Addressing, on the 21st November, the Barons of Exchequer in Ireland, Edward instructed them to forward to the Prince of Wales for use by the garrisons of Lochmaben, Dumfries, Ayr, and Linlithgow, large supplies of wheat, malt, and small and great fish.[8]

[1] Chancery Miscellaneous Portfolios, No. ⅘.
[2] *Ibid.*, No. ⅘.
[3] Exchequer Q. R. Memoranda, 30 Edward I., m. 10 dorso.
[4] Chancery Miscellaneous Portfolios, ⅘, ⅘.
[5] Tower Miscellaneous Rolls, No. 474.
[6] *Ibid.*
[7] Exchequer Q. R. Memoranda, 30 Edward I., m. 6.
[8] Patent, 30 Edward I., m. 36.

On the 7th December, he had large quantities of hay shipped at Newcastle for Blackness near Linlithgow; while on the 1st of January, 1400 foot soldiers, brought from England, were added to his force.[1]

The Prince of Wales joined his father at Linlithgow,[2] prior to the 30th of December, and on the 1st of January 1301-2, his step-mother, the Queen, handed him a golden goblet, in guerdon of her favour.[3]

Edward found that his campaign was attended with a serious cost. In Exchequer memoranda, dated 8th October 1301, the weekly expenses of the royal section of the army are noted as amounting to £751, 14s. 4d., apart from the pay which remained due to certain military leaders.[4] Not improbably the Prince of Wales incurred an equal expenditure.

Owing to a rigorous winter, Edward experienced at Linlithgow much personal discomfort, and his losses included a large number of valuable horses.[5] Quitting Linlithgow early in February, he marched southward. To his troops he made known that he was attended by a chaplain and chapel-clerks,[6] and that he bore with him in a coffer, a purse of silk, which contained a thorn of the Redeemer's crown, formerly the treasured possession of the Duke of Cornwall.[7]

At Roxburgh Castle on the 12th February, Edward obtained pledges from the wardens of the castles of Edinburgh, Roxburgh, Berwick, Jedburgh, Linlithgow, and Ayr, that they would defend these fortresses till the ensuing Pentecost. He also bound Sir

---

[1] Patent, 30 Edward I., m. 36; Close, 30 Edward I., m. 18 dorso.

[2] Chancery Miscellaneous Portfolios, No. $\frac{41}{166}$.

[3] Exchequer Q. R. Miscellanea (Wardrobe), No. $\frac{32}{26}$.

[4] Exchequer Q. R. Memoranda, 30 Edward I., m. 6.

[5] *Ibid.* (Army), No. $\frac{22}{27}$.

[6] *Ibid.*, m. 6.

[7] Exchequer Q. R. Miscellaneous (Wardrobe), No. $\frac{32}{25}$.

Alexander de Balliol to hold out Selkirk Forest against the Scots, and for that purpose to provide 1600 foot soldiers; also to rear in the Forest a peel or stronghold.[1] At Roxburgh he granted to Sir John Fitz Marmaduke, constable of the castle of Bothwell, the keeping of Renfrewshire or Strathgryffe.[2] And at Morpeth on the 23d February, he commanded the Earl of Ulster and other magnates in Ireland to provide for use in warfare against the Scots 500 men-at-arms on barbed horses; also 10,000 foot soldiers.[3]

Amidst these hostile manifestations, Edward had not discontinued his negotiations with Philip of France as to a prolongation of the Scottish peace. On the 14th October 1301, he definitely proposed a renewal of the truce[4]; and this was followed by the treaty of Asnieres, in which it was included.[5] At the conference at Tournay, which followed soon afterwards, Edward's commissioners agreed that hostilities against the Scots should cease till the 30th of November 1302. This treaty Edward approved at Linlithgow on the 26th of January 1301-2, when he also empowered his commissioners[6] to meet with those of France at the ensuing Easter in order to its full confirmation. To the treaty he subjoined a minute, in which he protested against the act of the French commissioners, who had described Baliol by the title of King; he further objected to the Scots being described as the "allies" of France.[7] Against the entire truce, he, at Devizes, on the 30th April, publicly protested.[8]

---

[1] Exchequer Q. R. Miscellanea (Army), No. $\frac{27}{27}$, $\frac{27}{57}$; Chancery Miscellaneous Portfolios, No. $\frac{4}{5}$.

[2] Exchequer Q. R. Miscellanea (Army), No. $\frac{27}{15}$.

[3] Privy Seals (Tower), 30 Edward I., File 3.

[4] Fœdera, new ed., i., 936.

[5] Chapter House (Scots Documents), Box 92, No. 34; Box 100, No. 127. Chancery Miscellaneous Portfolios, No. $\frac{41}{135}$.

[6] The English Commissioners were the Bishop of Chester, the Earl of Lincoln, the Archdeacon of Richmond, and John de Berwick, Canon of York (Chancery Miscellaneous Portfolios, No. $\frac{41}{11}$).

[7] Patent, 30 Edward I., m. 32, and schedule appended.

[8] Prynne, p. 876.

By means of Bishop Lamberton, Philip, on the 6th April 1302, communicated with the guardians and other magnates of Scotland in these terms :—" Philip, etc., to these noble persons, Robert de Brus, Earl of Carrick, and John Comyn the younger, guardians of the kingdom of Scotland, in the name of the illustrious King John, and to the bishops, abbots, priors, earls, barons, and other magnates, and the community, our chosen allies, etc. With sincere regard have we received your envoys, John, abbot of Jedburgh, and Sir John Wishart,[1] and have been intensely distressed by the evils which have malignantly been thrust upon your country. To your loyalty do we commend your illustrious king ; and, approving your brilliant valour in defence of your country, we entreat you to honourably persevere. And, in respect of the aid which is asked of us, we are not unmindful of the ancient league between your king and us, and we are carefully pondering on the ways and means to be employed on your behalf. In regard to these, considering the dangers of the road and the risks which occasionally chance to letters, we have expressed our views orally to William (Lamberton), bishop of St Andrews, who is entitled to full credence."[2]

Philip's letter, which was delivered by Lamberton to the Scottish guardians, reached not long afterwards the English Treasury. The transmitter was probably the young Earl of Carrick, who, disheartened by Philip's adhesion to the cause of Baliol, may thus have sought to advance himself by covertly communicating with Edward. Of this act there seems to be some degree of evidence in the fact that, within twenty-two days after the date of Philip's letter, Bruce re-approached Edward as

---

[1] Sir John Wishart was proprietor of Pitarrow and Conveth in the Mearns, and nephew of Bishop Wishart. At Elgin, on the 29th July 1296, he swore fealty to Edward, but in reality he did not abandon the national cause.

[2] Chancery Miscellaneous Portfolios, No. 11.

a homager. Prior to the 28th April, he is named as having come with some of his Carrick tenants to the king's peace,[1] while at that date Edward appears as granting "to the tenants of his liege Robert de Brus, Earl of Carrick, those lands in Cumberland lately escheated for rebellion."[2]

Having drawn apart the two guardians, Edward was, in relation to Scottish affairs, not less successful at the Court of Rome. For, on the 13th August 1302, the Pope Boniface VIII. charged Bishop Wishart, in an admonitory letter, to promptly desist from further opposing himself to English rule. To Wishart he wrote thus : "I have heard with astonishment that you, as *a rock of offence* and *a stone of stumbling*, have been the prime instigator and promoter of the fatal disputes which prevail between the Scottish nation and Edward, king of England, my dearly beloved son in Christ, to the displeasing of the Divine Majesty, to the hazard of your own honour and salvation, and to the inexpressible detriment of the kingdom of Scotland." "If these things are so," continued Boniface, "you have rendered yourself odious to God and man, and it befits you, by your most earnest endeavours after peace, to strive to obtain forgiveness." Boniface at the same time charged the other Scottish bishops to be at peace with the English king, menacing them in the event of disobedience with the apostolic malediction.[3]

To alienate from the Scots the support of Philip of France was Edward's next concern. Hitherto he had evinced his sympathy with the Flemings in their resistance to France, but he now offered to discontinue interesting himself in Flemish affairs, on condition that Philip withdrew his countenance from

[1] Tower Miscellaneous Rolls, No. $\frac{4.59}{0.0}$.   [2] Close, 30 Edward I., m. 13.
[3] Fœdera, new edit., i., 972.

the Scots. And in order to a speedy settlement of affairs he, on the 15th of August, intimated to Master John del Hospital, clerk, and Sir Gobert de Helleville, ambassadors of France, that up to the 18th of November he would permit any six Scotsmen named by them to pass through England to the court of France.[1] As covertly arranged, Philip's ambassadors named those Scotsmen whose absence from the kingdom Edward held as convenient to his purpose. These were Bishop Lamberton, Mathew de Crambeth, bishop of Dunkeld, John, Earl of Buchan, James the Steward, Sir John Soulis, Sir Ingram Umfraville, and Sir William Balliol.[2] Meanwhile, before the Scottish ambassadors arrived, a truce between England and France was arranged at Amiens on the 25th November, in which Edward, in enumerating his allies, omitted the name of the Earl of Flanders, while Philip in like manner excluded all reference to Baliol and the Scots. In the final treaty of peace, subscribed at Paris on the 20th May 1303, a similar course was followed. And now having, as he believed, deprived the Scots of every prop and refuge, and the truce being about to expire, Edward proceeded to prepare for their complete discomfiture.

Amidst the general defection in regard to Scottish interests, Wallace remained firm. Under his leadership, had Edward's recent expedition failed of its purpose, and the English king had strong reason to apprehend that on renewing hostilities he would, at the hands of the same skilful leader, be further repelled. Whether, as has been popularly alleged, he sought to induce the hero of the field of Stirling to abandon the patriotic cause, cannot certainly be known, but in reviewing Edward's usual

[1] Exchequer Q. R. Memoranda, 30 Edward I., m. 12.

[2] Fœdera, vol. ii., 929 ; Maitland, i., 461.

[3] Close, 31 Edward I., m. 19 dorso ; Fœdera, new edit., vol. i., part ii., p. 947 ; Tyrrel, vol. iii., 152.

[4] Exchequer Q. R. Miscellanea (Army), Nos. 11, 27, 22.

policy, it is not improbable that he made the attempt. And in this light Henry's episode as to Edward's queen holding a colloquy with the Patriot, and entreating his forbearance, may rest on an actual incident, since Edward may have induced Queen Margaret to send commissioners to Wallace in name of her brother, the French king, at the time, when through the interposition of Philip, a truce between Edward and the Scots was in active progress.[1]

Shortly after the reception of Philip's letter and message in April 1302, Wallace proceeded to France, but, finding that Philip had changed his policy, he forthwith returned to Scotland. According to the Minstrel, he on his return sailed up the Firth of Tay, and by means of a small boat effected a landing at the mouth of the Earn.[2] Here he was joined by his associates, among whom was Sir Simon Fraser, who, prior to the 14th of August, had renounced Edward's homage, and returned to the national cause.[3]

Soon after Fraser's desertion, Edward committed to prison Sir Alexander de Balliol, keeper of Selkirk Forest, on the plea that he had not, according to order, reared a peel in the forest. On renewing his homage, and granting his son as a hostage, he was afterwards liberated.[4]

Observing that the Scots were instituting a system of defence, Edward instructed that a course of desultory warfare, such as in the last campaign they had exercised against his troops, should now be directed against themselves. Accordingly, in a despatch dated the 14th of September, Sir John de Segrave, his lieutenant, expressed his readiness to make forays ; and on the 29th

---

[1] Henry, B. viii., ll. 1215-1496.
[2] *Ibid.*, B. xi., ll. 329, 330.
[3] Exchequer Q. R. Miscellanea (Army), Nos. 14, 27, 23.
[4] Tower Miscellaneous Rolls, No. 450 ; Close, 31 Edward I., m. 14.

of the same month Edward ordered him to pursue his intention thereanent, both at Stirling and Kirkintilloch.[1]

Writing from Roxburgh on the 7th January 1302-3, Sir William le Latimer, "le pere," informed the English chancellor that he and his company were in daily peril by the Scots.[2] And on the 20th January Edward instructed Sir Ralph Fitz William to render effective support to Sir John Segrave, his lieutenant, since the Scots had taken possession of several castles and towns, and unless forthwith checked were likely to penetrate into England. He also charged twenty-six of the Scottish barons to strengthen Segrave's force with horse and foot. In his despatches he intimated that he would forthwith assume the command in person, and that Sir Ralph de Manton, his cofferer, would make the necessary payments.[3]

In February 1302-3 Segrave assembled at Berwick an army of 20,000 men, including a large body of men-at-arms. He then moved northward in three divisions, leading the first personally, while he placed the second in command of Sir Ralph de Manton, and the third under the leadership of Sir Robert de Neville, who had acquired distinction in the Welsh wars.[4]

As the first division lay encamped at Roslin, on the morning of the 24th February, a youth called out that the Scots were near. Led by Wallace, assisted by Sir Simon Fraser, about 8000 foot soldiers had, after a rapid night march, arrived from Biggar, and so unexpectedly, that they captured in bed Segrave's son and brother.[5] A general engagement followed, when Segrave was

---

[1] Exchequer Q. R. Miscellanea (Army), No. $\frac{2}{4}\frac{7}{5}$; Royal Letters, No. 3116.

[2] Chancery Miscellaneous Portfolios, No. 11.

[3] Close, 31 Edward I., m. 18 dorso ; Fœdera, vol. i., new ed., part ii., p. 947.

[4] Wyntoun, vol. ii., p. 111 ; Hemingford, 197 ; Trivet, 336 ; Fœdera, vol. i., new ed., p. 608.

[5] Tyrrel, vol. iii., p. 153 ; Tyrrel, quoting Walsingham and the "Chron. Abingdonense," distinctly asserts that Wallace headed the Scots at the battle of Roslin (see Henry the Minstrel, B. vi., ll. 341).

repulsed and himself severely wounded. Among the prisoners secured by Wallace were sixteen knights and thirty esquires. As the second division came up the struggle was renewed, with a second victory to the Scots. The third division was defeated in turn, while Sir Ralph de Manton and Sir Robert de Neville were both found among the slain.[1]

The sequel of the defeat at Roslin has been differently reported by English chroniclers. According to Hemingford and Trivet, Sir Robert de Neville had, with his division, remained behind to attend mass, and on coming up, they, in a manner, repelled the Scots, and recovered many of the prisoners—while none of the third division were killed, or wounded, or taken captive.[2] Langtoft relates that Sir Ralph de Manton was captured by Sir Simon Fraser, and as he begged his life on account of his priestly office, received the answer, " This laced hauberk is no priestly habit. Where is thy alb, or hood ? You have often robbed us of our lawful earnings, and done us wanton wrong, and it is now our turn to sum up the account and exact payment." Then, adds Langtoft, Fraser despatched his prisoner—first striking off his hands, and then severing his head from his body.[3]

By the defeat at Roslin, Edward was bitterly exasperated, and in order to an effective renewal of the Scottish war, proceeded to disentangle himself from some continental complications. In terms of a proclamation which he issued on the 9th April, the northern and midland counties contributed 9500 foot soldiers, and these, on the 12th May, assembled at Roxburgh.[4]

---

[1] Fordun, xii., 2 ; Wyntoun, vol. ii., p. 117.

[2] Hemingford, i., 198 ; Trivet, 336 ; Matthew Westminster, 445 ; Walsingham, 87.

[3] Langtoft, vol. ii., pp. 319, 320. Sir Ralph de Manton had borrowed a black "bausan" horse for the Scottish expedition, which being destroyed in the king's service at Roslin, compensation for the loss was charged against the king (Exchequer Q. R. Miscellanea (Army), No. $\frac{3}{1}\frac{9}{1}$).

[4] Patent, 31 Edward I., m. 28.

To the same muster, the Earl of Carrick was expected to bring from Carrick and Galloway 1000 men, Sir John Siward from Nithsdale 300 foot, and the Earl of Angus a body of men-at-arms and 300 foot.[1] From Ireland the Earl of Ulster brought a contingent of 500 men.[2]

There were other preparations. At Lynn Regis were constructed two portable bridges, to be used in spanning the Forth. And a fleet of thirty vessels laden with provisions and war engines were despatched to the Scottish coast.[3]

Arranging his army in two divisions, Edward gave the command of the first to the Prince of Wales, who was expected to enter Scotland by Carlisle. With the second division he marched northward, by way of Morpeth,[4] and on the 21st of May he was joined at Roxburgh by his northern contingent.[5] On the 4th June he reached Edinburgh, and on the 6th rested at Linlithgow. From thence he marched to Stirling, and crossing the Forth by means of his portable bridges, arrived at Perth on the 10th June.[6]

At Perth Edward remained till the middle of July; he then marched to Dundee, and from thence to Montrose. He now summoned Sir Thomas Maule to surrender the castle of Brechin, and being met with a defiance, he waited at Montrose the landing of a portion of his fleet, which bore his war engines. At the commencement of the siege Maule evinced a daring spirit of resistance, by wiping with a towel the *débris* raised by a stone thrown into the stronghold. And when soon afterwards, on being severely injured by a missile, he was, by a member

---

[1] Exchequer Q. R. Miscellanea (Army), No. ²₁ˢ.

[2] Add. MSS., British Museum, 8835.

[3] Chancery Miscellaneous Portfolios, Nos. ⁸₁, ⁴₅, ¹₁, ⁴₁ ; Tower Miscellaneous Rolls, No. ¹⁸²₈.

[4] Prynne, 1015, 1016.

[5] *Ibid.*, 1017.

[6] Privy Seals (Tower), 31 Edward I., File 4 ; Fœdera, ii., 934 ; Hemingford, 205 ; Langtoft, 321 ; Prynne, *passim.*

of his staff, entreated to surrender, he peremptorily expressed his refusal. Dying of his wounds, the garrison capitulated.[1] Into the castle Edward propelled five waggon loads of lead, which he had stripped from the roof of the adjoining cathedral. This damage he made a show of compensating, by granting to the bishop of Brechin the sum of seventeen pounds.[2]

At Brechin Edward was joined by the Prince of Wales. By a course of desultory warfare Wallace had opposed the Prince's entrance into Scotland, and had smitten the English quarters at Annandale and Liddesdale.[3] The Prince had consequently deviated from his intended route, and proceeding to Roxburghshire, afterwards moved northward in the rear of his father. Leaving Kelso on the 26th of May, he reached Linlithgow on the 5th June, and on the 10th rested at Cambuskenneth. On the 22d June he arrived at Dundee, and after spending some time at Perth, reached Arbroath on the 1st of August.[4] From thence he proceeded to Brechin.

By his father instructed to profess a zeal for religion, the Prince contributed a penny daily as an "oblation." He also purchased "The Life of the Blessed Edward," with pictures and in ornate binding, for fifty-eight shillings; and, at his father's request, gave sixty pounds for a pearl-embroidered cope, as a gift to the Cardinal Peter of Spain. But his large income the Prince expended chiefly on his pleasures. At intervals in his northward journey he occupied himself in hunting and falconry, also in practising the game of dice, at which he was usually a loser. Addicted to practical jesting, he threw his fool into the water, much to the injury of his person.

---

[1] Matthew Westminster, 446; Liber Garderobæ, Edward I., fol. 15.

[2] Exchequer Q. R. Miscellanea (Army), No. $\frac{2.3}{6}$.

[3] Patent, 31 Edward I., m. 20.

[4] Prince of Wales' "Household Roll."

To denote the dignity of his rank, a caged lion was borne in his progress.[1]

Resuming his journey northward, Edward, on the 17th of August, sojourned in the castle of Kincardine.[2] At Aberdeen, on the 24th, he from hence proceeded to Banff, which he reached on the 4th of September;[3] he next entered the county of Moray. Reaching Kinloss about the 20th of September, he thence penetrated into Badenoch, where he occupied the castle of Lochindorb, a principal stronghold of the Comyns. There he caused the neighbouring barons and the occupants of the adjacent strongholds to render him homage.[4] Writes Wyntoun,—

> "And owre the Mownth[5] than alsa fast
> Till Lowchyndorbe than strawcht he past ;
> Thare swjowrnand a qwhill he bad
> Quhill he [the] North all wonnyn had."[6]

While at Lochindorb Castle, Edward liberated from the Tower William, Earl of Ross, whom he had there detained as a prisoner since the battle of Dunbar. As the earl had consented to join his standard, he caused him to be brought to Scotland with an honourable retinue, yet not without such a powerful guard as to prevent the possibility of his escape.[7] Returning to Kinloss Edward there remained till the 8th of October, when he removed to the great castle of Kildrummie.[8]

The Scottish deputies lingered at the court of France, being assured by Philip that, though their countrymen were not named

---

[1] Exchequer Q. R. Miscellanea (Wardrobe), No. $\frac{2.9}{2.7}$.

[2] Prynne, 1012.

[3] *Ibid.*, 1021.

[4] Fordun a Hearne, p. 989.

[5] The Mownth is an ancient appellation of the Grampians.

[6] Wyntoun, B. viii., ll. 2682-2685.

[7] Exchequer Q. R. Miscellanea (Army), Nos. $\frac{2.9}{2.5}$, $\frac{2.8}{3}$, $\frac{2.8}{3}$; Close, 31 Edward I., m. 2.

[8] According to Hemingford, Edward scorched the country as far as Caithness, and the statement is repeated by Hardyng.

in his treaty with Edward, he was deeply concerned in their welfare, and would, when his own affairs were fully settled, induce his brother of England to grant them liberty and peace. Satisfied with Philip's assurances, the deputies, on the 25th May 1303, communicated with the guardian, Sir John Comyn, in these words :—" Be not alarmed that the Scots are not mentioned in the treaty. The king of France will immediately send ambassadors to divert Edward from war, and to procure a truce for us, until the two kings can have a personal conference in France. At that conference a peace will be concluded beneficial to our nation. Of this the king of France has himself given us the most positive assurance. It was the opinion both of the English and French counsellors, that our peace would be negotiated with more facility, and on better terms, if the two kings were once united in friendship and affinity [by the marriage of the Prince of Wales and a daughter of Philip]. We therefore beseech and advise you to consent to such a truce as the king of France shall propose. But should Edward not consent, we earnestly entreat you to prosecute the war with vigour and unanimity. Marvel not that none of us return home at present. We would all have willingly returned, but the king of France will have us to remain till we can bring home intelligence of the result of this business; wherefore, for the Lord's sake, despair not. But if ever you acted with resolution, do so now. For, according to the Scriptures, whoso fainteth before he arrive at the goal, runneth in vain. You would much rejoice if you knew what reputation you have acquired all over the world by your late conflict with the English. The French ambassadors will be empowered to treat of peace, as well as to negotiate a truce. This, as the French counsellors inform us, is for the better despatch. Should such a treaty be proposed, conduct yourselves with all caution, lest the enemy overreach you." The deputies conclude by desiring the guardian to continue the pension granted to the wife of Sir John Soulis until their return, "lest her husband, one of their number, hitherto so diligent and faithful, should be drawn off from the public service." In reference to this request, Lord Hailes remarks that the lands of Souliston (now Saltoun) lay in East Lothian, which was then under Edward's control.[1]

Leaving the southern fortresses to the care of his followers, Wallace proceeded northward. Assembling a strong force, probably under the shelter of Torwood Forest, he laid siege to the castle of Stirling, which, having reduced, he placed under the care of Sir William Oliphant. The circumstances of the siege are unrecorded, but we are certainly aware that the castle was garrisoned by the English, when Edward passed through Stirling to Perth early in June; and there is evidence that, prior to the 10th of November, it was in the hands of the Scots.[2] Further, we learn that owing to seriously disquieting tidings which had reached him in the north, Edward returned southward by rapid marches, and on the 1st of November pitched his camp near the abbey of Cambuskenneth.[3] Learning that Wallace had moved to the Dunfermline woods,[4] he hastened thither. Writes Langtoft :—

[1] Fœdera, i., p. 955 ; Chapter House (Scots Documents), Box 14, No. 16. The suggestion of resistance becoming a necessity contained in the letter of the deputies appears clearly to have been due to Bishop Lamberton.

[2] See *postea*.

[3] Prynne, p. 1022.

[4] According to an ancient tradition the Patriot was accompanied to Dunfermline by his widowed mother, who there died, her remains being deposited in the Abbey churchyard. The spot of her interment, forty yards to the north of the Abbey church, and about sixty yards to the north-west of Queen Margaret's tomb, is denoted by a thorn tree. A local historian, writing in 1816, remarks that the tree had reached an immense size, and was seemingly of great age, about fifty years ago, when it was blown down by a storm, and replaced by a stem from the old one (Historical Account of Dunfermline by the Rev. Peter Chalmers, vol. i., p. 174).

> " Turn we now other weys vnto our owen geste,[1]
> And speke of the Waleys, that lies in the foreste.
> In the foreste he lendes [2] of Dounfermelyn,
> He praied alle his frendes, and other of his kyn,
> After that Yole [3] thei wilde biseke Edward,
> That he mot him yelde tille him, in a forward [4]
> That were honorable to kepe wod or beste,
> And with his scrite [5] fulle stable, and seled at the lest,
> To him and alle hise to haf in heritage,
> And non other wise, als terme tyme, and stage,
> Bot als a propire thing, that were conquest tille him.
> Whan thei brouht that tithing,[6] Edward was fulle grim,
> And bitauht him the fende,[7] als his traytoure in loud,
> And ever ilkon [8] his frende that him susteynd or fond.
> Thre hundredth marke he hette unto his warisoun [9]
> That with him so mette, or bring his hede to toun.
> Now flies William Waleis, of pes nought, he spedis
> In mores and mareis [10] with robberie him fedis." [11]

At Dunfermline Edward was joined by his Queen. She had remained at Tynemouth from the end of June till the 26th of September, when, resuming her journey northward, she reached Norham Castle by the middle of November.[12] Remaining at Berwick till the 13th of January,[13] she probably reached Dunfermline about six days afterwards. In token of her approach she sent to her husband the gift of a cup and pitcher of gold.[14]

Familiar with the skill of the Scottish leader, Edward in his camp arrangements at Dunfermline made provision against surprise. In commissioning Sir John Segrave, Sir Robert

[1] Affairs, narrative.

[2] Comes, enters.

[3] Yule, Christmas.

[4] Compact.

[5] Writing.

[6] Tidings.

[7] Called him the devil.

[8] Every one.

[9] Reward.

[10] Muirs and marshes.

[11] Langtoft, ii., 324. That Wallace ever intended to surrender himself to Edward is clearly apocryphal.

[12] Chancery Miscellaneous Portfolios, Nos. $\frac{41}{38}$, $\frac{41}{38}$; Tower Miscellaneous Rolls, Nos. $\frac{450}{61}$, $\frac{450}{43}$, $\frac{450}{32}$; Exchequer Q. R. Memoranda, 32 Edward I., m. 67 dorso.

[13] Tower Miscellaneous Rolls, No. $\frac{450}{47}$.

[14] Exchequer Q. R. Miscellanea (Wardrobe), No. $\frac{23}{23}$.

Clifford, and Sir William le Latimer to make raids, he restricted their movements within two and three leagues, while they became bound to avoid the company of strangers, and to seize all who might offer service, sending them to headquarters.[1]

The hope of Edward's forbearance, which Comyn, the guardian, may have cherished through the letter of the French king, was probably disturbed by the proceedings at his family castle of Lochindorb. And Wallace's activities may have further stimulated him to a sense of his responsibility. From whatever cause, Comyn appeared in arms at Linlithgow in September. At Linlithgow Sir Aymer de Valence commanded a detachment of English troops, and as in his despatch to Edward, dated the 26th of September, he expresses a hope that, by God's help, he may be successful in a certain enterprise, it may be inferred, in the light of subsequent events, that he hoped to induce the guardian to submit himself.[2] In the same letter he represents that for lack of funds military operations were impracticable. On the 9th he writes, that he had borrowed £20 from Sir Alexander Kennedy, canon of Glasgow, and that the treasurer, though repeatedly called upon, had not refunded the loan.[3] In a further despatch, dated the 28th September, De Valence reports that, while the Scots had mustered in great force, the loyal Irish contingent could obtain no food, and that they were consequently packing up their luggage to return home. He also refers to certain negotiations on the part of Sir John Menteith and Sir Alexander Meyners being stopped, owing to the scarcity, adding, that if the country to the south of the Forth was to be retained, supplies should be provided forthwith.[4]

[1] Tower Miscellaneous Rolls, $\frac{4}{5}\frac{5}{9}$.

[2] Chancery Miscellaneous Portfolios, No. 11.

[3] *Ibid.*, No. 11.

[4] From the original in the Public Record Office.

Having, as he believed, made secure against Wallace's escape from Dunfermline Forest, Edward proceeded to arrange for the recovery of Stirling Castle. On the 10th of November he instructed his sheriff at Edinburgh to send by sea to Inverkeithing, *en route* for Stirling, sixty carpenters and two hundred ditchers. But the impecuniosity of Edward's paymaster led to a reply, written on the sheriff's behalf, in which Edward was informed that skilful workmen would not proceed to Stirling unless borne hither by force, since their wages for work done at Linlithgow had not been satisfied. Edward was indignant, and writing to the sheriff from Dunfermline on the 21st November, he repeats his order, adding, that if carpenters could not be found at Edinburgh, they should be brought from Haddington or other parts.[1]

Negotiations with Comyn for his submission to Edward's authority, which began at Linlithgow, were systematically carried on. But the guardian, though personally willing to accept the English rule, was indisposed to occupy the position of one who had proved unfaithful to his country. With a body of troops the Prince of Wales remained at Perth, and it was concerted between Comyn and Sir Aymer de Valence that the former should move towards Perth with an army, while the latter should offer terms of peaceful accommodation. Accordingly, when Comyn drew near the town of Perth on the 22d of December,[2] De Valence approached him as soliciting terms. These were embodied in the following proposals :—

" 1. In regard to the fortresses, it is the King's intention that these should be kept at the charges of those to whom they belong, until a meeting of Parliament.

<hr>

[1] Exchequer Q. R. Miscellanea (Army), Nos. 22/11.   [2] Chancery Miscellaneous Portfolios, No. 31.

" 2. With respect to the bishop of Glasgow, it is the King's intention that he shall suffer banishment from Scotland for two or three years because of the great evils he hath occasioned.

" 3. With respect to William le Waleys, it is the King's intention that he be received to his will as he shall ordain.

" 4. The King demands that Sir David de Graham should be banished for half a year beyond the Tweed, in order to his 'penance' on account of his bearing himself falsely in respect to the conferences he has held with members of the King's Council.

" 5. It is the King's will that Sir Alexander of Lindeseye should have a certain 'penance' for his leaving the King, who had made him a knight.

" 6. That the Prince should bring with him the Earl of Lancaster, the Earl of Ulvester, the Earl of Warrewyk, Sir John de Bretaigne, Sir Hugh le Despensar, Sir Robert de Clifford, Sir William de Leyborne, Sir Alexander of Abernythy, and Sir Richard Syward ; and that the Earls of Stratherne and of Menetetht be commanded to accompany the Prince on the day on which he will come to Dunfermelyn. And that the Prince leave the town of St John [Perth] well fortified, and that he should in no wise depart therefrom until the town was so well garrisoned that it could not be taken by surprise nor be in peril, and that the workmen there could work in safety until his return ; and that he and the others who shall come with him, bring with them to the King the least company that they can both of people and of carriage, since thereby will be facilitated their speedy return.

" 7. With respect to the security to be given by the ambassadors, the King wills that they grant their letters-patent sealed with their seals ; and when Sir John Comyn shall have given homage and fealty to the King, the King will, by his letters-patent, agree to observe all the conditions

as they have been discussed and granted, and according to
the purport of the writ which the ambassadors shall have
made thereon.

" 8. It is the King's intention, that on the liberation of those
who have been taken in war, to grant freedom to those pledged
as hostages. Also that if a portion of the ransom money for
which these hostages were pledged be paid, the remainder
should be dispensed with and the whole discharged, and the
hostages released both on the one side and the other." [1]

These conditions were wholly at variance with terms such as
might have been offered to one who was sincere in upholding
the independence of his country, implying as they did the
actual surrender of every vestige of national liberty. Further,
by surrendering Wallace unconditionally into Edward's hands,
Comyn well knew that he was conveying him to certain death.
Nor was our hero's condition improved when Edward, in
revising the proposals, gave consent that all who, prior to the
16th of January,[2] should join the guardian in a surrender,
should escape the punishment of death, since Comyn would
certainly have gratified the English king by subjecting the
Patriot to a fatal sentence as a rebel to his personal authority.

Nearly six weeks were occupied in adjusting the proposals.
In order to escape imprisonment and forfeiture, Comyn
pledged himself to a year's voluntary exile. The Steward
became bound to surrender his castles and rents, and that
for two years he should retire to the south of the Trent; Sir
David Graham surrendered unconditionally; while of Sir Simon
Fraser and Thomas du Bois, it was demanded that they
should for three years absent themselves from Scotland, England,

[1] Chapter House (Scots Documents), Box 5,   [2] *Ibid.*, Box 5, No. 01 , Palgrave, p. 270.
No. 25; Palgrave's Documents, i., 283-285.

and France. In respect of others who had opposed his arms, Edward insisted that ransom should be exacted at his pleasure.

While the treaty negotiations were in progress, Comyn remained in his camp at Strathord, and there, on the 9th of February, sanctioned a document which effectually compromised the honour of his country. On the occasion Edward was represented by three delegates, the Earls of Pembroke and Ulster, and Sir Henry Percy. And of the Scottish barons who by their presence gave a further blow to the nation's liberties have been preserved the names of Sir Edward Comyn of Kilbride, Sir John de Vaux, Sir Godfrey de Rosse, Sir John de Maxwell "le einzniez," Sir Pierres de Prendregast, Sir Walter de Berkeleye of Kerdaan, Sir Hugh de Erth, Sir William de Erth, Sir James de Rosse, and Sir Walter de Rothevan (Ruthven), these becoming parties to the ratification.[1]

Wallace hovered in the vicinity of the English camp at Dunfermline till the end of February, when on quitting the place Edward dilapidated the elegant and spacious structure of the Benedictine monastery, lest it should be used for shelter by the Patriot and his followers.[2]

On leaving Dunfermline, Edward marched into eastern Fifeshire, whereupon the Patriot, leaving his place of shelter in the forest, conducted his followers westward, so as to bring relief to Sir William Oliphant, who, in retaining possession of the castle of Stirling, had suffered from a scarcity of provisions.

---

[1] Chapter House (Scots Documents), Box 100, No. 110 ; Exchequer Q. R. Memoranda, 34 Edward I., m. 30.

[2] Matthew Westminster, 446. The Westminster chronicler justifies Edward's barbarity in the destruction of the monastery, as the Scots, he alleges, had converted the house of God into a den of thieves, by holding therein rebellious parliaments. He adds that Edward graciously spared the church of the monastery, also a few monastic cells.

Informed of the movement, Edward on the 2d of March instructed the Prince of Wales to forthwith despatch Sir Alexander Abernethy, with forty men-at-arms, to intercept Wallace's party at the ford of Drip.[1] And replying to a question by Abernethy as to the terms which should attend Wallace's submission, Edward, writing from Kinghorn on the 3d of March, made answer that he must surrender unconditionally. Translated from the Norman French, his precise words are these :—"In reply to the matter wherein you have asked us to let you know whether it is our pleasure you should hold out to William le Waleys any words of peace, know this, that it is not our pleasure by any means that either to him, or to any other of his company, you hold out any word of peace, unless they place themselves absolutely and in all things at our will, without any exception whatever."[2]

Though Comyn's submission had all but subjected the kingdom to his control, Edward was not unaware that the recent treaty was incomplete without Parliamentary sanction. He therefore summoned a Parliament to meet him at St Andrews at Mid Lent, while he in the interval proceeded to subject to his authority certain fortified places in the county of Fife, including the castles of Aberdour and Wemyss.[3] From the fort of Kincaple, which he reached on the 11th March, he moved to St Andrews, entering the castle, of which the Prince of Wales was already in occupation.[4]

In the Parliament held at St Andrews, Edward insisted that a decree he had given forth abrogating the ancient laws of

---

[1] Royal Letters, No. 2582. Drip, a ford of the river Forth, near Craigforth, is now remarkable for an antique bridge by which it is spanned.

[2] Chancery Miscellaneous Rolls, No. 474.

[3] Royal Letters, 3260 ; Tower Miscellaneous Rolls, No. 474 ; Duchy of Lancaster (Royal Charters), No. 203 ; Chancery Miscellaneous Portfolios, Nos. 11, $\frac{4}{1}$.

[4] Chancery Miscellaneous Portfolios, Nos. 11, $\frac{4}{1}$.

Scotland and substituting those of England, should receive a legislative sanction. Next intimating that he had summoned to the Parliament Sir William Wallace, Sir Simon Fraser, and Sir William Oliphant, governor of Stirling Castle, he demanded that as they had not attended they should be forfeited and outlawed. At Edward's request Parliament also decreed that the siege of Stirling Castle should be actively proceeded with.[1]

Escaping the vigilance of Sir Alexander Abernethy and his troop, Wallace reached Stirling, when he proceeded to introduce provisions into the castle. The early history of the siege is otherwise unknown, further than that the defence must have been vigorously maintained, since the garrison successfully resisted all ordinary attempts for their dislodgment. Acting upon his experiences at Brechin, the Prince of Wales procured Edward's consent for stripping the lead from the refectory at St Andrews, also from the churches at Perth and Dunblane.[2]

Money for the soldiers' pay being the next requirement, Edward made an urgent appeal to his English treasurer, Walter de Langton, bishop of Lichfield. In his letter to the bishop, which is dated at St Andrews on the 22d of March, he intimates that on the Sunday after Easter, he would proceed personally to Stirling, and that consequently, and in order to the effective prosecution of the siege, he desired as much money as could possibly be raised. Such money, he added, the bishop should bring to him in person, more especially that messengers were expected to arrive from France—and that messages were to be despatched to the Pope—the bishop's advice with regard to these being also required.[3] To the bishop Edward on the 31st

---

[1] Fœdera, ii., 951; Trivet, 338; Fordun, xii., 3.

[2] Royal Letters, No. 2677; Liberate Roll, 33 Edward I., m. 6; Fordun a Hearne, p. 990.

In stripping the lead from the roofs of the churches, Edward caused that portion which covered the altars to be untouched.

[3] Royal Letters, No. 3513.

March addressed a further communication, charging him to procure from York, for use at the siege of Stirling, the materials for producing Greek fire, viz., a horseload of cotton thread, a load of quick sulphur, a load of saltpetre, and a load of arrows feathered and ironed.[1]

As these preparations were in progress, Edward on the 1st of April communicated from St Andrews with the Earls of Strathearn, Menteith, and Lennox, prohibiting them, on their allegiance, from holding any communication with the garrison, and from supplying them with provisions.

For aid in prosecuting the siege Edward next had recourse to the Earl of Carrick. The earl's recent proceedings must be noted. In April 1303, we find Edward requiring him to join his army at Roxburgh with a thousand men.[2] On the 14th July he is named as accepting, on the precept of Sir Aymer de Valence, a supply of grain in advance of his "wages."[3] On the 30th of December he is described as "Sheriff of Lanark,"[4] and on the 9th January 1303-4, he appears in command of the English garrison at Ayr.[5] On the 3d of March 1303-4, Edward addresses him jointly with Sir John Segrave, remarking facetiously that as "the cloak is well made," they should also "make the hood,"[6] meaning that, having made a good commencement in his royal service, they should diligently go forward. To testify his appreciation and respect, Edward on the 4th of March presented the earl with a sesterce of wine[7] from his stores at Linlithgow.

---

[1] Wardrobe Book of Edward I., p. 52 ; Stevenson's Documents, ii., 480. In producing the destructive appliances known as Greek fire, a mixture of sulphur and nitre was on blazing tow attached to arrows projected by the balista

[2] Exchequer Q. R. Miscellanea (Army), No. 3/18.

[3] Chancery Miscellaneous Portfolios, No. 4/37.

[4] Exchequer T. R. Miscellanea, No. 15/17.

[5] Exchequer Q. R. Miscellanea (Army), No. 31/6.

[6] Duchy of Lancaster (Royal Charters), No. 203

[7] Exchequer Q. R. Miscellanea (Army), No. 12/39.

On the 30th of March Bruce was, at Edward's instance, waited upon at Ayr by Sir John Botetorte, who reminded him that he had promised to grant for use in the siege at Stirling a stupendous battering-ram.[1] Bruce expressed his willingness to fulfil his engagement, but pleaded that the instrument was attached to a frame of such vast proportions, that its removal was impracticable. But Edward was not to be put off, and accordingly in a letter to Bruce, written at Inverkeithing on the 16th of April, he offered to aid in the transmission, and requested him to provide the needful appliances. He also called upon him to supply other engines, also stones and lead. Sir John Botetorte was then instructed to fetch the great engine, which lay at Inverkip.[2]

Edward left St Andrews on the 5th April, and proceeded by Wemyss and Kinghorn to Inverkeithing;[3] thence he marched to Tullibody, and on the 21st reached Stirling.[4]

Edward made known his arrival to the garrison by summoning the commander to surrender. To the demand Sir William Oliphant made answer that, consistently with his knightly honour, he dared not leave his post, since in maintaining it he was pledged to his master, Sir John Soulis, now in France. Sir William added, that if Edward would grant a cessation of hostilities, he would personally repair to France, and there ascertaining his master's will, would, on his return, deliver up the castle, if so permitted.[5] To the messengers Edward replied haughtily, "If he will not surrender the castle at once, let him keep it at his peril."

[1] Royal Letters, No. 2869.

[2] *Ibid.*, No. 2719; Stevenson's Documents, ii., 482, 483.

[3] Chancery Miscellaneous Portfolios, No. 11; Privy Seals (Tower), 32 Edward I., File 5; Royal Letters, No. 2677; Exchequer Q. R. Miscellanea (Army), No. 11.

[4] Privy Seals (Tower), 32 Edward I., File 5; Chancery Miscellaneous Portfolios, No. 11.

[5] Prynne's Edward I., p. 1051.

For the effective prosecution of the siege, Edward had secured most powerful appliances.   In Langtoft's words—

> "Threttene great engynes, of all the reame the best,
> Broulit thei to Strivilyne, the kastelle doun to kest."[1]

The Greek fire, of which the materials had been received from York, was used vigorously.   It was projected into the castle for eighteen successive days by eighteen trained persons, who each received as recompense 3d. daily.[2]   For a time Sir William Oliphant, with the aid of his lieutenant, Sir William Oliphant of Dupplin, maintained a vigorous defence by casting projectiles among the besiegers.[3]   These efforts Edward some time regarded with disdain, by frequently riding under the castle rock amidst showers of stones and javelins thrust from the ramparts.   But he had two important warnings, for in one of his rides an arrow pierced a chink of his mail and inflicted a wound,[4] while at another time a large stone fell near him with such force as to upset his horse and to seriously imperil his life.[5]

When the siege had continued about a month, Edward, on the 20th of May, despatched messengers to the sheriffs of York, Lincoln, and London, charging them to forward a supply of such projectiles as they could procure.   He directed a similar requisition to the governor of the Tower.[6]   And in order to a steady concentration of force he prohibited his knights, and others occupied in the siege, from engaging in tournaments or other sports.[7]

---

[1] Langtoft, 326; Exchequer Q. R. Miscellanea (Wardrobe), No. $\frac{2}{5}\frac{5}{}$.

[2] Memorandum in Public Record Office.   In the memorandum it is set forth that six shillings were expended in purchasing eighteen yards of canvas, and eighteenpence for sewing it in portions.

[3] Among the weapons used by the besieged was an espringal, which threw large darts, winged with brass (Matthew Westminster, 449).

[4] Matthew Westminster, 449.

[5] Walsingham, p. 89 ; Matthew Westminster, p. 449.

[6] Fœdera, new ed., i., 963.

[7] *Ibid.*, i., 964.

After a fruitless effort to reduce the castle, prosecuted for about two months, Edward devised a new mode of attack. On the 30th June he ordered the sheriff of York to provide forty cross-bowmen and forty carpenters.[1] The latter he employed in constructing several wooden towers, so contrived as horizontally to cast into the stronghold stones of two and three hundred-weight. One of these formidable appliances is by Langtoft described as a *loup-du-guerre*, or "war-wolf"—a name derisively adopted on account of the figure of a wolf being a principal charge in the seal of the place. In allusion to the power of his "war-wolf," Edward grimly remarked, that Oliphant and his friends might resist its ravages as best they could.[2] When the engine was completed, he caused an "oriole" to be made in his pavilion, so that the Queen, the Countess of Gloucester and Hertford, and other ladies of his court, might comfortably remark its effects.[3]

As the English king had anticipated, his "war-wolf" effected its purpose. The inner wall of the castle was penetrated, and other defensive works were thrown down and ruined. Sir William Oliphant now offered to capitulate on being assured of safety in life and limb, whereupon Edward despatched Sir John de Moubray and Sir Eustace le Poer to summon him to meet his commissioners at the gate of the castle. Edward's commissioners were the Earls of Gloucester and Lincoln, who agreed that the garrison should, on surrender, receive the honours of war.[4] But in the instrument of capitulation, dated the 24th of July, the terms of surrender are undefined, and Edward in consequence caused the brave Oliphant and twenty-five of his

---

[1] Close Roll, 32 Edward I., m. 8.

[2] Exchequer Q. R. Miscellanea (Army), No. $\frac{26}{12}$; Tytler's History, ed. 1869, i., 80.

[3] Wardrobe Account in the British Museum.

[4] Fordun a Hearne, 991; Wyntoun, vol. ii., p. 119.

companions, also two churchmen, to approach him in their shirts, and with ropes round their necks, and then, as he sat upon a throne, to implore his pardon on their bended knees. Edward next sentenced Oliphant and his companions to detention in English prisons.[1] He sent Oliphant to the Tower, Sir William Oliphant of Dupplin to Wallingford Castle, Hugh Oliphant to Colchester Castle, and Walter Oliphant to the prison at Winchester. These other members of the garrison he warded in other strongholds, viz.—Fergus de Ardrossan, Hugh de Ramsay, Thomas de Clenhull, Thomas de Lyllay, Patrick de Polleworthe, William Gyffard, Alan de Vypont, Andrew Wishart, Godfrey de Botillier, John le Naper, William Sherere, Hugh le Botillier, John de Kalgas, William de Anant, and Robert of Renfrew.[2]

When by the treaty of February Comyn had ceased to resist the English arms, Edward proceeded to communicate with the Scottish envoys in France. On the 17th of February he despatched safe conducts to Sir John Soulis, James the Steward, Mathew de Crambeth, bishop of Dunkeld, and to the bishop of St Andrews, authorising them, on their consenting to render fealty, to return home by way of England.[3] Two of the envoys rejected the terms, viz.—Sir John Soulis and the Steward. But Bishop Lamberton yielded, and on his return to Scotland, he, on the 5th May, rendered homage to Edward at Stirling, when, "by the king's special grace," he was restored to the temporalities of his see, which he consented to hold henceforth from the kings of England. In further token of submission, Lamberton declared in a legal instrument, that, having since his

---

[1] Fœdera, new ed., p. 966; Matthew Westminster, pp. 449, 450; Hemingford, i., 206. See also Trivet and Langtoft.

[2] Fœdera, new ed., 966; Chancery Miscellaneous Portfolios, No. $\frac{101}{57}$. The inmates of Stirling Castle on surrender were found to consist of 153 persons, of whom 13 were females, the wives and sisters of knights and barons.

[3] Privy Seals (Tower), 32 Edward I., File 2.

consecration drawn the revenues of his office without Edward's sanction, he would answer for the same when called upon.[1]

On the 24th July Edward planted in Stirling Castle an English garrison under the command of Sir John Lovel, one of his knights. He now marched to Edinburgh, where, on the 16th August, he lodged in the abbey of Holyrood. Next day he rested at Pentland, and on the 19th at Eddleston in Peeblesshire.[2] After a rapid march through Peebles, Traquair, and Selkirk, he, on the 24th, reached Yetholm.[3] At Brustewick, on the 8th December, he imposed a new tax[4] upon the kingdom. At Lincoln he celebrated Christmas with some religious rites, also with many mirthful festivities.[5]

[1] Exchequer T. R. Miscellanea, No. 4/6.

[2] Exchequer Q. R. Miscellanea (Army), Nos. 3/9, 4/3; Privy Seals (Tower), 32 Edward, I., File 17.

[3] Chancery Miscellaneous Portfolios, No. 4/2; Close, 32 Edward I., m. 13 *cedula.*

[4] Close Roll, 33 Edward I., m. 22.

[5] Mat. Westminster, 450; Hemingford, i., 206.

———o———

CHAPTER VII.

THE PATRIOT'S BETRAYAL AND DEATH.

URING a period of two weeks which elapsed between the surrender of Stirling Castle and the resumption of his journey southward, Edward was specially occupied; he was devising measures for the capture and destruction of one whose devotedness to his country could not be overcome, whether by policy or conflict. Having on his return from Dunfermline supplied provisions to Sir William Oliphant and the garrison at Stirling, Wallace seems to have found shelter for his followers in the moors and uplands of Dunblane. While in that locality, he had, in March 1303-4, a sharp skirmish with a body of English troops, under the leadership of Sir William le Latimer, Sir John de Segrave, and Sir Robert Clifford. And when, thereafter, Edward prosecuted the siege of Stirling, he seems to have from time to time attacked and cut off outlying portions of his army. On the 25th of July, five days after the surrender of the castle, Edward issued a proclamation whereby he provided that any person or persons who should, prior to the twentieth day after Christmas, seize and deliver up the person of Sir William Wallace, would receive a suitable token of his royal favour. And inasmuch as Sir John Comyn, Sir Alexander de Lindsay, Sir David Graham, and Sir Simon Fraser had consented to retire into exile, he would to any one of their number who should place Wallace in his hands, render acknowledgment, by abbreviating his exile, and diminishing his forfeiture or ransom. Edward also notified that, until Wallace was surrendered, the three Scottish envoys still in France should not be permitted to return.[1]

Edward had for some time contemplated that Wallace's person might be secured by means of betrayal. Some time in the year 1302, after the Patriot's return from his second visit to France, he granted to Edward de Keith letters-patent conveying to him "all the goods and chattels" he might gain from "Monsire Guilliam le Galeys (Wallace), the King's enemy, to his own profit and pleasure."[2] Keith, who was willing to deliver up his fellow countryman to his country's oppressor, was member of a family remarkable for their patriotism and honour, and whom he solely disgraced. His history is unknown further than that in right of his wife, Isabella de Synton, he, on the 23d of July 1305, was appointed hereditary sheriff of Selkirk.[3]

For Wallace's capture, Edward continued to put forth proclamations with offers of reward. One of these was addressed

---

[1] Chapter House (Scots Documents), Box 4, No. 4 ; Palgrave, pp. 267-277.

[2] Tower Miscellaneous Rolls, No. 4⁵⁄₂. In the instrument of grant, Keith is described as Edward's "dear servant."

[3] Chancery Miscellaneous Portfolios, No. ⁸⁄₁.

to his captains and governors in Scotland;[1] but at the same
time he privately conducted negotiations with those more
subservient to his purpose. Of these, one was Sir John de
Moubray, a man of considerable valour, but of vast infirmity of
purpose. An adherent of Baliol, he was taken prisoner by
Edward, and being confined in the Tower, he, on the 6th
November 1297, is named as receiving for maintenance an
allowance of fourpence daily.[2] From the Tower he was, on
the 16th July 1299, transferred to the prison of York.[3] And
when, in February 1303-4, the regent Comyn, who was his
relative, succumbed to Edward, he also submitted himself, and
at the same time undertook to secure Wallace as a prisoner.
In his attempt to execute his mission, he was aided by Ralph
de Haliburton, who, being one of the Scottish garrison at
Stirling, escaped from being committed to an English prison by
offering to assist in Wallace's capture.[4]

Ralph de Haliburton belonged to a family which held lands in
Berwickshire. Rendering homage to Edward in 1296, Sir Henry
de Haliburton also consented to remove his Scottish servants
from his lands in Northumberlandshire.[5] He subsequently
attached himself to the national party under Wallace, and
took part in the invasion of Northumberland, and of the other
northern counties, and was consequently, by an English Jury
at Newcastle, on the 17th February 1299-1300, forfeited as
"the king's enemy." Of lands in Northumberland, which he held
in right of his wife, he was deprived on the 2d December 1302.

---

[1] Fordun a Goodal, vol. ii., p. 223.

[2] Exchequer Q. R. Memoranda, 26 Edward I.,
m. 109.

[3] Close, 27 Edward I., m. 10 and 9.

[4] Ryley's *Placita*, 279 ; Chancery Miscellaneous Portfolios, No. ₁₀₇⁴⁴.

[5] Q. R. Ancient Misc. Sheriffs' Accounts,
Bundle 694 ; Chapter House Boxes, No. 210 ;
Roll, m. 27.

[6] Inq. p. m., 28 Edward I., No. 89 ; Privy
Seals (Tower), 30 Edward I., Files 5 and 9 ;
Leland's Collect., vol. i., p. 541.

But he afterwards changed sides, since in a letter addressed to the English government in 1306, he is named as willing to proceed to the north of the Grampians in the English interest.[1] Of this vacillating person, Ralph de Haliburton seems to have been a younger brother.

Another Scotsman tainted with inconstancy was Sir John Menteith. His patronymic was Stewart. Walter Stewart, third son of Walter, the third Steward of Scotland, married Mary, younger of the two daughters of Maurice, third Earl of Menteith, and of the union were born two sons, Alexander and John. Of these the latter abandoned the surname of Stewart, and assumed that of Menteith. Alexander, the elder brother, became sixth Earl of Menteith, but his line closed, when, in 1424, Murdoch, second Duke of Albany, Earl of Menteith and his three sons, were by James I. beheaded as conspirators against the crown.

John, second son of Walter Stewart, and grandson of the Steward, obtained the lands of Rusky in Perthshire. Under the Earl of Buchan he took part in the battle of Dunbar in April 1296, and having been made a prisoner, he was by Edward confined in the castle of Nottingham.[2] By consenting to serve under Edward abroad, he, on the 9th August 1297, obtained his release, and at the close of the Flanders campaign he returned to Scotland. He now attached himself to the national cause, and it is supposed that he fought under Wallace at the battle of Falkirk. But the statement of a modern writer,[3] that he on the eve of the battle joined his relative Sir John Stewart in a dispute with Wallace, is utterly baseless. The dispute it has been shown had no actual existence, and it

---

[1] Parliamentary Petitions, No. 9124.
[2] Close, 24 Edward I., m. 7 and 6.

[3] Duncan Stewart's History of Royal Family of Scotland, pp. 149-209.

appears that Menteith had not renounced the national cause up to October 1301, when, in a communication addressed to Edward of that date, John, son of Suffne, complains that his lands of Knapdale have been seized by John of Argyle on behalf of John of Menteith, "the king's enemy."[1] At what subsequent date Menteith returned to Edward's service, we are uninformed, but in a commission dated at St Andrews on the 20th of March 1303-4, we find that he was then appointed to the keepership of the castle, and sheriffdom, and burgh of Dunbarton. And in this commission Edward styles him "his lovite and faithful."[2]

On the surrender of Stirling Castle by Sir William Oliphant in July 1304, Wallace quitted the shores of the Forth, and with a single attendant sought shelter in the unfrequented wilds of the counties of Stirling and Lanark. Whether his place of refuge was included within the sheriffdom of Dunbarton is uncertain, but it would seem that, in the exercise of his functions, Menteith had conceived the notion of further recommending himself to his new master, by delivering into his hands the patriotic leader, under whom he had formerly served.

In the course of his wanderings, Wallace had reached the secluded district of Cadder, in the north-eastern border of Lanarkshire, and there he took shelter in a barn or cattle-shed then or since known as Robraystoun.[3] There, on the 5th of August 1305, he was surprised by a body of English soldiers, led by Menteith, at whose instance he was seized and fettered.

The place of Wallace's capture is an inconsiderable hollow lying between the modern mansion of Robraystoun and the farm of Mains immediately adjoining. There stood the fabric

[1] Chancery Miscellaneous Rolls, No. 474.

[2] Tower Miscellaneous Rolls, No. 471.

[3] A spring well which bears the Patriot's name is situated about a quarter of a mile to the north-eastward of Robrayston, in the corner of a field, bordering the parish road; it is enclosed by a modern wall.

in which the Patriot was seized, and up to the year 1825 a small portion of it still remained. Towards the close of the last century, an oak rafter, which had served as one of the supports of the original roof, protruded from one of the walls, but owing to its perilous aspect it was taken down and deposited in the farm yard. And in the year 1820, Mr Joseph Train, the antiquary, discovered in the walls butts of other rafters, and these, with the great beam preserved in the courtyard, he, with the farmer's permission, utilised in constructing a chair for presentation to Sir Walter Scott. Fashioned on an ancient model found in Hamilton Palace the chair was made to represent various Scottish emblems, including a figure of the national harp; and it is one of the art treasures now preserved at Abbotsford.

According to the Arundel MS., Wallace was captured "at Glasgow" in the house of one "Rawe Raa;"[1] and as it so happens that his place of capture is included within the diocese of Glasgow, it may be further concluded that Robraystoun is a simple adaptation of the words *Rob Raa's town*. In confirmation of this view, we find in the "Rental Book of the Diocese of Glasgow" an entry under the 19th July 1522, in which the place of the Patriot's seizure is styled "Rob Raystoun," while in the same register it is in 1538-39 designated Robraiston.[2]

Respecting the particulars of Wallace's arrest, Langtoft writes:

> "Sir John of Menetest sued William so nigh
> He tok him when he ween'd least, on night, his leman him bi ;
> That was through treason of Jack Short, his man
> He was the encheson that Sir John so him ran
> Jack's brother had he slain, the Waleis that is said
> The man Jack was fain to do William that braid."[3]

[1] Illustrations of Scottish History, Maitland Club.

[2] Rental Book of the Archbishop of Glasgow,

Grampian Club, 2 vols. 8vo, 1875 ; vol. i., pp. 84, 112, 164.

[3] Langtoft, ii., 320.

That a servant of the Patriot made known to Menteith his place of shelter is probably fictitious, but there is no doubt that the hero was captured during night. If we are to accept the Minstrel's authority, he was at the time of his capture attended by Kerlé or Kerlie, an attached adherent, who had fought under his standard at the battles of Loudoun Hill and Falkirk, and who, being taken captive with his chief, was forthwith slaughtered.[1] That Menteith was the hero's captor is distinctly affirmed in the Chronicle of Lancrcost,[2] and in the " Scala Cronica ";[3] it is also asserted by Fordun and Wyntoun. An attempt to exonerate the memory of Menteith, first made by Lord Hailes, and afterwards by some less conspicuous writers, has been conclusively disposed of by Mr Tytler.[4]

Taking part in foreign trade, Menteith, on the 20th November 1305, received from Edward letters of protection for Jaques Drilbrod, burgess of St Omer, and his two sons, in passing with goods through his dominions. In his letters Edward set forth that he had granted them reluctantly, and would not have yielded the privilege to any other petitioner.[5] The privilege was renewed and extended to three years.[6] Menteith received from Edward, on the 16th June 1306, the revenues of the earldom of Lennox ;[7] also the temporalities of the bishopric of Glasgow, in the county of Dunbarton, of which Bishop Wishart had been deprived.[8] When Robert the Bruce was in 1306 prosecuting his patriotic labours, Menteith undertook,

---

[1] Henry's Wallace, B. xi., ll. 1000-1016. Kerlé or Kerlie, the reputed associate of the Patriot, is said to have been a member of the family of Carrol or M'Kerlie of Cruggleton, in Galloway (see Paterson's " Wallace and his Times," 3d ed., Edinb. 1860, pp. 337-378).

[2] Chronicle of Lancrcost, p. 203.

[3] See Leland's Collections, vol. i., p. 541.

[4] See a statement of evidence against Menteith in Tytler's " History of Scotland," ed. 1869, vol. i., pp. 362-364, App. U.

[5] Privy Seals (Tower), 33 Edward I.

[6] Close Rolls, Edward I., m. 40.

[7] Sir Francis Palgrave's Transcripts, vol. 63, fol. 10.

[8] *Ibid.*, vol. 63, fol. 61.

jointly with Sir Hugh Bisset, to cut off by a fleet his retreat from the Western Isles.[1] And in July of the following year, he is described as with some others guarding, on Edward's behalf, the town of Ayr.[2] But Edward had only a few days ceased to live, when the captor of Wallace renounced the English interest, and attached himself to King Robert.

Laden with fetters Wallace was hastened to London under a powerful guard. Concerning his arrival in the English capital, and the subsequent proceedings, there are minute and ample details. These are derived from a manuscript composed in Latin, which bears to be a transcript[3] from the Cottonian MS., which in 1731 perished by fire. The original had belonged to an institution connected with the city of London, in which certain functionaries made record of important local events. In reference to Wallace the narrative has evidently been prepared by one who was personally cognizant of the events which he has described. In translation the narrative proceeds thus :—

"The same year [1305], on the 22d of August, Sir William Waleis, knight, a native of Scotland, came to London, and to meet him there went out a multitude both of men and women. He was lodged in the house of William de Leyre, a citizen of London, in the parish of All Hallows in the Ropery [Fenchurch Street]. And on the following day, being Monday, in the vigils of St Bartholomew [23d August], he was led on horseback to Westminster, John de Seagrave and Galfrid de Seagrave, knights, the Mayor, sheriffs, and aldermen of London following him, with many others both mounted and on foot. In the great hall of Westminster he was placed on the south bench, and crowned with leaves of laurel, since it was reported that he had asserted that he deserved to wear a crown in that hall. On being subjected to trial, he was, by Sir Peter Maluree, the king's justice, charged as a traitor to the king,

[1] Close, 35 Edward I., m. 14.

[2] Exchequer Q. R. Miscellanea (Army), No. 3/2.

[3] There are two copies of the transcript, one of which is contained in the Hargrave MS. 179, p. 292 ; the other and more correct, which we have used, is in the Additional MSS., 5444, fol. 138, c. 9.

when he replied that he was not a traitor to the king of England. The truth of other accusations he acknowledged, and at last the said Peter and the other justices gave sentence."

The recorder of the proceedings next presents Edward's warrant for the Patriot's trial; it is in these terms :—

" Edward, by the grace of God, King of England, Lord of Ireland, and Duke of Aquitaine, to his beloved and trusty John de Segrave, Peter Maluree, Ralph of Sandwyc, John of Bacnelle, and John le Blound, mayor of his city of London, greeting: Know ye that we have appointed you our justices for delivering our prison of our Tower of London of William le Waleis, according to the ordinance thereon enjoined by us upon you ; wherefor we charge you that at a day and place as four or three of you shall appoint, ye deliver our prison of the said William in the form prescribed. And you, the foresaid John de Segrave, in whose custody the foresaid William is specially placed, shall cause the foresaid William and his attachiament come before you at the foresaid day and place.—In witness whereof, we have made these our letters-patent. *Teste me ipso* at Ranrethe the 18th day of August, the 33d year of our reign.

" By brief of the Privy Seal." [1]

Proceeds the reporter :—

" In consequence of which brief, the foresaid justices proceeded to the delivery of the foresaid prison of the foresaid William, in manner as follows:—

> " The pleas at Westminster before John de Segrave, P. Maluree, R. de Sandwyc, John de Bacnelle, and John le Blound, mayor of the king's city of London, the Monday in the vigils of St Bartholomew, the 33d year of the king's reign.

" WILLIAM WALEIS, A NATIVE OF SCOTLAND, TAKEN CAPTIVE FOR SEDITION, HOMICIDES, DEPREDATIONS, FIRE-RAISING, AND SUNDRY OTHER FELONIES, was by the same judges found guilty, inasmuch as, after the king had made conquest of Scotland, as represented by John Baillol, the prelates, earls, barons, and his other enemies of the said country, and had by the forfeiture of the said John, and by conquest, brought into submission and subjugation all Scotsmen to his royal power, and, as their king, had publicly received the homages and fealties of the prelates, earls, barons, and a vast number of other persons, and had caused his peace to be proclaimed through the whole land, and appointed guardians of the country, also sheriffs, provosts, bailies,

---

[1] Privy Seals (Tower), 33 Edward I., File 4.

and others to maintain peace, and do justice; the foresaid William le Walcis, forgetful of his allegiance, seditiously made insurrection against the said king, having united and confederated with him a vast number of persons, and feloniously invaded and attacked the guardians and ministers of the said king, and attacked, and slew, and cut in pieces William of Hesebregg,[1] sheriff of Lanark; and with a multitude of armed men invaded the towns, cities, and castles of that country, and sent forth his briefs through the whole of Scotland as the briefs of the superior of that country; also held parliaments and assemblies, and expelled the guardians and officers of the foresaid king. Further, he in his boundless wickedness had counselled all the prelates, earls, and barons of that country who adhered to his party, that they should submit themselves to the fealty and lordship of the king of France, and furnish assistance to the destruction of the realm of England. Likewise that he, taking with him certain accomplices, penetrated into the English counties of Northumberland, Comberland, and Westmerland, and there wickedly slew all whom he found there loyal to the king, including priests and nuns; destroyed churches built to the honour of God and his saints; disturbed the bodies of the saints, and also cast down, burnt, and laid waste consecrated buildings and their relics, and put to a more terrible death than can be conceived, old men with young men, wives and widows, infants and sucklings. Further-more, he every day and hour had seditiously plotted the death of the king, and the destruction of his authority and royal dignity. And though, after such enormous and horrible acts, the king with a great army had invaded Scotland, and overthrown the foresaid William, carrying his standard against him in mortal war, and had mercifully caused the foresaid William to be recalled to his peace, he still wickedly and seditiously refused to submit himself, and accordingly was outlawed as a seducer, robber, and felon. And as it is unjust and contrary to the laws of England, that any one so outlawed and put out of the pale of the laws, and not afterwards restored to the king's peace, should be admitted to defend his case or make answer: it was adjudged that the foresaid William, for his manifest sedition, plotting the king's death, perpetrating annulment of his crown and dignity, and bearing banner against his liege lord, should be led from the palace of Westminster to the Tower of London, and from the Tower to Allegate, and so through the middle of the city to Elmes, and be there hanged and afterwards drawn, for the robberies, and homicides, and felonies which he had committed in the realm of England

---

[1] Probably an error for Heselregg on the part of the transcriber.

and country of Scotland: And because he was an outlaw and had not been restored to the king's peace, that he should be beheaded; and thereafter for the vast injury he did to God and Holy Church in burning churches, vessels, and biers, wherein the bodies of the saints and relics of them were placed; the heart, liver, and lungs, and all the inner parts of the said William, whereout of such perverse imaginations proceeded, should be cast into a fire and burned; and also because he had done the foresaid sedition, depredations, fire-raising, and homicides, and felonies, not only to the said king, but to the whole people of England and Scotland, the body of the said William should be cut and divided into four quarters, and the head set on the Bridge of London, in sight of those passing both by land and water; and one quarter suspended on the gibbet at Newcastle-on-Tyne, another quarter at Berwick, a third quarter at Stirling, and a fourth quarter at St Johnstoun, for the dread and chastisement of all that pass by and behold them."

Pursuant to sentence the condemned Patriot was dragged by horses from Westminster Hall to West Smithfield, where the revolting sentence was, in all its hideous barbarity, fully carried out.[1] The place of slaughter is included in the modern alley of Cow Lane, which covers the locality known as the Elms, where, in the thirteenth century, state criminals were executed.

The Patriot's martyrdom is referred to in a ballad written in the year following the event, when the head of Sir Simon Fraser was set up on London Bridge beside those of Wallace and Llewellyn—

" To warny alle the gentilmen, that liueth in Scotlonde
The Waleis wes to drawe, seththe he wes anhonge,   } to abyde.
Al quic biheveded, ys boweles ybrend,
The heved to Londone brugge wes send

.   .   .   .   .   .

" Sire Edward oure Kyng, that ful ys of pietè,
The Waleis quarters sende to his ouue contre,   } Ant drede."[2]
On four half to honge, huere myrour to be,
Ther-apon to thenche, that manie myhten se.

---

[1] There seems to be no authority for Henry's statements that Winchelsey, Archbishop of Canterbury, received Wallace to confession on the scaffold, and that with the permission of Sir Robert Clifford the hero was permitted, while being done to death, to look upon the pages of a Psalter, held open before him by a priest.

[2] MS. Harl., No. 2253, fol. 59, b.; Trivet, p. 340; Wyntoun, ed. 1879, iii., 288, Note.

According to the Chronicle of Lancercost, Wallace's slaughter and dismemberment were attended with an expenditure of £61, 10s. In terms of the sentence, the body of the hero was divided into four portions—that which included the right arm being exhibited at Newcastle, that bearing the left arm at Berwick, that bearing the right leg at Perth, that bearing the left leg at Aberdeen.[1] The duty of transmitting the remains to the several stations was confided to Sir John de Segrave, who, on Edward's order, was by John de Lincoln and Roger de Paris, sheriffs of London, refunded the cost of carriage.[2]

Having barbarously slaughtered the Scottish hero, and exposed in the principal towns his dismembered remains, Edward proceeded to recompense those who had abetted Menteith in securing his prisoner. Among certain memoranda in the Chapter House are these :—

> "4. Fait a remembrer des xl m^{a}rs q̃ deyvent estre dones a un
>   Valet q̃ espia Wiłł le Waleys.
> 5. Iт̃ de les lx m^{a}rs q̃ deyvent estre donez as autres, et le
>   Roi voet q̃ ces . . . lx . . .
>   qui fenrent a la p^{i}se du dit Willā p^r ptir entre eus.
> 6. Ð la тre. cest assaᵛ c łi p J. de Menceteтh."[3]

In translation these entries read thus :—

> "4. Cause to remember the forty marks which should be given
>   to a valet who had watched William le Waleys.
> 5. Item of the sixty marks that ought to be given to the others;
>   it is the king's will that these be divided among those
>   persons who were at the capture of the said William.
> 6. Item of land for J. de Menceteth, valued at £100."

<hr>

[1] Chron. of Lancercost, printed for the Maitland Club, p. 203. There is a discrepancy between the disposition of the hero's members narrated herein and that set forth in the Cottonian MS., formerly quoted,—Aberdeen being named as receiving one of the limbs instead of Stirling.

[2] Memoranda Roll, 33 and 34 Edward I., m. 76.

[3] Chapter House (Scots Documents), Box 100, No. 126 ; Palgrave's Documents, i., 295.

Though charged at his trial with acts of cruelty and revenge, Wallace was in reality mild, placable, and forbearing ; he granted quarter to his enemies, was courteous to women, and reverenced the priesthood. And his public life was in conformity to his private virtues, inasmuch as he alone of all persons of his rank who took part against Edward, remained consistent and faithful.

Wallace became a martyr for his country about the age of thirty-five. In relation to his memory, Sir James Balfour preserves the following epitaph :—

> "Fortunæ tetricæ domitor, vindexque
> [suorum
> Hic iacet immeritâ pressus sub invidiâ
> Ausa immane nefas, fraus effera, gentis
> [honorem
> Abstulit, et patriæ robora certa suæ."[1]

In translation the epitaph reads :—

> The conqueror of harsh fortune, and the avenger of
> his countrymen, lies here overwhelmed by unmer-
> ited envy. Unbridled guile, daring an inhuman
> wickedness, has snatched honour from his nation
> and removed the sure strength of his native land.

These lines on the Patriot are preserved by David Hume of Godscroft :—

> "Invida mors tristi Gulielmum funere Vallam,
> Quæ cuncta tollit, sustulit :
> Et tanto pro cive cinis, pro finibus urna est,
> Frigusque pro lorica obit.
> Ille quidem terras, loca se inferiora reliquit ;
> At fata factis supprimens,
> Parte sui meliore solum cœlumque pererrat ;
> Hoc spiritu, illud gloria :

[1] Balfour MS. in the Advocates' Library, No. 33, 2, 7.

> At tibi si inscriptum generoso pectus honesto
>   Fuisset, hostis proditi
> Artibus, Angle, tuis, in pœnas, parcior isses,
>   Nec oppidatim spargeres
> Membra viri sacranda adytis.   Sed scin' quid in ista
>   Immanitate viceris ?
> Ut Vallæ in cunctas oras sparguntur et horas
>   Laudes, tuumque dedecus."

To this epitaph Hume has appended the following metrical translation :—

> " Envious Death, who ruins all,
>   Hath wrought the sad lamented fall
>   Of Wallace, and no more remains
>   Of him, then what an urn contains.
>   Ashes for our Hero we have,
>   He, for his armour, a cold grave.
>   He left the earth—too low a state,
>   And by his worth o'ercame his fate ;
>   His soul death had not power to kill,—
>   His noble deeds the world do fill
>   With lasting trophies of his name.
>   O ! had'st thou virtue loved, or fame,
>   Thou could'st not have insulted so
>   Over a brave betrayed dead foe,
>   Edward, nor seen those limbs expos'd
>   To public shame,—fit to be clos'd,
>   As relics, in a holy shrine ;
>   But now the infamy is thine.
>   His end crowns him with glorious bays,
>   And stains the brightest of thy praise." [1]

[1] History of the Houses of Douglas and Angus, by David Hume of Godscroft.   Ed. 1644, pp. 22, 23.

———o———

CHAPTER VIII.

FROM THE DEATH OF WALLACE TO THE DEATH OF EDWARD.

"Thy spirit, Independence, let me share,
Lord of the lion heart and eagle eye !
Thy steps I follow with my bosom bare,
Nor heed the storm that howls along the sky."
—Dr Tobias Smollett.

IN effecting the death of Wallace, Edward believed that he had completed the final act of subjugating Scotland, and accordingly when, on the 20th October 1305, he instructed his chamberlain to apply the customs of the boat ferry at Stirling in re-erecting a bridge across the Forth which the Patriot had destroyed, he was satisfied that no further attempt would be made to subvert his authority.[1]

A scheme had already been promulgated for the absorption of the two countries into one kingdom, for at Lent 1304-5 it was ruled by a Convention of the Estates that Scotland should be represented in the English Parliament by ten commissioners—of these, two to be chosen by the bishops, two by the abbots, two by the earls, two by the barons, and two by the representatives of burghs. Under this arrangement, Edward had convened the several electoral bodies at Perth, when, as representatives to his English Parliament, were nominated the bishops of St Andrews and Dunkeld, the earls of Buchan and March, Sir John de Moubray, Sir Robert Keith, Sir Adam Gordon, and Sir John of Inchmartin. And when on the 13th of September the English

---

[1] Close Roll, 33 Edward I., m. 3.

Parliament assembled at London, all the commissioners attended, save the Earl of March, who, at Edward's command, was deprived, and his place supplied by Sir John Menteith. Adding to the Scottish commissioners twenty-two magnates of England, Edward thereby formed a council or executive for carrying out his royal decrees in the management of Scottish affairs.

The Scottish Council met on the 23d September 1305, when they established the government of Scotland on a new basis. As lieutenant, John de Bretagne, Edward's nephew, was confirmed in office, and natives of England were approved as chancellor, chamberlain, and comptroller. The Council next appointed four "pair" of Englishmen as district judges, two in Lothian, two in Galloway, two between the Forth and the Grampians, and two to the north of the Grampians. Resident sheriffs, they ruled, might belong to either of the two kingdoms, but should be appointed only by the king, and be made removable at his pleasure. They further determined that Edward should continue to appoint governors of all the castles and strongholds, with the exception of the castle of Kildrummie, which had been conferred on the Earl of Carrick.

Abolishing all the national statutes, the Council ruled that under the advice of "the good people of the country," all persons who opposed themselves to the new system should be sent to the king, to be confined in England south of the Trent. They also sanctioned that part of the capitulation of Strathord, which provided that Sir Alexander Lindsay should for six months absent himself from Scotland, and Sir Simon Fraser become for four years an exile both from this country and from France.[1]

In pretended evidence of clemency, Edward proceeded to

---

[1] "Ordonnance faite par Edouard Roi d'Angle-terre sur le gouvernement de la terre d'Escosse;" Acta Parl. Scot., vol. i.; Close Roll, 33 Edward I., m. 13 dorso cedulá; Ryley, 506.

modify his indemnities. From the clergy who had taken part against him, with the exception of the bishop of Glasgow, he was content to receive one year's rental, and from those civilians who had submitted prior to the treaty at Strathord, the rents of two years. From Sir Adam Gordon, Sir Simon Fraser, also from Sir John Comyn, the late guardian, he was willing to accept three years' rents; and from Sir William de Baliol and John Wishart, the rents of four years. And he was content that his exactions should be paid in moieties, each offender being allowed half his income till the penalties were discharged.[1] In further illustration of affected clemency, Edward liberated James the Steward from prison, on securing his acknowledgment that he had "by wicked counsel" made war upon "his lawful sovereign," and further on his absolute submission "in body, lands, and goods."[2]

We last found the Earl of Carrick assisting Edward in reducing Stirling Castle by a supply of powerful engines. At this time his father, the second Robert Bruce, was in failing health, and he sought to be on friendly terms with Edward, as, in the event of his father's death, he might otherwise be deprived of his English estates, and also fail to obtain service to his lands in Annandale.

Robert Bruce of Annandale died shortly before the 4th April 1304, since at that date Robert Bruce the younger, writing from Hatfield in Essex, entreated Edward's escheators at Essex, Middlesex, and Huntingdon to grant him service in lands which had belonged to his father. He also begged that he might have early service, as he desired to render speedily to the king the

[1] Fœdera, ii., 968.

[2] Close Roll, 33 Edward I., m. 5 dorso; also Memoranda Roll, 33 and 34 Edward I., m. 54. To the Memoranda Roll is appended a note, stating that on the 3d November, James the Steward appeared before the Lord Chancellor and others, and acknowledged the deed as his own.

customary homage.[1] By letter he informed Edward that, both in London and in the county of Essex, he had been endeavouring to procure horses and arms for himself and his followers, in order to advance the royal service, but without success, inasmuch as he had not yet become entitled to draw the rents of his estates; he therefore desired to learn the king's pleasure.[2] Under this plea he sought an excuse for not taking part personally in the siege of Stirling. And he did not present himself until his attendance was peremptorily ordered. At Stirling on the 1st of May, he received from Edward a writ directed to a jury for his service as heir to his father in the lands at Hatfield, Tottenham, and Writtle,[3] while, consequent on receiving his father's estates in Annandale, he rendered homage on the 14th of June.[4]

Though in attendance at Stirling as Edward's vassal, Bruce had already resolved to espouse the liberties of his country. Accordingly on the 11th of June, he, in the Abbey of Cambuskenneth, entered into a compact with Bishop Lamberton. That compact, drawn in Latin, was of the following purport :—

"In the year of our Lord 1304, on the day of the festival of the Holy Apostle Barnabas; the Reverend Father in Christ, William de Lamberton, by the grace of God, Bishop of St Andrews, and the noble Robert, Earl of Carrick, Lord of Annandale, having had a conference at the Abbey of Cambuskenneth in relation to impending dangers, they, in order to resist their enemies, enter into a friendly covenant. They engage to seek each other's safety in their common affairs and transactions against all persons opposed to them, also to assist

---

[1] Royal Letters, No. 2660.

[2] *Ibid.*, No. 3248.

[3] In one of the four inquests, the Earl of Carrick is described as twenty-two years old and upwards, and in a second as being twenty-eight, while a third sets forth his actual age, which was thirty.

[4] Privy Seals (Tower), 32 Edward I., File 8.

each other, both individually and by their adherents. They further agree that the one shall not enter on any arduous undertaking without consulting the other. Furthermore they become pledged that whoever should come to the knowledge of dangers impending over the other, should forewarn him, or cause him to be forewarned, and should use his utmost efforts to avert the same. And for the faithful performance of this compact, they, without any sort of reservation, bind themselves to each other by oath, also under the penalty of ten thousand pounds, to be applied for the recovery of the Holy Land."[1]

When at Lent 1304-5 Edward resolved that commissioners should be sent from Scotland to his English Parliament, he appointed the Earl of Carrick and Bishop Wishart of Glasgow to express his intention to the Scottish Estates.[2] But when the commissioners were chosen some months afterwards, he so arranged that Bruce and Wishart were unnamed. Assured, however, of Edward's favour, Bruce proceeded to London, probably in the hope that he might be appointed to the lieutenancy or other high office. How long he remained in London is uncertain, but early in February 1305-6, he departed hastily for Scotland. The cause of his sudden departure is a matter of conjecture. According to certain writers, he received from his friend, the Earl of Gloucester, a secret token that Edward contemplated his destruction. Wyntoun sets forth that he was arraigned by Edward for betraying his confidence,[3] but this statement is at entire variance with the fact that, on

---

[1] The duplicates of the original indenture have been lost, but a notarial instrument, in which its terms have been preserved, was drawn up at Newcastle-on-Tyne on the 9th August 1306, which on being shown to Bishop Lamberton, he acknowledged as authentic. The indenture is noticed by Lord Hailes (Annals, i., 342), but it has, as engrossed in the notarial instrument referred to, been published for the first time in an authentic form by Sir Francis Palgrave (Documents, etc.), vol. 1., pp. clvi., clvii., 323, 324.

[2] Close Roll, 33 Edward I., m. 13 dorso cedulâ.

[3] Wyntoun, B. viii., ll. 2804-2887.

the 8th of February, Edward issued a writ relieving him of a debt due by his father, for omitting to discharge a military obligation.[1]

With a single attendant, Bruce rode from London into Annandale. Reaching the Castle of Lochmaben, he was there informed by his brother Edward that the English Justiciars of the district were on an early day to hold at Dumfries an assembly of the barons. At this assembly Bruce presented himself, and there, either incidentally or by prearrangement, met Sir John Comyn, the ex-regent. With Comyn being on friendly terms, he invited him to a private interview in the church of the Greyfriars in reference to public affairs.[2] On Thursday, the 12th of February, the parties met at the place appointed, but as they were together approaching the high altar, Bruce used some strong words expressive of his belief that Comyn had betrayed him to the English king. This imputation Comyn met with a fierce and impetuous rejoinder, when, forgetful of the sacredness of the place, Bruce thrust at him with his dagger. But the next moment realizing his rashness, he hastened from the scene, and at the entrance of the church met his follower, Roger de Kirkpatrick. Addressing this person in the words "I doubt I have slain Comyn," he received the answer, "Do you doubt?—then I'll mak siccar." So saying Kirkpatrick rushed into the sacred edifice and completed the slaughter. The ex-regent was accompanied by his father's brother, Sir Robert Comyn, whom Kirkpatrick also slew.[3]

[1] Close Roll, 34, Edward I., m. 18.

[2] Trivet, 334; Hemingford, 219; Fordun a Hearne, iv., 992; Wyntoun, vol. ii., p. 122; Langtoft, ii., 330; Barbour's Bruce, Jamieson's edit., p. 18.

[3] Our narrative of the Comyn slaughter is substantially founded on the relation of Sir Thomas de Gray, the Northumbrian Knight, formerly quoted (Scala Cronica, 130). See also Leland's Collectanea, 502. It may be added that the crest of the "Kirkpatricks" or Kilpatricks, baronets of Closeburn, is a hand with a dagger erect in pale dropping blood, with the motto "I mak siccar."

According to Wyntoun, Bruce had formed the deliberate intention of revenging himself upon the ex-regent, whom he believed to have revealed to Edward a proposal he had made to him at Stirling, implying that the proposer was to strike for the crown.[1]

Barbour presents a different narrative. Bruce, he relates, in his journey from London had reached the Scottish border, when he intercepted a messenger of Comyn bearing letters to the English court compromising his master.

These surmises are evidently conjectural. Comyn was sister's son of the dethroned Baliol, and as he had formerly been guardian of the kingdom, it was most natural that Bruce should ascertain his sentiments before assuming arms against England. Whatever his motive really was in inviting him to a conference, we agree with Lord Hailes,[2] that he had in so doing no intention to commit violence, since he would not have deliberately chosen for that purpose the interior of a consecrated structure.

The slaughter was certainly unpremeditated. Comyn was of a haughty and choleric disposition, as appears from his personal attack upon Bruce in August 1299,[3] and the rude words uttered by him in the Greyfriars church had no doubt provoked the sally which resulted in his death.

Tidings of Bruce's act of slaughter were promptly conveyed to Edward, who, on the 24th of February, communicated with James de Dalilegh, his store-keeper at Dumfries, instructing him that as " Sir John Comyn and his uncle, Sir Robert Comyn, were murdered by persons who were seeking to subvert the peace of the kingdom," he should warn the lieges to avoid communication with them.[4]

---

[1] Wyntoun, B. viii., ll. 2767-2887.
[2] Hailes' Annals, i., 021.
[3] Scots Documents, Public Record Office; National MSS. of Scotland, ii., No. viii.
[4] Exchequer Q. R. Miscellanea (Army), No. $\frac{3}{7}$.

Returning to the castle of Lochmaben, Bruce intimated that he had assumed the sovereignty,—among his early adherents being his four brothers, Edward, Nigel, Thomas, and Alexander, his nephew, Thomas Randolph of Strathdon, afterwards Earl of Moray, and his brother-in-law, Christopher Seton. Soon afterwards he was joined by the Earls of Lennox and Athole, Bishops Lamberton and Wishart, David Moray, bishop of Moray,[1] and the abbot of Scone; subsequently by the Earl of Mentcith, Gilbert de la Haye of Errol, and his brother Hugh, Nigel Campbell of Argyleshire, Alexander Fraser, brother of Sir Simon Fraser, Sir John de Somerville of Linton, David of Inchmartin, Robert Boyd of Kilmarnock, and Robert Fleming.[2] Proceeding for coronation to the Abbey of Scone, he was in his progress joined by Sir James Douglas, whose fidelity and valour became afterwards conspicuous.[3]

At Scone, in the absence of the ancient coronation stone, Bruce was content to be enthroned in a modern chair, while his kingly robe was formed of one of Bishop Wishart's episcopal vestments, and a regal coronet adapted from a golden cincture worn by the abbot.[4] As chief of the clan Macduff, the Earl of Fife possessed the privilege of crowning the Scottish sovereign, but the earl had attached himself to Edward, while the Earl of Buchan, husband of his sister, Isabella, had also succumbed to the usurpation. But the Countess Isabella determined to discharge the function which under other circumstances would have

---

[1] David Moray, bishop of Moray, was founder of the Scots College at Paris. He represented to the people of his diocese that to render support to Robert the Bruce by arms was a duty as meritorious as to engage in a crusade (MS. Records, Lond., quoted by Lord Hailes, Annals, ii., 3, note).

[2] Matthew of Westminster, p. 452; Fordun a Hearne, vol. v., p. 998.

[3] Barbour's Bruce, p. 27.

[4] At Carlisle, on the 20th March 1306-7, Edward at his Queen's intercession extended a pardon to Geoffry de Coigners for concealing a certain coronet of gold, with which Robert de Brus lately caused himself to be crowned in Scotland (Patent Roll, 35 Edward I., m. 28; Fœdera, i., 1012).

fallen to her brother, or her husband, and so, hastening to Scone, she reached the place on the day subsequent to the ceremonial.[1] But in respect of her loyal intention, Bruce reseated himself in the coronation chair, and by her hands was crowned a second time.[2]

The earlier ceremony at Scone took place on the 27th March 1306, and a few days afterwards Bruce succeeded in displacing a number of the English sheriffs,[3] while Edward's nephew, John de Bretagne, retired in alarm from the lieutenancy.

Made aware that the insurrection had assumed formidable proportions, Edward commissioned Sir Aymer de Valence to muster "men-at-arms, horse, and foot,"[4] in order to its suppression. Next confiscating Bruce's possessions, he conferred on the Earl of Hereford and Essex "his castle of Lochmaben," also his lands in Annandale.[5] His possessions in Carrick he granted to Sir Henry Percy,[6] and his manor of Hert in Durham to Sir Robert Clifford ;[7] while he personally appropriated his lands in Essex.[8]

Appointing the Prince of Wales as De Valence's coadjutor, Edward summoned three hundred esquires to attend him at Westminster, so that as the Prince's chosen attendants they might receive military equipment. On the appointed day, these assembled at the palace, and having received knighthood at the high altar of Westminster Abbey, they were at a subsequent banquet made to witness a performance by the king, when he swore upon the Holy Scriptures, also on the heads of two swans, that when

---

[1] Hemingford, vol. i., p. 220.

[2] Trivet, p. 342; Matthew of Westminster, 454. In "Scala Cronica," the act of crowning Robert Bruce is assigned to Elizabeth, daughter of Roger de Quinci, Earl of Winchester, and widow of Alexander Comyn, father of John, Earl of Buchan, husband of the Countess Isabella.

[3] Fœdera, vol. ii., p. 988.

[4] Patent Roll, 34 Edward I., m. 28.

[5] Duchy of Lancaster (Royal Charters), No. 205 ; Chapter House (Scots Documents), Box 4, No. 13.

[6] Hemingford, p. 224.

[7] Patent Roll, 34 Edward I., m. 22.

[8] Exchequer Q. R. Memoranda, 34 Edward I., m. 4 dorso ; Close Roll, 34 Edward I., m. 7.

he had avenged the slaughter of the Comyns, and smitten the Scots, he would embark for Palestine, and there close his life.

Writing to Sir Aymer de Valence on the 24th May, Edward informs him that the Prince was about to join him with a strong force, and that he would follow personally.[1] On the 8th of June he congratulates De Valence on the capture of Bishop Wishart,[2] and in a dispatch written a few days afterwards, enjoins that the bishop should be sent to Berwick without any consideration being extended to him in respect of his office.[3] In further letters, Edward commends his lieutenant for despoiling the lands and goods of Sir Simon Fraser; and instructs him to similarly destroy the possessions of all who abetted him.[4]

Having repressed the English authority in Galloway,[5] Bruce proceeded northward. Finding that De Valence occupied the city of Perth, which he had strongly fortified, he challenged the lieutenant to meet him in the field. Encamping in the woods of Methven, about six miles distant, he proposed there to wait for reinforcements, but meanwhile he was suddenly assailed by De Valence at the head of his entire force.[6] De Valence attacked him in person, and would have secured him as his prisoner, but for the timely interposition of Sir Christopher Seton.[7] After a severe struggle the Scots were completely defeated, many of Bruce's principal adherents being cut down or made prisoners. Among the captives was Thomas Randolph, the king's nephew, who afterwards accepted Edward's fealty.[8]

---

[1] Sir Francis Palgrave's Transcripts, vol. 63, fol. 44.

[2] Chancery Miscellaneous Portfolios, No. 33.

[3] Sir Francis Palgrave's Transcripts, vol. 63, fol. 61 and fol. 10.

[4] *Ibid.*, vol. 63, fol. 58.

[5] Chron. Lanercost, p. 204.

[6] Chron. Abingdon, quoted in Tyrrel, vol. iii., p. 172.

[7] Barbour, pp. 35, 36; Leland, i., 542. According to an English authority, Bruce was at the battle of Methven thrice unhorsed, and on each occasion rescued by Sir Simon Fraser (Matthew of Westminster, p. 455).

[8] Prynne's Edward I., p. 1123; Barbour, 35-37.

By the discomfiture at Methven, which took place on the 19th June 1306, Bruce became almost powerless. With a small body of followers he took refuge in the forest of Athole, and from thence penetrated into Aberdeenshire. At Aberdeen he was met by his wife and her ladies, whom he conducted for safety into the wilds of Breadalbane.[1]

In the vicinity of Tyndrum, between Loch Awe and Loch Tay, Bruce resisted a new peril. Alexander of Argyle, Lord of Lorne, husband to an aunt of the slaughtered ex-regent, resolved to wreak revenge upon his slayer. Having occupied the mountain passes, he inveigled Bruce into a narrow passage between a lake and its abrupt bank. Here, as the king rode up, three persons rushed upon him, one seizing his bridle, a second passing his hand between the stirrup and his boot, and the third tightly seizing him from behind. The first assailant he struck dead, dragged the second to the ground, and vigorously turning in the saddle smote the third with his battle-axe.[2]

Bruce now sent his Queen and her ladies to the castle of Kildrummie under a strong guard; his own personal followers being reduced to about two hundred. But he was in the vicinity of Loch Lomond unexpectedly rejoined by the Earl of Lennox, who had since the disaster at Methven been seeking shelter in the wilds.

Having determined that Bruce should perish on the scaffold, Edward, on the 28th of June, instructed De Valence that the Earl of Carrick should, on his capture, be reserved pending his order;[3] and in the month of October following, he issued an injunction that all concerned in the slaughter of the Comyns should be hanged and drawn.[4]

[1] Barbour, i., 41.

[2] *Ibid.*, i., 43 ; Fordun, l. xll., c. ii.

[3] Sir Francis Palgrave's Transcripts, vol. 63, fol. 1. In the same dispatch Edward gave similar instructions respecting Sir Simon Fraser.

[4] Tyrrel, iii., 174 ; Fœdera, vol. i., Part ii., p. 995, new ed.

Though only in his sixty-fifth year, Edward suffered much from bodily weakness, and as he was extremely corpulent, he sat heavily on horseback, and moved slowly. Reaching Lanercost by slow stages, he was there, on the 7th October, seized with a dangerous illness, which confined him for the winter.[1]

Revenge and cruelty are rarely restrained by infirmity or sickness. Bruce's queen and daughter, and other female relatives and adherents having been made prisoners, Edward on the 7th November issued orders for their detention. The Countess of Buchan, who had crowned Bruce at Scone, he caused to be confined at Berwick Castle in an iron cage;[2] and in a cage suspended from a turret in the castle of Roxburgh, he confined Bruce's sister, Mary. The Scottish king's other sister, Christina, and his daughter, Marjory, he immured in a convent. As Bruce's wife was the sister of his ally, the Earl of Ulster, he was content to consign her to a common prison. He executed as traitors Nigel Bruce, the king's brother; also his adherents, Sir David de Inchmartin, Sir John de Cambo, Sir John de Somerville, Ralph de Herries, Alexander le Scrimgeour, Robert Wishart, Bernard de Mouat, Cuthbert de Carrick, William de Baa, William de Botharm, Ughtred le Mareschal, and Sir Christopher Seton.[3]

Among the adherents of the Scottish king present at the battle of Methven whom Edward sought specially to secure, was the Earl of Athole. In attempting to escape beyond seas, the Earl was driven back by a storm, and was consequently seized. As he was Edward's own kinsman, and was suffering from a severe and dangerous ailment, he hoped for mercy, but such was

---

[1] Fœdera, ii., 1005, 1017, 1025, 1027.

[2] Chapter House (Scots Documents), Box 1, No. 4; Fœdera, ii., 1013, 1014; Barbour's Bruce, p. 66.

[3] Assize Roll (York), 34 Edward I., m. 26, dorso.

resolutely denied him; he was by Edward's order gibbeted and disembowelled.[1]

Attacking a body of English soldiers in the neighbourhood of Stirling, Sir Simon Fraser was defeated, and made prisoner. By Edward's command, he was laden with irons, ignominiously paraded through the streets of London, and thereafter executed at Smithfield with every circumstance of barbarity.[2]

Having procured additional adherents, Bruce fortified the castle of Dunaverty, at the Mull of Kintyre; but some time prior to the 22d September it was besieged by John of Argyle,[3] who succeeded in reducing it. With difficulty Bruce effected his escape, and on the 29th January 1306-7, we find Edward pursuing him with a powerful fleet.[4]

Bruce now sailed for Norway,[5] and appealing to King Eric, whose second queen was his paternal aunt, Isabella Bruce, he obtained from him a fleet of galleys. He now surprised Brodick Castle, in Arran, dislodging the garrison in command of Sir John Hastings, an English knight. Occupying Arran, he from thence sent a messenger to the coast of Carrick, with instructions that if the country was well affected, he should kindle a fire on the cliffs at Turnberry. At the time specified a strong light appeared on the coast, and under the belief that it was the friendly signal, Bruce steered towards the shore. But his messenger, who met him on the strand, informed him that the fire was not of his kindling, and that Sir Henry Percy held Turnberry Castle with a powerful force.[6] Notwithstanding the misadventure, Bruce resolved to continue on the mainland, and in the first instance he set on fire a number of huts in which Percy

[1] Matthew of Westminster, p. 456.
[2] *Ibid.*
[3] Royal Letters, No. 3167.
[4] Close Roll, 35 Edward I., m. 14; Patent Roll, 35 Edward I., m. 39.
[5] Fabian's Chronicle, ed. 1559, p. 148.
[6] Barbour, 53, 84.

accommodated a portion of his troops; he also seized his war horses, and household plate.[1]

Bruce now retired to the uplands, in the hope of being there joined by his brothers, Thomas and Alexander, who were expected from Ireland with a powerful force. The brothers landed at Loch Ryan on the 9th February, but their movements being discovered by Duncan Macdowall, a local chief in the English interest, he suddenly attacked them with superior numbers. Both brothers were captured; also Sir Reginald Craufurd, who had accompanied them from Ireland, and although all were severely wounded, they were borne to Carlisle, and there, by Edward's order, subjected to the executioner.[2]

Bruce now sought shelter in the wilds of Nithsdale, but his retreat becoming known he was pursued by Sir John Botetorte at the head of seventy men-at-arms and two hundred archers. Contriving to escape into Ayrshire, he with an accession of followers gave battle to De Valence at Loudoun Hill, when he achieved a signal victory.[3]

The battle of Loudoun Hill was fought on the 10th of May 1307. And on the 15th of the same month, an abettor of the English rule, who concealed his name,[4] made report to headquarters in a missive written at Forfar, that Bruce, consequent on his recent success, had attained so a high place in popular favour, that should he march to Ross-shire or other northern parts the populace would certainly adhere to him. The writer therefore urged that a body of men-at-arms should be

[1] Hemingford, 225, 226; Matthew of Westminster, 456; Barbour, 92.

[2] Matthew of Westminster, 457, 458; Hemingford, 225; Trivet, 346; Fordun, xii., ii. According to Langtoft, Alexander Bruce was educated at Cambridge, where he attained educational distinction; he adds that he was Dean of Glasgow (Chronicles, vol. ii., p. 337).

[3] Barbour, 155.

[4] It was not uncommon for Edward's supporters in Scotland to conceal their names in transmitting intelligence, in view of the possible apprehension of their messengers.

forthwith sent to the northern districts in order to consolidate the royal authority. In conclusion he expressed a hope that God might prolong the king's life, adding, " for when we lose him, say they openly, all must be on one side, or they must die or leave the country, with all those that love the king, if other counsel and aid be not sent them." [1]

Edward left Lanercost at the close of February, moving by slow stages towards Carlisle, which he reached on the 10th March. He now experienced a severe attack of dysentery which confined him to his chamber till the end of June. On his recovery he reviewed his household troops, whom he addressed mirthfully ; [2] he then entered the cathedral, and there deposited the litter on which he had been borne, dedicating it to God. He now mounted his charger, and travelling one mile daily, reached on the fourth day the small hamlet of Burgh-upon-Sands, Unable to proceed further, he was conducted into a cottage, where he soon afterwards expired.

Edward died on the 7th July 1307. [3] Shortly before his death, he caused the Prince of Wales to renew the promise he had formerly exacted of him, that he would boil his body, and thereby detaching his bones, carry them in his progresses till such time as Scotland was subdued. [4] But the Prince dispensed with the ghastly commission, and conveying his father's remains to Westminster, there deposited them in the sepulchre of the kings.

So terminated the career of one of the most powerful of the English sovereigns, one who to an unworthy ambition prostrated talents and capabilities of a high order. In attempting the

[1] Chancery Miscellaneous Portfolios, No. 11.
[2] Fœdera, ii., 1046-1053.
[3] Fœdera, vol. i., part ii., 1018, new ed. ; Prynne's Edward I., p. 1202.
[4] Froissart, vol. i., chap. xxvii.

conquest of Scotland, he wholly misjudged the unbending character of a people who were ready to endure every privation so as to maintain their personal and national freedom. And the cruel and unwarranted slaughter of their chief served to stimulate them to a more ardent resistance, till at length under a leader second only to Wallace himself, they were enabled to shake off the yoke of foreign domination. The work of rescue inaugurated by Wallace at the battle of Stirling Bridge was, on the memorable 24th of June 1314, consummated by King Robert the Bruce on the field of Bannockburn.

APPENDICES.

APPENDIX I.

JOHN BLAIR.

John Blair, supposed to have been the hero's chaplain and biographer, is described as having had a noble ancestry;[1] and if, as is alleged, he was Wallace's school companion at Dundee, it may be assumed that he belonged to the Fifeshire family of the name. Prior to 1229 Alexander de Blair had a charter of the lands of Konakin or Kenly in Fife; he afterwards acquired by marriage the lands of Nydie, in the same county. His son, Sir William de Blair, steward of Fife in the reign of Alexander II., had two sons, Alexander and Walter. A gift to Duncan of Crambeth of the lands of Balbard, by the elder son, styled Sir Alexander de Blair, was confirmed by Symon, abbot of Dunfermline, about the year 1278. At the same time are named as members of that abbey, Adam, David, and George, sons of David and William de Blair.[2]

David, son of John de Blair in Fife, swore allegiance to Edward I. in 1296; he may have been the elder brother of the Patriot's associate.

In reference to John Blair, the chaplain, Henry writes thus :—

> " Maister Jhone Blayr was offt in that message,
> A worthy clerk, bath wyss and rycht sawage.—
> Lewyt he was befor in Paryss toune
> Amang maistris in science and renoune.
> Wallace and he at hayme in scule had beyne ;
> Sone eftirwart, as verité is seyne—
> He was the man that pryncipall wndirtuk
> That fyrst compild in dyt the Latyne buk
> Off Wallace lyff, rycht famous of renoune.

> .   .   .   .   .

[1] Dempster's Hist., Eccl. Gent. Scot., Edinb. 1829, i., 86.   [2] Register of Dunfermline, p., 213.

> " Eftyr the pruff geyffyn fra the Latyn buk
> Quhilk Maister Blayr in his tym undyrtuk,
> In fayr Latyn compild it till ane end ;
> With thir witnes the mar is to commend.
> Byschop Synclar than lord was off Dunkell,
> He gat this buk, and confermd it him sell
> For werray trew ; thar off he had no dreid,
> Himselff had seyn gret part of Wallace deid.
> His purpos was till haue send it to Rom
> Our fadyr off kyrk tharon to gyff his dom.
> Bot Maistir Blayr and als Schir Thomas Gray,
> Eftir Wallace thai lestit mony day,
> Thir twa knew best off gud Schir Wilyhamys deid
> Fra sexteyn yer quhill nyne and twenty yeid." [1]

The tradition to which the Minstrel alludes, that Blair composed a record of Wallace's principal exploits was probably well-founded; but it is evident that the composition in the original Latin had early disappeared, otherwise it had certainly been quoted by Fordun. To the Minstrel it was probably known through the medium of an imperfect version in the vernacular.

A statement by Dr George Mackenzie, that subsequent to the Patriot's death, Blair entered the monastery of Dunfermline under the name of Arnald Blair, rests on no historical basis.[2] The tract entitled "Relationes Quaedam Arnaldi Blair," printed in 1707 by Mr Andrew Symson, bookseller in Edinburgh, under the editorship of Sir Robert Sibbald, is an adaptation from the *Scotichronicon.*

---

[1] Henry's Wallace, B. v., ll. 538-546 ; B. xi., 1413-1425.

[2] Mackenzie's Lives of Writers of the Scots' Nation, Edinb. 1829, vol. i., p. 36.

———o———

II.

SIR WILLIAM DOUGLAS.

Between the years 1175 and 1199, William of Dufglas witnessed a charter by Joceline, bishop of Glasgow, to the monks of Kelso.[1] Of his six sons, Archibald the eldest had a third son, Sir William, to whom were born two sons, Hugh and William. Hugh took part at the battle of Largs in 1263; he succeeded to the family estate, and dying unmarried prior to 1288, the barony devolved on his brother William.

William Douglas became known as the Hardy. Having married Alianora, widow of William de Ferrars, an English baron, without obtaining the royal sanction, Edward I., in a missive addressed to the Guardians of Scotland on the 27th January 1288-9, ordered his arrest, also the seizure of his wife, in order that they might be compelled to answer for their contempt. Edward also charged the Sheriff of Northumberland to seize Douglas's possessions within the bounds of his sheriffdom, until he had made the usual submission. In his writ directed to the sheriff, Edward sets forth that Douglas had abducted his wife from Elena de Zusche's manor of Tranent, where she was awaiting her dower from the lands of her late husband. And on the 14th of July 1288, Edward instructed his escheator beyond the Trent to seize the lands and goods of John Wichard, whom he charged as an accomplice in effecting the abduction.[2] Douglas was some time warded in the castle of Leeds ; he was liberated on the 15th May 1290, on producing surety that he would duly submit himself.[3] On consenting to make payment of £100, he, on the 18th February 1290-1, received the royal pardon.[4] Attending the Parliament at Brigham in 1289, he signified his approval of the letter by which the Scottish community asserted their privileges. In July 1291, he swore fealty to Edward, at Thurston in Berwickshire. Warmly attaching

---

[1] Origines Parochiales Scotiæ, i., 155.

[2] Chancery Miscellaneous Portfolios, No. 11 ; Originalia, 17 Edward I., m. 3, 14.

[3] Close Roll, 18 Edward I., m. 11.

[4] Fine Roll, 19 Edward I., m. 16.

himself to Baliol's government, he furthered the league proposed between Scotland and France. He had command of Berwick Castle when in March 1296 it was attacked by Edward, and on capitulating was allowed to march out with military honours. After being some time warded in Berwick Castle, he, at Edinburgh on the 10th June, renounced his share in the league with France, and renewed to Edward his oath of homage.[1]

When in the prospect of being absent in Flanders Edward took measures to secure his authority in Scotland, he on the 24th May 1297 commissioned Sir William Douglas, with other Scottish barons, to co-operate on his behalf.[2] But Douglas had already made to Wallace overtures of help, and about the end of May he accompanied him to Scone, and took part in his attack on Ormesby, the English justiciary; he afterwards assisted in reducing the English garrisons at Sanquhar and Durrisdeer. But his support of the Patriot was of short continuance, since on the 9th July he joined in the capitulation at Irvine.[3] His submission was rejected, and after a period of imprisonment at Berwick, he was committed to the Tower, where he was laden with fetters.[4]

While Douglas was assailing the English garrisons in Dumfriesshire, the young Earl of Carrick, at Edward's request, wrecked his territories, and threw his wife and children into prison. And on the 12th June 1297, the sheriff of Essex by a royal order escheated his wife's lands situated in that county.[5]

Douglas died in prison prior to the 24th of January 1298-9. The fine of £100 imposed on him in connexion with his marriage not being fully paid, Edward on the 18th February 1304-5 gave instructions to the sheriff of Northumberland to levy the balance on his wife's lands.[6] In his barony, Douglas was succeeded by his eldest son, who, as the brave and faithful Sir James Douglas, is closely associated with the struggles and triumph of King Robert the Bruce.

[1] Ragman Roll, m. 1.

[2] Close Roll, 25 Edward I., m. 27.

[3] Scots Documents, Box 99, No. 13.

[4] Tower Miscellaneous Rolls, No. 474; Royal Letters, 3251; Exchequer Q. R. Memoranda, 26 Edward I., m. 63, 67 dorso; Close Roll, 25 Edward I., m. 4.

[5] Fine Roll, 25 Edward I., m. 12.

[6] Exchequer Q. R. Memoranda, 33 Edward I., m. 81 dorso.

III.

BISHOP WILLIAM FRASER OF ST ANDREWS.

Third son of Simon Fraser, of Oliver Castle, in Tweeddale, and brother of Sir Simon Fraser, the notable patriot, William Fraser took orders in the Church, and became Rector of Cadzow. In 1273 while holding office as Dean of Glasgow, he was appointed Chancellor of the kingdom. In 1279 he was advanced to the bishopric of St Andrews, receiving consecration from Pope Nicholas III. in the following year. On the 29th March 1286, immediately after the funeral of Alexander III., he, on behalf of the bishop of Glasgow and of the nobles and barons, despatched to Edward I. the Prior of the Dominicans at Perth, and Brother Arnold of the same order, to solicit his royal counsel and assistance.[1]

When by the clergy and nobles six guardians were appointed to Margaret of Norway, the young queen, Bishop Fraser was named first in order, his colleagues being the bishop of Glasgow, Duncan, Earl of Fife, Alexander, Earl of Buchan, John Comyn the younger, and James the Steward.

In the course of a journey through England to wait on King Edward at Gascony, early in 1289, Bishop Fraser and his suite were, by the sheriff of York, arrested at Doncaster. In connexion with the arrest, Edward ordered a judicial enquiry.[2]

As first of the guardians, Bishop Fraser supported Edward's proposal as to the marriage of the infant queen with his son, the Prince of Wales. By his co-guardians, he was, on the 3d October 1289, accredited conjunctly with the bishop of Glasgow, Robert Bruce, the elder, and John Comyn, to arrange with the ambassadors of the king of Norway as to the custody of the young queen.[3] He accordingly met them at Salisbury on the 6th of November, while at the Parliament at Brigham, held on the 14th March 1289-90, he continued his adherence to Edward's policy. When a rumour arose as to the

---

[1] Chancery Miscellaneous Rolls, No. 474.   [2] Patent Roll, 17 Edward I., m. 10 dorso; m. 37.
[3] Liber A. Chapter House, folio 127.

young queen's death, Bishop Fraser despatched to Edward a special communication. Dated on the 7th October 1290, that missive proceeds thus:—
"As was recently determined in your presence, the messengers sent by you, and some of the nobles of Scotland, met at Perth on the Sunday before the feast of St Michael, to hear and consider your reply to the things which were submitted to you; which reply being heard, the faithful nobility, and a certain portion of the commonalty of Scotland, rendered great thanks to your highness. We then, and your messengers, determined to proceed to Orkney, in order to treat with the ambassadors from Norway, for the due reception of our lady, the queen, when a dismal rumour reached us that she was dead; a rumour that troubles and distracts the kingdom of Scotland. As soon as Robert de Bruce heard of this, he came to our meeting at Perth, which he did not intend doing before. He is accompanied by a great retinue, but what his object is, we have not yet learnt. The Earls of Mar and Athole have raised troops, and some of the other nobles are attaching themselves to his party, so it is feared there will be a civil war and great bloodshed, unless the Most High bring us a remedy through your means. The Bishop of Durham, the Earl of Warren (Surrey), and we, have just heard that our lady the queen has recovered from her illness, but is still very infirm; on which account we have resolved to remain at Perth, or the neighbourhood, till we know certainly, from the knights who are gone to Orkney, the true state of our lady, which I heartily wish may be favourable. And should we receive such an account as we desire (which we expect daily), we will be prepared to proceed as we purposed, to the fulfilment of our design. If John de Baliol go to you, we advise you to treat him in such a way as to maintain your own honour and advantage. But if it turn out that our lady is dead (which God forbid!), let your Highness be pleased to come to our Border, to console our people, and hinder the effusion of blood; so that the faithful of our land may preserve their oath inviolate, and raise him to the throne who is entitled to it; yet so that he may be willing to follow your counsel. May God crown you with temporal and eternal felicity." [1]

In the superscription to his letter, Bishop Fraser approaches Edward by styling himself his "devoted chaplain," and it is probable that he wrote at

---

[1] Royal Letters, No. 1302; Fœdera, i., 741; National MSS. of Scotland, i., No. lxx.

the dictation of Bishop Bek, then in Scotland, and who early interested himself on behalf of Baliol. Fraser's support of Baliol becoming known to Robert Bruce of Annandale, led to the protest against his being continued as a guardian, contained in the celebrated document addressed to Edward by those members of the nobility who styled themselves "the seven Earls of Scotland." [1]

On the 9th May 1291, Edward granted a safe conduct to Bishops Fraser and Wishart, also to the nobles and magnates of Scotland, so that they might meet him at Norham, in relation to Scottish affairs.[2] From his duties as coroner of Northumberland, Edward on the 10th August 1291 relieved Stephen de Muscamp, since, as "familiar" to the bishop of St Andrews, he was constantly occupied in the bishop's household.[3]

Bishop Fraser strongly adhered to Baliol, even after his rupture with the English king. On behalf of Baliol's government he proceeded to France as the principal member of an embassy, for the renewal of the ancient league, also to negotiate a marriage between the royal houses of the two kingdoms. According to Fordun he did not return from his mission, but died at Carteville in France, in September 1297. His remains were consigned to the church of the Friars Predicant in Paris, while his heart, enclosed in a costly shrine, was conveyed to Scotland by his successor, Bishop Lamberton, and deposited in the cathedral of St Andrews.

[1] Chapter House, Scots Documents, Box 89, No. 22.

[2] Patent Roll, 19 Edward I., m. 14.

[3] Close Roll, 19 Edward I., m. 4.

IV.

SIR SIMON FRASER.

The representative of a Border family, Simon Fraser of Oliver Castle, in the county of Peebles, had three sons, Simon, Alexander, and William; also two daughters, one of whom married Sir Patrick Fleming, ancestor of the Earls of Wigton, and the other, Sir Gilbert Hay, progenitor of the noble family of Tweeddale. From Alexander, the second son, have descended the Barons of Saltoun and Lovat. William, the third son, became Bishop of St Andrews,[1] and on the death of Alexander III. was elected one of the six regents of the kingdom.

Simon, eldest son of Simon Fraser, succeeded to the patrimonial inheritance prior to the 23d July 1291, when he swore fealty to Edward I., on the great altar of the Abbey of Lindores.[2] On the 16th January 1292-3, he is named as one of the Scottish magnates, who in the preceding December had attested an act of homage to Edward by John Baliol.[3] Taken prisoner by the Earl of Surrey on the surrender of Dunbar Castle in April 1296, he seems to have remained in ward till the 13th October, when he renewed his homage to Edward on "the Holy Evangels."[4] On the 28th May 1297, he at Bramber in Sussex made oath that he would support Edward against the king of France, and presented as his surety his cousin, Sir Richard Fraser. To letters-patent attesting this act of fidelity, he and his relative attached their seals.[5] He accompanied the expedition to Flanders on the 22d August 1297, and in a letter from Ghent, dated 21st October thereafter, Edward gave instructions that his lands in England and Scotland should be restored to him.[6] In a missive, dated 1st May 1298, Edward warmly commends his services.[7]

---

[1] Patent Roll, 18 Edward I., m. 30.

[2] Chapter House, Scots Documents, Box 16, No. 2.

[3] *Ibid.*, Box 95, No. 6 ; Liber A., fol. 175b.

[4] *Ibid.*, Box 3, No. 40.

[5] Chapter House, Scots Documents, Box 99, No. 20.

[6] Privy Seals (Tower), 25 Edward I., File 2.

[7] Exchequer Q. R. Memoranda, 26 Edward I., m. 35.

In view of an expedition to Scotland, Edward, early in July 1298, gave command that extensive stores should be shipped from Berwick for the castle of Edinburgh ; and these he enjoined should be conveyed from Leith to the castle under the superintendence of Sir Walter de Huntercumbe or Sir Simon Fraser.[1] On the 22d of July, Fraser served under Edward at the battle of Falkirk ; he was then mounted on a charger, described as a " ferrand pomele," presented by the king.[2] As English Warden of Selkirk Forest, he subsequent to the battle resumed his function. But he had attached himself to the English interest simply from policy, and in reality was an abettor of the patriotic movement ; he therefore, in the Forest, extended shelter to that portion of the Scottish army which had escaped from the field of Falkirk, giving his special countenance to the illustrious leader. Professedly with a view to his more efficiently executing a mission in the royal service, but in reality to disarm suspicion, he on the 31st of July procured from the governor of Berwick an attestation of fidelity.[3] But despite his efforts to disguise his conduct, his divided allegiance did not escape observation. On the 9th August, John de Kingston, Constable of Edinburgh Castle, reports of him to Langton, the Treasurer, in these terms :—" As to the news of our neighbourhood, I have to tell you that the Earl of Buchan, the Bishop of St Andrews, and other earls and great lords, who were on the other side of the Scottish sea, have come to this side, and were at Glasgow on the day on which this letter was made ; and by . . . they intend to go towards the borders, as is reported among them and their people who are in the forest. And whereas Sir Simon Fraser comes to you in such haste, let me inform you, sire, that he has no need to be in such a great hurry, for there was not by any means such a great power of people who came into his jurisdiction but that they might have been stopped by the garrisons,[4] if Sir Simon had given them warning. And of this I warned him eight days before they came ; and before they were entered into the forest, it was reported that there was a treaty between them and Sir Simon, and that they had a con-

[1] From the Original Indenture in the Public Record Office.

[2] Roll of the horses of bannerets, knights, esquires and valets of the King's household, valued in the Scottish war (Exchequer Q. R. Miscellanea (Army), No. $\frac{8}{8}$).

[3] Royal Letters, No. 2893.

[4] Chain of forts from Oliver Castle by the Tweed to Berwick.

ference together, and ate and drank, and were on the best of terms. Wherefore, sire, it were well you should be very cautious as to the advice which he shall give you. And let me tell you, sire, that this same Sir Simon sent me a letter (whereof I send you a copy) the day when he set out from his charge, or the next day, and he wished that I should come thither to him ; to which I made such an answer, as I send you in writing, but I do not know whether it reached him or not. And he sent me other letters some time before I came thither to him, on the day on which our enemies came suddenly before our castle, and on which Sir Thomas de Arderne was taken; wherefore I fear that he is not of such good faith as he ought to be. Wherefore I beg of you and the rest of the king's council, to beware. I have to inform you, sire, that they of the forest have surrendered themselves to the Scotch." [1]

Informed of Fraser's defection, Edward resolved as a matter of policy to subject his fidelity to a further trial. Accordingly on the 25th of November he addressed him from Newcastle in the following missive :—" The King to his beloved and faithful Simon Fraser, greeting: Whereas we have charged our beloved and faithful John de Kingston, our constable of the castle of Edinburgh, and sheriff of the same place, to make a raid, which he cannot do with his own company without having more sufficient aid, and we take it much to heart that this expedition be made safely, well and effectually; we command, and pray, and charge you, that whensoever the said constable shall let you know, or shall command you—leaving all else without delay, and all kind of excuse, you come to him with twenty armed horses, doing whatever he shall enjoin you upon our part. For be it known to you that we are very anxious that the said expedition should succeed well, as has been said. And to do this fail not in any manner in which you are bound to us, and as you love our honour." [2] On the 1st of December, Edward by his Privy Council enjoined Sir Simon Fraser, together with the sheriffs of Roxburgh and Jedburgh, to make arrangements at Berwick, so that the safety of the garrison might be secured. The Privy Council also provided that Sir Simon and other officers " should spy out and cause to be spied out, all the news possible about the enemies and their plan," and severally communicate their discoveries to

---

[1] From the British Museum, Cott. Chart. xxiv., 18.   [2] Patent Roll, 27 Edward I., m. 40.

the constable of Edinburgh Castle so that they might join him in a foray.[1]

On the 27th March 1299, Fraser was restored to his forfeited possessions.[2] On the 16th July following, he took part at a meeting at York as to the garrisoning of the Scottish fortresses, and at the same time was, along with other Scottish magnates, commissioned to advise as to the delivery of certain notable Scottish prisoners.[3] In the English interest he was present at the siege of Carlaverock in July 1300, and on the 30th of October, Edward notified to him as "Warden of Selkirk Forest," the terms of his truce with the Scots.[4] During the same year, Sir Simon Fraser is named in the Wardrobe Account as receiving a salary, also his wife, Lady Mary, and his daughters, as residing by permission in the castle of Jedburgh, with a weekly allowance of one mark. In the year 1300, Edward granted warrant for a payment of twenty pounds to Sir Simon Fraser, in part of a sum due to him as certified by Sir Ralph de Manton, the cofferer.[5] In March 1300-1, Sir Simon is named as in attendance on Edward at Lincoln, but shortly after April 1302 he renounced his allegiance. And on the 13th August 1302, it is set forth that when he joined the Scots, he carried off from Wark, horses and armour, the property of Sir William of Durham.[6] On the 24th of February 1302-3, he surprised the English forces at Roslin under command of Sir Ralph de Manton, effecting a decisive victory.

On the 6th March 1303-4, Edward received tidings that "Sir Simon Fraser and William Wallace" had been routed at Hopprewe by Sir William Latymer, Sir John de Segrave, and Sir Robert de Clifford.[7] Nine days later, John of Moskelburgh, a Scotsman, is named as having received a recompense of ten shillings for guiding the three English leaders to a place in Lothian where Fraser and Wallace had found shelter.[8] On the 10th September, Boice de Burdil received four pounds to compensate him for the loss of two horses in his foray upon the followers of Fraser and Wallace.[9] Several Scotsmen in

---

[1] Exchequer, Treasury of Receipt Miscellanea, No. $\frac{43}{20}$ dorso.

[2] Patent Roll, 27 Edward I., m. 33.

[3] Close Roll, 27 Edward I., m. 10 ; also m. 9.

[4] Chapter House (Scots Documents), Box 100, Nos. 135, 136, 137, 138.

[5] Privy Seals (Tower), 29 Edward I., File 1.

[6] Exchequer Q. R. Miscellanea (Army), No. $\frac{26}{14}$.

[7] British Museum, Addit. MSS., No. 8835.

[8] *Ibid.*

[9] *Ibid.*

the English interest, who had watched the movements of the two Scottish leaders at Stirling and elsewhere, were also recompensed.

In 1305, when Scotland was re-subjected to English rule, Fraser offered to return to Edward's allegiance. This offer Edward agreed to accept on two conditions, first, that the petitioner should make his submission before Christmas, and secondly, that he would exile himself for a period of four years both from this country and from France.[1] Soon afterwards we find Fraser in full possession of Edward's favour; while not long thereafter he appears as a prominent supporter of King Robert the Bruce.

In a dispatch to Aymer de Valence of the 12th June 1306, Edward expresses satisfaction that he has wasted Fraser's lands in Selkirk Forest, and desires that his work of destruction may be continued.[2] And on the 28th June he instructs De Valence, that in the event of his capturing Sir Simon Fraser, he should send him to London strongly guarded.[3]

Soon afterwards Fraser was captured, and on his presenting an entreaty for Edward's clemency his messenger was executed.[4] Borne to London, he was brought to trial, and sentenced to suffer as a traitor. On the 7th September 1306, he was executed with every circumstance of barbarity, and his head attached to a long spear was thereafter exhibited on London Bridge.[5] A poem in relation to his death, composed a few years after the event, is preserved among the Harleian MSS.;[6] it has been published by Ritson.

---

[1] Close Roll, 33 Edward I., m. 13 dorso cedula.

[2] Sir Francis Palgrave's Transcripts, vol. 63, fol. 58.

[3] *Ibid.*, vol. 63, fol. 1.

[4] Assize Roll, York, 34 Edward I., No. $\frac{1}{20}$, 1.

[5] Harleian MSS., 206.

[6] *Ibid.*, No. 2203.

V.

BISHOP WILLIAM LAMBERTON OF ST ANDREWS.

Early in the eleventh century a Saxon named Lambert settled on lands in Berwickshire; his descendants assumed the name of Lamberton.

William de Lamberton flourished in the reign of David I., and Henry de Lamberton was one of the barons nominated by Robert the Bruce in 1292 to assist Edward I. in forming a judgment as to his claim for the throne. Robert de Lamberton swore fealty to Edward, at Berwick, in August 1296. William de Lamberton, the future bishop, was born at Kilmaurs in Ayrshire. Entering the Church, he became parson of Campsie. When chancellor of the diocese of Glasgow in 1296 he swore fealty to Edward.

On the death of Bishop William Fraser of St Andrews in September 1297, the Culdean chapter of the city nominated as his successor William Comyn, brother of the Earl of Buchan, Provost of the monastery at Kirkheugh.[1] The election was unwarranted, inasmuch as the privilege of nominating to the See which the Culdean chapter formerly enjoyed had fallen into abeyance. Several months after Comyn's nomination, Wallace, in his capacity of guardian, proceeded to St Andrews to effect Comyn's ejectment, while according to the Minstrel, Comyn, informed of his approach, "got away by sea." He would appear to have made a brief visit to the English court, and thereafter to have posted to Rome. Under Wallace's recommendation, the canons-regular of St Andrews now elected to the See William Lamberton, who hastened to procure Papal confirmation. At Rome Comyn arrived first, but only to find that the Pope, Boniface VIII., was hostile to his claim. Lamberton, on the other hand, was cordially received, and as his title was certified by the Scottish guardian, also by the French king, his election was confirmed.

Having been duly consecrated to his office, Lamberton was employed by the Pope in drafting a letter to Edward, in which he refused to sanction the pretence that Scotland was a fief of the English crown.

---

[1] The Culdean monastery of Kirkheugh at St Andrews consisted of a Provost and twelve prebendaries.

From Rome the bishop proceeded to Paris, in the hope of inducing Philip to provide for the independence of Scotland in his treaty with Edward, then in progress. And by letters to Wallace he empowered him to utilize a principal portion of his episcopal revenues for the defence of the country.[1] Having at the court of France failed to secure the contemplated benefits, Lamberton proceeded to Flanders, accompanied by Sir John Soulis and other Scottish barons in a journey homeward. His movement, and that of his associates, becoming known, Edward instructed "masters of vessels" and others to intercept their passage.[2]

When in 1299 Wallace resigned the guardianship, Bishop Lamberton, the Earl of Carrick, and John Comyn the younger, were jointly appointed to the office. And on the 15th November the bishop and his colleagues addressed a letter to Edward from the Forest of Torre, in which they offered to submit all questions between the kingdoms to the mediation of the French king.[3]

On behalf of the guardians Lamberton proceeded to France in 1301 to further entreat Philip's co-operation, and he returned to Scotland in the following spring, bearing from the French king an important communication. In his letter Philip informed the Scottish guardians, bishops, nobles, and the entire community, that he was moved "to the very marrow" by the evils inflicted upon their country, and that, in virtue of the old league between the kingdoms, he was most desirous of rendering help, but, as risks attended the transmission of written communications, he had preferred to convey his intentions orally by the bishop of St Andrews, who would doubtless faithfully report them.[4]

Bearing to the French king the grateful acknowledgments of the guardians and barons, Lamberton returned to Paris, and from that city on the 25th of May 1303 he addressed a letter to his constituents urging them to vigorously resist the Edwardian rule.[5] His letter was accompanied with an assurance under Philip's seal that terms of peace between him and Edward would not be finally adjusted till the interests of Scotland were secured.[6]

By a mandate issued at Dunfermline on the 17th February 1303-4, Edward

---

[1] Palgrave's Documents, clxv., clxvi.

[2] Patent Roll, Edward I., m. 20, 22.

[3] Chapter House (Scots Documents), Box 14, No. 14.

[4] Chancery Miscellaneous Portfolios, No. 11.

[5] Chapter House (Scots Documents), Box 14, No. 16.

[6] Royal Letters, No. 2566.

instructed his chancellor, William de Grenefield, to prepare under the Great Seal, letters of safe conduct to several Scottish magnates who had returned to his allegiance.[1] And by a writ dated the 2d of May 1304, he restored to the bishop the temporalities of his See, calling upon Sir Richard Siward to deliver up to him the castle and regality of St Andrews, and the sheriffs of the midland and northern counties to re-invest him in his lands and goods.[2] But Lamberton's submission to Edward was insincere, for on the 11th June—that is, within forty days after his restoration to his temporalities—he, at the abbey of Cambuskenneth, entered into an indenture with the Earl of Carrick in which they became bound to assist each other in effecting the deliverance of the kingdom.

In the Compotus of James de Dalileye and John de Westone, rendered to Edward on the 28th February 1304-5, these provincial agents include in their expenditure a disbursement of sixty-six shillings as the expenses of Ralph de Pentland and John de Pollok, who, accompanied by two grooms and a clerk, had proceeded from Aberdeen to Montrose to arrest a vessel of the bishop of St Andrews, reported to be laden with the goods of rebel merchants. The merchants and others in the bishop's service were, it is added, liberated in the month of August, as the bishop had come to the king's peace.[3]

Shortly after the 15th of September 1305, Bishop Lamberton attended at Westminster as one of the commissioners whom Edward had authorised to represent Scotland in the English Parliament.[4] And on the 16th February 1305-6, Edward empowered him, with three others, to administer his affairs in Scotland until at Easter his nephew, John of Bretagne, would assume office as his lieutenant.[5]

Lamberton's arrangement with the Earl of Carrick had been carefully concealed, hence Edward was startled by the intelligence that the bishop was prominently concerned in Bruce's coronation at Scone; and in a letter to Aymer de Valence, dated 26th May 1306, he consequently ordered his arrest.[6] And in a missive to De Valence, dated the 8th of June, he, while expressing his satisfaction that Bishop Wishart had been captured, renewed his instruction for

---

[1] Privy Seals (Tower), 32 Edward I., File 2.

[2] Chapter House (Scots Documents), Box 1, No. 7.

[3] Exchequer T. R. Miscellanea (Placita, Rentals, etc.), No. $\frac{9 \cdot 0 \cdot 2}{2 \cdot 1 \cdot 8}$.

[4] Close Roll, 33 Edward I., m. 13 dorso cedulâ.

[5] Patent Roll, 34 Edward I., m. 35.

[6] Sir Francis Palgrave's Transcripts, vol. 63, fol. 53.

Lamberton's seizure, assigning as a reason that, while he had appointed him chief of the guardians, he had proved viciously faithless. About the same time Edward escheated the bishop's temporalities, and conferred the custody of the castle of St Andrews on Sir Henry de Beaumont, one of his knights.[1]

On the 9th June 1306, Bishop Lamberton, now a prisoner, conveyed to Aymer de Valence his solemn assurance that he had no concern in the slaughter of the Comyns,[2] while in order to his liberation, he on the 22d June produced a mainprise, in which Henry de Sinclair and two other barons became his sureties that he would answer when called upon.[3] Refused a release, the bishop was conveyed to Berwick and from thence to Newcastle; and under a warrant dated the 7th of August, he was, along with the bishop of Glasgow and the abbot of Scone, warded in Nottingham Castle.[4] Soon afterwards he was under a secret order laden with irons, and sent for confinement in the castle of Winchester.[5] By another warrant, also of the 7th of August, Edward restricted his aliment to sixpence per day, with some subsidiary allowances for a chaplain and serving boy. In the warrants he is described as the betrayer of the king.[6]

When Lamberton was taken prisoner, there was found on his person a duplicate of the indenture, into which on the 11th June 1304 he had entered with the Earl of Carrick; he was consequently at Newcastle, on the 9th August, subjected to a judicial examination. In his deposition, he acknowledged that at Stirling on the 4th May 1304 he had sworn fealty to Edward, and that in the following month he had entered into a covenant with Bruce. And on being urged to explain why he made concealment of his league when he was admitted to the English Privy Council, he answered that the obligation had passed from his memory. In reply to the query as to why he, as a councillor of the king of England, had assisted at Bruce's coronation, he replied that he sought thereby to offer him sympathy under the menaces which oppressed him. But he denied the imputation of having delivered up to Bruce, Andrew, son and heir of the Steward of Scotland, whom Edward had

---

[1] Chancery Miscellaneous Portfolios, No. $\frac{2}{11}$.

[2] Chapter House (Scots Documents), Portfolio 1, No. 23.

[3] Royal Letters, No. 4515.

[4] Chapter House (Scots Documents), Box i., No. 5.

[5] Close Roll, 34 Edward I., m. 6.

[6] *Ibid.*, 31 Edward I., m. 6 dorso.

entrusted to his keeping.[1] He acknowledged that he had admitted Bruce to the sacrament of the Mass subsequent to the slaughter of the Comyns; also that he had rendered fealty to him after his coronation.

To the Pope, Clement V., Edward had represented the Earl of Carrick as guilty of murder and sacrilege; he had also complained of Bishop Lamberton as one of his abettors. As in reference to Lamberton, Clement answered evasively,[2] Edward proceeded to entreat the Pope for his spiritual degradation. In a memorial to Clement he set forth that the bishop had, when chancellor of Glasgow in 1296, rendered him the oath of fealty upon the Gospel, the cross Neyth,[3] and the black rood of Scotland, and that nevertheless he had taken part with William Wallace, and being by his aid elected bishop of St Andrews, had used his episcopal authority in seeking to subvert his (the petitioner's) supremacy in Scotland. Edward further set forth, that when he had personally regained his ascendancy in Scotland in the year 1304, the bishop renewed his allegiance, and had in consequence been restored to his temporalities. Yet he had, after Bruce had slaughtered the Comyns, taken part in his coronation, and had also surrendered to him an important hostage. Moreover, proceeded Edward, the bishop had, on the restoration of his authority in the north, made submission to Aymer de Valence, but on being allowed to return to his See, had forthwith assisted Bruce both with men and money. In conclusion, Edward informed the Pope that he could not fulfil his intention of proceeding to the Holy Land until the bishops of St Andrews and Glasgow were effectually restrained.[4]

Edward died in 1307, and in the following year Edward II. gave instructions that Lamberton's episcopal revenues should be paid into his exchequer, the bishop being allowed £100 for yearly maintenance.[5] He was liberated on the 23d of May 1308, on producing five sureties that he would remain peacefully in the county of Northampton.[6] On the 11th of August he rendered fealty to Edward II., and on the following day granted him a bond for 6000 marks,

---

[1] Chapter House (Scots Documents), Portfolio 4, No. 5.

[2] Papal Bulls.

[3] This cross was reputed to be a portion of the true cross, and it was named Gnayth, or Neyth, as a monk of this name was believed to have brought it from Palestine.

[4] Chapter House (Scots Documents), Portfolio 4, No. 6.

[5] Fœdera, vol. iii., p. 81.

[6] Close Roll, 1 Edward II., m. 2.

of which the moiety was by half-yearly instalments to be paid within three years to the English chamberlain in Scotland.[1]

To a Papal rescript urging Lamberton's liberation, Edward II. replied on the 4th of December 1309, with the intimation that the bishop had been set free.[2]

On his return to Scotland, Lamberton resumed his efforts in the national defence. On the 24th February 1308-9 he, as president of an assemblage of his clergy at Dundee, strongly asserted Bruce's title to the throne.[3] This act was evidently unknown to the English government, since on the 15th of the following June Lamberton had Edward's letters of protection to enable him to attend the English Parliament at Stanford.[4] And when the bishop was, prior to the 24th of June 1311, summoned to attend the General Council of Vienne, we find Edward II. instructing his chancellor to entreat the Pope to dispense with his attendance, as his presence in Scotland was essential to the continuance in that country of the English rule.[5]

In October 1313, Patric, Earl of March, and Sir Adam de Gordon, represented to the English government that they had for upwards of three years been subjected to a course of oppression by the English garrisons at Roxburgh and Berwick. They also set forth that the garrison of Berwick had seized eight tuns of wine belonging to Bishop Lamberton, and had insulted and menaced the bishop personally.[6] In November 1313 the bishop attended Edward II. at Westminster, and on the 30th of the same month received from him letters of protection for a journey on the king's business to the court of France.[7] And on the 25th September 1314, being three months after the battle of Bannockburn, he appears as receiving a safe-conduct from the English king so that he might proceed abroad on his personal affairs.[8]

Grateful for being permitted to return to his diocese, while other Scottish prisoners in England were much less favoured, Lamberton devoted himself towards furthering an alliance between the kingdoms. But his strong attachment to King Robert Bruce at length aroused the aversion of Edward II.,

[1] Chapter House (Scots Documents), Box 96, No. 10.

[2] French and Roman Roll, 2 Edward II., m. 6.

[3] Lord Hailes' Annals, iii., 215-218.

[4] Patent Roll, 2 Edward II., p. 1, m. 1.

[5] Privy Seals (Tower), 5 Edward II., File 2.

[6] Tower Miscellaneous Rolls, No. 459.

[7] Patent Roll, Edward II., p. 1, m. 2, 3.

[8] *Ibid.*, p. 1, m. 20.

who in June 1318 entreated Pope John XXII. to remove him from office. Unmoved by the hostile demonstration, the bishop pursued his conciliatory policy; and in the year 1323 he attended the English court as an envoy for the extension of a treaty.[1]

Bishop Lamberton completed the cathedral of St Andrews, which on the 5th June 1318 was consecrated in presence of King Robert. He died in 1328, and his remains were deposited in his cathedral, at the north side of the great altar.

[1] Tower Miscellaneous Rolls, No. 459; Privy Seals (Tower), 16 Edward II., File 3; Close Roll, 17 Edward II., m. 43.

VI.

BISHOP ROBERT WISHART OF GLASGOW.

The surname of Guiscard or Wischard, an appellative implying skill or prowess, was conferred on Robert, son of Tancred de Hauteville of Normandy, afterwards Duke of Calabria, who died on the 27th July 1085. Guiscard was also the surname of the Norman kings of Apulia in the twelfth and thirteenth centuries. John Wychard is named as a small landowner in the Hundred de la Mewe, Buckinghamshire, in the reign of Henry II. (1216-72), and in the reign of Edward I. persons named Wyschard or Wischart appear as landowners in Shropshire, also in the counties of Essex, Oxford, Buckingham, and Warwick.[1]

From the south, members of the House of Wischard penetrated into Scotland prior to the twelfth century. John Wischard was sheriff of Kincardineshire in the reign of Alexander II. (1214-49). To a charter by which this sovereign confirmed a grant to the monks of Arbroath by Walter and Christian Lundyn, spouses, the witnesses are John Wischard "vicecomes de Moernes," and his son John.[2] The same persons are witnesses to a charter by which Robert and Richenda Warnebald, spouses, grant to the kirk of St Thomas, of Arbroath, certain lands in the parish of Fordoun,[3] which charter is confirmed by Alexander II. on the 20th March 1238.

John Wischard, sheriff of Kincardineshire, had three sons, John, William, and Adam. John, the eldest son, was knighted by Alexander II., and from Adam, abbot of Arbroath, received the lands of Conveth (Laurencekirk), Halkertoun, and Scottistoun, in the county of Kincardine. His great-grandson, also Sir John, received the lands of Pitarrow in Kincardineshire, and among his notable descendants were James Wishart, Justice-Clerk to James IV.; George Wishart, the martyr; John Wishart, collector-general of

---

[1] Rotuli Hundredorum, vol. i. and ii. ; Testa de Nevill, *passim.*

[2] Register of Aberbrothoc, p. 97.

[3] *Ibid.,* pp. 198, 199.

teinds at the Reformation, and William Wishart, father and son, both distinguished Principals of the University of Edinburgh.[1]

William, second son of John Wischard, sheriff of Kincardineshire, entered the Church; and in 1256, while holding office as Archdeacon of St Andrews, was appointed Chancellor of the kingdom. In 1270 he was elected bishop of Glasgow, but in the same year was postulated to St Andrews. On the solicitation of Edward I., Pope Gregory X. dispensed with his proceeding to Rome for consecration. At St Andrews he founded the Dominican monastery, and reared the nave of the cathedral; he also exercised an important influence in public affairs. He died in 1278.[2]

Adam, third son of the sheriff of Kincardineshire, acquired the lands of Ballandarg, Logie, and Kennyneil, in the county of Forfar.[3] He had, with other children, two sons, John and Robert. "John Wychard del Miernes," supposed to be the elder son, swore fealty to Edward at Elgin on the 29th July 1296.[4]

Robert, the younger son, entered the church under the auspices of his uncle, Bishop Wishart of St Andrews. Having served as archdeacon of St Andrews within the bounds of Lothian, he was in 1270 elected bishop of Glasgow, when his uncle Bishop William was from that See transferred to the bishopric of St Andrews. According to the chartulary of Melrose he received consecration at the hands of the bishops of Aberdeen, Moray, and Dunblane. A Privy Councillor to Alexander III., he was, on the death of that sovereign, appointed one of the six guardians of the kingdom.

To Edward's proposal for the marriage of the infant queen Margaret with the Prince of Wales, Bishop Wishart yielded a cordial assent, and in prospect of the union he, as a representative of the Guardians, consented to place the national strongholds in Edward's hands.[5] On the 9th May 1291, he received from Edward a safe conduct to enable him to proceed to Norham, there to engage in conference relative to the national affairs;[6] and on the

---

[1] For a full account of the Scottish house of Wishart, *see* Life of George Wishart, Edinburgh, 1876, 8vo.

[2] Fordun's Scotichronicon, lib. x., c. 28; Spottiswoode's History, Edinburgh 1851, vol. i., pp. 91, 93.

[3] Dalrymple's Historical Collections, 217; Reg. of Aberbrothoc, 332.

[4] Ragman Roll, m. 17, 18.

[5] Patent Roll, 18 Edward I., m. 8.

[6] *Ibid.*, m. 14.

24th December 1292, he appended his seal to an instrument whereby Baliol acknowledged Edward as his liege-lord.[1]

Towards Bishop Wishart Edward began to evince a special liberality; he in October 1294 granted him the escheats, wards, and other privileges connected with certain lands of the earldom of Fife, till Duncan, the youthful earl, should attain his majority;[2] he also allowed him to possess the lands of Calder, in Fife. In a letter to his keeper in Fife, Edward distinguishes the bishop as his "dear friend."[3]

A patriot by conviction, Bishop Wishart lacked fixity of conduct. When in 1295 Baliol renounced Edward's allegiance, he also withdrew his fealty, and thereafter prominently furthered the league with France, as a member of Baliol's government. But when Baliol was feudally degraded and deprived of his crown, he, on the 26th July 1296, waited on Edward at Elgin, and there renewing his homage, expressed his regret for his recent tergiversation.[4]

Within a year after his submission at Elgin, Bishop Wishart reappears prominently in the national cause. As an enemy of the English king, his episcopal palace was in the summer of 1297 besieged by Bishop Bek, and early in July he is found in the camp at Irvine, a confederate of the Earl of Carrick, the Steward, Sir William Douglas, and others, who had assembled to resist the English arms. But in consideration that a powerful force under Percy and Clifford hovered near, he counselled submission, and succeeded in inducing the several leaders to signify their acceptance of the English rule, in the treaty of Irvine. In connexion with that treaty, he, on the 9th July, joined the Steward and Alexander de Lindsay as guarantees for the good conduct of the Earl of Carrick, until such time as he should surrender his daughter Marjory as a hostage.[5] Wallace avenged the bishop's time-serving policy, by entering his episcopal residence, and carrying off his nephews and a portion of his goods.[6]

Prior to the 23d of July 1297, the bishop in a familiar letter thanks Cressingham for communicating with him by Sir Reginald de Craufurd, and asks him to give credence to his clerk, Master Walter Camoys, also to Sir

---

[1] Chapter House (Scots Documents), Box 95, No. 6; Liber A., Chapter House, folio 175 b.

[2] Chancery Miscellaneous Portfolios, No. 11.

[3] Privy Seals (Tower), 22 Edward I., Bundle 3.

[4] Fœdera, i., 843.

[5] Chapter House (Scots Documents), Portfolio 4, No. 6.

[6] Hemingford, i., 124.

Reginald.[1] Writing to Edward from Berwick on the 1st August, the Earl of Surrey reports that within a week he expected that the bishop of Glasgow would, along with the Earl of Carrick and the Steward, fulfil his covenant.[2]

During the protectorate of Wallace, and for several years afterwards, Bishop Wishart supported Edward's authority. But prior to January 1303 he must have returned to the national party, for at that time we find Edward issuing instructions relative to the conditions on which his submission should be received. In Edward's writ he is associated with "William le Walcys, Sir David de Graham, Sir Alexander de Lindesaye, and Sir John Comyn."[3] Having renewed his homage, he seems to have been received cordially, since, on the 10th April 1304, Edward thanks him "dearly" for appointing his clerk, P. de Donewyz, as prebendary of Old Roxburgh.[4] On the 16th May and the 29th July, Edward addressed him special messages, and on the 1st August he is named as despatching a special messenger to Edward.[5]

Wishart next appears on the national side. In October 1304 Sir Nicholas Hastang, an English ecclesiastic, who held the church living at Ayr, represented to the English Privy Council that Wishart had ousted him from the prebend of Renfrew, while he was a hostage among the Scots for his brother, Sir Robert Hastang, sheriff of Roxburgh. In his memorial Sir Nicholas set forth that when the king ordered his being re-invested in his revenues, the bishop, "who was with the Scottish enemies," had "deigned no reply." Various proceedings followed, and as Wishart would not yield, the English warden was instructed to retain the petitioner in his office.[6] In the Compotus for escheats rendered by James de Dalilegh, on the 20th November 1304, Sir Robert Hastang, in connexion with the county of Peebles, accounts for £10 from farm of the vills of Stobo and Draych, and for 46s. 8d. from the farm of the mill of Stobo, both of which had belonged to "the rebel bishop of Glasgow."[7]

Wishart again espoused the English interest. Accordingly, when at Lent 1305 Edward was prosecuting his arrangements for the representation of the

<hr>

[1] Royal Letters, No. 3362.

[2] *Ibid.*, No. 3263.

[3] Chapter House (Scots Documents), Box 5, No. 25.

[4] Chancery Miscellaneous Portfolios, No. 11.

[5] British Museum, Addit. MSS., No. 8835; Bain's Calendar of Scottish Documents, iv., pp. 482, 483.

[6] Patent Roll, 27 Edward I., m. 15; C. Miscellaneous Portfolios, No. 11.

[7] Exchequer Q. R. Miscellanea, No. $\frac{9}{21}$.

Scottish Estates in the English Parliament, he communicated with Bishop Wishart and the Earl of Carrick, expressing his desire that the Scots should elect a certain number of commissioners to the Parliament to be held at Westminster after midsummer.[1]

A year later, Wishart enacted a further change, for when in the spring of 1306 Robert Bruce asserted his claim to the throne, he became his active adherent. As a bishop he assoilzied him from his acts of slaughter within a consecrated edifice. He also supplied from his repositories robes and other adornments for the coronation at Scone. By this procedure he deeply incensed Edward, who on the 26th of May instructed his lieutenant, Aymer de Valence, to make every effort for his arrest.[2] Soon afterwards Wishart was captured at Cupar-Fife, the garrison of the castle of that place, which he commanded, being forced to surrender. To Edward his seizure was so gratifying, that, writing to De Valence on the 16th of June, he remarked that he was as much pleased as if the Earl of Carrick had been apprehended personally.[3] He instructed that the bishop should, under a strong guard, be sent to Berwick, and that without any regard to his estate as a prelate or clerk.[4]

About the time of Wishart's arrest, Edward also secured as a prisoner Bishop Lamberton of St Andrews, and on the 7th of July he gave command that both prelates should, laden with irons, be imprisoned—Lamberton in Winchester Castle, and Wishart in the castle of Porchester.[5] Thereafter Edward addressed several letters to the Pope, charging the bishops with perjury and rebellion. In support of his charge against Wishart, he signified that he had on six occasions sworn fealty to him.[6]

Failing to accomplish Wishart's clerical degradation, Edward kept him in close confinement to the close of his reign. In reply to a message from the Pope, Edward II, on the 4th December 1308, set forth that inasmuch as

---

[1] Close Roll, 33 Edward I., m. 13 dorso cedulâ.

[2] Sir Francis Palgrave's Transcripts, vol. 63, fol. 53.

[3] *Ibid.*, vol. 63, fol. 61.

[4] *Ibid.*, vol. 63, fol. 10.

[5] Close Roll, 34 Edward I., m. 6.

[6] Chapter House (Scots Documents), Port-

folio 4, Nos. 2-6. Among the English archives is a letter in Norman French, purporting to be from Bishop Wishart, in which he begs Edward to allow him to remain in England till the " ryote " of the Scots be put down. The genuineness of the letter is more than doubtful (Royal Letters, No. 2782).

Wishart had been guilty of lese-majesty and other offences against the late king and himself, his return to Scotland was disallowed.[1] Learning that Wishart had renewed his entreaties at the court of Rome, Edward, in January 1310-11, authorised the bishop of Worcester, his chancellor in Scotland, also the Earl of Lincoln, the guardian, to resist his efforts by reminding the Pope of his violated oaths.[2] As a further step, Edward, on the 23d of April, requested the Pope to deprive Wishart of his See, and to appoint as his successor Stephen de Segrave, an English churchman.[3]

Though unheeding Edward's demand for Wishart's ecclesiastical degradation, the Pope, Clement V., was unwilling, in the interests of the imprisoned prelate, to incur the open hostility of the English sovereign. He therefore adopted the intermediate course of summoning Wishart to Rome, and afterwards of returning him to Edward's keeping, with instructions that he should be subjected to a less rigorous restraint. Consequent on this decree, Edward, on the 20th November 1313, consigned the bishop to the care of the prior of Ely, with the injunction that he should not be allowed to leave the priory without a sufficient escort.[4]

At the battle of Bannockburn, fought on the 24th of June 1314, the Earl of Essex and Hereford fell a prisoner in the hands of the Scots, and on the 2d of October thereafter, he was exchanged for the Scottish king's wife, daughter, sister, and nephew, also for the bishop of Glasgow.[5]

Owing to the rigorous character of his long imprisonment, Bishop Wishart became blind. Surviving his release about two years, he died on the 26th November 1316. Apart from his largely concerning himself in civil affairs, he promoted the erection of his cathedral. It was one of the charges brought against him by Edward I. that he had used timber granted him for building a steeple to his cathedral, in constructing engines of war against certain English strongholds, especially the castle of Kirkintilloch.

[1] French and Roman Roll, 2 Edward II., m. 6.
[2] Privy Seals (Tower), 4 Edward II., File 1.
[3] *Ibid.*, File 7.
[4] Close Roll, 7 Edward II., m. 17 dorso.
[5] Patent Roll, Edward II., p. 1, m. 18.

VII.

SIR THOMAS CHARTERIS.

In the castle of Kinfauns is exhibited a two-handed sword, which, according to tradition, was wielded by Thomas de Charteris, one of Wallace's principal adherents. According to Henry, Charteris was the representative of the ancient family of Longueville in France, and was by the French king deprived of his rank and estates for slaying a nobleman at court. He had consequently adopted the life of a pirate, and engaging in desperate enterprises become known as "the Red Rover." Attacking the vessel in which Wallace was sailing in one of his voyages to France, he was captured through the Patriot's valour. Making him prisoner, Wallace was moved by the story of his misfortunes, and recommending him to King Philip, obtained his pardon. Moved with gratitude, Longueville accompanied his benefactor to Scotland, and under the name of Charteris became his companion in arms.[1]

This narrative is entirely fictitious. Prior to Wallace's period the family of Charteris occupied in Scotland a prominent position. A son of the Earl of Chartres accompanied William of Normandy in his invasion of England; and his son or grandson settled in Scotland during the reign of David I., receiving the lands of Amisfield in Dumfriesshire. The representative of the Amisfield house, Sir Thomas de Charteris, was in 1280 appointed by Alexander III. Chancellor of the kingdom; he died in 1296. In the same year his son, Andrew de Charteris, rendered homage to Edward, but renouncing his allegiance two years afterwards, his lands of Amisfield were, in September 1298, conferred upon the Earl of Warwick.[2]

Among Edward's homagers in 1296 are Osbern de Chartres of the county of Peebles, Robert de Chartres of the county of Dumfries, and Thomas de Chartres of the county of Roxburgh. As Sir Thomas de Chartres, the last, is described in an Inquisition dated at Dunfermline, 2d January 1303-4, as

---

[1] Henry's Wallace, B. ix.　　　　[2] Chapter House (Scots Documents), Box 93, No. 16.

having died to the north of the Grampians in November 1302 out of Edward's peace;[1] he was evidently that adherent of the Patriot whom the Minstrel has clothed in a fictitious guise. His son, William, who had joined his father in the national cause, returned to Edward's allegiance.[2]

Sir Patrick Charteris of Kinfauns is named as one of the barons who were present at the conflict on the North Inch of Perth in 1396 between the members of the clans Chattan and Kay.

[1] Exchequer T. R. Miscellanea (Placita, etc.), No. 4/6.   [2] *Ibid.*

VIII.

ALEXANDER SCRIMGEOUR.

According to Crawfurd, the surname of Skirmischur was in 1107 conferred by Alexander I. on Sir Alexander Carron, a valiant knight, who vigorously had overwhelmed and scattered a body of northern rebels.[1] King Alexander also bestowed on his faithful knight, and the heirs-male of his body, the office of standard-bearer to the king, together with an escutcheon bearing gules, a lion rampant, or, in the dexter paw, a crooked sword, proper, and for motto the word *dissipate* or disperse.

Alexander Skirmischur or Scrimgeour, a descendant of Sir Alexander Skirmischur, the first royal standard-bearer, joined Wallace at the siege of the castle of Dundee in September 1297, and on the Patriot's departure to encounter Surrey in the field of Stirling, continued the blockade until the garrison surrendered. In recognition of his important service, Wallace, as guardian of the kingdom, conferred on him the office of Constable of Dundee, the office being made hereditary in his family. By the instrument of grant (which is given in the text of the present work, pp. 146, 147) he received the lands at Dundee styled *campus superior*, but afterwards known as Upper Dudhope.

To the national cause Alexander Scrimgeour faithfully adhered. After the death of Wallace, he joined the standard of King Robert the Bruce, but he soon fell into the hands of the English. With other persons of rank he was, by Edward's order, executed at York in August 1306.[2] His son Nicholas received from King Robert a charter of the office of standard-bearer, along with the lands of Hillfield and others in the barony of Inverkeithing.[3] The representative of Wallace's associate, Sir John Scrimgeour, royal standard-bearer, fell at the battle of Halidon-hill in 1333. Sir James Scrimgeour, also royal standard-bearer, took part with the Regent Albany

---

[1] Peerage, p. 115.

[2] Assize Roll, York, 34 Edward I., $\frac{N}{26}$ } 1.

[3] Robertson's Index 20, No. 115; 22, No. 52.

against Donald, lord of the Isles, at the battle of Harlaw in 1411, and fell in the conflict. By Wyntoun he is celebrated thus :—

> " Schir James Scremgeoure of Dundee,
>   Comendit a famous knycht wes he,
> The Kingis banneoure of fé,
>   A lord that wele aucht lovit be." [1]

In the ballad of "The Battle of Harlaw," he is commemorated in these lines :—

> " Sir James Scrimgeor of Duddlap, knight,
>   Gret constabill of fair Dunde,
> Unto the dulefull death was dicht,
>   The Kingis chief banner-man was he,
>   A valziant man of chevalrie."

James Scrimgeour, seventh constable of Dundee, acquired from Lord Grey, on the 27th April 1495, the lands of Lower Dudhope, together with the custom or tax payable on young horses brought into Dundee for sale.

Sir James Scrimgeour, tenth constable, was, in January 1584, charged to depart from the realm, as an adherent of the Earl of Angus, one of the lords engaged with the Earl of Gowrie in the Raid of Ruthven. On the 25th November 1587, he received at Holyrood a charter of his estates under the Great Seal, restricting their destination,—while the grants made by Alexander I. to Sir Alexander Skirmischur first of the name, and subsequent royal grants and immunities, were fully confirmed.[2] Sir James was one of the commissioners who, in June 1589, proceeded to Denmark to complete the negotiations for the marriage of James VI. with the Princess Anne. He was a member of the commission appointed in 1604 to treat as to a political union with England; he died in 1612. By him, as is believed, was erected the castle of Dudhope, which, in a view of Dundee published about the year 1680, appears a considerable fortalice. In Dudhope Castle Sir John Scrimgeour, eleventh constable, had the privilege of accommodating James VI. for a night during his visit to Scotland in 1617. By the Parliament of 1621 he was chosen a lord of the Articles, and in the same year he voted for the five articles of Perth. A favourite of Charles I., he was by that sovereign, on the

---

[1] Wyntoun's Chronicle, B. ix., ll. 3125-3128.   [2] Nisbet's System of Heraldry, vol. ii., App., p. 49.

15th November 1641, created Baron Scrimgeour of Inverkeithing and Viscount of Dudhope; he died on the 7th March 1643. He married Margaret Seton, of the family of Parbroath, by whom he had a son, James, second Viscount of Dudhope, who died of a wound received at the battle of Marston Moor on the 2d July 1644. His elder son, John, joined in the Duke of Hamilton's engagement in 1648 for the rescue of Charles I.; he also attended Charles II. at the battle of Worcester, and afterwards joined the standard of General Middleton. He was taken prisoner by the English in November 1654. At the Restoration, he, in reward of service, was created Earl of Dundee, his patent being dated 8th September 1660. He died 23d June 1668 without issue, and his titles became extinct.

The representation of the family devolved on the Scrimgeours of Birkhill, whose male heir, Henry Scrymgeour Wedderburn of Wedderburn, now holds the hereditary office of royal standard-bearer in Scotland. The more notable members of the ancient house include the names of the learned Henry Scrimgeour, Professor of Philosophy at Geneva, who was born at Dundee in 1506, and died at Geneva in 1572; also of Dr Alexander Scrimgeour, Professor of Humanity, and afterwards of Philosophy, in the University of St Andrews.

----o----

IX.

SIR RICHARD LUNDIN.

From Malcolm IV., who reigned from 1153 to 1166, Philip and Malcolm de Lundin, brothers, received grants of land—the former a barony styled Lundin, near Largo in Fife; the latter, the lands of Lundie in the county of Forfar. Thomas de Lundin, son of Malcolm, was appointed by King William the Lion, royal door-ward or usher, and consequent on the office becoming hereditary, his branch of the family assumed the surname of Durward. King William confirmed a charter of gift by Thomas, son of Malcolm of Lundin, by which he bestowed on the monastery of Cupar one mark of silver from his lands of Balelmeryremath [Balmerino]. The granter uses in his charter these words: "And if I should go the way of all flesh in the kingdom of Scotland, my body shall be conveyed to Cupar, and there deposited in the cloister before the door of the church, in the spot I have chosen." His remains were deposited in the cloister in 1231. Alan de Lundin, son of Thomas, was justiciary of Scotland; he married an illegitimate daughter of Alexander II., when he obtained the title of Earl of Athole. He died in 1275, and with him terminated the male representation of his branch.

Philip de Lundin, who received from Malcolm IV. the barony of Lundin in Fife, had a son Walter, who is believed to have been father of Thomas, who in 1220 granted a charter to the nuns of North Berwick. The daughter and heiress of Thomas wedded Robert, a natural son of William the Lion, who, assuming the name of Lundin, is in the reign of Alexander II. described as *Dominus Robertus de Lundin, frater illustris regis Alexandri.* Apparently the next baron was Peter, for in 1296 is named Margaret, relict of Pieres de Lundin of the county of Fife.

Richard, or Sir Richard de Lundin, was the next representative of the Fifeshire family. He originally upheld the cause of Baliol, but quitted the Scottish camp at Irvine in July 1297, when the several leaders were in conflict. Joining the English army, he took a conspicuous part under Surrey at the battle of Stirling. According to Hemingford, he, prior to the engagement, exhorted Surrey to proceed cautiously in making his attack, but his counsel was, on the advice of Cressingham, unwisely rejected. Thereafter Lundin's name disappears from the national history.

Thomas de Lundin was about the year 1450 sheriff of Fifeshire. In 1457 is named Sir John Lundin of Lundin, who seems to have married, first, Isobel Wemyss; and secondly, Catherine, daughter of Lord Drummond. His descendant, styled John Lundie of Lundie, went on pilgrimage in 1507, and Walter, the elder son of this person, became a promoter of the Reformation; he died in 1569. By his wife Elizabeth, daughter of Lord Lindsay, Walter Lundie had a son, William, who succeeded to the family estate, and also strongly upheld the Reformed doctrines.

Margaret Lundie, heiress of the barony of Lundin, married in 1643 Robert Maitland, brother of the first Earl of Lauderdale, who assumed the name of Lundie. Their daughter, Sophia, married in 1670 John Drummond, second son of James, third Earl of Perth, who in 1686 was created Earl of Melfort and Viscount Forth. A descendant of the marriage, James Drummond, acquired the family estates, and was created Baron Drummond. He was succeeded by his daughter Clementina Sarah Drummond, who married in 1807 Peter R. Burrell, afterwards Baron Willoughby de Eresby. At Drummond Castle, in Perthshire, Lady Willoughby's representative preserves a two-handed sword, which is supposed to have been used by Sir Richard Lundin at the battle of Stirling.[1]

---

[1] For further particulars respecting the family of Lundin of Lundin, *see* Wood's "East Neuk of Fife," 1862, 12mo, pp. 239-243.

X.

PATRIC, EARL OF MARCH.

Patric Dunbar, ninth Earl of March, was descended from Gospatric, governor of Northumberland, who, deprived by William the Norman of his office on account of his supporting the Danes, retired to Scotland, and there, in 1072, received from Malcolm III. the castle of Dunbar and the adjacent lands. His representatives in Scotland were styled Earls of Dunbar or March, but were more generally known by the latter title.

Patric de Dunbar, son of Patric, seventh earl, was born in 1242, and on his father's death in August 1289, succeeded as eighth earl. As one of the nobles he consented to the young queen, Margaret of Norway, being pledged in marriage to the Prince of Wales, and on the queen's death became a competitor for the crown as great-grandson of Ilda, daughter of William the Lion.[1]

When Baliol refused to comply with Edward's demands, the Earl of March withdrew his allegiance, but his wife continued to adhere to the national cause.[2] In the castle of Dunbar, which in his absence her husband had entrusted to her keeping, she gave entertainment to her brother, the Earl of Buchan and his principal adherents on their return from their expedition into England, till she was compelled to surrender the stronghold after the battle of Dunbar.

In August 1296 the Earl of March became one of the sureties to a mainprise, that Gilbert de Umfraville, son of the Earl of Angus, would render submission to Edward's will, in respect of his contempt in striking Hugh de Louther in presence of the Parliament at Berwick.[3]

When Wallace, in his capacity as guardian, summoned a convention at

---

[1] Chapter House (Scots Documents), Box 88, No. 20.

[2] About the year 1282 the Earl espoused Marjory, daughter of Alexander Comyn, Earl of Buchan.

[3] Close Roll, 24 Edward I., m. 4.

Perth, the Earl of March refused to attend, and in his declinature he contemptuously styled the guardian "king of Kyll"—that is, king of the woods—the word *Coille*, pronounced Kyle, signifying a forest.[1] On the 19th November 1298, he was appointed by Edward captain of his forces and castles in the eastern district to the south of the Forth.[2]

In July 1300 the Earl of March, along with Patric Dunbar, his elder son, took part in the siege of Carlaverock. On the 12th February 1301-2, he undertook to retain the custodiership of the county and castle of Ayr, on being provided with forty men-at-arms.[3] On the 21st of the same month, he conveyed to his troops in the castle, a supply of provisions consequent on a menaced siege by the Scots.[4] And on the 30th August 1302, he covenanted to keep the castle and sheriffdom of Ayr from the 1st of September till "Nowel" [Yule] on receiving £100 to meet expenditure.[5]

Though the possessor of large estates, the Earl of March fell into pecuniary embarrassment. On the 11th May 1303, he "impignorated" with Thomas of Tyndale for £26 sterling, certain "jewels" described as consisting of six silver dishes, a silver flagon, a pair of basins, a silver pitcher, and a silver-gilt cup with stand and cover.[6] And not long afterwards James de Dalilegh, one of Edward's escheators in Scotland, made complaint that the earl had appropriated a portion of his goods forfeited to the crown, with the result that the restoration was ordered.[7]

In a letter written at Inverkeithing on the 2d March 1303-4, Edward reproved the earl for his slackness in marching against the enemy, and commanded him to forthwith proceed to Dunipace, so as to intercept the Scots in their anticipated movement towards the castle of Stirling. Edward also enjoined the earl to exercise a strict vigilance so as to prevent the Scots from making a sally from Stirling Castle into the unprotected districts to the north of the Forth.[8]

The Earl of March was in 1305 elected one of the Scottish commissioners

---

[1] Carrick's Life of Sir William Wallace, edit. 1840, p. 115.

[2] Patent Roll, 26 Edward I., m. 2.

[3] Exchequer Q. R. Miscellanea (Army), No. 1½.

[4] Chancery Miscellaneous Portfolios, No. 3/4.

[5] Exchequer Q. R. Miscellanea (Army), No. 7/8.

[6] *Ibid.*, No. 1/2.

[7] Miscellaneous Portfolios, No. 11.

[8] Royal Letters, No. 3260.

to the English Parliament, but as he failed to attend, Sir John Menteith was by Edward nominated as his successor.[1]

When King Robert the Bruce commenced his insurrection in 1306, Edward appointed the Earl of March to aid in its suppression.   He was, prior to the 1st of June 1307, reappointed to the command at Ayr.[2]   He died on the 10th October 1308, and his son Patric, then in his twenty-fourth year, was served as his heir.[3]

[1] Close Roll, 33 Edward I., m. 13 dorso cedulâ.

[2] Exchequer Q. R. Miscellanea (Army), No. $\frac{3}{8}$.

[3] Bain's Calendar of Documents relating to Scotland, vol. iii., p. 15.

XI.

BISHOP ANTHONY BEK.

Younger son of Walter Bek, Baron of Eresby, Anthony Bek received the sign of the cross when in 1270 he consented to accompany Prince Edward [afterwards Edward I.] to the Holy Land,[1] and when in June 1272 Edward made his will at Acre, he named him as one of his executors.[2] In 1273 Edward nominated him Archdeacon of Durham, and in 1275 appointed him Constable of the Tower. He was present in the Parliament at Westminster on the 29th September 1278 when Alexander III. rendered homage to Edward for his English baronies.[3] Elected on the 9th July 1283 Bishop of Durham, he was, on the 9th of January 1283-4, consecrated by the Archbishop of Canterbury in the king's presence. On the occasion of his being enthroned, the official of the Archbishop of York and the Prior of Durham contested the right of performing the office, when he settled the dispute by dispensing with both functionaries, and accepting the mitre from the hands of his brother, Thomas Bek, bishop of St Davids.[4]

To the discharge of the sacerdotal function, Anthony Bek gave little or no attention, continuing to chiefly occupy himself in civil or military affairs. In the competition for the Scottish throne he advised Edward to prefer Baliol to Bruce, inasmuch as the former was more compliant. Between Edward and his barons, also between the king and his children, he frequently mediated.[5]

Possessed of ample revenues, Bishop Bek secured a lordly following. In the northern wars he was attended by twenty-six standard-bearers, one hundred and forty knights, five hundred horse, and one thousand foot, which last he marched under the consecrated banner of St Cuthbert. On the 11th March 1287-8, he sent to Edward the Divine blessing and his own, with the request that Sir William Heron, the king's servant in the north, might be

---

[1] Dugdale's Baronage, i., 426.
[2] Royal Wills, p. 18.
[3] Rot. Parl., i., 224.

[4] Surtees' History of Durham, 54.
[5] *Ibid.*

excused answering to a plea, on the ground that he was on the way to Scotland to seize evil-doers. The letter is given forth as issued in the fifth year of his consecration.[1] On the 1st September 1288, he was empowered by Edward to grant a safe conduct to the ambassadors of King Eric of Norway ;[2] and on the 20th February 1289-90, he received the royal authority for assuming possession of lands at Penrith and Tyndale which had belonged to the deceased Alexander III. of Scotland.[3]

On the 20th June 1290, Edward named Bishop Bek one of his plenipotentiaries in Scottish affairs ;[4] when he was also authorised to receive to the king's allegiance, the inhabitants of the Scottish Isles.[5] In July 1290, the Mayor and community of Berwick complained of him for oppressing them by his followers, and his letters as a plenipotentiary were consequently suspended. On the 27th of August he received certain manors in consideration that he had bestowed annuities amounting to £400 on several Norwegian magnates, who were expected to persuade their sovereign to entrust his infant daughter, the Scottish queen, to Edward's keeping.[6] On the 28th August Edward notified to the guardians, also to the clergy and community of Scotland, that he had appointed Bishop Bek lieutenant to their infant queen; also to his son Edward, her intended husband.[7] On the first September he accredited the bishop, conjointly with the Earl of Surrey and Henry de Newark, Dean of York, to wait upon the Scottish queen at Orkney, and there to confer with her father's envoys.[8] On the 1st of September, Bek acquired a loan of £4000 or £5000 for Edward's use.[9]

Sending a substitute to Orkney, Bek, attended by the abbot of Welbeck as his secretary, proceeded to St Andrews, there to enter upon his office as lieutenant. Arriving towards the close of September, he took up his abode at Leuchars Castle, one of the residences of Bishop Fraser. At his suggestion, Fraser on the 7th October communicated with Edward, in a letter in which he, in reference to a rumour as to the young queen's death, gave counsel that in the event of the tidings proving correct, he should march to the Border

---

[1] Royal Letters, No. 2631.
[2] Chapter House, Lib. A., fol. 150.
[3] Patent, 18 Edward I., m. 35.
[4] *Ibid.*, 19.
[5] *Ibid.*

[6] *Ibid.*, 9.
[7] *Ibid.*
[8] Liber A., Chapter House, fol. 149, 150.
[9] *Ibid.*, fol. 150.

with an army.   He also reported that the Lord of Annandale was causing an agitation, and advised that if Baliol presented himself at court, he should be received courteously.

At Norham Castle on the 4th June 1291, Bishop Bek was the first subscribing of the several witnesses to an instrument, whereby nine of the competitors for the Scottish throne consented to feudally invest Edward I. in the realm, pending his decision; also to the instrument attesting the execution.[1]   On the 28th December he again proceeded to Scotland on Edward's service.[2]

While absent in Scotland, Bek was, on the 23d July 1292, excommunicated by the archbishop of York, but he soon afterwards had his revenge by throwing the archbishop into prison, and refusing his liberation till he had paid a forfeit of 4000 marks.[3]   Differing with the prior of Durham, Bek deprived and ejected him, but in reprisal the prior seized his adversary's temporalities.   These Bek recovered by the authority of Parliament, while his Palatine rights were confirmed to him by the Itinerant Justices.   On the 25th June 1294, Edward confirmed in his favour the manors of Penrith, Scotteby, Carlaton, Langwathby, and others, which had been granted in liferent by John Baliol.[4]

On receiving from Baliol an unconditional surrender, Edward empowered Bishop Bek to effect his final degradation.   This the bishop accomplished by conducting the degraded king to the churchyard of Stracathro, near Brechin, and there, on the 7th of July 1296, causing him to undergo a degrading ceremony.   Three days afterwards, he as Edward's delegate received from Baliol a full renunciation of his crown and royal dignity.[5]

Bishop Bek's unsuccessful attempt to quell the insurrection under Wallace in 1297, attended with his defeat in the streets of Glasgow, is set forth in our principal narrative.   At the battle of Falkirk he commanded the second division of the English army, his followers including thirty-nine bannerets.

With his royal patron, Bek was ultimately at variance.   He took part in the popular movement against the king, led by the Earl Marshal and the Earl

---

[1] Chapter House (Scots Documents), Box 16, Nos. 13-16.

[2] Patent, 19 Edward I., m. 25.

[3] Rot. Parl., i., 102 *et seq.*

[4] Patent, 22 Edward I., m. 3.

[5] Chapter House (Scots Documents), Box 17, No. 4.

of Hereford; and when by Edward charged with ingratitude, he urged in his defence that the policy he upheld conduced better than Edward's own to the material welfare both of the sovereign and the people. Being cited to the court of Rome on the charge of unlawfully dismissing the prior of Durham, he attended in great pomp, and received from the Pope an approval of his conduct. But on his return he found that his vassals had complained of his misrule, and that Edward, on the charge of his quitting the kingdom without permission, was proceeding to deprive him of his Palatinate. In July 1301, Edward conferred his temporalities on Sir Robert Clifford, and charged him, in the affair of the prior of Durham, with procuring writs from Rome so as to infringe on the dignity of the crown.

In a missive dated at Stirling on the 10th May 1303, Edward commanded Bishop Bek to deliver up to Nicholas de Graham his heritage and that of his wife, of which the bishop had illegally possessed himself.[1] On the 26th March 1304, Edward charged him by his chancellor, William le Grenefield, to restore the church of Haltwhistle to the abbot and convent of Arbroath.[2] And on the 13th June of the same year, he commanded him to restore the fishing of Wodhorn to the monastery of Kelso.[3]

By the favour of Edward II., Bek was restored to his former dignity, while he received from the Pope the title of Patriarch of Jerusalem, and also attained the sovereignty of the Isle of Man. Holding high court at Durham, he claimed a royal rank, causing all the followers of the nobles to approach him upon their knees, and the knights to attend him uncovered. Indulging an excessive prodigality, he moved from one manor to another with a numerous following, gorgeously attired. He reared a castle at Somerton, in Lincolnshire, enlarged Barnard Castle and the castle of Alnwick, and constructed a manor-house at Eltham, in Kent. He died at Eltham on the 3d March 1310-11, and his remains were conveyed to Durham, and there deposited in the cathedral. His joint heirs were Robert de Willoughby, son of Alice, his elder sister, and John de Harcourt, son of his second sister, Margaret.[4]

---

[1] Close Roll, 31 Edward I., m. 11.

[2] Privy Seals (Tower), 32 Edward I., File 3.

[3] *Ibid.*, file 8.

[4] Surtees' History of Durham, *passim.*

XII.

JOHN, EARL OF WARREN AND SURREY.

Son of William, Earl of Warren and Surrey, by his second wife, Maud, widow of Hugh Bigot, Earl of Norfolk, the subject of this memoir succeeded to his father's honours in 1240 at the age of five years. Obtaining the favour of Henry III., he was early advanced to important offices. At the battle of Lewes on the 13th May 1264, he held a command in the royal army, but along with the Earl of Pembroke quitted his post at the commencement of the action, and took refuge first at Pevensay Castle and afterwards in France. Subsequently he joined the Earl of Gloucester on behalf of the king, and took part with the royal troops at the battle of Evesham. In 1268 he had a violent dispute with the Earl of Lincoln, and about the same period, while contending at law with Alan, Lord Zouche, he made a personal attack on his opponent and his son in Westminster Hall, wounding the latter seriously. To avenge this public outrage, Prince Edward (afterwards Edward I.) pursued him with a strong force, when he took refuge in his castle at Reigate. Afterwards submitting himself, he consented to pay a penalty of 10,000 marks, in certain annual instalments.

Subsequent to the funeral of Henry III. in 1272, the Earl of Warren and Surrey entered the Abbey of Westminster, and there at the high altar swore allegiance to Edward I. And visiting him at Reigate, Edward, in acknowledgment of his hospitality, caused his fine to be reduced by 1000 marks.[1]

Though in his hot youth he had outraged the proprieties so as to incur the severe censure of the court, Warren contrived to fully regain the royal favour. On the 20th March 1277-8, he was, along with the archbishops of Canterbury and York, and the Earls of Gloucester and Lincoln, appointed to escort Alexander III. of Scotland and his retinue to the English court.[2]

---

[1] Close Roll, 9 Edward I., m. 5 dorso.   [2] Royal Letters, No. 1286.

Other important commissions followed. On the 14th February 1289-90, he was appointed ambassador to Scotland;[1] on the 28th of August 1290, Edward's procurator in arranging the contract of marriage between the Prince of Wales and the infant Queen Margaret;[2] and on the 1st September one of the English commissioners appointed to receive at Orkney the young Queen and her father's envoys.[3]

Having in the spring of 1296 accompanied Edward in his expedition to Scotland, Warren was, at the head of a body of troops, sent from Berwick to reduce the castle of Dunbar. In its vicinity he, on the 27th April, encountered the Scottish army under the Earl of Buchan, when he obtained a signal victory. By Edward he was soon afterwards appointed as his lieutenant in Scotland, and in this capacity he, on the 31st January 1296-7, undertook to prevent any one leaving the kingdom by land or sea without the royal permission, also to arrest all persons bearing letters.[4]

In a letter to Edward dated at Berwick on the 1st of August 1297, the earl informed him that within a week he expected the bishop of Glasgow, the Earl of Carrick, and the Steward to complete the covenants stipulated in the treaty of Irvine; he also reported that the country generally was submissive and orderly.[5] Consequent on this intelligence, Edward arranged to relieve him of his command, in order to his taking part in the expedition to Flanders; naming as his successor, Brian Fitz-Alan of Yorkshire. But Fitz-Alan being expected to undertake the lieutenancy with a diminished revenue, declined the appointment, and as a rumour prevailed as to a new insurrection, Warren was recalled.[6]

On learning the reduction by Wallace of the northern strongholds, the earl collected from the northern English counties a powerful force, and therewith marched from Berwick about the end of August. Informed of the movement, Wallace abandoned the siege of the castle of Dundee, and conducted his followers rapidly to Stirling so as to attack the invaders at the passage of the Forth. Having reached the locality through a defile of the Ochils, the Patriot encamped his followers on the north-eastern slope of the Abbey Craig,

---

[1] Patent Roll, 18 Edward I., m. 38.

[2] *Ibid.*, m. 9.

[3] Chapter House, Liber. A., fol. 149.

[4] Close Roll, 25 Edward I., m. 25 dorso.

[5] Royal Letters, No. 3263.

[6] *Ibid.*, No. 2586 ; Close Roll, 25 Edward I., m. 5 dorso.

and from thence, by a deft movement, succeeded in overwhelming a large body of Surrey's troops which had crossed the Forth at Kildean,—the remaining portion flying in consternation. To the Scots the victory was so decisive as for a time to repair every previous discomfiture, and to place the government of the kingdom in the hands of the victor. Yet it is to be remarked, as illustrative of the English policy, that Surrey's disaster upon the 11th September is unnoticed in the State papers, while in a letter which, on his return from Flanders, Edward addressed " to his earls and barons " who had in Scotland fought under the Earl of Surrey, he simply thanks them for their services without any allusion to their defeat.[1]

In a military order, dated 19th December 1298, Edward granted to the Earl of Surrey, as captain of a new expedition to Scotland, the sum of £1538, 6s. 8d., with one hundred barbed horse.[2]

In the year 1300 Surrey commanded the second squadron at the siege of Carlaverock. He was, in 1301, appointed along with the Earl of Warwick and others to treat with the agents of Philip of France, relative to a peace proposed between England and Scotland. He about the same time took part with the English barons in their celebrated letter to the Pope.

The Earl of Surrey died on the 27th September 1304. According to Langtoft his death took place in Scotland, but we learn from the registry of the Priory at Lewes that the event occurred at Kennington. His remains were deposited in the Abbey of Lewes, in the choir before the high altar. The earl married in his twelfth year Alice, daughter of Hugh de Brun, Count of March, and uterine sister of Henry III.; she died 9th February 1291. Of the marriage was born a son, William, who died in his father's lifetime leaving a posthumous son, John, who succeeded to the earldom. Of the earl's two daughters, Eleanor the elder espoused Henry, Lord Percy; Isabella, the younger daughter, married John Baliol, afterwards King of Scotland. On the 18th November 1299, the Earl of Surrey took in ward his grandson, Edward Baliol,[3] who subsequently became a prisoner in the hands of Earl John, with whom he remained till the 20th of September 1310, when he was committed to the keeping of Thomas and Edmund, brothers of Edward II.[4]

<hr>

[1] Patent Rolls, 26 Edward I., m. 22.

[2] Exchequer Q. R. Memoranda, 26 Edward I., m. 106 dorso.

[3] Close Roll, 27 Edward I., m. 1.

[4] Patent Roll, 4 Edward II., p 1, m. 14.

XIII.

SIR HENRY PERCY.

Henry de Percy was third son of Henry, Lord Percy, by his wife Eleanor, daughter of John, Earl of Warren and Surrey; he succeeded to the family barony soon after the year 1272, on the death of his brother John, who died young. Accompanying the English army to Scotland in the spring of 1296, he was by Edward I. knighted before Berwick. He was present at the battle of Dunbar,[1] and thereafter attended Edward in his northern expedition. On the 28th August 1296, Alexander, Earl of Menteith, and Alexander de Abernethy acknowledge their indebtedness to him in the loan of a hundred marks, and authorise him to levy the same on their lands in Menteith and elsewhere.[2] On the 8th September 1296, he was appointed warden of Galloway, and custodier of the castles of Ayr, Wigtown, Cruggelton, and Botel [Buittle]; and soon afterwards the Constable of Carlisle Castle was instructed to grant him access into that stronghold.[3] On the 4th June 1297, he and Sir Robert Clifford were sent into Scotland in command of a powerful force, their commission empowering them to arrest, imprison, and put to death, all persons engaged in insurrection.[4]

After the surrender of the Scottish leaders at Irvine, Sir Henry Percy and his colleague, on the 9th July 1297, received the submission of Bishop Wishart of Glasgow, the Earl of Carrick, James the Steward, and others.[5] On the 19th December 1298, he undertook to supply for the proposed expedition against the Scots a troop of fifty barbed horse.[6] And on the 20th February 1298-9, he, in acknowledgment of service, received from Edward lands in England and Scotland which had belonged to the late Ingelram de Balliol.[7]

Sir Henry Percy took part in the siege of Carlaverock in July 1300. From Edward he afterwards received lands in Aberdeenshire, and in a letter written at St Andrews on the 29th March 1304, the English king enjoined the Bishop

[1] Siege of Carlaverock, by N. H. Nicholas.

[2] Close Roll, 24 Edward I., m. 7 dorso.

[3] Exchequer L. T. R., "Nomina Villarum," No. 455; Close Roll, 24 Edward I., m. 3.

[4] Patent Roll, 25 Edward I., Part i., m. 6.

[5] Royal Letters, No. 3250.

[6] Exchequer Q. R. Memoranda, 26 Edward I., m. 106 dorso.

[7] Patent Roll, 27 Edward I., m. 36; Fine Roll, Edward I., m. 22.

of Aberdeen to admit to benefices within his diocese those clergy only who had received presentations from him.[1]   And on the 10th October 1305, Edward, in a mandate granting the restoration of lands to certain Scotsmen who had returned to his allegiance, made exception in regard to the possessions of the late Ingelram de Balliol, which he had granted to Percy, unless Ingelram de Umfraville, the nearest of kin, should seek to recover them by a legal process.[2]

When, on the 5th April 1306, Edward appointed Aymer de Valence to lead an army into Scotland against Robert the Bruce, he enjoined Sir Henry Percy, then in Galloway, to muster his troops.[3]   On the 29th June Percy is named as lieutenant at Carlisle;[4] and in the exercise of this office he, on the 25th July, ordered James de Dalilegh, keeper of the stores at that place, to forthwith send to Girvan two war engines, while he stoutly remonstrated with him for his neglect in providing victuals.[5]   In February 1306-7, he was surprised by King Robert at Turnberry Castle, when a number of huts occupied by his troops were destroyed.   On the 6th of February he received a letter from Edward urging him to make a report by a special messenger.[6]

Sir Henry Percy was summoned to attend the coronation of Edward II. at Westminster on the 25th February 1308-9.   He afterwards made purchase of Alnwick Castle, which became his chief residence; it has continued in the hands of his representatives, the Dukes of Northumberland.   In 1309 he was appointed Constable of York Castle.   When Piers de Gaveston surrendered the castle of Scarborough in May 1312, on the promise that his life would be spared, Percy was associated with those who made and violated the condition. Under the belief that Gaveston had been put to death directly at his instance, Edward II. issued warrants for his apprehension and forfeiture; he afterwards received pardon.

At the battle of Bannockburn Percy was one of Edward's staff; he escaped unhurt.   He died in 1315, and his remains were deposited in Fountain's Abbey. By his wife, Alianora, daughter of John, Earl of Arundel, who survived him, he had several children.   Henry, his eldest son and successor, was much employed in military affairs by Edward II., and afterwards by Edward III.

---

[1] Royal Letters, No. 3520.
[2] Close Roll, 33 Edward I., m. 6.
[3] Patent Roll, 34 Edward I., m. 28.
[4] Exchequer Q. R. Miscellanea (Army), No. $\frac{3}{2}$.
[5] *Ibid.*
[6] Privy Seals (Tower), 35 Edward I., File 1.

XIV.

SIR ROBERT CLIFFORD.

Robert de Clifford, son of a baron of the same name, was born in April 1274. In 1280 he succeeded his father, who was killed by an accident; and six years later, he inherited from his paternal grandfather the baronial honours of his house. By devoting himself to military pursuits he attracted the favour of Edward I.; he accompanied the king to Scotland in the spring of 1296, and was present at the battle of Dunbar. Appointed Warden of the Scottish March at the head of 500 foot and 140 men-at-arms, he was, on the 2d April 1296, authorised to receive hostages from suspected persons in Selkirk Forest, Cavers Muir, and the vales of Liddel, Esk, Annan, Moffat, and Nith, also in Galloway.[1] Recognising his military proficiency, Edward, on the 4th June 1297, commissioned him jointly with Sir Henry Percy, to arrest, imprison, and "justify" all disturbers of the peace in Scotland.[2] He now entered Scotland from Carlisle in command of one hundred men-at-arms, also of a large body of foot, chiefly natives of Cumberland. To the people of Cumberland he, on the 24th June, along with Sir Henry Percy, granted an assurance that their act in voluntarily serving against the Scots should not be construed into an acknowledgment that such service might at any time thereafter be demanded of them by the king.[3]

Towards the end of June, Clifford marched to Ayr with the view of assisting Sir Henry Percy in attacking the Scots, who had, under the Earl of Carrick, the Steward, Sir William Douglas, and other leaders, assembled at Irvine. On the 9th July he received their submission.[4]

During the winter of 1297-8, Clifford made two inroads into Annandale, when he ravaged the estates of the Earl of Carrick, and burned the town of Annan and the adjacent villages.[5] On the 20th November 1298, he is named

---

[1] Chancery Miscellaneous Rolls, No. 474.
[2] Patent Roll, 25 Edward I., part i., m. 6.
[3] Privy Seals (Tower), 25 Edward I., File 2.
[4] Royal Letters, No. 3250.
[5] Hemingford, i., 137.

as governor of the castle of Dumfries, and on the 25th of the same month, "the good men" of Annandale are ordered to obey him.[1] In a military order dated 23d April 1299, he is described as "Captain of Carlisle,"[2] and in this capacity he appears as providing for the defence of Lochmaben Castle, when, from the 1st to the 25th of August 1299, it was besieged by the Earl of Carrick.[3] On the 23d September 1299, he is named as Constable of the castle of Nottingham.[4] At the siege of Carlaverock in July 1300, he so distinguished himself, that on the surrender Edward appointed him Constable of the stronghold.

In the celebrated letter from the English barons to Pope Boniface in February 1301, Clifford is described as "Castellanus de Appelby," and in a compotus of April 1301, he is styled "joint hereditary sheriff of Appleby Castle."[5] He continued in command of the English garrisons in Annandale till 1303, when Edward employed him as a principal officer. In a memorandum written at Dunfermline in that year, Edward charges him to exercise a special vigilance lest strangers should intermix with his followers.[6]

On the outbreak of Bruce's insurrection, Edward, on the 5th April 1306, issued letters authorising Clifford to take command of troops raised in the palatinate of Durham, and to co-operate with Sir Henry Percy at the head of troops from Lancaster, Westmoreland, and Cumberland.[7] And on the 26th May Edward bestowed on him for good service, the manor of Hert, in the bishopric of Durham, "formerly a possession of the Earl of Carrick."[8] Also in further appreciation of service, Edward granted him in the following February lands in the county of Cumberland seized from Sir Christopher Seton.[9]

As he was dying, Edward entreated Sir Robert Clifford to oppose the return to England of Piers Gaveston, his son the Prince of Wales' unworthy associate.

Received into the confidence of Edward II., Clifford was by him appointed governor of Nottingham Castle; he was also constituted Earl Marshal, and

---

[1] Exchequer Q. R. Miscellanea (Army), No. 28/9, m. 9; Patent Roll, 27 Edward I., m. 41.

[2] Patent Roll, 27 Edward I., m. 28.

[3] Exchequer Q. R. Miscellanea (Army), No. 28/8.

[4] Close Roll, 27 Edward I., m. 5.

[5] Exchequer Q. R. Memoranda, 29 Edward I., m. 70.

[6] Tower Miscellaneous Rolls, No. 405/8.

[7] Patent Roll, 34 Edward I., m. 28.

[8] *Ibid.*, m. 22.

[9] Charter, 35 Edward I., m. 15.

Justiciar of the Forest *ultra* Trent. In connexion with the last office, he, on the 25th September 1307, received the royal command to allow the men of Galloway to feed their flocks and herds in Englewood forest, whether they had sought refuge from " Robert de Brus and his accomplices." [1]

By a warrant dated 20th December 1309, Edward II. appointed Sir Robert Clifford his warden in Scotland, with a retinue of 100 men-at-arms and 300 foot.[2] In the exercise of his function, he in December 1310 invited King Robert the Bruce to meet him at Selkirk, but the project did not succeed.[3] He accompanied Edward to Bannockburn on the 24th June 1314, and was there mortally wounded. On the 24th September, Edward II. empowered the royal victualler at Carlisle to issue a tun of wine to the executors of the late Sir Robert de Clifford, to be used at the interment of his remains.[4] His remains were deposited in Shapp Abbey, in Westmoreland.

Sir Robert Clifford married Maud, daughter and co-heir of Thomas de Clare, steward of Waltham Forest, son of Thomas, younger son of Richard de Clare, Earl of Gloucester and Hertford; she survived him, and married, secondly, Robert, Baron Welles. Sir Robert had four sons, Roger, Robert, John, and Andrew; also a daughter, Idonea, who married Henry, Lord Clifford. Roger, the eldest son, inherited his father's barony, and dying without issue, was succeeded by his younger brother Robert, ancestor of the Earls of Cumberland.

[1] Close Roll, 1 Edward II., m. 19.
[2] Exchequer Q. R. Miscellanea, No. $\frac{0\,0\,0}{1\,1}$.
[3] Chancery Miscellaneous Portfolios, No. 11.
[4] Exchequer Q. R. Miscellanea (Army), No. $\frac{4\,4}{2\,2}$.

XV.

HUGH DE CRESSINGHAM.

Hugh de Cressingham bore on his seal the legend "Sigillum Hugonis, filii Willelmi de Cressingham;" but the twelve jurors who served on an inquest as to his succession, declared that his birth was illegitimate.

Taking orders, Cressingham was appointed rector of Ruddely, also prebendary of several churches. Having served as Chief Justiciary of York, he was, on the 3d November 1292, constituted along with William de Ormesby and three others, an itinerant justice in the district of Carlisle. In November 1292, there sought justice from him and his colleagues William le Walcys, who had a writ of novel disscisin against Adam, son of Alan of Ulvesby, and John, son of Adam le Walcys, as to a tenement in Ulvesby; also Robert de Bruce, senior, and Cristiane, his wife, who complained that Geoffrey de Moubray refused to keep an agreement entered into on the 9th September 1261 between her and Adam de Gesemuthe, her former husband, and the respondent's uncle, in regard to certain tenements at Bolton.[1]

On the 16th August 1294, Cressingham received the benefice of Levyngton, in Cumberland, which by forfeiture had passed to the crown.[2] Early in March 1295-6, Edward appointed him to the office of treasurer in Scotland, and on the 28th of the same month he was charged by the Privy Council to compensate the friars of Coldstream for losses sustained by them during the march of the English army to Berwick.[3] Confirmed in the treasurership on the 6th September 1296, Cressingham had, on the 16th day of the same month, the rolls of Exchequer at Edinburgh Castle delivered to him at Berwick; he is in the indenture of delivery styled "Sir Hugh de Cressingham."[4] By letters from Edward, dated 6th March 1296-7, he was instructed to open a court at Berwick after the model of the Exchequer Court

---

[1] Assize Roll, Cumberland, 20 Edward I., m. 25, 1.

[2] Chancery Miscellaneous Rolls, 474.

[3] Exchequer Q. R. Miscellanea (Army), No. 2/2.

[4] Exchequer L. T. R. "Nomina Villarum," No. 455; T. R. Miscellanea (Placita, Rentals, etc.), No. 4/5.

at Westminster.[1] By the hands of John of Mar, a Carmelite friar, he, on the 1st of April 1297, made report to Edward, then at Forde, in Devonshire, concerning his transactions in Scotland.[2] And on the 24th of May thereafter, Edward, in letters to the Earl of Carrick, John, brother of the Steward, and other Scottish barons, enjoined them to act upon certain instructions, which Hugh de Cressingham and Osbert de Spaldington would convey to them orally.[3] By Edward's letters-patent dated 4th June 1297, Cressingham was instructed to aid Sir Henry Percy and Sir Robert Clifford in arresting and imprisoning, also in putting to death, all persons who opposed themselves to the royal authority.[4] And on the 25th of June, Cressingham received by Edward's order the sum of £2000, to be used by him in restoring tranquillity.[5]

Prior to the 23d of July 1297, Bishop Wishart of Glasgow thanked Cressingham by letter for communicating with him through Sir Reginald Craufurd, and made request that he would give credence to his clerk, Master Walter Camoys, also to Sir Reginald.[6] In dispatches dated from Berwick on the 23d and 24th July, Cressingham informed Edward that while the Scots had generally submitted, Wallace continued to hold out; he also reported as to the difficulty of raising money in Scotland, owing to the unsettled condition of the country.[7] On the 24th of July another letter was despatched to the court, in which the writer, who, though undesigned, is evidently Osbert de Spaldington, informs Edward that the church of Douglas, with a revenue of 200 marks, is vacant, and begs that it may be conferred upon Cressingham.[8] And in a communication to Edward, dated the 4th of August, De Spaldington entreats that Cressingham might receive, at least temporarily, the office of lieutenant of Scotland, in succession to the Earl of Surrey.[9] Meanwhile Edward had appointed Brian Fitz-Alan as Surrey's successor, and on the 5th of August we find Cressingham communicating with Edward that his nominee was unwilling to accept office on the reduced emolument proposed to him.[10]

When, towards the close of August, Surrey, who had resumed the

---

[1] Excheq. Q. R. Memoranda, 25 Edw. I., m. 15.
[2] British Museum, Addit. MSS., No. 7965.
[3] Close Roll, 25 Edward I., m. 27.
[4] Patent, 25 Edward I., part i., m. 6.
[5] Exchequer Q. R. Memoranda, 25 Edward I., m. 100.

[6] Royal Letters, No. 3362.
[7] Tower Miscellaneous Rolls, No. 474.
[8] Royal Letters, No. 3251.
[9] Chancery Miscellaneous Portfolios, No. 11.
[10] Tower Miscellaneous Rolls, No. 474.

lieutenancy, assembled an army at Berwick, in order to suppress the insurrection under Wallace, Cressingham joined his staff. When remarking the strong position of the Scots, Surrey hesitated to attack them on the field of Stirling, Cressingham overcame his scruples, and by inducing him to engage in battle, led to his disastrous defeat. Cressingham was among the slain, and having rendered himself odious in inflicting a burdensome taxation, the Scots mutilated his remains.[1] On the 18th September, being seven days after his death, a writ was issued at St Paul's church, London, ordering an inquisition by twelve jurors to determine as to his heir. The jurors found that as a bastard he had no legal heir; therefore his possessions, which were chiefly in the counties of Norfolk and Suffolk, were conveyed to the crown.[2] At Michaelmas 1304 and subsequently, was instituted by the English treasurer in Scotland a judicial inquiry as to a sum of £300 or £400 in Cressingham's possession, but which after his death had gone amissing. Of the several witnesses examined in the inquiry the depositions have been preserved, and these serve to show that the money was after Cressingham's death deposited in Werkworth Castle, and afterwards transferred to the castle of Durham.[3]

[1] Trivet, 307; Hemingford, 130; Chron. Lanercost, 190.

[2] Inq. p. m., 25 Edward I., No. 34; Fine, 25 Edward I., m. 5.

[3] Exchequer Q. R. Memoranda, 33 Edward I., m. 37.

————o————

XVI.

AYMER DE VALENCE, EARL OF PEMBROKE.

Isabel, daughter and heiress of Aylmer, Count of Angoulême, second queen of John, king of England, and mother of Henry III., married secondly Hugh le Brun, Count of the Marches of Aquitaine, with issue William de Valence, who by his uterine brother, Henry III., was created Earl of Pembroke. The earl had three sons and three daughters. Of the sons, the two elder predeceased him, dying young and unmarried; and on his death, which took place on the 13th of June 1296, he was succeeded by Aymer, his third son.[1] Though claiming rank above all the barons, excepting Henry of Lancaster, Aymer de Valence dispensed with his father's title to the close of the reign of Edward I. Engaged in the expedition to Flanders, he was appointed by Edward as his commissioner to ratify an agreement between him and Florence, Count of Holland, relative to some auxiliaries from the count in that war. Subsequently he became one of Edward's ambassadors in negotiating the treaty with Philip of France; and in the Scottish war which followed he was intrusted with an important command. He accompanied Edward on the field at Falkirk in July 1298, and he is afterwards named as having in that engagement sustained the loss of a black charger worth sixty marks.[2] In June 1300 he took part in the siege of Carlaverock, and on the 30th October of the same year, was instructed to defend against the Scots the castles of Selkirk and Bothwell.[3] Edward granted him on the 10th August 1301, also to his heirs, a charter of land in Scotland of the estimated value of £1000, including the castle and barony of Bothwell, forfeited by William de Moray.[4]

On the 1st January 1301-2, Aymer de Valence, as commissioner for Edward's queen, Margaret of France, placed in the king's hands at Linlithgow

---

[1] Exchequer, Treasury of Receipt, Miscellanea, No. 1⅓.

[2] Exchequer Q. R. Miscellanea (Army), No. ³⁷.

[3] Tower Miscellaneous Rolls, No. ⁴⁴⁄₉.

[4] Chapter House (Scots Documents), Box 93, No. 1.

a gold goblet and two silver platters.[1] On the 12th February thereafter, he became bound to preserve Bothwell Castle against the Scots.[2] Consequent on a Scottish raid into Annandale and Liddesdale, he was, on the 14th June 1303, charged to assist Sir Walter de Huntercumbe in the defence of Berwick.[3] As Sir Aymer de Valence, he is, on the 14th July 1303, described as English lieutenant in Scotland, to the south of the Forth.[4] And in this capacity he despatched from Linlithgow, on the 26th September 1303, a letter to William de Grenefeld, the chancellor, apprizing him that he was in treaty with the Scottish magnates, with a view to securing their submission to English rule, and that though not quite certain, he hoped to succeed in his effort.[5]

In November 1303, De Valence held command of the English troops encamped at Dunfermline, and subsequently of the force stationed at Perth.[6] Having returned to Dunfermline, he, in February 1303-4, was sent from thence, with other knights, to receive the Prince of Wales at Perth on his arrival in that city. Shortly prior to the month of July 1305, he was granted by Edward the lands of Boharm in the counties of Banff and Elgin, formerly in possession of the Earl of Athole.[7]

Henry the Minstrel asserts that De Valence in the church of "Ruglane" or Rutherglen made payment to Sir John Menteith of three thousand pounds, on his consenting to effect Wallace's capture.[8] The statement is clearly fictitious.

By the slaughter of John Comyn, husband of De Valence's sister, Robert Bruce initiated his revolt against Anglican usurpation; while by appointing De Valence as his lieutenant in suppressing the new insurrection, Edward was led to expect that the desire of vengeance would intensify his military ardour. In his commission, which is dated 5th April 1306, Edward appoints him lieutenant and captain, " to put down the rebellion of Robert de Brus, late Earl of Carrick, who has betrayed his confidence and murdered his liege, John Comyn of Badenach ;" he then charges all men-at-arms, horse and foot, to muster at his command.[9] And on the 15th of April, Edward instructs

---

[1] Exchequer Q. R. Miscellanea (Wardrobe), No. 23.

[2] *Ibid.* (Army), No. 27.

[3] Patent Rolls, 31 Edward I., m. 20.

[4] Chancery Miscellaneous Portfolios, No. 14.

[5] *Ibid.*, No. 11.

[6] Exchequer, Treasury of Receipt, Miscellanea, No. 12; Chancery Miscellaneous Portfolios, No. 14.

[7] Parliamentary Petitions, No. 271.

[8] Henry's Wallace, B. xi., ll. 791-848.

[9] Patent Roll, 34 Edward I., m. 28.

John de Sandale, his chamberlain in Scotland, to furnish his lieutenant with the necessary supplies.[1]

In Edward's letters to De Valence we trace the latter's military progress. On the 24th of May, Edward informs him that he is pleased he is to commence his expedition; and two days later he asks him to co-operate with the strong force he would find at Carlisle, under command of the Prince of Wales.[2] On the 8th June, he signifies his satisfaction that Bishop Wishart had been made a prisoner, and his anxiety that his lieutenant would also capture the bishop of St Andrews.[3] Writing on the 12th June, he commends the operation of laying waste Sir Simon Fraser's lands in the Forest of Selkirk, and expresses a hope that his lieutenant will wreak similar destruction among the lands and goods of the whole of Bruce's adherents.[4] In four other letters, all written in June, Edward instructs De Valence as to the conveyance to England of the captured bishops of Glasgow and St Andrews, also as to the forfeiture of their temporalities.[5]

On the 19th of June, De Valence defeated Bruce at the battle of Methven, and among others secured as a prisoner his nephew, Sir Thomas Randolph, whom Edward instructed should be kept in sure ward.[6]

On the 4th October 1306, Edward granted to De Valence a charter of the castle and manor of Selkirk, the demesne lands of Traquair, the burgh and mills of Peebles, together with the Forest of Selkirk; he also appointed him heritable sheriff of the counties of Peebles and Selkirk.[7]

Having recovered from his disaster at Methven, Robert Bruce appeared strongly posted in the neighbourhood of Ayr, while De Valence, who lay encamped in the vicinity, being in constant dread of an attack, communicated with Edward less frequently. Apprehending a renewal of resistance, Edward, on the 6th February 1306-7, ordered the Bishop of Chester, his treasurer in Scotland, to charge De Valence on his allegiance to make an early report; and as a spur to his breaking silence, to suggest to him that the king had learned he had done so badly that he was ashamed to write. On the 11th of

---

[1] Close Roll, 34 Edward I., m. 16.

[2] Sir Francis Palgrave's Transcripts, vol. 63, fol. 44, 53.

[3] Chancery Miscellaneous Portfolios, No. 4¹.

[4] Sir Francis Palgrave's Transcripts, vol. 63, fol. 58.

[5] *Ibid.*, vol. 63, fol. 10, 47, 61.

[6] *Ibid.*, vol. 63, fol. 49.

[7] Chapter House (Scots Documents), Box 91, No. 9.

February, Edward commanded his lieutenant personally to no longer conceal from him the true position.[1] When before the close of March he acknowledged the royal missive, he had to report that at Bruce's hands he had experienced a defeat.

Writing on the 1st of June 1307 to James de Dalilegh, keeper of the English stores at Carlisle, De Valence reminds him that it was agreed that the Earl of March and "the other good people of Ayr" should have 300 foot, and that he should furnish the necessary pay; and also provide masons and carpenters to repair the castle and private dwellings. As lieutenant of Scotland, he on the 11th of June renewed his order.[2]

When early in July 1307, Edward found that his end was drawing near, he entreated De Valence to render his support to the government of his son. Subsequent to Edward's death, he was summoned to Parliament as Earl of Pembroke, and at the coronation of Edward II. he, as a mark of honour, was privileged to carry the king's left boot.

On the 22d November 1307, Lord Pembroke was empowered to convey the captive Earl of Strathearn from Rochester Castle to York.[3] In his office of lieutenant, superseded by John of Brittany, Earl of Richmond, he was, under his authority and in virtue of royal letters dated 12th December 1307, restored to the possession of lands in the counties of Selkirk and Tweeddale, which had, on account of the tenants giving their adherence to the Scottish king, been appropriated by the English government.[4]

In March 1309 Lord Pembroke was one of several peers appointed to regulate the royal household. And on the 16th June of the same year, he was commissioned by Edward II. to meet him at Berwick on the 8th of September, to proceed with him against the Scots.[5] On the 6th of August 1312, he was with several others accredited by Edward II. to the Pope on a secret mission. In the letters, of which they were bearers, the Pope was informed that they were authorised to orally inform him of important matters which concerned his honour.[6] At the battle of Bannockburn, fought on the

---

[1] Privy Seals (Tower), 35 Edward I., File 1; Close Roll, 35 Edward I., m. 14 dorso.

[2] Exchequer Q. R. Miscellanea (Army), No. $\frac{8}{8}$.

[3] Close Roll, 1 Edward II., m. 16; Patent, 1 Edward II., p. i., m. 10.

[4] Close Roll, 1 Edward II., m. 13.

[5] National MSS. of Scotland, Part ii., No. xx.

[6] French and Roman Roll, 4-10 Edward II., m. 19.

24th of June 1314, he, as an esquire of the royal person, remained by the king's bridle.[1]

In July 1315, Lord Pembroke appears as Warden of the English Border. In attempting to ravage Scotland, he was repulsed.[2] In a letter written at Westminster on the 17th of June 1317, he is invited by Edward II. to come to him speedily, as he is "that day leaving for the north on the Scottish war."[3] Writing from Leicester on the 13th of July, Edward informs him that the Scots were mustering in great numbers, and had already penetrated into England; he therefore begs that he will join him with an armed force.[4]

Lord Pembroke was one of the English commissioners who on the 22d December 1319 settled a truce between the kingdoms. In this truce it was agreed on the part of King Robert that no new fortresses should be constructed in the counties of Berwick, Roxburgh, and Dumfries.[5] When three years afterwards there prevailed a warfare on the borders, Edward II., on the 31st March 1322, authorised the keepers of the Great Seal to prepare writs at Lord Pembroke's dictation, in order to provide means for the repulse of the invaders.[6] And in a letter written at Rivaux on the 13th October he entreated Pembroke to resist a body of Scots who had penetrated to North Allerton.[7]

Pembroke's latter history is uncertain. According to one account, he in 1323 accompanied Isabella, queen of Edward II., to France, and was there incidentally killed at a tournament given by him to celebrate his marriage with his third wife. According to Dugdale, he was murdered on the 23d June 1324, in revenge for his conduct towards his relative, the Earl of Lancaster. He was thrice married—first, to Beatrix, daughter of Ralph de Noel, Constable of France; secondly, to a daughter of the Earl of Barre; and thirdly, to Mary de St Paul, daughter of Guy de Chastillon, Count of St Paul. His last countess founded in 1347 Pembroke College, Cambridge. She was likewise a benefactress to several religious houses.

The Earl of Pembroke's remains were deposited in Westminster Abbey,

---

[1] Barbour's Bruce, xi., 172-179.

[2] Sir Francis Palgrave's Transcripts, vol. 63, pp. 52, 63.

[3] *Ibid.*, p. 54.

[4] *Ibid.*, p. 8.

[5] Royal Letters, No. 4340.

[6] Privy Seals (Tower), 15 Edward II., File 1.

[7] Sir Francis Palgrave's Transcripts, vol. 63, p. 60.

where he is commemorated by an elegant monument. He died without issue. Of his three sisters, Anne, the eldest, married, first, Maurice Fitz-Gerald; secondly, Hugh de Baliol; thirdly, John de Avennes. She died without issue. His two other sisters were Isabel, who married Sir Robert Hastang, English marshal of Berwick, and Johanna, who married John Comyn, the regent,[1] both with issue. On the 24th November 1324, Edward II. instructed his escheators to assign a provision to Maria, widow of the Earl of Pembroke, consequent on the contention thereanent on the part of "John de Hastingges, Johanna, wife of David de Strabolgi, Earl of Athole, and Elizabeth Comyn, cousins and heirs of the late earl."[2] In the matter of Lord Pembroke's succession there followed further conflict, inasmuch as David, Earl of Athole, son and heir of Johanna, Countess of Athole, " heir to a quarter of the inheritance of the late earl," complained that Hugh de Despenser, father and son, had, on the part of Elizabeth Comyn and the heir of John de Hastyngs, the other co-heirs, obtained all the best castles and manors, leaving Johanna with lands in Northumberland, which were over-valued, while the petitioner, being in Gascony in the king's service at the time of his mother's death, was unable to challenge the proceedings.[3]

---

[1] Royal Letters, No. 1706. On the 30th July 1297, Aymer de Valence is, along with Bishop Bek and Sir John Comyn of Badenoch, signatory to a mainprise for the liberation of his brother-in-law, John Comyn the younger (Close Roll, Edward I., m. 7 dorso).

[2] Close Roll, 18 Edward II., m. 22.

[3] Privy Seals (Tower), 3 Edward III., File 8.

XVII.

SIR BRIAN FITZ-ALAN.

In the lordship of Bedale in Yorkshire, Brian Fitz-Alan in 1276 succeeded his father, who bore the same name. In 1282, and again in 1287, he served with Edward in Wales. Under Edward's sanction, he in 1291 transformed his mansion at Kilwardeby into a fortified castle. And on the 13th June of the same year, he received a commission from Edward to act as one of the guardians of Scotland.[1]

With the consent of the regents, also of the competitors for the crown, the castles and strongholds of Scotland were, on the 11th June 1291, transferred to Edward, who thereupon appointed as keepers, natives of England. To Brian Fitz-Alan he assigned the custodiership of the castles of Dundee, Forfar, Roxburgh, and Jedburgh.

At Braid, near Edinburgh, on the 21st October 1291, Fitz-Alan granted to the Chamberlain of Scotland, by the hands of Richard, his clerk, a receipt for £20 sterling, in part payment of his salary for his custodiership of the several castles.[2] In the Compotus of Walter de Langton, keeper of the Royal Wardrobe, rendered in November 1291, he is denoted as receiving, as keeper of the castles of Forfar and Dundee, a daily allowance of fifteen shillings.[3] And in January 1291-2, he granted to the Chamberlain a receipt for £60 in part payment of his recompense as keeper of the castles of Roxburgh and Jedburgh.[4]

In February 1291-2, Fitz-Alan informed Edward by letter that William de Dumfries, Rector of Kinross, who had been promoted from the office of clerk of the rolls to that of Chancellor, had not received from the English Chancery his letters of institution. Consequent on the report, Edward instructed his English Chancellor, the Bishop of Bath and Wells, to prepare

---

[1] Chapter House (Scots Documents), Box 16, No. 9.

[2] *Ibid.*, Box 100, No. 187.

[3] Pipe Roll, 21 Edward I., m. 24.

[4] Chapter House (Scots Documents), Box 100, No. 187.

a commission and despatch it to Fitz-Alan, that it might receive the Scottish Seal.[1]

On the 10th of July 1296, Fitz-Alan witnessed the act whereby Baliol made his surrender of the crown. Nominated lieutenant of Scotland in succession to the Earl of Surrey on a reduced salary, he, in a letter dated 5th August 1297, refused the office. But his letter was accompanied by a communication of the same date, in which, on his behalf, Hugh de Cressingham, the Treasurer, expressed his readiness to undertake the government on the former pay.[2] He was appointed accordingly, but in respect of the progress of the northern insurrection, Surrey was restored to his command.[3]

In July 1300, Fitz-Alan took part in the siege of Carlaverock. In February 1300-1, he joined the English barons in their letter to the Pope. His seal attached to that document presents a whimsical assemblage of animals, these consisting of two birds, a rabbit, a stag, and a boar, all looking to the dexter, except the last, which is regarded as the chief, and is inscribed " Tot capita tot sentencie." [4]

In the year 1302, Margaret, widow of Robert de Ros of Warke, complained to the government of Edward I. that the bishop of Durham had ejected her from the manors of Belestre and Playmelor in Tyndale and granted them to Sir Brian Fitz-Alan.[5] In March 1302-3, Sir Brian is named as serving with the English army in Forfarshire.[6] He died in 1303, and his remains were deposited in the church of Bedale, where an elegant monument was erected to his memory. He had two daughters, Maud and Katherine: the former married, first, Sir Gilbert Stapleton, and secondly, Thomas Sheffield; the latter espoused John, Lord Grey of Rotherfield.

---

[1] Royal Letters, No. 1308; Privy Seals (Tower), 20 Edward I., No. 1.

[2] Royal Letters, No. 2586; Tower Miscellaneous Rolls, No. 474.

[3] Privy Seals (Tower), 25 Edward I., File 6.

[4] From an allusion in the Poem, "The Siege of Carlaverock," it would appear that Fitz-Alan had a controversy with Hugh Poyntz in the matter of arms, and that he had adopted his peculiar heraldic devices in order to expose to ridicule the claims or pretensions of his rival.

[5] Chancery Miscellaneous Portfolios, No. $\frac{14\ 7}{60}$.

[6] Exchequer Q. R. Miscellanea (Wardrobe), No. $\frac{3\ 7}{12}$, m. 5 d.

XVIII.

SIR WALTER DE HUNTERCUMBE.

Walter de Huntercumbe succeeded to his father's lands in Northumberland
in 1271. Soon thereafter he married Alice, third daughter and co-heiress of
Hugh de Bolebec, who in 1274 was served one of the co-heirs of Richard de
Montfichet, his grandmother's brother. On the 12th December 1276, he was
summoned to serve with the army in Wales, and similar summonses were
addressed to him at intervals. About the end of October 1279, he became
one of two " mainpernors " for John Baliol to satisfy the king for his trespass
in doing homage to the bishop of Durham for Barnard Castle, if it is found
that the homage is due to the crown.[1] On the 4th June 1290, he, by royal
warrant, received the custody of the Isle of Man.[2]

On the 28th August 1296, Huntercumbe was, by Walter de Ibernia, charged
with being privy to the removal of sixteen oxen and sixteen cows from his
pastures in Aberdeenshire. Huntercumbe denied the charge, and a trial was
ordered.[3] He appears as keeper of Edinburgh Castle on the 24th July 1298,[4]
and on the 25th of November of the same year he was in the command
superseded by John de Kyngston.[5] Thereafter appointed Warden of the
Marches, he on the 1st of December was instructed to join Sir Simon Fraser
and others in making a foray with two hundred men-at-arms.[6] In an
instrument, undated, but evidently written not long afterwards, he seeks to
be reimbursed for corn and cattle he had got for his troops when appointed to
office, while he sets forth that his private means were exhausted, and that
Northumberland was in the greatest danger from the Scots.[7] He was allowed

[1] Close Roll, 7 Edward I., m. 3 dorso
cedula.

[2] Patent Roll, 18 Edward I., m. 28.

[3] Chapter House (Scots Documents), Box 93,
m. 9.

[4] Exchequer Q. R. Miscellanea (Army), No.
$\frac{2}{3}$, m. 10.

[5] Patent Roll, 27 Edward I., m. 40.

[6] Exchequer, Treasury of Receipt Miscellanea,
No. $\frac{4}{5}$ dorso.

[7] Tower Miscellaneous Rolls, No. 459.

£10 as compensation for "a black nag," killed by the Scots at Flete in August 1299.[1]

Walter de Huntercumbe took part in the siege of Carlaverock in July 1300. On the 14th June 1303, he was commanded to muster all the horse and foot in Northumberland, so as to resist an apprehended inroad of the Scots, who had attacked the English garrisons in Annandale.[2] In 1306 he applied for a remission of scutage on account of his military services, setting forth in his memorial that in the first Scottish campaign he had served at Berwick with twenty horse; and in the second, under the Earl of Surrey at Stirling, with thirty-two; also with thirty at Le Vaire Chapelle, in the retinue of the Bishop of Durham. He likewise represented that he had sent eighteen horse to a recent battle, though not present in person, owing to his discharging duty as Warden of the Marches. He died in 1312, about the age of sixty-four. Twice married, he had no issue, and in his estates was succeeded by Nicholas Newband, his nephew, son of his sister Gunnora.

[1] Wardrobe Accounts, 28 Edward I.   [2] Patent Roll, 31 Edward I., m. 20.

—o—

XIX.

SIR JOHN SEGRAVE.

Sir John Segrave was the eldest son of Nicholas Segrave, a valiant English baron, on whose death, about the year 1294, he at the age of thirty-nine succeeded to the family estate. By Edward I. he in 1295 was, in reward of distinguished military service in Wales, appointed Constable of the army. According to Dugdale, he in 1296 became bound by indenture to Roger le Bigot, Earl of Norfolk, the Earl Marshal, to serve him with a small body of knights, he in acknowledgment of service receiving the manor of Lodene, in Norfolk.

Sir John Segrave accompanied Edward to Scotland in 1296, and on the 30th August of that year, he received from William de Murray of Tullibardine a bond for £20 of borrowed money.[1] He is believed to have served under Edward at the battle of Falkirk. At the siege of Carlaverock in July 1300 he acted as Marshal, and in virtue of his office when the castle was taken, his banner was displayed from the battlements.[2] At Carlaverock on the 14th July 1300, he, as "lieutenant of the Earl Marshal," certified that Sir Robert Malest was there in person.[3] Pending proposals for a truce, he was, on the 30th October 1300, instructed by Edward to provide the English garrisons at Roxburgh, Edinburgh, Linlithgow, Stirling, and Kirkintilloch, with men and victuals, and to see that the castellans were ready to make an attack.[4]

On the 5th August 1302, Segrave was appointed Warden of Berwick Castle, and in this capacity he pledged himself to make forays with thirty men-at-arms.[5] When riding out of Berwick with a small escort, he was attacked by a party of Scots, who succeeded in taking him prisoner.[6] He regained his liberty, and on the 20th of January 1302-3, was by Edward appointed as his lieutenant in Scotland, with special instructions to proceed against a body of

---

[1] Close Roll, 24 Edward I., m. 7 dorso.

[2] Langtoft's Chronicle, p. 309.

[3] Tower Miscellaneous Rolls, No. $\frac{150}{118}$.

[4] *Ibid.*, No. $\frac{450}{4}$.

[5] Exchequer Q. R. Miscellanea (Army), m. 15, No. $\frac{37}{16}$.

[6] Langtoft's Chronicle, p. 319.

"rebels," accused of occupying certain castles and towns, and of perpetrating various excesses.[1]

In an inquisition held at Lanark on the 20th January 1302-3, Segrave is described as possessing the lands of Elemston, in the barony of Strathaven.[2] Occupying the castle of Roslin during the battle fought in its vicinity on the 24th February 1302-3, he was made a prisoner by the Scots, and several years afterwards in addressing Parliament for redress of grievances, he set forth that when he was captured at Roslin he left the castle well furnished, and on his return found it empty.[3] When in attendance on Edward at Dunfermline in 1303, he was specially enjoined to watch his followers, and arrest any strangers who might offer to join them.[4] About the month of March 1303-4, he, guided by a spy, discovered Sir William Wallace and Sir Simon Fraser at Hopprewe, in Tweeddale,[5] where he successfully attacked them. In September 1304, he appears as Warden of Lothian; afterwards in the same year as justiciary of Scotland to the south of the Forth.[6]

On the 18th August 1305, Edward appointed Segrave one of his justiciars for Wallace's trial at Westminster,[7] also after the execution at Smithfield to bear the Patriot's mangled remains to Scotland, there to be exhibited as objects of terror. For "the carriage of the body of William le Waleys to Scotland," he received a payment of fifteen shillings.[8]

Having appointed him as his lieutenant of Scotland on the 28th October 1305,[9] Edward in the same year instructed Segrave to acquire the lands of Polmaise, on the south of the Forth, near Stirling, for the erection of a stronghold.[10] By Edward II. he was continued in his office as lieutenant, and in the exercise of his function was, on the 6th October 1309, enjoined to seize all the Templars in Scotland, and to subject them to ward pending the will of the Inquisitor Depute appointed by the Pope to investigate the charges brought against them.[11]

---

[1] Close Roll, 31 Edward I., m. 18 dorso.

[2] Chapter House (Scots Documents), Box 94, No. 8.

[3] Parliamentary Petitions, No. 4430-1.

[4] Tower Miscellaneous Rolls, No. $\frac{4}{p}\frac{5}{8}\frac{9}{}$.

[5] British Museum, Addit. MSS., No. 8835.

[6] Chancery Miscellaneous Portfolios, Nos. $\frac{4}{6}\frac{1}{2}$, $\frac{4}{7}\frac{1}{6}\frac{1}{4}$.

[7] Privy Seals (Tower), 33 Edward I., File 4.

[8] Exchequer L. T. R. Memoranda, 33 and 34 Edward I., m. 76 dorso.

[9] Patent Roll, 33 Edward I., part 2, m. 7 dorso.

[10] Chancery Miscellaneous Portfolios, No. $\frac{4}{7}\frac{1}{6}$.

[11] Close Roll, 3 Edward II., m. 19.

At the battle of Bannockburn, fought on the 24th June 1314, Segrave was taken prisoner by the Scots. He was on the following November liberated on a heavy ransom, also in exchange for Sir Thomas Morham, a Scottish knight, who was a prisoner in the Tower.[1]

In a royal writ, dated 18th January 1315-6, Sir John Segrave is described as " Constable of Nottingham Castle."[2] On the 14th July 1316 he received from Edward II. a grant of £1000 for good service, also towards repayment of the ransom required of him by the Scots. But from the sum granted him he was called upon to deduct certain moneys he was due to the king while he held the offices of keeper of the Forest *ultra* Trent, and of constable of Nottingham Castle.[3] Sir John afterwards gave offence to the king, owing to his concern in the escape of Lord Mortimer from the Tower in 1325. Sent to Gascony to conduct some military operation, he was there attacked by an epidemic, to which he succumbed. He died about the age of seventy. By his wife Christian, daughter of Sir Hugh de Plessets, he had two sons, Stephen and John, who both predeceased him. John, son of his elder son Stephen, succeeded to the barony.

[1] Close Roll, 8 Edward II., m. 28.   [2] *Ibid.*, 9 Edward II., m. 20.

[3] *Ibid.*, 10 Edward II., m. 31.

XX.

SIR RICHARD SIWARD.[1]

In the year 1236, King Henry III. published a manifesto denying that he had, by collusion, induced the imprisonment of Richard Siward, or that he had entered into any convention with him contrary to the duty which he owed to the King of Scots. Concerning the transaction thus referred to, we are not further informed. Between Siward and the Earl of Cornwall there was some contention which Henry endeavoured to suppress, but having failed to effect a reconciliation, he exiled Siward from his court.[1]

Sir Richard Siward, son or grandson of Richard Siward, of the reign of Henry, possessed lands in Hampshire, at Northampton, and in Tyndale. He also held lands in the south of Scotland. When in the exercise of his claim as overlord Edward I. obtained possession of the Scottish fortresses, he gave the castles of Dumfries, Wigtown, and Kirkcudbright in keeping to Sir Richard, who, in respect of his services, was allowed by the guardians a payment of forty marks.[2] Apart from his special function as custodier of the southern strongholds, Siward was one of Edward's personal attendants; and on the 16th January 1292-3 he witnessed an indenture whereby the English king received from Baliol a renewal of his allegiance.[3]

On the 22d April 1294, Sir Richard Siward obtained a grant of the tax on the marriage of the widow of Simon Fraser; and in the same year he is among the Scottish barons commanded by Edward to be in readiness to attend him in his expedition to Gascony.[4] As a baron of Scotland, he adhered to Baliol, and having in April 1295 renounced Edward's allegiance, he was in consequence deprived of his English possessions. On subsequently yielding his submission, Edward, on the 6th of December 1295, empowered the sheriffs of

---

[1] Fœdera, i., 370; M. Paris, 274; Hailes' Annals, i., 332.

[2] Chancery Miscellaneous Rolls, No. 474.

[3] Chapter House (Scots Documents), Box 95, No. 6; Liber A., Chapter House, fol. 175, 176.

[4] Fœdera, ii., 643.

Southampton and Northampton to restore to him his lands and goods.[1] But Siward's submission was only temporary, for subsequent to December we find him commanding the castle of Dunbar in Baliol's interest.[2]

In his surrender of the castle of Dunbar on the 28th April 1296, Siward has been charged with treachery, but this imputation is satisfactorily disposed of by Lord Hailes, who shows that the surrender ensued consequent on an agreement previously made, that he would deliver it up if it was not relieved within three days.[3]

After the surrender at Dunbar, Siward was committed to the Tower, his fellow-prisoners being the Earls of Ross, Athole, and Menteith, John Comyn the younger, and other prominent Scotsmen.[4] On the 4th of September 1296, Edward gave an allowance to his wife Maria, also to "eleven other Scottish women," whose husbands were detained in English prisons.[5] Having consented to serve with the English army in Flanders, Siward was liberated on the 30th July 1297, the Bishop of Durham and others entering on a mainprise for his fidelity, while he delivered his son John as a hostage.[6] Consequent on this new submission, Edward instructed the sheriff of Northampton to restore his possessions.[7]

In Flanders Siward acquitted himself so efficiently, that in token of his "good service," Edward, on the 29th May 1298, instructed the Constable of Bristol Castle to remove the fetters from his imprisoned son Richard; also to allow him a separate apartment and a privy chamber.[8]

At the close of the Flanders campaign, Siward was permitted by Edward to return to Scotland. Proceeding to repair his castle of Tibbers,[9] he sought co-operation from his cousin, Sir John de St John, who, on the 27th August 1298, begged Sir Ralph de Manton, the English cofferer in Scotland, to grant the necessary help.[10] By Edward's order, Siward received an advance of £100.[11]

---

[1] Close Roll, 24 Edward I., m. 12.

[2] Q. R. Ancient Misc. (Sheriffs' Accounts), Bundle No. 694.

[3] Hailes' Annals, i., 262.

[4] Close Roll, 24 Edward I., m. 7 and 6.

[5] Exchequer L. T. R. "Nomina Villarum," No. 455.

[6] Close Roll (Tower), 25 Edward I., m. 7 dorso.

[7] Close Roll, 25 Edward I., m. 9.

[8] *Ibid.*, 26 Edward I., m. 8.

[9] Tibbers Castle, now a ruin, is situated on the margin of the Nith, near the village of Carronbridge, in the parish of Morton, Dumfriesshire.

[10] Tower Miscellaneous Rolls, No. 474.

[11] Exchequer Q. R. Memoranda, 30 Edward I., m. 16.

In a roll of horses used in the Scottish War from May to October 1298 is this entry: "Sir Richard Siward has a horse for his own riding by gift from the king." [1]   In December 1298, Siward is associated with the Earl of Carrick and others as consenting to supply Edward with troops for continuing the war. [2]   On the 3d April 1299, he was appointed warden of Nithsdale. [3]   On the 24th of November 1299, his son, John, was consigned as a prisoner to Chester Castle. [4]   To Edward, Sir Richard personally remained faithful.   In the Wardrobe Accounts of 1299, he appears as receiving £41, 5s. for his services at Lochmaben Castle ; also certain allowances as the value of a horse killed at Kirkcudbright, and for a robe or winter dress.   On the 29th September 1302, he was allowed, as warden of Galloway and Annandale, a prest of £20 beyond his usual pay. [5]   Soon afterwards he reports to Sir Ralph de Manton that he had not above ten men-at-arms at Lochmaben or Dumfries, but that the country is quiet, and the Earl of Carrick had gone to Parliament. [6]   On the 19th March 1302-3, he is described as sheriff of Fife, [7] and in this capacity he was, on the 4th May 1304, enjoined to restore to Bishop Lamberton of St Andrews his forfeited temporalities. [8]

While retaining his office as sheriff of Fife, Sir Richard Siward continued to exercise his military duties in Nithsdale. [9]   Subsequent to the 15th September 1305, he was appointed sheriff of Dumfries. [10]   His castle of Tibbers was, on behalf of Robert Bruce, occupied in 1306 by John de Seton, who was taken prisoner and executed. [11]   Against Bruce Siward contended vigorously, and he is named with other Scotsmen as receiving from Edward II., on the 20th of May 1308, special thanks for faithful service. [12]   He died prior to the 20th April 1311, since in a warrant of that date, Edward II. allows his widow to appoint approved attorneys to attend to her dower from her late husband's lands in England, as, owing to feeble health, she was unable to proceed thither personally. [13]

---

[1] Exchequer Q. R. Miscellanea (Army), No. $\frac{2}{3}\frac{2}{3}$.

[2] Tower Miscellaneous Rolls, No. 474.

[3] Patent Roll, 27 Edward I., m. 28.

[4] Liberate Roll, 28 Edward I., m. 8.

[5] Royal Letters, No. 2723.

[6] Tower Miscellaneous Rolls, No. $\frac{4\,5\,0}{7\,1}$.

[7] Exchequer T. R. Miscellanea, No. $\frac{1}{8}\frac{3}{8}$.

[8] Chapter House (Scots Documents), Box 100, No. 100.

[9] Exchequer Q. R. Miscellanea (Army), No. $\frac{2}{1}\frac{}{8}$.

[10] Close Roll, 33 Edward I., m. 13 dorso cedulâ.

[11] Assize Roll, York, 34 Edward I., $\frac{N}{26}$ } 1.

[12] Close Roll, 1 Edward II., m. 4 dorso.

[13] Privy Seals (Tower), 4 Edward II., File 7.

Sir Richard had two sons, John and Richard. After suffering imprisonment for opposing the Edwardian rule, Richard latterly served under his father in Nithsdale in upholding the English domination. In January 1314-5, John Siward sold to Thomas, Earl of Lancaster and Leicester, all his goods and chattels now in the manor of Chelveston, for the sum of forty pounds.[1]

[1] Duchy of Lancaster Charter, Box G., No. 120.

—o—

CORRIGENDA.

Vol. I., p. 293, l. 23, *for* " for " *read* " from."

    "   "   l. 33, *before* " thoroughly " *insert* " not."

    "   p. 294, l. 2, *for* " their " *read* " the."

    "   "   l. 15, *for* " land " *read* " law."

INDEX.

ABBEY CRAIG, I., 259-262, 264, 266, 273-275 ; II., 129.
Abbotsford, chair of wood from Robraystoun at, II., 230.
Abdies, lands of, I., 210.
Aberbrothoc, abbey of, II., 90.
Abercorn castle, II., 161.
Abercrombie, Margaret, I., 178.
Aberdeen, destruction of the English troops and shipping there, II., 123.
    Statue of Wallace in, I., 258.
Aberdour, certain acres at, I., 210.
Aberdour castle, II., 217.
Abernethy, Treaty of, II., 6.
Achewaltoun, family of, I., 171.
Adair, Sir Robert, I., 141.
Adam the Carpenter, I., 11.
Adamhill, the laird of, I., 55.
    lands of, I., 50, 52.
Aghynlek (Auchinleck), Adam of, I., 15.
Agmondesham, Walter de, II., 124, 150, 151.
Agnew, Colonel Andrew, of Lochryan, I., 79.
    Eleanor, I., 79, 80.
    Robert Vaus, of Barnbarroch, I., 85.
    Robert Vaus, younger of Barnbarroch, I., 85.
Aissone, Euphan, I., 191.
Alan, Brian Fitz, governor of the castles of Dundee, Roxburgh, Jedburgh, and Forfar, II., 97.
Alan the Durward, II., 11.
Alan of St Edmunds, II., 150.
Alanson, Adam, Provost of Dunbarton, I., 13.
Albany, Robert, Duke of, I., 23, 35, 39, 92.
Alenstoun, Janet, I., 189.
Alexander II., I., 4, 197 ; II., 8.
Alexander III., I., 4, 267 ; II., 10, 11, 16-18.
Alexander, elder son of Alexander III., II., 17, 18.
Alexander, Thomas, portioner of Drumeldrie, I., 206.
    Sir William, Secretary for Scotland, I., 58.
Algeo, Margaret, I., 131.
Alison, Sir Archibald, Bart., I., 275, 282.
Alnwick, castle of, II., 7.

Alston, Frances Charlotte, I., 115.
    George, of Craighead, I., 114.
    Isabella Anne, I., 114.
    Katherine Mary, I., 114.
    Margaret Frances, I., 114.
    Robert Charles, I., 114.
    Violet Mary, I., 115.
Altikane, the lands of Nether, I., 154.
Amisfield castle, II., 170.
Anderson, Margaret, I., 207, 222.
Angus, Earl of, I., 56, 119, 146.
Annandale, Marquis of, I., 198.
Annesley, Major-General Lyttleton, I., 297.
Arbuthnot, church of, II., 169.
Argyle, Robert bishop of, I., 44.
    the Earl of, I., 119.
Arnot, Rev. Dr David, I., 275.
Arran, Earl of, I., 45, 53 ; II., 168.
Athole, Duke of, I., 275.
Atkinson, Edward, Lieutenant, I., 225.
Auchinbothie, lands of, I., 19, 23.
Auchincruive, castle of, II., 105.
    family of, I., 11.
Auchinleck, church of, I., 8.
Auchinvole, the lands of, I., 195.
Auchinweit, family of, I., 162.
Auldhall, lands of, I., 153.
Auldtoun, Gilbert of, I., 182.
    Roger of, I., 182.
Ayr, families at, I., 173.
    Friar Preachers at, I., 13-35, 45.
    the new castle of, II., 165, 196.
    Wallace tower in, I., 257.

BAILLIE, Hon. Charles, I., 270, 273.
    Sir William, I., 22.
Baillies of Lamington, I., 22.
Baird, Alicia, I., 76.
    General Sir David, I., 76.
    Elizabeth, I., 77.
    Matthew, I., 74.
    Robert, of Newbyth, I., 77.
    William, of Newbyth, I., 76.
Bakun, William, II., 161.

Balcarres, Colin, Earl of, I., 206.
Balcormo, lands of, I., 207.
Ballatho, Easter and Wester, I., 196.
Ballendaloch in Stirlingshire, II., 94.
Baliol, John, II., 57, 58, 60, 67, 70, 71.
Balliol, Sir Alexander de, II., 203.
Ballmekeran, lands of, I., 13.
Barcaskine, lands of, I., 166.
Barclay, James, I., 128.
Bargour, family of, I., 172.
Barleith, land of, I., 159.
Barmure, lands of, I., 11.
Barnbarroch, Lord, I., 54, 96, 122.
Barnwell, parish church of, I., 117.
Barnwell Hill, I., 259.
Barr, Adam, "Custumar of Ayr," I., 35.
Barr Hill, I., 305.
Barras, lands of, I., 17.
Bartholomew, Roger, II., 59.
Beaton, Cardinal, I., 240.
Beaufort, Lady Joan, I., 213.
Beaumont, Sir Henry de, II., 189.
Becket, Thomas à, II., 90.
Beg, John, I., 13.
Bek, Bishop of Durham, II., 118.
Bell, Henry Glassford, I., 266, 276, 286.
     Jane Colquhoun, I., 89.
     John, of Enterkine, I., 89.
Bell o' the Brae, II., 118.
Bellenden, Sir John, of Auchnoule, I., 47.
Bellomylne (Ballomylne), lands of, I., 203.
Benane, Little, lands of, I., 34.
Benestede, John de, II., 169.
Berwick, town of, II., 8, 69, 135.
Biggar, Major John, of Woolmet, I., 66, 67.
     Sir Walter de, I., 14, 15.
     William, of Woolmet, I., 78.
Bilston Burn, I., 305.
Binney, Barnabas, M.D., I., 216.
Binning, Sir William, I., 179.
Bisset, Baldred, II., 184.
Blackhall, Agnes, I., 242.
Blackie, Professor John Stuart, I., 272.
Blackwood-yards, lands of, I., 94.
Blair, Sir Adam, of Carberrie, I., 71, 180.
     Sir Adam, of Elphingston, I., 66.
     David, of Adamton, I., 152.
     Elizabeth, I., 172.
     James, in Schaw, I., 161.
     John, of Adamton, I., 21, 125.
     John, of Hillhouse, I., 152.
     John, of Middle Auchinane, I., 173.
Blakeford, William of, I., 34.
Blantyre, Stephen of, I., 4.
     Walter, first Lord, I., 138.
Boghead, lands of, I., 29.
Boig, Christian, I., 203.
Bolden, William of, I., 15.
Boniface VIII., II., 184, 190, 192, 201.
Bonkyl, castle of, II., 194.

Bordland, lands of, I., 97.
Borthwick, Margaret, I., 156.
Boswell, Andrew, I., 210.
     Christian, I., 210.
     David, of Auchinleck, I., 99.
     Janet, I., 210.
     John, of Balmuto, I., 209.
Bothwell, barony of, II., 194.
Bothwell castle, I., 305; II., 196.
Bothwell, Patrick, Earl of, I., 213.
     Richard, I., 12.
Boyd, Robert, lord, I., 50, 137.
     Agnes, I., 123.
     Colonel David, of Turgillon, I., 97.
     Robert, I., 28, 44.
     Sir Robert, II., 118.
     Mr Robert, minister of Paisley, I., 192.
     Steven, of Temple, I., 176.
     Sir Thomas, of Bonshaw, I., 66.
Boyle, David, of Halkshill, I., 128.
     Grizel, of Kelburn, I., 128.
     Maria, I., 128.
     William, I., 129.
Braddill, Ann Maria, I., 231.
     George, of Belfast, I., 231.
     Harriet, I., 231.
Bradford, Tace, I., 215.
     William, Attorney General, I., 215.
     Colonel William, I., 215.
Braid, Edward, II., 161.
Braiddaill, the lands of, I., 182.
Braidfoot, Marion, I., 21.
Brechin, Patrick, bishop of, I., 17.
Brechin, castle of, II., 123, 206.
Brighouse, lands of, I., 155, 160.
Bright, Benjamin Heywood, I., 181.
     Mary, I., 181.
Brisbane, William, of Montfode, I., 78.
Brogan, the lands of, I., 220.
Brown, Barclay, I., 108.
     George, of Capelrig, I., 108.
Bruce, Alexander, I., 250.
     Alexander, II., 252.
     Andrew de, I., 117.
     Christina, II., 250.
     Edward, I., 15.
     Janet, I., 128.
     Mary, II., 250.
     Nigel, II., 250.
     Thomas, I., 250; II., 252.
     Sir William, of Stenhouse, I., 128.
Buccleuch, Anne, Countess of, I., 67.
Buchan, John, Earl of, I., 13, 14.
     John Comyn, Earl of, II., 72.
Buchanan, Agnes, I., 105.
     George, I., 295.
     James, I., 105.
Burgoyne, Harriet Sophia, I., 233.
     Captain F. W., I., 233.
     Captain William, I., 231.

Burghjarg, lands of, I., 184.
Burnbank, lands of, I., 56.
Burnett, Sir Thomas, Edinburgh, I., 179.
Burns, Gilbert, I., 81, 83.
    Robert, I., 148 ; II., 105.
    William, I., 296.
Bute, the Marquis of, I., 19, 293, 294.
Buttergask, Sir Andrew of, I., 13.
Byers, Margaret, I., 205.
Bysset, Thomas, II., 168.

Cairnhill, lands of, I., 32, 92, 93, 99, 100, 133.
Callander, Alexander, Earl of, I., 167.
Cambridge, H.R.H. the Duke of, I., 275, 276.
Cambuskenneth Abbey, II., 93.
Camcescau, the lands of, I., 165.
Cameron, Janet de, I., 93.
    Janet, I., 196.
Camoys, Master Walter de, II., 125.
Campbell, Alexander, I., 31.
    Alexander, of Monzie, I., 269.
    Archibald, younger of Cammo, I., 116.
    Archibald Graham, of Shirvan, I., 113.
    Sir Archibald, I., 31.
    Archibald, of Succoth, I., 30.
    Captain Charles Vereker Hamilton, I., 105.
    Sir Duncan, I., 251.
    Elizabeth, I., 31.
    Mrs Helen, of Succoth, I., 32.
    George, of Auchmunnoch, I., 162.
    Sir Hugh, of Cessnock, I., 100, 133.
    Sir Hugh, of Loudoun, I., 43, 44, 54, 93.
    Islay, President of the Court of Session, I., 30.
    John, of Wester Loudoun, I., 44.
    John, younger of Succoth, I., 30.
    Jonet, "Lady Barskimming," I., 97.
    Sir Matthew of Loudoun, Sheriff of Ayr, I., 47, 50, 51, 56, 146, 251.
    Ord Graham, I., 113.
    Admiral Sir Patrick, K.C.B., I., 77.
    Richard Frederick Fotheringham, of Craigie, I., 91.
Camyshill, lands of, I., 41.
Carbellow, Nether, lands of, I., 163.
Cargill, Mr Donald, I., 144.
    Sir Edward, curate of Symington, I., 135.
Carlaverock castle, II., 180, 185.
Carleton, Alice, I., 224.
    Sir Thomas, I., 224.
Carlisle castle, II., 9.
Carlyle, Thomas, Bust of, I., 295.
Carmichael, family of, I., 165.
    Alexander, burgess of Dundee, I., 217.
    Katherine, I., 180.
Carnegie, Mr Andrew, of New York, I., 294.
Carrick, Countess of, I., 12.
    Robert, Earl of, II., 241-254.
    bailiwick of, I., 249.

Carstares, William, I., 201.
Cartland Crags, II., 111.
Carzeill, lands of, I., 186.
Cashogil, land of, I., 97.
Cassillis, lands of, I., 14.
Cassiltoun, lands of, I., 163.
Cassingray, lands of, I., 206, 207.
Castlemains, lands of, I., 148.
Cathcart, the lords, I., 18.
    Allan, lord, I., 47, 95.
    (Cathkert), Alan de, I., 17, 18.
    Allan, in Broomhill, I., 123.
    Elizabeth, I., 43.
    Elizabeth, I., 224.
    Helen, I., 173.
Cessnock, the estate of, I., 106.
Chalmer, Jean, I., 133.
    James, of Gaitgirth, I., 133.
    John, I., 135.
Charles II., I., 124, 143, 144, 194.
Charteris, Robert, printer, Edinburgh, I., 176.
Chartres, Andrew de, II., 170.
Chatelherault, the Duke of, I., 119.
Cheislie, Catherine, of Dalry, I., 171.
Christie, Mr William, I., 298.
Clark, Alexander, I., 29.
Cleghorn woods, II., 112.
Cleland, James, II., 107.
Clerk, Jean, I., 218.
Clermistoun, South, lands of, I., 170.
Clifford, Sir Robert, II., 120, 145, 170, 188.
Clifton, Charles Frederick, I., 252.
Cloncaird and Busbie, the estates of, I., 113, 116.
Closeburn, churchyard of, I., 186.
Cnokfubyll or Dalyell, lands of, I., 16.
Coanwood, lordship of East and West, I., 224.
Cochrane, Mr Baillie, afterwards Lord Lamington, I., 271.
    Sir John, of Ochiltree, I., 66.
Cochran, Margaret, I., 163.
Cochrane, Sir William, I., 140.
Cockburn, Archibald, of Hornfendean, I., 180.
    John, of Ormiston, I., 119.
    Robina, I., 180.
Coilsfield, plantations of, I., 117.
Coldingham, Abbey of, I., 6.
    lands at, I., 183.
Colquhoun of Luss, the family of, I., 18.
Colquhoun, Sir James, Bart. of Luss, I., 101.
    Janet, I., 107.
    Sir John, of Luss, I., 93.
    John, writer, I., 140.
    Robert of, I., 17, 18, 35.
    Robert, of St Christopher, I., 107.
    William Dalziel, I., 31.
Colvil, Alexander, I., 65.
Colvill, Robert, I., 8.
Colville, James, lord, I., 207.
Comyn, John, Earl of Buchan, II., 124.
    Sir John, II., 213-216.

Comyn, John, of Badenoch, II., 58, 156.
  William, of St Andrews, II., 148.
Connell, Sir John, I., 31.
Coombes, Mercy, I., 226.
Cooper, Samuel, of Failford, I., 113.
Cornella, Maria Antonia Soler de, I., 231.
Corsbie House, I., 253 ; II., 103.
Corsflat, lands of, I., 131.
Corshall, lands of, I., 137.
Corstorphine, lands of, I., 166.
Coucy, Mary de, II., 12.
Coustonn, Isobel, I., 203.
Cowan, Alison, I., 176.
  Henry, I., 254.
Craigie castle, I., 52, 89, 90.
Craigie, lands of, I., 10, 33, 34, 41, 87, 91.
Craigmilne, lands of, I., 246.
Craufurd, Galfrid de, I., 249.
  Sir Gregan, I., 249.
  Hugh, sheriff of Ayrshire, I., 249.
  Hugh, of Kilbirnie, I., 28.
  Sir John de, I., 249.
  Katherine, I., 28.
  Margaret, I., 20, 250 ; II., 88.
  Reginald de, I., 249.
  Sir Reginald, I., 20, 249, 250.
  Susanna, I., 251.
  Walter de, I., 249.
  Andrew, I., 67.
  John, younger of Crawfurdland, I., 97.
Crawford Lindsay, I., 201.
Crawfurd, Robert, of Crawfurdland, I., 147.
Cressingham, Hugh de, I., 250 ; II., 117, 124-
  126, 133.
Crichton, Elizabeth, I., 148.
  William, I., 148.
Crosseby, John de, II., 169.
Culzenach, lands of, I., 100.
Cumyn, Isobel, I., 220.
Cunningham, Sir Alexander, Bart., I., 86.
  Alexander, yr. of Craigends, I., 101.
  Alexander, I., 134.
  Ann, I., 86.
  Captain Archibald, I., 107.
  Catherine, I., 24.
  Sir David, I., 134.
  Elizabeth, I., 134.
  John, of Barndarroch, I., 179.
  John, of Cambuskeith, I., 243.
  John, of Enterkin, I., 178.
  John, of Hill, I., 155.
  Lilias, I., 101.
  Margaret, I., 243.
  Mary, "Lady Bar," I., 98.
  Sir William, I., 230.
  William of, I., 23.
  William, I., 68.
  William, of Craigends, I., 101.
Cunyngham, Adam, of Caprontoun, I., 42.
  Adam, I., 42.

Cunyngham, Lady Margaret, I., 45.
Cunynghame, James, in Kinghorn, I., 209.
  Dame Margaret, I., 49.
Cuthbert, Elizabeth, I., 221.

Dalgarno, II., 168.
Dalmahoy, lands of, I., 170.
Dalmelling, lands of, I., 46.
Dalmellington, lands of, I., 17.
Dalry, lands of, I., 16.
Dalrympil, James of, "Custumar of Ayr," I., 35.
Dalyell of Motherwell, lands of, I., 16-18.
  James, Master of Work, I., 121.
Dalziel, General Thomas, I., 142.
Darien expedition, I., 179, 180.
Darnley, John, lord, I., 39, 92, 125.
David I., I., 2.
David II., I., 8, 9, 12, 13, 16, 118.
Davidson, Professor John, of St Andrews, I., 96.
Demaliverene, Anna, I., 189.
Denholm, Jean, I., 195.
Dickson, Elspeth, I., 183.
  Dr Thomas, I., 209.
Dodds, James, of London, I., 270, 271, 280, 289.
Donald, Mr Patrick, priest, I., 201.
Donaldson, Christian, I., 203.
Douglas, church of, II., 126.
  James, Marquis of, I., 166.
  James, Earl of, I., 35.
Douglas and Mar, William, first Earl of, I., 15.
Douglas, William, Earl of, I., 17.
  Sir William, II., 126, 127.
  Archibald I., 15.
  Eleonora, I., 15.
  Elizabeth, I., 25.
  Lady Elizabeth, I., 56.
  Gavin, I., 154.
  James, of Heriotmuir, I., 36.
  Lady Jane, I., 213.
Dowray, lands of, I., 56.
Drumalloch, family of, I., 171.
Drumferne (Drumiferne), lands of, I., 13, 16.
Drumgrane (Drumgrain), lands of, I., 11-27.
Drumlanrig, William, lord, I., 100.
Drummond, David, of the family of Concraig, I.,
  144.
  Elizabeth, I., 144.
  William, of Rockdale Lodge, Stirling, I.,
  259, 296.
Drumtennant, lands of, I., 203.
Dryburgh, Abbacy of, I., 134.
Dufraissee, Clementina, I., 231.
Dullares, family of, I., 160.
Dunbar, the castle of, I., 92.
Dunbar, Marjory, I., 127.
  William, the poet, I., 154.
Dunbarton castle, I., 297.
Duncan, James, of Mosesfield, I., 256.
Dundaff Linn, I., 305.
Dundee, castle of, II., 95, 97, 135.

Dundonald, church of, I., 7.
 lands and barony of, I., 138-140.
 Earls of, I., 140.
 William, Earl of, I., 66.
Dundrennan, William, Abbot of, I., 37.
Dunfermline Abbey, I., 197 ; II., 216.
Dunipace, lands of, II., 90, 102.
Dunkeld, John, Bishop of, I., 3.
Dunlop, Mrs. I., 83.
 Agnes Eleanor, I., 83, 84.
 Alexander of, I., 80, 85.
 Anthony, I., 86.
 Frances, I., 85, 86.
 Frances Magdalene, I., 86.
 Francis, I., 81, 85.
 Henry, I., 86.
 Major-General James, I., 85.
 Sir James, Bart., I., 86.
 James, of, I., 80.
 Sir John, Bart., I., 86.
 John, I., 80, 81, 83, 86.
 John Andrew, I., 86.
 Keith, I., 85.
 Margaret, I., 85.
 Rachel, I., 85.
 Robert, I., 86.
 Susan, I., 84.
 Wallace-Francis, I., 86.
Dunnottar castle, siege of, II., 123.
Duns, Rev. Professor, D.D., I., 295.
Durham, monks of, I., 6.
Durisdeer, barony of, I., 33.
Durris, Kincardineshire, I., 13.
Duval, General, I., 231.
 Margaret, I., 231.

EASTER CRAIG, lands of, I., 56.
Eccles, John, of that Ilk, I., 41.
Edgar, King, I., 2, 6.
Edmonstone, Alison, I., 67.
 Sir John of, I., 15.
Eglinton, Sir Hugh de, I., 8.
 Alexander, tenth Earl of, I., 148.
 Hugh, first Earl of, I., 44.
 Hugh, third Earl of, I., 94.
Elderslie, lands of, I., 8, 19, 24, 25, 29, 30, 68, 77, 169.
Elgin, Earl of, 261.
Elienton (Ilelington), lands of, I., 24.
Elliot, Admiral George, I., 77.
Ellis, Henrietta, I., 227.
 Major, I., 227.
Elphinstone, John, lord, I., 166.
Errol, Earl of, I., 220.
Erskine, Sir Robert, I., 14.
Erskine, Robert of, I., 17.
Erthbyset, of Slamannan, I., 17.
Eton, lands of, I., 5.

FAIL, loch, I., 117.
 Monastery of, I., 9, 117, 122.

Fairlie, Lady Cunningham, I., 109.
Fairny, Easter, lands of, I., 203.
Falkirk, battle of, II., 155-158.
Faslane, II., 113.
Felrig, I., 185.
Ferguslie, lands of, I., 26.
Ferguson, Christian, I., 222.
Ferguson, Isobel, I., 211.
 James, I., 211.
Fergusson, Sir James, of Kilkerran, I., 271.
Ferrier, Major Archibald, I., 104.
 Grizel, I., 104.
 Jane, I., 104.
 Colonel John, of Cairnhill, I., 104.
 Lilias, I., 104.
 Margaret, I., 104.
 Sophia, I., 104.
 Walter, of Somerford, I., 104.
 William, I., 104.
Fife, Duncan, Earl of, II., 58.
 Robert, Earl of, I., 17.
Findlater, Earl of, I., 134.
Fleming, Agnes, I., 240.
 Malcolm, Lord, I., 240.
 Sir Malcolm, I., 13.
 Marjory, I., 8.
Forbes, Margaret, I., 110.
 Sir William, Bart., I., 110.
Forest Kirk, II., 146.
Forfar, castle of, II., 123.
Forrest, Robert, I., 257.
Forrester, Bailie, I., 296.
Forret, Archibald, I., 191.
Forster, Eleanor, I., 230.
 Thomas, of Adderstone, I., 230.
Fraser, Sir Simon, I., 171, 238.
French, David, M.P., I., 226.
 Elizabeth, I., 226.
 Robert, I., 226.
Frissel, Margaret, I., 185,
Fullarton, Euphame, I., 75.
 George, of Dreghorn, I., 100.
 Major John, I., 128.
 William, I., 75-100.
Fullerton, Ann, I., 180.
 Barbara, I., 100.
 Jean, I., 152.
 John de, I., 125.
 Patrick, I., 180.
Fulton, lands of, I., 23.
Fyntreth forest, I., 197.

GADGIRTH, Laird of, I., 45.
Galbraith, Hugh of, I., 12.
Gallostra, M. Jose, I., 232.
Galloway, Earl of, I., 56.
 Thomas, I., 209.
Galrigs, lands of, I., 152.
Gameline, Bishop, of St Andrews, II., 93.
Gardiner, Robert, I., 239.

Gargunnock, peel of, II., 114.
Garibaldi, General, I., 108.
Garleton Cave, I., 304.
Garvine, Thomas, I., 165.
Gass, lands of, I., 40.
Gemmell, Euphemia, I., 70, 71.
   William, I., 70, 71.
Gibsone, Elizabeth, I., 246.
Gilchrist, Mr James, I., 74.
Gilfillan, Rev. George, I., 272.
Gillan, Rev. Dr Robert, I., 269, 274, 279.
Gillon, Andrew, of Wallhouse, I., 105.
   Georgina Vereker, I., 105.
   Julia Mary, I., 105.
   Captain William, I., 105.
Gilmour, Sir John, I., 67.
Gladney, lands of, I., 204.
Glasford, John, I., 100.
Glasgow, Robert, of Mountgreenan, I., 85.
Glencairn, Earl of, I., 45.
Glencorse, II., 162.
Glenfinlas, forest of, I., 241.
Glentig, lands of, I., 154.
Gloag, Sheriff, I., 299.
Godeney, lands of, I., 11.
Gogar, Over, lands of, I., 176.
Gordon, Elizabeth, I., 230.
   Jane, Duchess of, I., 87.
   Colonel John, I., 230.
   John, I., 232.
   Marie Victorine, I., 232.
Gore, Fanny, I., 223.
Gort, Viscount, I., 104.
Gourlay, Ingelram de, I., 205.
   Marion, I., 205.
   Sir Thomas, I., 205.
Graham, Sir David de, I., 22.
   Sir David, II., 175.
   Isabella, I., 225.
   Janet, I., 193.
   John, of Claverhouse, I., 72, 167.
   Sir John the, II., 110, 111, 157.
   Katherine, I., 24.
   Patrick de, II., 58.
Grahamston, II., 158.
Gray, Lord, I., 211.
Graystocke, Henry de, II., 169.
Greg, Isobel, I., 131.
   Mr James, I., 131.
Greynrig, land of, I., 15.
Griffith, Colonel, I., 275.
Grimston, E. H., I., 77.
   Eleanor, I., 77.
Gunning, Robert Halliday, M.D., I., 295.
Guthrie, Isobel, I., 220.
   Janet, I., 151.

HACKENCROW, lands of, I., 7.
Haldane, James, I., 256.
Haldchingleston, lands of, I., 11.

Haliburton, Sir Henry de, II., 135.
Halkburne, lands of, I., 164, 183.
Halkerston, Margaret, I., 211.
Halls of Airth, I., 166.
Hamilton, Lord Claud, I., 52, 138.
   Duke of, I., 87.
   Allan, I., 25, 26.
   Eupham, I., 94, 95.
   Gavin, I., 94, 97.
   Mr James, I., 191.
   Lady Jane, I., 94.
   Jane Lilias Ferrier, I., 105.
   Janet, I., 25.
   Sir John, I., 27.
   John, of Barnewell, I., 152.
   John Prendergast Ferrier, I., 105.
   John Wallace, I., 106.
   Margaret, I., 26, 27, 192.
   Montgomerie, I., 112.
   Thomas Wallace Ferrier, I., 105.
   Mr Thomas, I., 257.
   Captain Walter Ferrier, I., 105.
   Sir William, of Sanquhar, I., 47.
   William, I., 98.
   William Archibald Ferrier, I., 105.
   William Ferrier, of Westport, I., 104.
Harbert, John, I., 167.
Harrington, Sir John, I., 36.
Hastings, Marquess of, I., 252.
Hastings, Sir Robert, I., 22.
Havecestertun, William of, I., 4.
Hay, Sir David, I., 8.
Heggie, Katherine, I., 207.
Helington, lands of, 25-29.
Hemans, Mrs, I., 255.
Henderson, Alexander, I., 204.
Henri, James, of Bernaldean, I., 84.
Hepburn, Lady Margaret, I., 213.
   Sir Patrick, I., 16.
Herries, Lord, I., 138.
Hesilrig, family of, II., 111-113.
Hettonu, lands of, I., 17.
Hillhouse, lands of, I., 161.
Hodges, Eliza Maria, I., 111.
   Parry, I., 111.
Hogg, James, I., 255.
Hoil, lands of, I., 152.
Holmstoue, family of, I., 146.
Home, Sir Andrew, I., 76.
   John, I., 87.
Hope, Colonel James, I., 226.
   Lady Jane, I., 226.
Hopetoun, Earl of, I., 226.
Hopkirk, Thomas, of Dalbeth, I., 256.
Hoppringle, Isobel, I., 42.
Houstoun, family of, I., 130.
   Sir John, I., 101.
   Andrew, of Jordanhill, I., 112.
   Elizabeth, I., 130.
   Friar William, I., 113.

Howison, John, of Braehead, I., 213.
Howlaris, lands of, I., 183.
Hozier, Colonel Wallace, I., 107.
    William, of Newland, I., 107.
Hume, David, I., 87.
Hungerford, Colonel, I., 232.
Hunter's Club, I., 87.
Huntly, Earl of, I., 119, 236.
Hürter, Marie Katherine, I., 115.

Inglis, Thomas, of Murdieston, I., 130.
    Tarvit, John of, I., 197.
Inglistoun, family of, I., 166.
    lands of, I., 10, 33, 167, 170.
Innerwick, barony of, I., 33.
Inverchaolan, church of, I., 117.
Inverkip, castle of, II., 196.
Inverness, castle of, I., 52.
Inverquharity, lands of, II., 94.

Jaye, Brian le, II., 158.
Johnstone, lands of, I., 130, 131.

Keith, Edward, II., 226.
Kelly, lands of, I., 106, 109.
Kelso, abbey of, I., 2, 3, 5, 182.
Kelsoland, John, lord of, I., 23.
Kennedie, Jonet, I., 159.
Kennedy, Agnes, I., 79.
    Alexander, of Bargeny, I., 44.
    Alexander, I., 154.
    Anne, I., 173, 174.
    Francis, I., 80.
    Gilbert, lord, I., 40, 154.
    Gilbert, I., 146.
    Hugh, of Balkeire, I., 159.
    bishop James, I., 154.
    Sir James, I., 154.
    James, of Garden Rose, I., 174.
    Jean, I., 30.
    John, I., 14.
    Katherine, I., 40, 41.
    Margaret, I., 44, 147.
    Marion, I., 40, 154, 184.
    Dr Thomas, I., 30.
    Thomas, of Dunure, I., 72.
    Walter, I., 154.
Kent, Robert de, I., 5.
Ker, Euphemia, I., 63.
    —— of Littledean, I., 63.
Ketliston, William of, I., 4.
    lands of, I., 4.
Kildean, II., 114.
Kildrummie, castle of, II., 208, 249.
Kilmarnock, Earl of, I., 66, 166.
Kilmaurs, Alexander, lord, I., 92.
    James, lord, I., 134.
Kilspindie, II., 98, 99.
Kilsyth, Viscount, I., 194.
Kincaple, fort of, II., 217.

Kincardine, forest of, II., 114.
Kincardine castle, II., 208.
King, Colonel, I., 107.
    James, I., 107.
    Jessie, I., 107.
    John, I., 107.
    Thomas, of Drums, I., 107.
Kinghorn, I., 4.
King's Case, hospital of, I., 38, 39.
Kingston, John de, II., 170.
Kinloss Abbey, II., 208.
Kinneries, lands of, I., 218.
Kinros, Sir John de, I., 9.
Kinross, bailie, I., 298, 303.
Kintyre, I., 166.
Kirk, Agnes, I., 211, 212.
Kirkaldy, Sir William, of Grange, I., 95.
Kirkby, John de, II., 171.
Kirkpatrick, Janet, I., 186.
Kirkton, church of, II., 169.
Kirkwood, Sir Finlay, I., 41.
Knaresdale, I., 224, 225.
Knight, John, I., 123.
Knockewart, I., 95.
Knokdoleane, fortalice of, I., 52.
Knokindaill, I., 50, 52, 55.
Knox, John, I., 95, 119-121, 295.
Kyle, I., 34, 35.
Kyle-Stewart, I., 7, 28, 29, 54, 127.

Laich Brumehill, I., 189.
Laighlyne, woods at, II., 105.
Lamberton, Bishop, I., 6; II., 149, 172, 176,
    177, 200, 223.
Lang, Rev. J. P., I., 208.
Langton, John de, II., 169.
Lapslie, Rev. James, I., 256.
Lauder, Allan, I., 9.
Laurie, Mr John, I., 73.
Law, James, of Brunton, I., 180.
    Janet, I., 180.
Lawmond, John, of that Ilk, I., 23.
Lawtie, David, I., 130.
Leckie, Susanna, I., 81.
Legge, Alexander, I., 230.
    Ellinor, I., 230.
Leipar, Katherine, I., 210.
Lennox, duke of, I., 54.
    Earl of, II., 129, 133, 146.
    John, Earl of, I., 43, 92.
    Maldonen, Earl of, I., 4, 8.
    Matthew, Earl of, I., 41.
Leslie, Lieutenant-General David, I., 176.
    George, of that Ilk, I., 177.
    Professor, I., 208.
Lincoln, Richard of, I., 5.
Lindesay, Margaret, I., 10.
    Sir John de, I., 10.
Lindores, Abbey of, I., 197; II., 96, 98.
Lindsays, the, of Craigie, I., 33, 118.

Lindsay, Sir Alexander, II., 122, 126, 168, 240.
    Sir David, I., 154.
    Sir John, I., 113.
    Sir John, of Balcarres, I., 156.
    Margaret, I., 33, 131.
    Simon de, II., 170.
    Walter de, I., 12, 33.
Linton, Edward, II., 162.
Liston, Mr Patrick, I., 73.
Litill, Edward, II., 107.
Livingstone, Dr David, I., 295.
    John, I., 229.
Lloyd, Frances Mary, I., 77.
    Henry, I., 77.
Lochindorb, castle of, II., 208.
Lochmaben, castle and town of, II., 195.
Lockenhit Moor, I., 186.
Lockhart, Christian, I., 40.
    John, I., 95.
    Susannah, I., 103.
Logan, Janet, I., 43.
    Sir Robert, I., 43.
    Sheriff, I., 272.
Lord, Corbetta, I., 227.
    Edward, I., 227.
Lorne, Marquis of, I., 258.
Loudoun castle, I., 84.
Loudoun Hill, battle of, I., 18 ; II., 102.
Loudoun, Earl of, I., 251, 252.
    Edith Maud, Countess of, I., 252.
    Margaret de, I., 249.
    Marjory, I., 179.
    Dame Sophia, I., 72.
Louis, Catherine, I., 170.
    Mr James, I., 170.
Lovat, Countess of, I., 53.
Lovet, Sir John, II., 224.
Lumsden, Anne, I., 223.
Lundin, Sir Richard, II., 121.
Lyon, Laurence, I., 126.

Macalister, Charles, I., 216.
M'An, Margaret, I., 220.
M'Connell, Elizabeth, I., 186.
M'Dougal, Jean, I., 67.
    Patrick, I., 67.
Macdougal, Rosina, I., 158.
M'Dougal, Uthred, I., 181.
Macfarlane, Andrew, I., 67.
    Christian, I., 66.
    John, I., 67, 259.
M'Ilvaine, Rebecca, I., 215.
    William, M.D., I., 215.
M'Ilwraith, Colonel, I., 230.
Mackenzie, Henry, I., 87.
    William, I., 77.
M'Kerrell, Jean, I., 100.
    John, I., 100, 243.
M'Millan, Andrew, I., 168.
Macnamara, Captain T., R.N., I., 223.

MacNeil, John, I., 31.
M'Nickell, John, I., 55.
Macpherson, Cluny, I., 270.
Macrae, James, I., 102.
MacWard, Mr Robert, I., 144.
Makdowall, Dougal, I., 250.
Makgill, David, I., 206.
    James, I., 206.
    Janet, I., 206.
Maddox, Joshua, I., 214.
    Mary, I., 214.
Mair, Margaret, I., 222.
Maitland, Sir James, Bart., I., 298, 303.
    William, I., 47.
Manton, Sir Ralph de, II., 205.
Mar, Charles, Earl of, I., 149.
March, Patrick, Earl of, II., 117, 170, 189.
Marchmont, Patrick, Earl of, I., 76.
Margaret, Countess of Carrick, I., 12.
Margoliouth, Dr, I., 1.
Marshall, Barbara Agnes, I., 106.
    James, I., 106.
Maule, Sir Thomas, II., 206, 207.
Maxwell, Edward, I., 57.
    Eglintoune, I., 87.
    Elizabeth, I., 26.
    Gabriel, I., 26.
    George, I., 57.
    Colonel Hamilton, I., 87.
    John, lord, I., 56.
    John, seventh lord, I., 57.
    Sir John, Bart., I., 108, 265.
    John, I., 57.
    Katherine, I., 138.
    Margaret, I., 57.
    Mary, I., 26.
    Sir William Stirling, Bart., I., 273.
Melfort, John, Duke of, I., 72.
    Earl and Countess of, I., 71.
Melmett, Anne Catherine Thirion, I., 87.
Melrose, abbey of, I., 11, 117, 182.
Melville, Viscount, I., 226.
    Sir John, I., 265.
    Mr Andrew, I., 156.
Menteith, Sir John, I., 229, 300.
Menzies, Alexander, I., 234.
    Jean, I., 75, 76.
    William, I., 75.
Mercer, Andrew, I., 196.
    Mr Lawrence, I., 203.
Mersington, Lord, I., 244.
Mirrie, Margaret, I., 242.
Moigne, Margery, II., 59.
Moncrieff, John, I., 240.
Montgomery, Christian de, I., 14.
Montgomerie, Hugh, lord, I., 41, 134.
    Robert, I., 140.
Montgomery, Janet, I., 93, 94.
    John of, I., 34.
    Marjory de, I., 14.

Montgomery, Thomas, I., 126.
Moray, Archibald Douglas, Earl of, I., 36.
    James, Earl of, I., 47.
    Sir Andrew, II., 132, 136-138, 145.
    Sir Thomas de, I., 16.
More, Elizabeth, 127, 128.
Morris, Margaret Emily, I., 108.
    Major Robert, I., 108.
Morton, James, Earl of, I., 47, 95, 213.
Mossgavill, Lady, I., 123.
Motherwell, William, I., 256.
Monbray, Geoffry de, II., 170.
    Sir John, II., 227.
Murdoch, Anna, I., 107.
    Anna Isabella, I., 108.
    Barclay Alison, I., 108.
    Frances Maxwell, I., 107.
    Frances Wallace, I., 108.
    George, I., 108.
    Isabella, I., 107.
    James, I., 107.
    James Barclay, I., 108.
    Janet Colquhoun, I., 107.
    John, I., 106, 107.
    John Wallace, I., 107.
    Robert Wallace, I., 108.
    Thomas William, I., 108.
Mure, James, I., 98.
    Mungo, I., 44.
Murray, Adam, I., 213.
    Sir Alexander, Bart., I., 72.
    John, I., 213.
Mydford, William, II., 96.
Myreton, Sir Andrew, Bart., I., 170.

Napier, Alexander, I., 37, 236.
    John, I., 208.
Neil, Gabriel, I., 259.
Neilson, Janet, I., 133.
Neish, Walter, I., 193.
Nesbit, Mr John, I., 161.
Neville, Sir Robert de, II., 205.
Newbotle, Lord, I., 97.
Nichol, Richard of, I., 5.
Nightingale, Colonel, I., 297, 298, 303.
Nithsdale, John, Earl of, I., 70.
Nugent, Captain Laurence, I., 80, 153.

Ochiltree, Andrew Stewart, lord, I., 46.
Ogilvie, John, I., 191.
Oliphant, Hugh, II., 223.
    Walter, II., 223.
    Sir William, II., 218, 220, 221, 223.
Ormesby, William de, II., 114, 145.
Ormond, Hugh, Earl of, I., 36.
Oswald, Richard, I., 18.
Oxenford, Viscount, I., 206.

Paisley, abbey of, I., 4, 7, 8, 11, 12, 23, 34, 37.
    Claude, lord of, I., 146, 151.

Paisley, James, Master of, I., 146.
Park, Patric, I., 259.
Parker, Fanny, I., 115.
    Rev. William, I., 115.
Paterson, David, I., 149.
    James, I., 150.
Patrick, Margaret, I., 207.
    William, I., 258, 296.
Pennington, Sir John, I., 36.
Percy, Sir Henry de, II., 101, 102.
Perochon, Joseph Elias, I., 83.
Peters, Rev. Alexander, I., 234.
Pitcairn, Dr Archibald, I., 79.
Porter, William, I., 127.
Porterfield, Jean, I., 107.
    John, I., 107.
Pouray, Adam, II., 169.
Preston, Steven, I., 42.
Pringle, John, of Stitchel, I., 65.

Queensberry, lands of, I., 152.
    Duke of, I., 167.
    Earl of, I., 99, 100, 124.
Querle, Thomas de, II., 169.

Radernie, lands of, I., 207.
Randall, Mary Sancroft, I., 105.
    Samuel, I., 105.
Rate, Thomas de, I., 16.
Rede, John, I., 135.
Redesdale, lands of, II., 90.
Reid, Adam, I., 43, 162.
    Hugh, I., 257.
Rhynd, lands of, I., 113.
Riccarton, lands of, I., 7, 10, 23, 34, 89 ; II., 104.
Riddel, John Sims, I., 216.
Ridley, Hugh, I., 225.
Ritchie, Henry, I., 113.
    James, I., 112.
Robert Loan, lands of, I., 38, 153, 161.
Robertson, James, I., 180.
Robraystoun, II., 229, 230.
Rochead, John Thomas, I., 274.
Rodger, Robert, I., 88.
    William, I., 88.
Roger, Rev. Andrew, I., 74.
    bishop of St Andrews, I., 249.
    chaplain at Dunipace, II., 94.
    the clerk, II., 95.
Rogers, Rev. Dr Charles, I., 297-299.
Rollo, Davida Paterson, I., 149.
Ronald, Bailie, I., 298, 303.
Roodman, Helen, I., 133.
Rooke, Rev. Frederick John, I., 150.
    Captain Frederick William, R.N., I., 149.
Roseneath castle, II., 113.
Roslin, castle of, II., 204, 205.
Roslin Muir, I., 72.
Ross, William, Earl of, II., 208.
    Sir John, I., 130.

Ross, George, I., 41.
Rothbury, forest of, II., 142.
Roxburgh castle, II., 125, 135.
Rullion Green, battle of, I., 142.
Rutherford, Dame Margaret, I., 135.
Rysewaeth, lands of, I., 25.
Rytre, lands of, I., 10.

St Andrews, castle of, II., 217.
St Clair, William de, II., 58.
St Duthac's Monastery, II., 139.
St Finan, church of, I., 11, 23.
St George, I., 71.
St John, Sir John de, II., 58, 182, 189.
Sampson, John, II., 160.
Sandilands, Alison, I., 119.
    Sir James, I., 16, 18.
    James of, I., 17.
Sanquhar, I., 7 ; II., 168.
Sanquhar-Hamilton, lands of, I., 39, 49.
Sark, battle of, I., 36.
Sauchton, lands of, I., 166.
Sawers, John, I., 296.
Schaw, Sir James, I., 93.
    John, of Haly, I., 95.
    John, of Sornbeg, I., 94, 96.
Scheillis, Archibald, I., 191.
Scone, II., 58, 114.
Scott, Sir Patrick, I., 134.
    Sir Walter, I., 38, 295.
    Sir William, I., 134.
    Margaret, I., 127, 169.
    Mary, I., 218.
Seaton, Sir John, I., 176.
Segrave, Sir John, II., 188, 204.
Selkirk, forest of, II., 162.
Sempill, James, I., 139.
Seton Stenart, Lady, I., 299.
Setoun (Seytoun), Dame Margaret, I., 46, 52, 151.
Shaw, John, I., 155.
Shewaltoun, lands of, I., 125, 129.
Shippen, Alice Lee, I., 215.
Shyrdrum, lands of, I., 197.
Simpringham, convent of, I., 8, 11.
Simpson, Thomas, I., 225.
Sitwell, Sir George, Bart., I., 31.
Skene, Andrew, I., 233.
    John, I., 71.
Smith, John, I., 23.
    William, I., 157.
Smollet, George, I., 170.
Soulis, Sir John, II., 58, 223.
    Sir William de, II., 58.
Southesk, Margaret, countess of, I., 150.
Sowerbye, John, I., 225.
Spaldington, Sir Osbert de, II., 126.
Speirs, Alexander, I., 32.
Spitalsheills, lands of, I., 37, 38.
Spottiswoode, John, I., 77.
Stamfoord, Henry, Earl of, I., 76.

Stein, Grace, I., 111, 112.
    John, M.P., I., 111.
Stenton, lands of, I., 4.
Stephens, Elizabeth, I., 105.
Stevenson, Alexander, I., 213.
    David Watson, R.S.A., I., 293-295, 298.
    William Grant, I., 258.
Steward, James the, II., 58, 122, 129, 133, 223.
Stewart, Alexander, I., 56, 139.
    Sir Archibald, of Castlemilk, I., 98.
    Sir John, of Bonkill, II., 156, 157.
    Sir John, of Minto, I., 138.
    Lady Margaret, I., 34.
    Margaret, I., 131, 139, 184, 185, 198.
    William, of Haling, I., 155.
    William, of Raith, I., 161.
Stirling Bridge, battle of, II., 129-134.
Stirling castle, I., 297 ; II., 135, 178, 218-223.
Stirling, John de, II., 170.
Strathclyde, I., 2 ; II., 5, 6.
Strathern, Earl of, I., 9.
Symington, church of, I., 117.
Symson, Andrew, I., 78.
Sywyld, lands of, I., 16.

Tait, Craufurd, I., 31.
    James, I., 31.
    John, I., 31, 55.
    Thomas, I., 50-52, 130, 155.
    Colonel Thomas Forsyth, I., 31.
Tarbolton, I., 9, 14, 54, 117.
Tarvit, mill of, I., 197.
Tathys, land of, I., 15.
Tennant, Charles, I., 114.
Thorn, Sir Robert, II., 111.
Thornlie (Thornylee), lands of, I., 9, 33, 34, 37, 40.
Thurston, lands of, I., 9, 33.
Tibber's castle, II., 168.
Torphichen, Priory of, II., 146, 158, 161.
Torthorwald, church of, I., 117.
Torwood castle, II., 94, 100.
Torwood, forest of, II., 102.
Torwoodhead, lands of, I., 106.
Towers, William, I., 16.
Tullibaggis, lands of, I., 196.
Tulloch, Walter, I., 34.
Turnberry castle, II., 196, 197.
Turnbull, Rev. George, I., 200.
Twenge, Sir Marmaduke, II., 133-135.
Tynyngham, Sir Adam, I., 15.

Umfraville, Gilbert de, II., 91-93, 170.
    Sir Ingram, II., 92, 93, 103.
    Sir Robert de, II., 90.
Underwood, lands of, I., 165.
Urquhart, castle of, II., 124.

Valence, Sir Aymer de, II., 189, 194.
Vallas, Annie Olivia, I., 114.

Vallas, George, I., 114.
Vaux, Sir John de, II., 189.
Vchterbauuok, lands of, I., 12.
Vereker, Hon. Georgina, I., 104.
Vernon, Admiral, I., 102.

WAKE, Sir Charles, Bart., I., 31.
Waleis, William le, I., 4.
Waleys, Adam le, counte de Arc, II., 102.
    Aleyn, tenant le Roi du counte de Arc, II.,
        102.
    Nicol le, del counte de Arc, II., 102.
Walker, Agnes, I., 172.
Wallace, Adam, I., 7, 36, 39, 41, 42, 92, 119,
        121, 122, 130, 146, 161, 173, 182, 185,
        189, 196, 236.
    Adam, of Cairnhill, I., 35.
    Adam, of Cambuseescan, I., 164.
    Sir Adam, of Craigie, I., 93.
    Adam, of Newtoun, I., 173.
Valleis, Waleys (Wallace), Adam, of Riccarton,
        I., 7, 8, 19 ; II., 88.
Wallace, Adam, of Rowhill, I., 162.
    Agnes, I., 66, 67, 71, 89, 109, 127, 140,
        152, 163, 164, 169, 176, 186, 210, 211,
        213, 218, 243.
    Agnes, Eleonora Alexandra Frances, I., 88.
    Sir Alan, I., 11.
Waleys (Wallace), Alan (Aleyn) de, I., 3, 11,
        12.
Wallace, Albany, of Lambley, I., 224.
    Albany, I., 227.
    Captain Albany French, I., 228.
    Albany John, I., 227.
    Alexander, I., 24, 43, 101, 109, 123, 128, 149,
        157, 162, 178, 179, 183, 186, 189, 194,
        203, 207, 210, 212, 218, 221, 222, 224,
        234, 242.
    Rev. Alexander, I., 202.
    Dr Alexander William, I., 209.
    Algernon Charles, I., 232.
    Alice Fanny Maude, I., 228.
    Alison, I., 210.
    Rev. Allan, I., 223.
    Allan, I., 27, 45, 192.
Walass (Wallace), Sir Andrew of, I., 197.
Wallace, Andrew, of Forthside, I., 195.
Wallas (Wallace), Andrew, bailie of Edinburgh,
        I., 175, 178, 180, 203, 214, 220-223.
Wallace, Ann, I., 108, 149.
    Anna, I., 101, 178, 179, 231.
    Anna Maria, I., 232.
    Annabell, I., 48, 123, 140.
    Anne, I., 134, 144, 211, 223, 226, 242.
    Anthony, I., 220.
    Archibald, of Failford, I., 124.
    Rev. Archibald, I., 246.
    Archibald, I., 103, 116, 154, 184, 188, 196,
        203, 206, 211, 212, 214, 229.
    Archibald C., I., 209.

Wallace, Baptista, I., 234.
    Barbara, I., 242.
    Bartholomew, I., 137.
    Bessie, I., 126.
    Bethia, I., 212.
    Bruce, I., 128, 131.
    Bryce, I., 177, 192.
    Catherine, I., 55-57, 127.
    Catherine Josephine Concha, I., 232.
    Dr Charles, I., 219.
    Charles, I., 185, 212.
    Charles Albany Ellis, I., 228.
    Major Charles James Stewart, I., 228.
    Charles Malcolm, I., 228.
    Charles Mansel, I., 227.
    Colonel Charles Tennant, I., 114, 115.
    Charlotte, I., 209, 232.
    Christian, I., 101, 107, 203, 213, 222.
    Clementina, I., 232.
    Clementina Josephine, I., 233.
    Corry Janetta, I., 227.
    Cosmo, I., 222.
    Cuthbert, I., 175.
    Cyril David, I., 232.
    Daniel, I., 133, 182, 190.
    David, I., 133, 149, 151, 180, 197, 203, 206,
        207, 209-211, 218.
    Captain David, I., 219.
    David, of Dankeith, I., 173.
    David, of Polduff, I., 203.
    David, of Shewaltoun, I., 125.
    Diana, I., 222.
    Dorothea, I., 185.
    Sir Duncan, I., 14-17.
Wallas, Walas (Wallace), Duncan, I., 15, 176,
        193.
Wallace, Edith Helen, I., 233.
    Edward, I., 46, 126-129, 179, 184, 196.
    Edward, of Achewaltoun, I., 171.
    Edward, of Shewaltoun, I., 125-128, 138,
        173.
    Edward, younger of Shewaltoun, I., 134.
    Edward Charles Lloyd, I., 223.
    Edwin, I., 205.
    Elderslie, I., 215.
    Eleonora Anne, I., 114.
    Elina, I., 232.
    Eliza, I., 226, 228, 230, 232.
    Elizabeth, I., 28, 63, 71, 101, 131, 148,
        149, 164, 190, 200, 203, 215, 216, 225,
        226, 231.
    Elizabeth Mary Emily, I., 228.
    Ellen, I., 230, 232.
    Ellinor Harriet, I., 113.
    Elspeth (Elspet), I., 183, 203, 209.
    Emma, I., 226.
    Epenetus, M.D., I., 235.
    Esther, I., 29.
    Ethel Maud, I., 233.
    Eupham, I., 66.

Wallace, Euphan, I., 78.
  Dame Euphemia, I., 72.
  Euphemia, I., 71, 72.
  Fanny, I., 114, 115.
  Fanny Lalla, I., 232.
  Florence Dora Anna, I., 228.
  Frances, I., 112.
  Frances Anna (Mrs Dunlop), I., 80, 81, 83.
  Frances Colquhoun, I., 107.
  Frances Mary, I., 115.
  Francis, I., 40, 234.
  Francis Gore, I., 223.
  Lieutenant-Colonel Francis James, I., 89.
  Frederick William Burgoyne, I., 233.
  Gabriel, I., 25.
  Geillis, I., 26, 176, 193.
  Sir George, I., 182.
  Rev. George, I., 223, 229.
  Captain George, I., 239.
  George, of Bogside, I., 126, 161.
  George, of Eardiston, I., 181.
  George, of Elderslie, I., 23, 24, 42, 133.
  George, of Muncastle, I., 171.
  George, of Symington, I., 118.
  George, of Wallacetown, I., 163.
  George, I., 101, 157, 163, 164, 179, 181, 200,
    201, 206, 209, 210, 222, 223, 231, 232.
  George Gordon, I., 89.
  Gordon, I., 231.
  Grizel, I., 71, 72.
  Harriet, I., 231.
  Harry, I., 63, 222.
  Heimine Marie Jeanne, I., 115.
  Helen, Lady Elderslie, I., 29.
  Helen, I., 28-30, 94, 123, 127, 144, 155, 161,
    211, 213.
  Helen Grace, I., 233.
  Henrietta Adeliza, I., 228.
  Henrietta Elizabeth, I., 227.
  Henrietta Ellis, I., 227.
Walleys-Waleis, Henry le, Mayor of London, I., 3.
Wallace, Henry, of Lambley, I., 224.
  Henry, I., 4, 65, 210, 227.
  Henry Charles, I., 115.
  Captain Henry Ritchie, I., 114, 115.
  Henry Ritchie Cooper, of Busbie and Clou-
    caird, I., 113, 115.
  Hew, I., 64, 65, 99, 131, 161, 178, 230.
  Hew, of Boghead, I., 146, 161.
  Hew, of Cairnhill, I., 45, 47, 50, 53, 93-96,
    155.
  Hew, of Camcescan, I., 164.
  Hew, of Craigie, I., 161, 177.
  Hew, of Musurde, I., 45.
  Hew, of Underwood, I., 109.
  Hew, of Whirrlefurd, I., 53.
  Hilda Harriet, I., 233.
  Major-General Hill, I., 232, 233.
  Hill, I., 230, 231.
  Colonel Hope, I., 226.

Wallace, Horace Binney, I., 216.
  Captain Houstoun, I., 149.
  Sir Hugh, of Craigie, I., 29, 34, 37, 62-65,
    133, 159.
  Sir Hugh, of Woolmet, I., 78.
  Sir Hugh, I., 35, 41, 66, 67.
  Hugh, of Auchinweit, I., 162.
  Hugh, of Nether Bargour, I., 172.
  Hugh, of Biscany, I., 112.
  Captain Hugh, of Biscany, I., 112.
  Lieutenant Hugh Ritchie, of Biscany, I.,
    112, 113.
  Hugh, of Boghead, I., 163-165.
  Hugh, of Craigie, I., 34, 59, 61, 62, 118.
  Hugh, of Elderslie, I., 29, 68.
  Hugh, of Ingliston, I., 30, 78, 167-171.
  Hugh de Meneturde, I., 137.
  Hugh, of Newton, I., 37, 39, 42.
  Hugh, of Smythston, I., 36, 40.
  Hugh, of Strabrakane, I., 154.
  Hugh, of Underwood, I., 99, 165.
  Hugh, of Wallacetown, I., 163.
  Captain Hugh, I., 67.
  Hugh, I., 24, 29, 34, 35, 37, 41, 42, 57, 58,
    63, 66, 67, 78, 97, 98, 101, 109, 135, 146,
    147, 153, 157, 158, 160, 164, 166, 169, 170,
    172-174, 178, 180, 192, 222, 229, 243.
  Hugh Harry Ritchie, I., 116.
  Hugh James, I., 113.
  Hugh Robert, I., 115, 116.
  Isabel, I., 55, 99, 169.
  Isabella, I., 212, 223.
  Isobel, I., 43, 56, 203, 206, 211, 234.
  Colonel James, of Auchans, I., 140-145.
  James, of Bardrain, I., 192.
  James, of Boghead, I., 123, 165.
  James, of Cairnhill, I., 93.
  James, of Dallowie, I., 63.
  James, of Dullares, I., 160.
  James, younger of Dullares, I., 160.
  James, of Felrig, I., 185.
  James, of Ferguslie, afterwards of "Loran-
    bauk," I., 192.
  James, of Johnstone, I., 131.
  James, of Milnholm, I., 194, 195.
  James, of Muirhead, I., 25, 163.
  James, of Prestwickshaw, I., 173.
  James, of Wallacetown, I., 163.
  Rev. James, I., 228, 246.
  Sir James, I., 220.
  General Sir James Maxwell, I., 110, 111.
  General James, I., 235.
  Captain James, I., 241.
  James, I., 26-28, 43, 45, 56, 97, 100, 101,
    128, 131, 134, 136, 138, 139, 141, 163, 174,
    177, 179, 184, 192-194, 196, 203, 206, 207,
    218, 220-223, 225, 226, 234-236.
  James Charles Stuart, I., 228.
  Lieutenant James Ritchie, R.N., I., 113.
  Jane, I., 147, 149, 212, 223, 231.

Wallace, Janet, I., 28, 107, 134, 140, 147, 151, 154, 155, 163, 164, 176, 193, 203, 211, 212, 234.
Janet Lucretia (Lady Cunningham Fairlie), I., 108, 109.
Jasper, I., 204.
Jean, I., 76, 99, 127, 131, 153, 242.
Jeanette Ritchie, I., 113.
Jeannette, I., 179.
Sir John, of Cairnhill (Carnell), I., 99, 123, 152, 161, 165.
Sir John, of Craigie (Cragyn), I., 36, 37, 146.
Sir John, of Riccarton, I., 8, 9.
Walays (Wallace), John, lord of Riccarton, I., 8, 9.
Wallace, Sir John, I., 4, 9, 33, 34, 36, 37, 136.
General Sir John Alexander Agnew, I., 87, 88.
John, M.D., surgeon-major, I., 223.
Rev. John, I., 245.
Captain John, I., 103, 179, 230, 243-245.
John, of Auchans and Dundonald, I., 53, 138.
John, of Brighouse, I., 157, 158.
John, of Burnbank, I., 39, 49, 98, 159, 160.
John, of Camsiscan (Camsescan), I., 79, 164, 165.
John, of Cairnhill (Carnell), I., 26, 56, 93, 98, 157, 159, 189.
John, of Colp, I., 222.
John, of Craigie, I., 24, 25, 39, 41-43, 45-57, 122, 138, 146, 230.
John, younger of Craigie, I., 25, 46.
John, of Corsflat, I., 26, 131, 191.
John, of Duffall, I., 180.
John, of Dundonald, I., 55, 123, 126, 138, 139.
John, of Elderslie, I., 23, 28, 30, 101, 187.
John, of Ferguslie, I., 26, 192.
John, of Glentig, I., 154.
John, of Grangemure, I., 183.
Waleys (Wallace), John, of Hayton or Ayton, I., 6.
Wallace, John, of Hillhouse, I., 136.
John, of Holmstone, I., 147.
John, of Hope Farm, I., 214.
John, of Kelly, I., 107.
John, of Menfuird, I., 137, 139.
John, younger of Menfuird, I., 137.
John, of Muncastle, I., 171.
John, of Munktounhill, I., 25.
John, of Neilstonside, I., 29.
Walays (Wallace), John, of Riccarton, I., 9.
Wallace, John, of Rowhill, I., 162.
John, M.D., of Wallacetoun, I., 163.
John, I., 5, 10, 24-28, 30, 35, 40-47, 55-57, 63, 65, 67, 78, 89, 97, 99-101, 106, 109, 112, 118, 125-127, 131, 137, 144, 147, 151, 161-164, 171, 174-180, 182-188, 191, 194, 197, 203-207, 209-211, 213, 215, 216, 218, 319, 221, 222, 225-227, 233, 234, 236, 239, 240, 243.
John George Frederick Hope-, I., 226.

Wallace, John Henry Albany French, I., 228.
John Ritchie, I., 114.
John Tennant, I., 114, 115.
Jonet, I., 184.
Jonette, I., 133.
Joseph, I., 230-233.
Joshua Maddox, I., 214, 215.
Katherine, I., 65, 184, 190, 210.
Katherine Anne, I., 115.
Katherine Mary, I., 114.
Lady, I., 87.
Lady Elizabeth, I., 43.
"Lambarte, of Sewalton," I., 125.
Laurence, I., 79, 127, 175, 179.
Lewis Alexander, I., 181.
Lilias, I., 103, 104, 107.
Louisa, I., 226, 230.
Louisa Eliza, I., 228.
Louisa Elizabeth, I., 228.
Mabel Henrietta, I., 228.
Magdalene, I., 101, 223.
Sir Malcolm, brother of the Patriot, I., 22, 23.
Malcolm, of Auchinbothie and Elderslie, II., 88, 102.
Malcolm, of Elderslie, I., 20, 250.
Malcolm, of Riccarton, I., 8.
Malcolm, I., 8, 19, 20, 22, 193.
Marcella, I., 230.
Margaret, I., 65, 75-77, 93, 94, 101, 112, 123, 131, 134, 147, 149, 155, 161, 164, 169, 176, 183, 184, 186, 203, 209, 210, 218, 222, 223, 243.
Margaret Christina, I., 114.
Margaret Louisa Bethune, I., 115.
Margaret de la Val, I., 232.
Maria, I., 231.
Marion, I., 18, 35, 45, 131, 134, 218, 220.
Marjory, I., 219.
Marshall, I., 216.
Martha, I., 45.
Martin, I., 209.
Mary, I., 107, 140, 149, 157, 191, 222, 223, 226, 235.
Mary Anne French, I., 227.
Mary Binney, I., 216.
Mary Blanche Annie, I., 228.
Mary Cox, I., 215.
Mary Coxe, I., 215.
Mary Eliza Owen, I., 227.
Mary Jane, I., 223.
Mary Maddox, I., 215.
Mary Rose Charlotte, I., 232.
Matilda, I., 230.
Matthew, of Auchans, I., 140.
Matthew, of Craigie, I., 41, 42.
Matthew, of Dundonald, I., 139.
Matthew, of Torschaw, I., 55.
Matthew, of Underwood, I., 97, 99.
Dr Matthew, I., 200.
Matthew, I., 41-43, 99, 162, 165, 197, 198.

Wallace, Mercy, I., 228.
Michael, of Washford (Washfuird), I., 46, 173.
Michael, I., 27, 28, 45, 46, 49, 51. 55, 101, 109, 123, 128, 129, 157, 173, 174, 177, 187.
Montagu Hill Clement, I., 233.
Moyses, I., 175.
Wallace National Monument, I., 108.
Wallace Oak, I., 20.
Wallis (Wallace), Field-Marshal Count Oliver, I., 57.
Wallace, Patrick, of Pouderlawfield, I., 217.
Patrick, I., 24, 42, 133, 175, 184, 188, 209-211, 217, 218, 239, 246.
Wallas (Wallace), Paul, I., 118, 197.
Wallace, Percy Maxwell, I., 223.
Philip de, I., 7.
Rachel, I., 66, 67, 78, 128, 129, 164.
Rachel Budd, I., 215.
Rebecca, I., 157.
Rebecca Blackwell-Willing, I., 216.
Waleyss (Wallace), Sir Richard, of Riccarton, I., 11 ; II., 104, 107.
Richard, of Riccarton, I., 7, 11.
Richard, of Hackencrow (Auchincruive), I., 11.
Walcis (Wallace), Richard, I., 3, 5, 7, 11, 12, 182, 201, 237.
Wallace, Richard, younger, I., 7.
Richard Ellis, I., 227.
Ridge, obelisk at, II., 157.
Sir Robert, Knight, I., 13, 14.
Robert, of Bargour, I., 172.
Robert, of Barnwell, I., 162.
Robert, younger of Barnwell, I., 162.
Robert, of Beechmount, I., 230.
Robert, of Brighouse, I., 155, 158.
Robert, of Cairnhill, I., 99-101, 134, 160, 164.
Robert, younger of Cairnhill, I., 165.
Robert, of Carmichael, I., 165.
Robert, of Corsflat, I., 191.
Robert, of Drumalloch, I., 171.
Robert, of Failford, I., 124.
Robert, of Galrigs, I., 152.
Robert, of Holmstoun, I., 98, 146-148, 150, 174 ; II., 94.
Robert, of Johnstone, I., 130.
Robert, of Kelly, I., 109, 110.
Robert, of Over Leitchland, I., 192.
Robert, younger of Shewaltoun, I., 126.
Bishop Robert, of the Isles, I., 169.
Wallis (Wallace), Archdeacon Robert, of St Andrews, I., 201.
Wallace, Robert, D.D., I., 198-200.
Colonel Robert Clerk, I., 227.
Major Robert, I., 149, 181, 231.
Major Robert Hugh, R.A., I., 114, 115.
Captain Robert, I., 227.

Wallace, Robert, M.P., I., 204, 205.
Robert, I., 3, 11-14, 45, 49, 53, 56, 97, 99-101, 114, 125, 127, 131, 149, 151, 156, 157, 162, 164, 165, 171, 173, 176-181, 183, 184, 186, 192, 194, 204-206, 210, 219, 230-232, 235, 237.
Robert Agnew, I., 89.
Robert Bruce, I., 89.
Robert Edward, I., 227.
Robert Francis, I., 115.
Robert French Algernon, I., 228.
Robert Paterson, I., 148.
Rollo, I., 149.
Rose, I., 223.
Samuel, I., 178, 233, 234.
Wallace Seat in Laighlyne woods, II., 105.
Wallace, Shippen, I., 215.
Waulis (Wallace), Simon, I., 182.
Walleys (Wallace), Sir Stephen le, I., 3.
Waleys (Wallace), Stephen de, I., 3.
Wallace, Susan Bradford, I., 215, 216.
Wallace Sword, I., 297-303.
Sybilla, I., 242.
Thomas, Baron, I., 226.
Waleys (Wallace), Thomas le, del Counte de Fyf, I., 197.
Wallace, Sir Thomas, Bart., of Craigie, I., 29, 30, 66-68, 77-80, 90, 100, 124, 169, 174, 178, 243.
Sir Thomas Dunlop, Bart., of Craigie, I., 86, 87.
Sir Thomas, Lord Justice-Clerk, I., 69, 70.
Wallas (Wallace), Sir Thomas, vicar of Spyne (Spynie), I., 220.
Wallace, Thomas, of Asholme, I., 225.
Thomas, of Cairnhill, I., 28, 187.
Thomas, of Craigie, I., 134.
Thomas, of Elderslie, I., 76, 78.
Thomas, younger of "Faill" or Failford, I., 124.
Thomas, of Lambley, I., 224, 225.
Captain Thomas, I., 103.
Thomas, I., 23, 27, 30, 32, 37, 39, 40, 56, 66-68, 71, 75, 78, 80, 87, 101, 109, 112, 114, 128, 138, 157, 164, 169, 175, 178, 184, 186, 190, 193, 202, 218, 220, 222, 225, 226, 240, 241.
Thomas Alexander, I., 228.
Thomas French, I., 226, 227.
Thomas Hull, I., 227.
Thomas T., I., 227.
Walter, I., 179, 203.
"the laird of Wolmet," I., 148.
attendant of Archbishop Sharp, I., 204.
Wilfred Osborne Gordon, I., 232.
William, Lord of Craigie (Cragyn), I., 18, 35.
Sir William, of Craigie, I., 40, 41, 72, 74, 75, 171, 179.
William, minister of Fail, I., 130.
William, minister of Failford, I., 52, 55, 122, 123, 159.

Wallace, William, minister at Symountoun, I., 123.
Colonel William, I., 103.
Lieutenant-Colonel William, I., 112.
William, of Auchinweit, I., 162.
William, of Barnwell, I., 162.
William, of Brighouse, I., 55, 155, 157, 160.
William, of Burnebank, I., 63.
William, younger of Burnbank, I., 159, 160.
William, of Busbie and Cloncaird, I., 113.
William, of Cairnhill (Carnell), I., 93, 97, 101, 102.
William, of Cambuscescan, I., 164.
William, of Craigie, I., 25, 35, 40.
William, younger of Craigie, I., 169.
William, of Caversbank, I., 172.
William, of Dullares (Dulleries), I., 56, 159, 160.
William, of Dundonald, I., 138.
William, of Elderslie, I., 24, 26, 28, 126, 131, 133, 136, 192.
William, younger of Elderslie, I., 26, 56, 57, 123, 151, 161.
William, of Failford, I., 66, 72, 124, 139, 159.
William, of Galrigs, I., 152, 153.
William, of Garnell, I., 126.
William, of Helington, I., 66, 133, 147, 169.
William, younger of Holmstone, I., 147.
William, of Hope Farm, I., 214.
William, of Johnstone, I., 25, 26, 130, 131.
William, younger of Johnstone, I., 26, 130, 131.
William, of Little Cessnock, I., 146.
William, of Mainholm, I., 166.
William, of Neilstonside, I., 27, 192.
William, of Prestwickschaws, I., 155.
William, of Sauchrie, I., 172.
William, of Shewaltoun, I., 127, 128.
William, of Smithstown, I., 124.
William, of Wallacetown, I., 163.
William, of Whytehouse, I., 173.
William, I., 12, 13, 20, 21, 24-29, 34, 37, 40, 41, 43-46, 49-51, 56, 64-66, 71, 72, 78, 97-101, 109, 118, 123, 126, 127, 131, 133-138, 144, 148, 152, 155, 160, 163-165, 169, 172, 175, 178, 180, 183, 184, 186, 189, 191, 193, 195, 196, 201, 203-209, 212-214, 218-223, 227, 229, 230, 232-234, 236-238, 240, 242, 245.
William Bradford, I., 215, 216.
William Frederick, I., 232.
William John, I., 115.
William M'Ilvaine, I., 215.
William Thomas Francis Agnew, I., 89.

Walltoun, lands of, I., 172.
Walter the Steward, I., 7, 8, 11.
Wardroper, Thomas, I., 240.
Warwick, Guy, Earl of, II., 169, 170.
Washington, General, II., 94.
Watt, James, I., 295.
Wauchope, Andrew, of Niddrie-Marischal, I., 75-77.
Colonel Andrew Gilbert, of Niddrie, I., 77.
Colonel William, I., 77.
Alice, I., 77.
Andrew, I., 76, 77.
George, I., 77.
Harriet Elizabeth Frances, I., 77.
John, I., 76, 77.
Robert, I., 77.
William, I., 76.
William John, I., 77.
Waus, Sir Patrick, of Barnbarroch, I., 96, 139.
Weir, Christian, I., 234.
James, of Blackwood, I., 94.
Welsh, John, I., 156.
Wemyss, Sir Michael of, I., 197.
Westmeath, George Frederick, Earl of, I., 226.
Weston, Bartholomew, I., 215.
Wexford and Marress, lands of, I., 126, 129.
White, Stevin, I., 159.
Whitehill, lands of, I., 106.
Wigtown, John, Earl of, I., 246.
Malcolm, Earl of, I., 13.
Marjory, Countess of, I., 8.
William the Lion, I., 7, 205 ; II., 7, 8.
Williams, Richard, I., 31.
Williamson, John, I., 180.
Willing, George, I., 216.
Willoughby, George, I., 232.
Margaret, I., 232.
Wilson, John, of Hillpark, I., 108.
Professor John, I., 258.
John, I., 101.
James, I., 186.
Windymill, lands of, I., 25.
Wishart, Robert, Bishop of Glasgow, I., 250 ; II., 58, 118, 122, 125, 201.
Wodehouse, Robert de, II., 169.
Wright, John, of Broom, II., 131.

Yellowlees, Provost, I., 298, 302, 303.
Yester, John, lord, I., 176.
Yule, General Patrick, I., 304.